SHE'S IN
HIS BLOOD....

D0441310

Praise for Katie MacAlister's
Dark Ones Novels

In the Company of Vampires

"Katie MacAlister is an excellent writer and never ceases to amaze us with her quick, aka witty, wit and amazing romantic tales . . . a funny but masterfully written romantic tale with all the paranormal types you could want and more."　　　　—Night Owl Romance

"This is trademark MacAlister, full of quirky characters and wacky plot twists. Fans of the funny, madcap Dark Ones series will not be disappointed with this entry."
　　　　　　　　　　　　　　　　　—*Romantic Times*

"Zany [and] clever."　　　　　—*Midwest Book Review*

"An excellent read. . . . Hysterical and surprisingly realistic, considering it includes witches, deities, vampires, and Viking ghosts, *In the Company of Vampires* delivers a great story and excellent characterization."
　　　　　　　　　　　　　　　　　　—Fresh Fiction

Crouching Vampire, Hidden Fang

"The fantastic follow-up to *Zen and the Art of Vampires*! . . . Not a book to be missed by lovers of paranormal romance. One of the best I have read so far."
　　　　　　　　　　　　　　　　—Enchanting Reviews

"Ms. MacAlister entertains readers with a captivating romance, supernatural politics, and her always present touch of humor."　　　　　—Darque Reviews

"A fantastic duo of stories from Katie MacAlister. . . . She continues to write strong and super spunky characters that women will love to read about. If you are a fan of Mary Janice Davidson's Betsy series, then I think you will definitely enjoy *Zen and the Art of Vampires* and *Crouching Vampire, Hidden Fang*."—Joyfully Reviewed

continued . . .

"The story line is fast-paced, filled with humor and action as Katie MacAlister balances the two nicely."
—*Midwest Book Review*

"Stay true to the spirit of the series, tell a good story, and readers will follow you anywhere. I certainly will follow Katie MacAlister to her next Dark Ones book."
—Romance Novel TV

Zen and the Art of Vampires

"A jocular, action-packed tale. . . . [a] wonderful, zany series."
—*Midwest Book Review*

"Has all of the paranormal action, romance, and humor that fans of the author look for in her books. This is a fast-moving read with sizzling chemistry and a touch of suspense."
—Darque Reviews

"Pia Thomason just might be my favorite heroine ever . . . an entrancing story, and a very good escape."
—The Romance Reader

"I completely loved *Zen and the Art of Vampires*! . . . The chemistry between Pia and Kristoff sizzles all the way through the novel. . . . I don't think I can wait for the next Dark Ones installment! Please hurry, Katie!!"
—Romance Junkies

"Steamy."
—*Booklist*

The Last of the Red-Hot Vampires

"MacAlister's fast-paced romp is a delight with all its quirky twists and turns, which even include a murder mystery."
—*Booklist*

"A wild, zany romantic fantasy. . . . Paranormal romance readers will enjoy this madcap tale of the logical physicist who finds love."
—The Best Reviews

"A fascinating paranormal read that will captivate you."
—Romance Reviews Today

"A pleasurable afternoon of reading."
—The Romance Reader

"The sexy humor, wild secondary characters, and outlandish events make her novels pure escapist pleasure!" —*Romantic Times*

"A fabulous urban fantasy.... The story line is fast-paced from the onset and never slows down.... Fans will enjoy visiting the chaotic, charming world of Ms. MacAlister, where the unbelievable becomes believable."
—*Midwest Book Review*

"Laugh-out-loud funny! ...A whimsical, upbeat, humor-filled paranormal romance ... delightful."
—Romance Junkies

Praise for Katie MacAlister's
Light Dragon Novels

The Unbearable Lightness of Dragons

"Magic, mystery, and humor abound in this novel making it a must read ... kudos to another stellar book, Ms. Katie M." —Night Owl Romance

"Katie MacAlister has always been a favorite of mine, and her latest series again shows me why.... If you are a lover of dragons, MacAlister's new series will definitely keep you entertained!"
—The Romance Readers Connection

"A wondrous story full of magic and romance.... I cannot wait to see what happens next in the lives of the dragons." —Fresh Fiction

"An action-packed and sexy paranormal romance.... The combination of dragons, demons, witty repartee, adventure, visions, magical mayhem, sexy scenes, and romance adds up to a truly entertaining tale that I hated to see end." —Romance Junkies

MUCH ADO
ABOUT
VAMPIRES

A Dark Ones Novel

Katie MacAlister

A SIGNET BOOK

SIGNET
Published by New American Library, a division of
Penguin Group (USA) Inc., 375 Hudson Street,
New York, New York 10014, USA
Penguin Group (Canada), 90 Eglinton Avenue East, Suite 700, Toronto,
Ontario M4P 2Y3, Canada (a division of Pearson Penguin Canada Inc.)
Penguin Books Ltd., 80 Strand, London WC2R 0RL, England
Penguin Ireland, 25 St. Stephen's Green, Dublin 2,
Ireland (a division of Penguin Books Ltd.)
Penguin Group (Australia), 250 Camberwell Road, Camberwell, Victoria 3124,
Australia (a division of Pearson Australia Group Pty. Ltd.)
Penguin Books India Pvt. Ltd., 11 Community Centre, Panchsheel Park,
New Delhi - 110 017, India
Penguin Group (NZ), 67 Apollo Drive, Rosedale, Auckland 0632,
New Zealand (a division of Pearson New Zealand Ltd.)
Penguin Books (South Africa) (Pty.) Ltd., 24 Sturdee Avenue,
Rosebank, Johannesburg 2196, South Africa

Penguin Books Ltd., Registered Offices:
80 Strand, London WC2R 0RL, England

First published by Signet, an imprint of New American Library,
a division of Penguin Group (USA) Inc.

First Printing, October 2011
10 9 8 7 6 5 4 3 2 1

For eight years, the editorial hand guiding my books belonged to Laura Cifelli, a charming woman with a wickedly funny sense of humor that frequently had me snorting beverages out of my nose (I quickly learned never to drink when on the phone with her). Although Laura decided to leave publishing, I am truly grateful for all her help, support, and shared admiration of dishy guys. I am blessed to have known her, and happily dedicate Alec to her. Er . . . Alec's book. She already got grabby with Baltic. She doesn't really need Alec, too. . . .

Thanks for everything, Laura!

Author's Note

Hello, and welcome to Alec and Cora's book!

"Who's Alec?" I hear some of you asking. Others of you might be familiar with Alec, but have no clue who Cora is. Since this book features characters from previous books, a novella, and a short story, I thought I'd make sure everyone was on the same page—ha! author humor!—before you get started.

Alec Darwin was introduced in *Zen and the Art of Vampires*, along with his buddy Kristoff and Kristoff's Beloved, Pia. That story was larger than could be reasonably put into one book, so the story spilled over into a sequel, *Crouching Vampire, Hidden Fang*.

I always intended to write Alec's story, since he was a man who suffered greatly during his long life, but didn't see a way to do that until I sat down to write a short story to explain the loss of his Beloved so many centuries ago. That story, "My Heart Will Go On and On", tells the tale of Corazon Ferreira's evening to remember, and led to Cora being a secondary character in the novella *Unleashed* (found in the *Cupid Cats* anthology).

Still with me? If not, you can find the "My Heart Will Go On and On" short story at the back of this book. You don't have to read it in order to understand what happens in *Much Ado About Vampires*, but the good folks at New American Library and I thought it might be nice to include it, since until now it's only been available online.

I hope you enjoy seeing Alec and Cora finally get together after all that groundwork!

Katie MacAlister

Prologue

Alec Darwin was dying, or as close to it as one could be without having that last little spark of life flitter away into nothingness.

He closed his eyes and lay back, shifting slightly when a rock dug into the small of his back. Should he go to the trouble of trying to remove it, he wondered absently, so he could lie for eternity in comfort? Or was such a trivial thing worth the effort? Did he even have the strength to do it? It had been all he could do to stagger to the area he had the previous day cleared of small, pointed rocks, his final resting place.

His shoulder shifted in mild irritation. The rock ground into his kidney, the pain of it distracting him from his plan. Dammit, he hadn't seen a rock when he fell to the ground, his strength draining from him as his body squeezed the last morsel of energy from the remaining teaspoon or two of blood that was slowly absorbed into his dying flesh.

He was supposed to be cherishing his martyrdom as he lay dying in the Akasha, not thinking about a damned rock the size of a watermelon digging into his back. He was supposed to be thinking of the pathetic tragedy of a life that he had been forced to live, unenlivened with any sort of joy or happiness, or even hope. He shouldn't be wondering whether if he rolled over onto his side, the damned rock would let him die in peace.

If only his Beloved hadn't died. If only he'd come to her a few minutes earlier, he could have been there when that idiot reaper lost control. If only he'd bedded her and Joined the minute he knew she was his Beloved, rather than allowing her to give in to her mortal sensibilities, demanding he court her.

A last breath passed his lips as he tried to hold on to the image of her face, his one true love, the woman who had been put on the earth to save him, and who had died the victim of a senseless accident that was directly responsible for his death at that moment.

Awareness slid away from him, the rock ceasing to be an annoyance, the last few sparks between his brain cells providing not the image of his Beloved, as he so desperately wanted, but that of a woman who had lain in a faint at his feet a few months previously.

Chapter One

The dream started the way it always started.

"What do you see, Corazon?"

The voice that spoke so calmly belonged to Barbara, the hypnotherapist whom Patsy had hired for our "Girls' Night In" semiannual party.

"Mud. I see mud. Well, mud and grass and stuff like that. But mostly just mud."

"Are you sure she's under?" Patsy asked, her voice filled with suspicion. Pats was always a doubter. "She doesn't look hypnotized to me. CORA! Can you hear me?"

"I'd have to be five miles away not to hear you. I'm hypnotized, you idiot, not deaf." I glared at her. She glared at me glaring at her.

"Wait just one second. . . ." Patsy stopped glaring and pointed dramatically at where I lay prone on the couch. "You're not supposed to hear me!"

"Is she supposed to know she's hypnotized?"

That was Terri, the third member of our little trio of terror, as my ex-husband used to call us.

The bastard.

"Her knowing doesn't negate the regression, does it?" Terri asked Barbara.

"Hypnotism isn't a magical state of unknowing," Barbara said calmly. "She is simply relaxed, in touch with her true inner spirit, and has opened up her mind to the many memories of lifetimes past. I assure you that she is properly hypnotized."

"Let me get a pin and poke her with it," Patsy said, bustling over to a bookcase crammed full of books and various other items. "If she reacts, we'll know she's faking it."

"No one is poking me with anything!" I sat up, prepared to sprint to safety if she so much as came near me with anything sharp and pointy.

"Please, ladies." I didn't see Barbara show any signs of rushing, but I knew she wanted to hurry us along so she could leave. "We have limited time. Corazon is in a light trance, also referred to as an alpha state. Through that, she has tapped into her higher self, her true Infinite Being, a state in which she is free to bypass the boundaries of time."

"Yeah. Bypassing all that stuff," I said, lying back down on the couch. Even though it was a dream, and I knew it was a dream, my stomach started to tighten at what was to come. "So sit back and watch the show. What do I do now, Barbara?"

"Look around you. Examine your surroundings. Tell us what you see, what you feel."

"I see mud. I feel mud. I *am* the mud."

"There has to be more to her past life than mud, surely," Terri said, munching on popcorn.

My stomach turned over. *It was coming.* He *was coming. I felt it, felt the horror just on the edges of my consciousness.*

"Are there any buildings or other structures around to give you an idea of what year you are reliving?" Barbara asked.

"Um . . . nothing on the left side other than forest. I seem to be standing on a dirt path of some sort. Let me walk to the top of this little hill—oh! Wow! There's a town down below. And it looks like there's a castle way up on a tall cliff in the distance. Lots of tiny little people are running around in some fields outside of the town. Cool! It's like a medieval village or something. Think I'll go down to say hi."

"Excellent," Barbara said. "Now tell me, how do you feel?"

Sick. Scared. Terrified.

"Well," my voice said, not reflecting any of the dream emotions, "kind of hungry. No, really hungry. Kind of an intense hunger, throbbing inside me. Oh great, I'm a peasant, aren't I? I'm a poor starving peasant who stands around in mud. Lovely."

"We are not here to make judgments on our past selves," Barbara said primly.

"Geesh, Cora," Patsy said, sitting on my feet. "Terri turned out to be Cleopatra's personal maid, and I was one of Caesar's concubines. You're letting down the team, babe. The least you could do is be a medieval princess in a big pointy hat or something."

I couldn't . . . because of him.

Loathing rippled through me as my voice continued. "I have shoes on. Peasants didn't wear shoes, did they?"

"Some did, I'm sure," Terri said, stuffing a handful of popcorn into her mouth.

"Can you walk to the town?" Barbara asked. "Perhaps we can find out who you are if we know where you are."

"Yeah. I'm going down the hill now."

A low rumble from behind me had me clutching the cushions of the couch. "Hey, watch where you're—oh my god. Oh my god! OMIGOD!"

"What? What's happened?" Barbara asked, sounding suddenly worried.

She should.

"A woman with an oxcart just ran me over."

"What?" Patsy shrieked.

"She ran me over. Her oxen were running amok or something. They just came barreling down the hill behind me and ran right over the top of me. Holy Swiss on rye! Now the oxen are trampling me, and the lady in the cart is screaming and—Jehoshaphat! My head just came off! It just came right off! Ack!"

I knew in my dream state that Terri sat staring at me, her eyes huge, a handful of popcorn frozen just beyond her mouth as she gawked at the words that came unbidden from my mouth.

If only she knew.

"Oh, my. I don't—I've never had anyone die during a regression," Barbara said, sounding stressed. "I'm not quite sure how to proceed."

"You're . . . decapitated?" Patsy asked. "Are you sure?"

"I'm sure, Pats. My head's separated from my body, which is covered in ox hoofprints. A wheel went over my neck, I think. It . . . urgh. That's just really gross. Why the hell do I get the reincarnations where I'm killed by two bulls and a cart? Why can't I be Cleopatra's concubine?"

"Personal maid, not concubine," Terri corrected, stuffing the popcorn into her mouth and chewing frantically. "Are you absolutely certain you're dead? Maybe it looks worse than it is."

Oh, it's going to get much, much worse, the dream part of my mind said.

Goose bumps rose on my arms.

"My head is three feet away from my body. I think

that's a pretty good indicator of death—good god! Now what's she doing?"

"The ox?" Patsy asked.

"No, the driver. She's not doing what I think she's doing, is she?"

"I don't know," Terri said, setting down the popcorn so she could scoot over closer to me.

"This is very unusual," Barbara muttered to herself.

"What's the lady doing?" Patsy said, prodding my knee.

"She's trying to stick my head back onto my body. Lady, that's not going to do any good. No, you can't tie it on, either. Ha. Told you so. Oh, don't drop me in the mud! Sheesh! Like I wasn't muddy enough? What a butterfingers. Now she's chasing the oxen, who just bolted for a field. Oh, no, she's coming back. Her arms are waving around like she's yelling, only I can't hear anything. It must be the shock of having my head severed by a cart wheel."

"This is just too surreal," Terri said. "Do you think she purposely ran you down?"

"I don't think so. She seems kind of goofy. She just tripped over my leg and fell onto my head. Oh man! I think she broke my nose! God almighty, this is like some horrible Marx Brothers meets Leatherface sort of movie. Holy runaway oxen, Batman!"

"What?" Terri and Patsy asked at the same time.

"She's doing something. Something weird."

"Oh my god—is she making love to your lifeless corpse?" Terri asked. "I saw a show on HBO about that!"

"No, she's not molesting me. She's standing above me waving her hands around and chanting or something. What the—she's like—hoo!"

He was coming. He was just out of my sight, just beyond the curve of the hill.

He was death.

"Don't get upset," Barbara said. "You are in no personal danger. Just describe what you're seeing calmly, and in detail."

"I don't know about you, but I consider a decapitation and barbecue as some sort of personal danger."

"Barbecue?" Patsy asked. "Someone's roasting a pig or something?"

"No. The ox lady waved her hands around, and all of a sudden this silver light was there, all over my body, singeing it around the edges. Oh, great. Here comes someone." *No!* my mind screamed. *Not again! Please god, not again!* "Hey, you, mister, would you stop the lady from doing the light thing? She's burnt off half of my hair."

"This is the most bizarre thing I've ever heard," Terri told Patsy. "You have the *best* parties!

"It's all in the planning," Patsy said, prodding my knee again. "What's going on now, Cora?"

"The guy just saw me. He did a little stagger to the side. I think it's because the lady tried to hide my head behind her, and my ear flew off and landed at his feet. Now he's picking it up. He's yelling at her. She's pointing to the oxen in the field, but he looks really pissed. Yeah, you tell her, mister. She has no right driving if she can't handle her cows."

My heart wept at what was coming.

"This would make a great film," Patsy said thoughtfully. "I wonder if we could write a screenplay. We could make millions."

"Well, now the guy has my head, and he's shaking it at the lady, still yelling at her. Whoops. Chunk of hair came loose. My head is bouncing down the hill. Guy and lady are chasing it. Hee hee hee. OK, that's really funny in a horrible sort of way. Ah. Good for you, sir.

He caught me again, and now he's taking me back to my body, hauling the ox lady with him. Whoa! Whoa, whoa, whoa!"

I struggled to get out of the dream, just as I struggled every time. It never did any good. The scene was determined to play out as it first had.

"Did he drop your head again?" Terri asked, her eyes wide.

Panic flooded me. "No, he just . . . holy shit! I want out of here! Take me out of this dream or whatever it is! Wake me up!"

"Remain calm," Barbara said in a soothing voice. "The images you see are in the past, and cannot harm you now."

"What's going on? What did the guy do?" Terri asked.

"I want to wake up! Right now!" I said, clawing the couch to sit up.

"Very well. I'm going to count backwards to one, and when I reach that number, you will awaken feeling refreshed and quite serene. Five, four, three, two, one. Welcome back, Corazon."

"You OK?" Patsy asked as I sat up, gasping, my blood all but curdling at the memory of what I'd witnessed.

"Yeah. I think so."

"What happened at the end?" Terri asked. "You looked scared to death."

"You'd be scared, too, if you saw a vampire kill someone!"

I sat up in bed, torn from the dream at last, gasping and blinking as the dream memory faded and I realized I was safe, in my own little apartment, alone, without the green-eyed, dark-haired monster who had killed a woman before my eyes.

I slumped back against the pillow, wondering why I kept dreaming about Patsy's party and experiencing the awful past-life scene again and again. Why were the dreams increasing in frequency? Why was I doomed to relive the experience over and over again, the sense of dread and horror so great I could taste it on my tongue?

Sleep, I knew from sad experience, would be useless. I got to my feet, headed for the bathroom. I'd brush my teeth to get rid of the taste of my own fear, and go sit with a book until I was too numb with exhaustion to stay awake any longer.

And I'd pray that the green-eyed vampire stayed out of my dreams.

"And then Dee said, 'Darlin', if you're going to rise to the top, you have to work for it. That goes for sex as well as anything else.' Well, you know how he is, Cora—he's such a joker, and of course, I *was* on top at that moment, but I'm sure you don't want to hear about that."

"Why on earth would you think I didn't want to hear about you and my ex-husband having sex?" I gritted my teeth at both the conversation and the ruts that riddled the long dirt drive up to the Astley house.

The car bounced on a particularly bad one, causing me to cling to the dashboard, as Diamond, with one hand waving airily, didn't seem to notice the appalling state of the drive. "It's not like it's something you haven't done before, unless Dee never asked you to play Cowgirl and the One-legged Itinerant Rodeo Clown, and given how much he loves that, I'm positive he did. But that's neither here nor there, really, is it?"

"No, it isn't," I said, my lips twitching despite myself.

She was silent for a minute before sliding me a questioning look. "You're not angry with me about something, are you, Corazon? Is it Dee? Is it because we didn't ask you to the wedding? Dee thought it was best we didn't have a big ceremony, since your divorce had just become final that very day, so we went to Vegas."

"No," I said on a sigh. "It's not the wedding, and it's not anything you've done, including marrying my ex. Not really. Our marriage was over before you came along. It's just . . ." I stopped, not wanting to bare my soul to her. I wanted so much to hate Diamond, to despise her husband-stealing self, her perfect blond hair, her svelte figure, her miraculous rise through the real estate ranks from receptionist to top agent while I still slaved away as a lowly assistant-cum-secretary . . . but unfortunately, I couldn't hate her, couldn't despise her, couldn't even work up so much as a mild dislike. She kept the notoriously roving eye of Dermott, my ex-husband of three years, fixed firmly on herself, charmed everyone she came in contact with, and had a sunny disposition that simply would not be quelled, no matter how much I tried snubbing her.

"Lonely?" she asked with a perception that made me uncomfortable.

"I just miss my sister," I said, but we both knew it was a lame excuse. "Even though Jas lived in Washington, we used to talk almost every day."

"Didn't she marry a Scotsman?"

"Yes." I grimaced as we hit a particularly bad rut, my head smacking on the roof of the car. Diamond didn't need to know just what type of a Scot Jacintha's new husband really was. Or the truth about Jas herself, for that matter.

"That must be very hard on you, having her so far away. You don't have any men friends?"

For some bizarre reason, my mind turned to the dark-haired, green-eyed murderer. I would have to be dead not to have noticed that a bloodsucking fiend he might be, but he was also extremely easy on the eyes. "No. No boyfriend."

"That stinks."

I gave up all pretense of dignity. "It really does. I can't tell you how hard it is to find a man these days. They're all so . . . I don't know, shallow. They're just into themselves, or their jobs, and none of them seem to have any real depth. Is it so much to ask that a man be comfortable with himself? That he be able to look beyond his own needs and desires once in a while? All I ever find are guys with agendas."

"Have you tried one of those online dating places?" Diamond asked as we crept down the long drive, past a wildly unkempt lawn dotted with downed branches from nearby scraggly alder trees. "I have a friend who had great luck with one."

"Tried them. Dated the guys. Dumped them shortly thereafter," I said grimly, staring out the window with an Eeyore sense of satisfaction at my misery.

"I'll have to put my mind to it," Diamond said after another minute of silence. "You're a nice girl, Corazon. You deserve to be happy."

I sighed morosely, not bothering to voice my agreement. I sounded pathetic enough without that.

"I think you should take Dee's advice," she added.

"What advice would that be?" I asked, faintly startled at the idea of taking my ex's advice about anything, let alone my love life.

"That rising-to-the-top business. This job, now," she said, nodding toward the looming house that cut with mottled black fingers into the sunny California sky, "this is a perfect example of how one can rise to the top. If you handled it right, it could do big things for you."

"I'm not the agent; you are."

"You can be my coagent," she said, with a decisive

little nod. "I think it would be a good thing for you to get out from behind the desk and start meeting people. I see lots of men in my job, successful men, just the sort you need."

I glanced at the house, unable to keep from smiling to myself. "I appreciate the offer, Diamond, I really do, but I just don't think that some sexy, urbane man is going to want either this house or me."

"You don't know until you try. I'll tell Dee that you're going to handle the sale of this house. It'll do you good, and he won't make a fuss when I tell him how much you need a man."

I groaned to myself. That's all I needed—Dermott knowing how desperate I was for a man in my life. Still, it was a nice offer, and I didn't want to hurt Diamond's feelings by turning it down. "I'll think about it."

"You'll do more than think about it—you'll make this your debut into the fabulous world of real estate. And, of course, man hunting."

I laughed and pulled my hair back into a ponytail, checking my digital camera to make sure I had enough charge on the battery to take a good four or five dozen pictures. "It's just a derelict house that's been tied up in some huge probate battle for decades. It's hardly going to work miracles either for my career or love life."

"You'd be surprised what it could do," she said with a little smile of her perfectly plumped lips.

She glanced at me as we bounced our way to a halt at the side of the monstrous old Victorian house. Once, perhaps, it had been the home of a lumber baron or railroad magnate. . . . Now it was falling down, its wood weathered and mottled with peeling paint, the windows boarded over, bits of shingles from the roof scattered around the unkempt and overgrown grounds.

"Don't believe me?" Diamond asked.

"'Fraid not."

Her blue eyes narrowed on me. "You're not one of those skeptics, are you? The people who don't believe in anything supernatural?"

I clamped my lips together to keep from laughing hysterically. Part of me, what my mother used to call my little devil, wanted to tell her that anyone who had a shape-shifting sister married to a vampire could hardly be a skeptic. I squelched my devil and just smiled. "Not particularly, no."

"Oh, good. I know I should be more tolerant, but really, how people can close their minds to the wonders of the world is beyond me. My great-grandmother once told me that a closed mind would be the death of me, and do you know, she was right? The only time I closed my mind to the possibilities, I died."

I stared at her as she got out of the car, wondering if I had heard her correctly. "You . . . *died*?" I asked, getting out, as well.

"Yes. I got in trouble with—" She shot me a quick, unreadable look. "Well, let's just say I got in trouble, and I paid the price for it. Although the near-death experience was very interesting, I learned my lesson, and ever since then, I've kept my mind open to everything and everyone, humans and other beings." She hoisted her bag and pulled out her camera, giving the house an assessing look as she jangled a set of keys. "My, this is a big one, isn't it? There should be four floors. How about you shoot the basement and first floor, and I'll do the second and attic?"

"That's fine. Er . . ." I followed after her as she tripped lightly up the front steps to the big double doors. I picked my way carefully, not trusting the half-rotted boards of the steps and porch to hold up under my more substantial weight. "When you say *other beings*, you wouldn't happen to include vampires in that, would you? Or, what do they call them . . . er . . . ?"

"Dark Ones?" She unlocked the door, pausing on the threshold to close her eyes and breathe deeply. "I always try to attune myself to the house before entering. It gives me a better idea of what sort of family would be perfect within its walls. How very odd. This house feels like someone of a dark nature was here a long time ago. . . . Hmm." She entered, tossing me an amused look over her shoulder. "Of course I believe in Dark Ones. I haven't met one, but that doesn't mean they don't exist. Are you interested in them?"

I thought of the large, blond, extremely deadly man my sister had married just a month before. I thought of his bigger, more deadly brother. I thought of the dark-haired murderer of my dreams. "Kind of. Not really, no. In a way."

She laughed and waved me forward into the house. "I don't blame you. They're fascinating, aren't they? Much more so than movies and books lead you to believe. Dark Ones are . . . ooh, so many things. Sexy. Mysterious. Sensuous. You know about Beloveds, don't you? How there's only one woman to redeem each Dark One, and they have to go through seven steps to save him, and that once they do, they're bound together forever and ever?"

"Yes," I said, my devil once again prodding me to do more than smile. "I know about Beloveds."

"Isn't it just the most romantic thing ever? I wonder what it would be like to have one as your lover. Wouldn't you think they would be intense? Kind of overwhelming, but in a good way?"

I remembered how Avery seemed wholly absorbed in Jas. "I think 'intense' is a good description."

"And then there's the bad-boy image. Who doesn't

love a bad boy? Who doesn't want to redeem them, make them whole again, show them the power of love?" She sighed, then giggled and poked me on the arm. "Listen to us! Mooning over vampires just like a couple of teenagers with a sparkle fetish! Mysterious and romantic they may be, but they're not for the likes of us. Shall we get started?"

My nose wrinkled as I looked around the entry hall. Directly across from the door was a staircase leading up to murky gloom, the pale fingers of light that managed to fight their way in through the boards on the windows not doing much to light the interior. To my right was a large room that seemed to stretch the length of the house, the dark, stained wallpaper making odd patterns that seemed almost to move when seen peripherally. To the left was a narrow hall with several doors, no doubt leading to smaller rooms. Thankfully, the house was empty of all furniture, nothing but a few torn shreds of ancient newspaper and bits of twine lying in desolation on age-stained wood floors to mark its removal.

"Mice," I said, rubbing my nose against the smell of stale rodent droppings.

"Probably, but it doesn't smell too fresh. Dee says the house was fumigated last month, so there shouldn't be anything alive in here but us. At least . . ." She paused at the foot of the stairs, her face tight for a moment before she shook her head. "No, there's nothing here but us. I must be imagining things."

"Oh, *that's* not going to give me the creeps," I said, rubbing my arms as I looked around the gloomy room.

Diamond just laughed and ran up the stairs, turning on her camera as she did so. "Don't forget to get several different angles of each room. I'd like to piece together each room's photos into a panorama if possible. Buyers love panoramas."

"Anyone would have to be insane to want to buy this monstrosity," I muttered to myself as I twitched my shoulder aside just in time to avoid hitting a massive cobweb that drifted down from an ornate, but filthy, brass light fixture. "I can only imagine what a barrel of laughs the basement is going to be."

"Just imagine it all fixed up, filled with people and laughter," Diamond called as she started up the second flight.

"If one single mouse so much as sticks his nose out of the wall at me, I'm leaving!" I bellowed up the stairs.

A faint sound of her tinkling laughter was my only answer. Dammit, she even laughed nicer than me. Hers was all lightness while mine came out throaty, as if I were a five-pack-a-day smoker.

"My life sucks," I said to no one as I stomped loudly toward the back of the hallway, checking each room before heading toward the door Diamond had indicated led to the basement. "Everyone has hooked up but me. And what do I have, house? Huh? What do I have? I'll tell you what I have," I said in a loud voice as I grabbed the doorknob. "I have a job that's going nowhere, a deranged vampire murderer trying to drive mc insane, and abso-friggin'-lutely no man on the horizons. I swear, what I wouldn't give to meet someone—urf!"

The force of a brick wall bursting through the basement doorway and slamming straight into me not only drove all the air from my body but sent me flying backward, the brick wall falling with me in a tangle of arms and legs, and heads clunking together painfully. My camera fell to the floor, and the tinkle of coins and the smashing of glass warned that the contents of my purse had spilled out under the force of the impact.

It took me a few seconds to shake the stars from my aching head, but that gave my lungs time to reinflate after the brick wall—which I was amazed to see turned out to be a man—rolled off me.

He spoke in some lyrical language, stopping himself to grab my hand and yank me to my feet. "I'm sorry, I didn't know you were there. Get out."

"Huh?" I said, rubbing my forehead where it had smacked against his. "Who are you? What are you doing here? We were told the house was empty."

The man cast a glance over his shoulder to where a narrow stairway descended into the yawning blackness of the basement. "Get out now! He knows I found the exit that led to this place!"

"Who knows you're here? Oh, man, if my camera is broken—" I ignored the man when he ran toward the front door, instead squatting to scoop up the small collection of coins, my now broken compact mirror, a tube of lipstick, and some sort of gray-striped flat round stone edged in gold, with a gold dragon embossed on one side. "What on earth is this? Hey, mister, this must be—holy Mary and all the apostles!"

Another man emerged from the blackness of the basement, but instinctively I knew this was no normal man, not with the way power and fury were rolling off him in almost visible waves. I clutched my things to my chest, stumbling backward to get out of his way, ignoring the pain of the coins and broken compact as they cut into the flesh of my palm, my eyes huge as his attention was momentarily directed my way. I froze, unable to breathe, but was instantly dismissed as he turned toward the front door, raising one hand as he bellowed out a word.

"Desino!"

Automatically, I translated the word from Latin to English—*halt*—and for a second, it seemed as if the world had stopped rotating. Everything seemed to hold its breath. Time just stopped dead as I stared in horrified wonder at the man. A sudden dizziness overtook me as the air in the house was suddenly contracted, then exploded outward with the velocity and volume of a nuclear explosion.

I fell to the ground, my arms around my head, as the walls of the house itself groaned. I was going to die right then and there, without even finding someone to love.

"Damn," I whispered to my knees, and consigned my soul to heaven.

Chapter Two

Heaven, it seemed, didn't want me. I realized this when the furious, frightening man stalked past me toward the man with whom I'd collided, the same man who was even now trying desperately to wrench open the front door.

"You dare steal from me!"

The powerful man's voice was as terrible as a nightmare, shrill and piercing little bits of my soul, making it feel as if it were being ripped from me.

"I would never do anything so heinous, Lord Bael," the other man said, dropping to his knees in a penitent position when he realized the door wouldn't open. "It was my master. He covets your tools, not I."

"Your master is a dead man," the one named Bael said, his words wrapped in such horrible tones, I didn't for one minute doubt the veracity of the prophecy. "What is your name?"

"Ulfur, my lord."

I watched the scene with terrified amazement. Was the powerful man named Bael some sort of a peer? He had a British accent, so maybe he was some visiting dignitary. I wracked my brain trying to remember who owned this house before it got tangled up in probate. Maybe the Bael person was the owner? If that was so, why hadn't he contacted the agency to let us know he was going to be present for the initial inspection?

"Who is your master?"

"Alphonse de Marco."

"I do not know this name. Where are my tools?"

"I do not have them, my lord," Ulfur said, spreading his hands wide. He had a bit of an accent, too, something Scandinavian. Slowly I got to my feet, still clutching my purse and its spilled contents, watching the men warily, my gaze lingering for a minute on the larger of the two. He had short brown hair and a worried-looking face that was more interesting than handsome, and wore a pair of jeans and a dark brown leather jacket. From beneath the back of his jacket, I got a glimpse of something shiny, something bulky.

Clearly Ulfur was lying and up to no good. He'd no doubt taken something from the basement. I glanced down to my hands where the gold-chased stone was clutched with the coins, and amended that to he'd taken something valuable from the basement. It behooved me to tell the owner what Ulfur had done, but I couldn't bring myself to speak. The English peer was just too . . . wrong. His presence felt bad, like he shouldn't be there. Almost like he foreshadowed disaster.

"Where are they?"

The volume of his voice dropped, but I felt physical pain at Bael's words, just as if they were etched with acid.

"I do not know, my lord," Ulfur said again, his head bowed now. "I know only that my master sent me to find them before the lichmaster Ailwin did so."

"Ailwin," Bael snarled, and I heard the rain of glass, as if his very words had smashed the windows nearest us. "*That* name I do know. Jecha!"

My eyeballs just about popped out of my head when, as if by magic, a large, muscular woman suddenly appeared before the peer. "My lord Bael?" she said, bowing low. "What is your pleasure?"

"Ailwin," Bael said, the word flaying me like a whip. I backed up down the hall, toward what I knew was the kitchen. I didn't know what was going on, but it brought up all sorts of unpleasant memories from a trip to visit my sister earlier this year, and I'd be damned if I got caught up in something weird again.

I bumped into something that moved, and almost shrieked, wheeling around to see Diamond making shooing gestures toward me. "I did both floors upstairs. Are you done here?"

"Am I . . . no!"

"No?" She frowned. "Oh, for pity's sake . . . don't tell me you saw a mouse!"

"No. I saw them."

"Them who?"

"The people out front. The two men who came up from the basement."

"What people? Cora, are you teasing me? I told you that this house was empty."

"Yeah, well, tell that to the basement people."

"*Tch,*" she said, pulling open the basement door. "Let me go down and see for myself."

"They're up here now," I called after her disappearing figure, but she evidently decided to ignore me.

I tiptoed down the hallway until I could see the front doors. Bael was grinding out some horrible instructions about locating and torturing the person named Ailwin, going into sickening detail about what he'd like done.

"Go," Bael said, waving his hand toward the woman, and just like that, she was gone. "As for you . . ."

Ulfur had half turned toward me, angling himself so

his back was to the wall, no doubt to keep anyone from seeing that he had an object stuffed into the back of his jacket.

I bit my lip, unsure if I should say something, or just let it go. I didn't condone stealing at all, but . . . my little devil urged me to turn around and walk out of the house, to leave the two men alone, but my conscience wouldn't let me. It was obvious the strange stone I held must belong to the Englishman, and that meant I had to return it.

I started toward him with the intention of doing just that when Bael threw wide his arms and, with a voice filled with fury, screamed, *"Abi in malam crucem, confer te in exsilium, appropinquabit enim judicium Bael!"*

"Go to torment, go into banishment, for the judgment of Bael is at hand," I whispered in translation, and just like that, I was slammed by a wall of power as the floor fell out from beneath my feet.

A scream was literally ripped from my throat as I plummeted into blackness, but it was a short-lived scream, one that turned to, "Ow! Ow, ow, ow! Jesus wept!" For the second time in a few minutes, I shook stars from my eyes and pushed myself into a sitting position, wincing when my hands, still clutching my things, came into contact with sharp, pointy rocks. "What the *hell*?"

"Not Abaddon, no," a weary voice came from behind me. I got to my knees and looked over a large, craggy boulder that squatted next to me. The man named Ulfur lay facedown on the rocky ground. "Worse. We're in the Akasha."

"How . . . what . . . huh?" I looked around as I got painfully to my feet. We seemed to be on some sort of horrible windswept, rocky moor. Or at least what I thought of as a moor, never having seen one in person.

But this place . . . it brought a new level of angst to the word "desolate." The wind seemed to carry with it the voices of a thousand tormented souls, the ground, stones, and sparse vegetation all the same shade of dusty brown. It was very rocky—not soft, smooth rocks, but sharp, pointed ones that jabbed up out of the earth as if they were straining to escape. "What's an Akasha?"

Ulfur groaned as he rolled over, brushing himself off as he sat up. "The Akashic Plain, more frequently known as the Akasha, is what mortals think of as limbo. It's a place of punishment, of permanent banishment, and before you ask, yes, it is possible to leave it, but you have to be summoned out. I think my face is broken."

"Limbo? How did we get here? We were in the house. . . . Ow. What the devil . . ." I tossed my handful of coins, flinching as I pulled a thin sliver of gold from where it had pierced my finger. "Oh, holy Chihuahua, that hurts. Ugh. I broke the rock you stole."

"The what?" Ulfur touched his forehead, his fingers pulling away red.

"The rock you dropped when you crashed into me. The one you stole from that English dude. All the little gold parts are twisted up, and the gray stone is in about a dozen little pieces."

He jerked upright at that, one hand scrabbling behind him to find whatever it was he had stuffed beneath his coat. What he pulled out was a flattened goldfish disk, discolored and stained. "The Anima! Oh, no . . ."

"You know, there's a limit to how many unbelievable, confusing things I'm willing to entertain in any given hour, and I think this hour has far surpassed that limit. What the heck is an Anima? And why did you steal it? And who was that English guy, why did he feel so wrong, how did we get here, where exactly is this Akasha place, and most importantly of all, how do I get back to the house?"

"Those are a lot of questions," Ulfur said, his shoulders slumping as he touched one torn edge of the flattened gold. "I'm dead. That's all there is to it. I'm dead. Again." He looked up at me, and I noticed that he had absolutely black eyes, no difference between iris and pupil. "The Occio is destroyed, as well?"

"Who knows? I certainly don't," I said, giving up and sitting down on the least pointy part of the boulder between us. "I just want to find a first aid kit so I don't get tetanus or something like that, and then get out of here. Oh, and chocolate wouldn't hurt, either. I'd take some chocolate."

"Let me see," Ulfur said, stumbling over to where I sat. I held out my hand. "No, not your hand, the Occio."

"The rock?" I held out my other hand, the one with the bits of twisted gold and broken bits of gray stone.

He frowned at it, touching one of the pieces with the tip of a finger. "I don't understand it. This is a Tool of Bael. Why would it be destroyed?"

"It's not a tool. It's like a . . . I don't know, pendant or something." I looked around the bleak landscape, wondering what sort of weird being the Englishman was that he could either make me insane or magically teleport me somewhere. "Who's Bael when he's at home, anyway?"

Ulfur's black-eyed gaze met mine—he was about to answer my question when he suddenly squinted at me. "You're . . . glowing."

"I beg your pardon?"

"You're glowing. There's a sort of shadowed glow about you."

I held up a hand. "You know what I think? I think we're both nuts, me because I let myself get caught in weirdness again, and you because you are seeing things."

"I'm not seeing things, not in the sense you mean. You're glowing."

"Look, Ulfur—" I stopped in the middle of telling him that there was no way on god's green earth that I was glowing, when I noticed something odd about him.

"Hey," I said, pointing at him. "You're glowing."

He looked down at himself. "This doesn't make any more sense than the Tools being destroyed. Why would we both glow just because we were banished to the Akasha?"

"Yeah, about that," I said, getting up off my rock to circle him. I'd be damned if he didn't have a faint blackish glow around him, almost like a corona. "When you say 'banished,' what exactly do you mean?"

"Bael, the premier prince of Abaddon, banished us here. Or rather, he banished me, and you must have gotten caught in his power during the banishment. He spoke some sort of a curse when he did it—"

"Abi in malam crucem, confer te in exsilium, appropinquabit enim judicium Bael," I repeated.

Ulfur's eyebrows rose.

"Basically it means go to hell, you're banished by Bael's judgment. I went to a Catholic school," I explained when he looked impressed at my knowledge of Latin. "I can say 'of the Antichrist' in ten different languages."

"How very . . . useful."

"Premier prince? That Englishman was a prince? I figured he must be someone important because you and that big chick were 'my lording' him all over the place, but a prince? Wow. I'm going to have to tell Jas that I saw a real prince. He seemed kind of . . . evil . . . for a prince."

"He is evil," Ulfur said, slumping onto my place on the rock. "The title 'prince' is an honorific, nothing more. He's the head demon lord of Abaddon."

"Abaddon being . . . ?"

"Its closest approximation would be hell."

I gawked at him, my skin crawling with sudden horror. "That guy was the devil?"

"No. Not in the mortal sense. Abaddon isn't what you know of as hell—it's . . . well, it's Abaddon. Mortals based their concept of hell on it, just as they based their concept of heaven on the Court of Divine Blood, but they are not the same thing. Abaddon is ruled by seven princes, seven demon lords."

"And the Bael guy, the man with the wicked fashion sense and plummy English voice, heads the whole place up?" I tried to stop my brain from squirreling around at the fact that the devil had looked at me, had walked right past me, and had evidently been so pissed at the man before me, I'd gotten swept along in his wrath, but I just couldn't resolve the idea of Satan and the man in the blue suit.

"Yes."

I breathed deeply for about two minutes, then said, "OK. There's a guy named Bael, and you stole a couple of pretty things from him. Why, Ulfur, did you steal a couple of pretty things from the man who rules hell?"

"My master made me." He looked about as dejected as you could get. My heart went out to him despite the fact that I was now in serious trouble because of him. "I'm a lich. When my master gives me a command, I follow it. I am bound to him."

I pursed my lips, wondering if I wanted to know what a lich was. I decided that so long as I had met Satan, I might as well hear everything. "And a lich is what?"

"I was a spirit. An Ilargi stole my soul, and had me resurrected. When soulless spirits are resurrected, they become liches."

"The things you learn when you least expect them," I said, filing away the lich info. "So this boss of yours told you to steal something from the big mucky-muck of hell? Is he insane, too, or just sadistic?"

"Both. I just don't understand why the Tools were destroyed. It doesn't make—" He stopped suddenly, his eyes opening wide, but before he could say anything more, he just blinked out of existence.

I stared in disbelief at the rock where a second before Ulfur sat, finally gathering my tattered wits together enough to wave my hands through the air, but he didn't just go out of my vision; he was gone.

"Well, hell," I said, my brain giving up at that point and more or less simply curling up into a fetal ball and whimpering softly to itself.

"Not hell, Akasha," a woman's voice corrected me. I turned to see two people approaching, one of whom, at least, I recognized.

"Diamond!" The relief I felt on seeing her cheerful little blond self was almost overwhelming. Until, that is, I realized that if I was seeing her there, it must mean she had been banished with Ulfur and me. "Oh no, not you, too?"

"There you are! Margaretta told me that she'd find you, and here we are. Isn't this exciting, Cora? We're in the Akasha!"

I looked from Diamond to the little woman who stood next to her. She was under four feet tall, had a bright, slightly brittle smile on her face, and was holding a pamphlet, which she gave to me.

"Good morning, and welcome to the Akasha. I am, as your friend said, Margaretta. I'm the greeter here. If you consult the pamphlet, you'll find in it many useful details about the Akasha, such as what you can expect during your banishment, a history of the notable figures who inhabit these regions, as well as a biography of our Hashmallim of the month. You'll see that this month we're featuring Hashmallim."

I looked at the pamphlet she shoved into my hands. Sure enough, there was a section titled "Get to Know Your Gaolers," followed by a subtitle of "Hashmallim of the Month: Hashmallim." Beneath that was the picture of a large black blob. "Uh . . . what's a Hashmallim?"

"The Hashmallim are the Court of Divine Blood's police force, and they rule over the Akasha."

"You have a policeman of the month here?" I couldn't help myself from asking. It all just seemed too bizarre for words.

"Hashmallim of the month, yes. As you can see, Hashmallim gave a particularly interesting interview regarding the subject of perpetual torment."

A question trembled on the tip of my tongue. After a few moments' struggle, I decided I couldn't hold it back any longer. "Just out of idle curiosity, what was the previous Hashmallim called?"

"Last month's Hashmallim of the month?" Margaretta thought for a few seconds. "That would be Hashmallim."

I nodded. It was what I had expected. "They're all named Hashmallim, aren't they?"

"Oh, yes. That is what they are," the little woman told me earnestly.

"I've always wanted to see one up close, but my grandmother wouldn't let me," Diamond said, looking thoughtful for a few seconds before taking my arm. "Oh, Cora, Margaretta says that they're having a 'Meet Your Fellow Damned' breakfast, and I think we should go. You never know who we could meet—Margaretta says the meet and greets are always very popular, so we'll want to get in right away to get a nice table. That way we can eyeball who's there. Wouldn't it be romantic if you had to be banished to the Akasha in order to find your one true love?"

"You can't be serious," I asked her, squeezing the last morsel of disbelief from my emotional center. "Why aren't you screaming and yelling about being here? Why aren't you freaking out? Why aren't you asking what's going on?"

She tipped her head to the side. "Why should I freak out? This is a chance in a lifetime, Corazon. Not many people get to actually visit the Akasha."

I glanced at the little woman. "The man who was with me, Ulfur, he said something about the only way you can get out of this place is if someone summons you. Is that right?"

"Yes, it's right. Although I should note that unless you have some sort of a bond with the Summoner, it's not easy to remove a member of the Otherworld from the Akasha. It's policy, you see. Now, you mortals, you're different."

"We are?" My hopes leaped up with a happy little song on their lips. "You mean we can leave?"

"Oh, no," she said, shaking her head and glancing at her watch. "It would hardly be a place of perpetual punishment if you could just walk out, would it? I'm sorry, but I'm going to have to cut this short if I want to see the lich you mentioned before I have to give the welcome speech at the meet-and-greet breakfast. It'll be held to the south, by the way, in the fifth quadrant, at the lodge level in the Hall of Burning Flesh."

"Fifth quadrant?" I asked, watching as Margaretta made a tick mark on a list of names and bustled off. "Hall of Burning Flesh?"

"Sounds like such fun! Are you coming?" Diamond asked, trailing after Margaretta.

"Er . . . no, I think I'll pass on the flesh-burning breakfast."

"Pfft," Diamond said, giving me a cheery wave. "This isn't Abaddon, after all. I'm sure they won't burn anyone's flesh at the breakfast. That would be totally unhygienic. See you later!"

I looked upward, at the sky, as if an answer to all my woes would be written there, but there was nothing but brownish gray sky that led down to the stark, inhospitable landscape. "Could this day get any weirder?"

No one answered me, for which I was strangely relieved. I decided that if I had a better chance than most at getting out of the (probably quite literally) godforsaken spot, then I'd best be looking around to find that way out.

I wandered around for what could well have been days. I know it was at least a few hours, because my shoes were beginning to show wear from the sharp rocks. The color of the sky didn't change, however, and I didn't seem to find any way out of the rocky-moor area, assuming Margaretta wasn't full of bull about there being welcome breakfasts in what sounded like the civilized part of the Akasha.

"I swear I'm going around in circles," I muttered under my breath as I glared suspiciously at a car-sized boulder vaguely in the shape of a hand flipping the bird. "You look familiar. Right. I'm going to go that way this

time." I moved around the rude rock and came to a
dead stop. Lying on the ground snuggled up next to the
base of the boulder was a man. At least I thought it was
a man.

"Hey. You OK?" I asked, not wanting to get close,
but at the same time wanting to make sure he wasn't
hurt or something. "Mister? Dammit."

I crept closer, my skin twitchy as I neared him, the
devil in my mind pointing out that it was just last week
that I'd watched a horror movie where a body that
looked dead actually wasn't, and had leaped up in a
manner guaranteed to cause incontinence in viewers,
subsequently ripping the unwary couple who stumbled
over it to shreds with long, razorlike claws.

I checked the guy's hands, but there didn't seem to
be any signs of claws. As I neared him, I adjusted my
image of someone who might need help, to someone
who was long past it.

"Oh, you poor guy." I squatted down next to his
head, taking in his gray skin, and cheeks so sunken, the
cheekbones stood out in painful relief. His mouth was a
slash of gray the same color as his flesh. He wore what
was probably a very expensive weathered black suit coat
and pants, but was now covered in the same brown dirt
that tinted everything in the Akasha. His hands bore
long, sensitive-looking fingers, the sinews that stood out
on the backs of his hands lending credence to the fact
that he was dead. "Did you die out here all by yourself?
I wonder."

There were no obvious signs of injury, no blood, no
mangled limbs. . . . It was as if he'd simply lain down and
died. A strange sense of sorrow filled me at the sight of
the man. He looked almost familiar, but as I studied his
face, I realized that it must have been a trick of the
shadows. Still, I felt an inexplicable, frustrated need to

help him. Perhaps there was someone I could call to take care of his remains? Someone who would clean him up and give him a decent burial. I brushed back a lock of hair that lay across his forehead. His hair was dark brown, almost black, sweeping back from the brow down to about ear length. "When you were alive, I bet you were quite the hunk," I said, gently combing his hair into a semblance of order, wishing I could wash the dirt from his face.

Without thinking, my fingers trailed down the length of his jaw, his slight stubble rasping softly.

"*Very* hunky," I said, unable to keep from noticing the gently blunted chin, and barest hint of a chin dimple that had he been alive, would have driven me wild. His nose was long and narrow, but with a couple of little bumps in it that most likely owed their existence to acts of violence. "Were you a fighter rather than a lover, then?"

A brown beetle emerged from under his open shirt, wandering out across his collarbone. I picked it off, lifting up his shirt a little to peer underneath and make sure there were no more insects inside it.

My fingers traced the curve of a thick pectoral muscle.

"OK, I've changed my mind. You weren't just hunky—you were mind-numbingly gorgeous. What did you do to end up here? And why did you die?" I sighed, and tidied up his shirt, standing up to look around. "Let me see if I can't find someone—hey! You! Yes, you! How many yous do you think there are around here?"

About a hundred feet away, a slight woman with a hunted look on her face was dashing around the rocks in a serpentine manner, tossing a worried look over her shoulder. She glanced toward me, pausing with the body language that said she was going to bolt any second. "Run!" she said, waving a hand vaguely. "There's a wrath demon on the hunt!"

"Bully for him. There's a dead guy here who needs our help."

"No one can die in the Akasha," the woman said, glancing behind her again.

"Well, someone has, and he needs a proper burial. Are there some sort of funeral-home people here?"

"No one dies in the Akasha," she repeated, stepping toward me a half-dozen feet. She peered over the edge of the boulder. "Oh, him. He's not dead. He's a Dark One. He simply has no blood left."

"He's a vampire?" I looked down at the man, aghast. "What's he doing here?"

"Nothing, unless someone feeds him, and no one is crazy enough to do that. Dark Ones are not to be messed with." She looked over her shoulder again, suddenly jetting off, throwing back at me, "And neither are wrath demons! If you know what's good for you, you'll get out of here!"

I looked in the direction she had pointed, but didn't see a sign of any movement. Still, if something scary was coming, it would be best to move along.

"I'm sorry," I told the comatose vampire. "It's nothing personal, but my brother-in-law aside, I haven't had good experiences with you guys."

I hurried off in the direction that the woman had taken, my feet slowing as I thought back about the brush of the vampire's hair against my fingers. It was long and silky, despite being coated with dirt. And the stubble on that sexy chin had felt soft, yet abrasive enough to make my fingertips tingle. Likewise the soft brown hairs of his chest when I had picked off the beetle. It struck me then that his flesh hadn't been deathly cold. . . . It was cool, below room temperature, but not the icy chill of death.

"Poor guy," I said again, turning back to look at the

obscene rock. I couldn't believe I was feeling any sort of empathy for a bloodsucking fiend, but somehow, the shrunken, gray-skinned man who lay back there didn't seem at all to be the fiendish short. He was . . . needy.

"No one will feed you," I said, gnawing on my lower lip. The savvy part of my mind told me to run far, far away from the vampire. I knew how deadly they could be—I had almost nightly reminders of that. But the idiot part of my brain, the part that fell for con artists, and lost puppies, and kids who cried in stores because they couldn't have a toy, that part commanded my feet to take me back the way I'd just come.

"This is stupid," I told the man when I got back to him. "You're a vampire. You're nothing but trouble. I'm not going to feed you and have you go kill someone." I knelt next to him, wondering how one went about feeding a comatose vampire. It wasn't something that came up much at the office. I pried open his lips and smooshed my wrist up against his teeth, prodding him on the shoulder as I said, "Mister? Soup's on. So to speak. Oh, god, what am I doing? I can't believe I'm actually trying to save you. Only . . . if you're as powerful as I think you are, then you can get Diamond and me out of here. OK? Do we have a deal? I give you blood and you get us out of the Akasha? One bite for yes, two for no, all right?"

The vampire just lay there, his eyes closed, his hair begging to be stroked. How on earth did one resuscitate a vampire? Mouth-to-mouth? I removed my wrist from his mouth, eyeing his lips with concern. He wasn't dead, but it seemed somewhat creepy to just slap my mouth on his and breathe for him. What if there were beetles in his mouth?

"Urgh," I said, shivering. "Too icky. I'd better look before I try that."

If anyone told me that one day I'd be kneeling in

limbo, prying open the mouth of an almost-dead vampire to see if insects had invaded him, I'd have laughed myself silly. It didn't strike me at all as funny as I angled the man's head first one way, and then another, trying to get enough light to see into his mouth. With a muttered apology, I wiped off my forefinger as best I could, and swept it around his mouth to make sure there were no lurking bugs.

His mouth was surprisingly warm, not moist the way a mouth should be, but slightly humid. I sat staring down at him, my index finger in his mouth, a sudden jolt of awareness hitting me that I was ashamed to admit was akin to arousal.

It got worse when he started sucking on my finger.

"Oh, my," I said, staring in amazement as his neck muscles worked. "Mercy. I think . . . oh, man. Mister? You there?"

I pried up one eyelid, but his eyes were rolled back. Still, he must have some sort of an awareness if his suckle reflex had been triggered.

"What could work on a finger can work for a wrist," I told him, gently removing my finger, letting it trail along his parched lower lip. I was going to edge my wrist between his teeth, but some urge deep inside me instead had me bending over him, holding my hair out of the way with one hand as I angled my neck down over his mouth. A strange awareness prickled along my skin as his dry, cool lips touched my neck. I waited a minute, but he did nothing. With a sigh, I scooted down until I was partially draped over his body, my hair spread over him like a screen as I shifted in tiny little movements until my nose was buried in the dusty silken coolness of his hair. I slid a hand under his neck, pressing his mouth to my flesh, my whole body tight and tense, as if I were waiting for a blow.

A soft exhalation of his breath warmed my skin for a moment, followed by a brief rasp of his tongue. "Go ahead," I told him, breathing in the scent from his hair, ignoring the musty smell of the dirt to revel in the woodsy, earthy scent that seemed to sink in through my pores.

Pain suddenly flared in my neck, pain that quickly turned to heat that rippled outward, flowing down through my veins. I moaned, clutching his head to me, the sensation of life flowing from me to him more arousing than anything I'd ever felt in my life. No wonder Jacintha didn't mind when Avery needed to feed from her—this was the most erotic sensation I'd ever felt, and that was with a comatose vampire. What would it be like when he was awake?

The impaired side of my mind cackled to itself that I could even contemplate feeding the vampire after he was on his feet again, but at that moment, I would have been willing to sign away all common sense in order to stay just as I was.

Two hands suddenly gripped my arms, the fingers biting into my flesh, holding me against him as he continued to feed, the sensation of his mouth making my breasts grow hot and heavy, and much more secret parts sit up and take notice.

Suddenly, I was on my back, the rocks beneath me digging painfully into my back, the vampire's body heavy on mine, but none of that mattered. It was his mouth that my entire awareness was focused on, his wonderfully hot mouth still on my neck as he drank deeply, and I had the oddest feeling that I could actually sense the blood flowing through his body, replenishing him, like water poured over parched earth. It soaked into every atom of his being, and with each passing moment, I felt myself soaring on a sort of high, a blissful awareness that I was fulfilling a need that had, until that moment, lain dormant in both of us.

My hands slipped from his head as I gave myself up to him, floating away on a fluffy cloud of euphoria, content with life at long last.

Chapter Three

Alec couldn't believe what he was seeing. He had rolled over to find a woman in his arms. She lay on top of him now, her head limp against his neck, her heart slowly beating, yet at the same time he could swear he felt it beating within him, as well.

Someone had fed him. Someone, this woman lying across him, had, for an unknown reason, fed him.

"Who are you?" he asked, his voice harsh and rough from his coma.

She didn't answer; she just lay across his torso, her body warm on his. He closed his eyes for a moment at the pain that awareness brought with it.

Dammit, he wasn't even allowed to escape the hell of his life through near death. He was to have no peace, no relief; not even the insensibility of a coma was to be granted to him. His heart, or what remained of it, was sick with the knowledge that he had an eternity of even more torment to exist through.

"All right," he told the woman, shoving at her arm. "You've done what you were sent to do. I'm awake and miserable. Get off me."

She made no move, just continued to lie there on top of him.

And the damned rock still dug into his back.

He sighed, wondering how much more torment he could survive before going stark, staring mad. Insanity seemed like the only route open to him, the only escape of the torment of his life, and yet, his pride had always held him back from just simply going mad. Now he wondered if it wasn't easier than existing for each excruciating second.

"You're hurting me. Not that you probably care, but I'd like to get up and smash a certain rock to gravel, so if you'd kindly remove yourself from me, I'd appreciate it."

The woman still didn't move, and it struck Alec at that moment that her heartbeat was too slow, her body too heavy on his.

"Miss?" he said, prodding the woman.

She lay limply on him, her breath shallow on his neck. For a moment, he closed his eyes, breathing in the scent of her. She smelled like wildflowers after a rain, clean and pure and sweet as honey. Unable to stop himself, he turned his face into her hair and breathed deeply, pulling her scent into his lungs, burning it to his memory.

Something inside him thrummed as the deep hunger awoke again. He inhaled deeply again, wanting to feed on her, wanting to take within himself the warmth he knew she held, the sweet, spicy taste of her blood still on his tongue. If he turned his head just a little more, he could reach her shoulder. He could drink until he was full. He could take everything she had to offer, every last sip of life, and roll her off him. She deserved it for torturing him this way. If only she didn't smell so damned good . . .

He growled a few oaths to himself as he shifted her

off him, letting her roll into the spot he had chosen for his final resting place, crushing that foul rock into nothing before examining his torturer.

She was mortal, apparently in her early thirties, with brown hair, arched eyebrows, and a delicately boned face that was covered in freckles. Her lips were slightly parted, and he had to fight with himself to keep from bending over her to taste their pink sweetness. With a connoisseur's eye, he cataloged the rest of her—large breasts, broad hips, probably slightly over medium height, big-boned . . . not at all the type of woman he found attractive. He preferred his women on the slight side, delicate and frail. This woman, while not an Amazon, looked every bit the phrase "hearty peasant stock."

Hearty peasant stock or not, he knew he'd taken too much of her blood. Her heartbeat was steady, but it had probably been a close thing. He wanted to tell himself that it didn't matter, that she was clearly there as part of his punishment, but guilt pricked him nonetheless.

Guilt and something else. He caught himself enjoying the sweep of her hips, the rounded weight of her breasts beneath a washed-out blue tank top. Her arms were also freckled, and for some reason, that pleased him.

"Wake up," he told the woman, placing his hands on her arms and shaking her slightly. "I'm tired of looking at your hips. You will awaken now."

She said nothing, just lay there, unconscious. He frowned at her, his gaze straying once more to her breasts, down to the curve of her dusty jeans. He would not be attracted to his tormentor.

"Wake up!" he said louder, and shook her again. "If you don't wake up, I will slap you."

Her chest rose and fell with a shallow pattern of breathing.

"There are times when I'd give anything to never have been born," he muttered, staring at her mouth before tapping her on the cheek.

She didn't move.

He tapped a little harder.

Her forehead wrinkled in a frown. "Ow."

He smiled. "Are you awake now?"

The frown grew, although her eyes remained shut tight. "No. Go away. I was floating. I want to float again."

"You're done floating. Wake up."

Her eyes screwed up. Just what he needed, a stubborn torturer. "Don't want to. Want to float."

"By the saints, woman, that wasn't floating. I almost killed you."

Her eyelashes fluttered a little, but remained closed. Color was returning to her cheeks, he noticed, his gaze once again on her mouth. Lips like strawberry cream, he thought, then gave her another little shake. "It's time for you to wake up now. You've floated long enough."

A little smile turned up the corners of her mouth. "I like your voice. It's sexy. If I can't float, talk some more."

You don't know what you're saying. I took too much blood, and almost killed you.

Blood? Oh, yes, I remember that. You're the vampire who looked like three-day-old roadkill.

Alec jerked backward. She couldn't have just done what he thought she had done . . . could she? Only Beloveds or someone with a close family tie could do that, and lord knew, his family and Beloved died out centuries ago.

Thanks to you, I no longer look like roadkill, he said, eyeing her.

That's good. She stretched and opened her eyes.

"Oh, pretty," the woman said, reaching up to touch his face. "I always wanted to have green eyes."

You shouldn't. You have lovely dark eyes. They're very exotic. What the hell was going on here? Why was she able to talk to him this way? It made no sense, unless the fact that he had been so close to death and she had fed him had established a blood bond.

They're plain old brown. She blinked a couple of times, her eyes widening, surprise and no little amount of wariness filling her mind. "Uh . . . how did you do that?"

"I don't know." He examined her face again, finding its delicate lines more pleasing with every perusal. "I don't recognize you, yet you seem familiar somehow."

"Maybe we knew each other in a past life," she joked, rolling herself up to a sitting position.

As soon as she spoke, she froze, staring at him with huge, horrified eyes.

"What is wrong with you?" he asked, not used to women gawking at him as if he were a monstrous beast.

"Vampire," she whispered, tickling a memory in the back of his mind.

He saw again the pooled light from the front of his house in California as it spilled onto the tiled front walk, remembered the three women who had too much to drink, and had evidently picked his house to visit. He remembered also the woman who took one look at him, screamed, "Vampire!" and fainted at his feet. "You were at my house a couple of months ago, weren't you?"

"Oh my god, I didn't recognize you." The woman tried to backpedal, to crawl backward, but the boulder was in the way. All she did was succeed in plastering herself up against it. "I didn't realize it was you, or I wouldn't have—"

"Wouldn't have what?" he asked, his eyes narrowing. "Tortured me? Dragged me back to awareness? Made my life once again an endless cycle of damnation?"

"Fed you," she said, making Alec shake his head.

"Where do you know me from?" he asked, not believing her pretense of innocence.

"I saw you kill a woman," she said, glancing to her right, obviously weighing up the chances of her success escaping him.

"Slim to none if I didn't want you to," he told her, and smiled, making her press herself back against the rock as he leaned forward, catching again her scent of wildflowers. "And at this moment, I don't want you to leave. What woman?"

Her mouth dropped open a smidgen. He couldn't resist rubbing his thumb over her lower lip, gently pushing it upward until she glared at him, brushing away his hand.

"You mean you've killed so many you don't know which one?"

He shrugged. "I've killed a couple of reapers when it was them or me, yes. Are you with the Brotherhood?"

"No, I'm a lapsed Catholic," she answered, her gaze moving over him. *You look better. Your color is back, and you look even more handsome than I imagined. You're downright simmering with sensuality, as a matter of fact. Just being close to you makes me dizzy with all sorts of emotions that I really do not want to have.*

His eyebrows rose a little at the candor of her inner monologue. *I didn't think I was particularly simmering, but I will admit that despite your actions, you intrigue me sexually.*

Her eyes got huge again as she blushed. "Oh my god, you could hear that?"

"Of course."

"Even the bit about me being dizzy?"

"Even that." He frowned. "You appear embarrassed.

Why would you project to me if you did not wish me to hear your thoughts?"

"I didn't project! My brain just thought those things up without my permission."

He gave a mental headshake. Surely she didn't expect him to fall for that?

"I think I'd better leave." She got to her feet, immediately staggering into him, her legs buckling beneath her.

"You're too weak yet," Alec said, catching her before she toppled over. He could feel her head swim with lack of blood. "You lost too much blood. Why didn't you stop me before I took too much?"

She let him push her back down onto the ground, gently guiding her head down between her knees. "I didn't know you didn't have an auto stop when you were full up."

"I do, but replenishing all the blood I lost would have killed you. What is your name?"

"Cora. Corazon Ferreira. Do you know my sister?"

"Corazon," he said, rolling the word around his mouth. It meant "heart," a fitting name for a woman who was so determined to stab him in his. "Spanish?"

"Hispanic. Mom and Dad came from Chihuahua. The place, not the dogs, of course. What . . . er . . . what is your name? Patsy never told me."

"Patsy? Ah, my former neighbor. I'm Alec. How did you know I was a Dark One?"

"Dammit!" she snapped, looking irritated.

"Pardon?"

"'Alec' is one of my favorite men's names! Now you've gone and ruined it for me."

What a very strange woman she was, not at all like a tormentor. Those big eyes, and that delicate face, and a mouth that was starting to hold an unholy fascination for him . . . and then there was the rest of her. He grew hard thinking about the rest of her. With an effort, he focused his attention on the maddening, desirable woman before him. "You're deranged, aren't you?"

"Not quite yet, but I wouldn't be surprised if you pushed me over the edge," she answered darkly, adding, "Alec what?" *Dear god, you're sexy. You're a vampire, but you're so incredibly sexy. I just want to . . . what on earth am I thinking? You're evil!*

Not particularly, no.

You're undead!

Not since you fed me.

You're a murderer! A vampire murderer! A seductive, sensual vampire murderer with gorgeous eyes and perfect hair and oh, holy mother, you can hear me, can't you?

Yes.

Grah! Stop reading my mind!

"Darwin," he said.

She looked like she was the one who was being driven insane. "What?"

"My name. It's Alec Darwin. I do hope I haven't ruined Darwin for you, as well."

She just looked at him as if he were speaking in tongues.

"How do you know me, Corazon?"

She blinked a couple of times, and he had the oddest feeling she was withdrawing mentally. "Darwin doesn't sound like a German name. You sound German. Do you happen to know a Scottish vampire named Avery?"

"Sins of the saints, woman!" His temper snapped, in no little part due to her scent, which was driving him wild with need. "Answer my question!"

"Don't you touch me, you murdering bloodsucker!"

she screamed, clawing her way up the rock until she stood clutching it to keep from keeling over.

Alec felt no real fear in her, just a sense of wariness, and something that he knew instinctively she was hiding from him. No doubt it was her connection with whoever had sent her to torment him. "What have I ever done to you? I don't even know you, and you act like I'm some sort of leper. I said I was sorry about taking too much of your blood, but I believe the extenuating circumstances have been explained."

"*What* did you do?" she asked him, plainly agog. "What did you *do*?"

"That's what I asked, several times now, as a matter of fact." His irritation at her faded with the knowledge that he was enjoying himself. Talking with her might be frustrating, but it was also stimulating, serving to eliminate the boredom that hung so heavily over him while he was being completely and utterly miserable.

She stomped over the three steps to where he stood, poking him on the shoulder. "You killed a woman!"

"So you said. Which one?" He wondered whether if he kissed her right then, she would kiss him back, or slap him. Perhaps she'd do both.

She poked him again. "Who knows? She was driving an oxcart."

"A what?" Those lips were meant for kissing, even when they were tightened into a line, as they were now. He felt himself grow harder as her scent wrapped itself around him. He wished her legs would do the same.

"Oxcart. You know, a cart . . . with oxen. And she ran over me and cut off my head, and then you came along, and—"

"What the hell are you talking about?" he interrupted, distracted almost to madness by the hot need that swelled inside him. It was tied to the hunger, part of it, yet separate. He stood watching her as she spoke, her hands waving in the air, her mouth—oh, that mouth—singing a sweet siren lure.

What was this strange sense of want? he wondered to himself. He had felt hunger for blood before, of course. He'd felt the need for sex, as well. He'd even indulged himself with human relationships whenever the loneliness got to be too much to bear. But this strange sense of possession tied to her was all wrong. He didn't want her, not really. He wanted her blood, nothing more.

She poked him again and he took her hand, the touch swamping him with the knowledge that he was lying to himself.

"It was a long time ago, all right? Like . . . at least a couple of hundred years ago. The ox lady was dressed in some sort of a brown skirt and leather bodice. And there was a town, and some sort of a castle on a hill, and you were wearing . . ." Cora bit her lower lip, hiding her thoughts from him.

I like your Adam's apple.

Well, not hiding those thoughts. *You truly are the strangest woman I ever met.*

I know. Why do I want so badly to kiss you even knowing you killed that woman right there in front of me?

Instantly, his gaze dropped to that sweet mouth. *I have an even better question. Who the hell are you?*

"My name is Corazon Esmeralda Ferreira, and I am a secretary with my ex-husband's real estate agency. I am thirty-two, have a sister who's married to a vampire, and I saw you kill a woman."

"An ox woman, yes, I know. What is the name of the Dark One?"

"Avery Scott. Why did you attack her, Alec? Why did you bite her and bleed her dry?" She wrapped her arms around herself, moving away from him, the faintest hint of horror filling her eyes. "Why did you take what you wanted from her, and just leave her body there on the road like she was nothing?"

"I don't know what it is you're . . ." He started to shake his head, then suddenly stopped. From the depths of his memory, he drew forth the scene she had described. He felt again the heat of the sun on him as he went to woo his Beloved, the scent of the newly turned earth, the sound of cattle lowing peacefully in the distant town where Eleanor lived. It was all idyllic, pastoral . . . until he came across the woman who had just killed his salvation. Slowly, he said, "A woman with an oxcart."

"You attacked her." Cora stared at him, clearly willing him to make the horror go away.

"How do you know what I did?"

"I had a . . . for lack of a better word, a vision."

He said nothing, just closed his eyes, pain swamping him. He was aware that Cora had moved toward him, but stopped, making a little sound of frustration. He acknowledged it, but the bone-deep anguish the memory of that time stirred still held him tight in its grip.

"She killed my Beloved," he said, swaying slightly at all he had lost. Sorrow, agony, and pain burned deep in him, spilling out onto her, but he was unable to stop it. She didn't run from him, however. She moved forward, wrapping her arms and her scent and the light of her soul around him, cradling him as if he were a hurt child. "She killed her before we had Joined, leaving me behind. She took everything from me, my heart, hope . . . life. All that was left me was suffering."

Concern washed over him like a soothing balm, her warmth touching all the dark places of his heart, and even though he knew she kept a little piece of herself back from him, he was stunned with the realization of what she was giving him.

She gave him compassion, heartfelt human compassion, the sweetest of all gifts that he could have received. He accepted it, acknowledging what it cost her, knowing she didn't want to feel emotions for him, but also knowing they shared a bond, even if it was only one of blood.

It was too much for him. He turned his face into her hair, his arms sliding around her to hold her body tightly to his, needing to feel her, needing to taste her . . . just needing her. His mouth was hot on the flesh of her neck, of her shoulders, his mind filled with the satisfying knowledge that she wanted him with the same need. *How can you taste so good? No other woman has tasted this way. You drive me wild with hunger.*

Vampire, she said, trying to rally a resistance in her own mind, but that faded almost instantly into awareness of him. *Bloodsucker.*

Tormentor. Temptress.

You killed that woman, she accused, trying one last attempt to convince herself.

She killed everything I was.

She bit gently on his ear, her lips caressing his jaw. *I can feel what she did to you. I can feel the agony. How can you live with so much pain inside you?*

I don't live. I merely exist. Christ, you are so sweet, he murmured, wanting to claim those luscious lips. *So good. I want you, mi corazón. I want your heat. I want the sweetness that resides within you.*

Go ahead, she told him, her body moving against him in a way that he knew would spell disaster. If she rubbed her belly against him just one more time, he was going to disappoint them both. *Take it, Alec. I want you to.*

He nipped at the skin of her shoulder, wanting more than anything in the world to drink from her, to join himself to her in the most elemental way a Dark One could experience, the hunger chewing him up inside, a fresh torment added to an already miserable existence.

You've lost too much blood, he said, his mouth moving along her shoulder to her neck, moaning to himself at the temptation the beat of her pulse posed. *I want it like I've never wanted anything, but I will not harm you again.*

She made a wordless noise of protest, her body twining against his as she clutched his back, clearly offering herself to him.

No, mi querida, *I cannot allow you to do this.*

She tensed for a moment, and he knew she misinterpreted him. *Mi querida* . . . "my beloved."

Does that word bother you? he asked. *I did not mean it as you believe.*

No, it's just . . . no. I don't mind.

He was mildly puzzled by the shadow of something she kept hidden from him, but the scent and feel and taste of her claimed his full attention. *Christ, how I want you. You are so smooth; you taste so sweet. . . . God give me strength, I can't resist you unless you make me stop.*

She hesitated but, after a moment of struggling with herself, admitted, *I don't want you to stop.*

Alec couldn't keep from kissing her, his mouth brushing against her lips in a way that he could feel made her mindless with pleasure. Her fingers dug into the cloth of his jacket as his tongue traced her lower lip.

"Cielito," he said, and she melted against him, her damned hips grinding against him with urgent little movements. Mi cielito lindo, *let me in. If I cannot have your blood, I must taste you again.*

I'm hardly heaven, and definitely not beautiful, she told him, but parted her lips nonetheless. He reveled in the taste of her as his tongue swept in, finding all her secrets, tasting her sweetness. Her breasts strained against him, her hips moving restlessly now, and when she touched his tongue with hers, he thought it was all over.

I want you, she told him with a sense of wonder that had him believing she didn't know she was projecting again. *I want you more than I've ever wanted another man. I physically ache to have you inside me. I want to kiss you forever. I want to feed you, to give you life, and none of that makes sense! You are a vampire, but oh, how I want you.*

Christ, woman, if you keep thinking things like that . . . he moaned into her mind, so close to taking what she offered. *By the saints, I want you, too. You're making me mad with need. And if you touch me there just one more time, I won't be able to stop.*

She wiggled against him, stroking her hand boldly down his chest.

That's it! You are more than any man can bear. You have no one but yourself to blame for this.

She sucked his tongue, drawing a groan deep from his throat. His hands moved around from caressing her delicious ass to the front of her jeans, tugging the zipper and sliding his hands over those wickedly wanton hips.

I shouldn't be doing this. It's wrong, so very wrong. I should stop you. Oh Mother Mary, right there! She clutched his shoulders as his fingers slid beneath her underwear, pushing it out of the way, discovering all her warm secrets.

It may not be wise, but it certainly isn't wrong, he said, groaning when she reached for his belt buckle, her hands stroking his fly before releasing him into her hands.

It is wrong . . . but I really don't care at this moment. My god, you're hot.

Only for you, mi corazón. His hips moved impulsively as she stroked him. *Do you know what you are doing to me?*

I can feel it, she said, panting into his mind. *I can feel what you feel. This is amazing. This is wonderful. This is . . . oh, you* really *like this, don't you?*

His eyes rolled back in his head for a few seconds before he growled at her, deep from his chest.

"And what of you, temptress? Do you like this?" he asked, his fingers parting her, finding areas with gentle brushes of his fingertips that he knew were driving her mad with ecstasy. Her mouth burned on his, her tongue twining around his in a way that almost pushed him beyond control. *Tell me what you want,* mi cielito.

More, she demanded, *I want more.*

He broke off the kiss, her eyes glazed with passion. "Do you know what you are asking?" His voice was rough with emotion, the erotic images in her mind mirroring his.

"Yes. I don't care. I just want you. Right here. Right now."

She found a rhythm that made him grit his teeth with the need to not end it all in her hands, his pleasure spiraling wildly out of control until he could bear it no longer. He pressed her against the rock, lifting her hips to him, the hot center of her beckoning to him. He slid into her with a groan of purest pleasure, one that was echoed by her as she shifted her hips, taking him even deeper.

Please tell me you're close, he all but begged as she bucked against him, her legs wrapped around his thighs. *I won't last long. And if you don't stop thinking things like that, I'm not going to last, period.*

Now! she yelled into his mind. *Do it now!*

He thrust hard against her, mindless to everything but the need for completion, the burning hunger that roared out of control when her muscles grabbed him, spasming around him as she found her pleasure.

Feed! she demanded, her fingers digging into his shoulders, her back arched against him as the tremors of her orgasm locked her muscles tight.

He couldn't have stopped himself if the world were ending. He bit the spot behind her ear that seemed to beckon to him, feeling her jerk against him for a second before relaxing with a sigh of rapture as he drank. He shared the sensation with her, so she could feel the power of feeding, and that fulfillment joined with his arousal until he thrust deep within her, his climax so powerful, it left him drained of every emotion but one.

And that he refused to acknowledge.

Chapter Four

The moment Alec's orgasm claimed him was the moment the truly reprehensible part of my mind pointed out two things that it felt were important—the first was that I had just had mind-blowingly fabulous sex with a murderous vampire, and the second was that I'd just had mind-blowingly fabulous sex with a murderous vampire . . . right out in the middle of the Akasha. That last point was driven home when in the distance I heard a scream of anger.

Alec pulled back, his breath as rough as mine, the sense of shared fulfillment fading as we stared at each other.

"Good lord. I had sex with you. Right here. Where anyone could have seen us." The taste of him lingered in my mouth, a sweet taste, one I doubted I'd ever get enough of.

Stop it! I yelled at my little devil. *Stop pointing things out like that! For god's sake, look what you made me do—I had sex with a vampire!*

"You don't have to say the word "vampire" like it's revolting. We prefer 'Dark One,' anyway," he said, withdrawing from me with an audibly wet noise that had me wincing in embarrassment.

"Sorry," I murmured. "I was a little bit . . . enthusiastic."

To my utter surprise—and inner delight—he grinned as he tucked himself away. "You weren't the only one who was *enthusiastic*, *querida*."

I bent to retrieve my underwear and jeans, not able to look him in the eye after my wholly irresponsible and completely uncharacteristic behavior, still a little weirded out by his choosing *querida* as a term of endearment.

It was clear he didn't understand that I was the woman who had been killed, hadn't put together the pieces of the puzzle I'd so disjointedly spilled. And although god knew I was physically attracted to him, the last thing I wanted was to be in Jacintha's position—bound to him forever.

Why not? the devil inside me asked before I hushed it up, worried Alec might overhear it. *You're here. You're lonely. He's in pain. You could comfort him. He'd be grateful for that. He might even come to love you.*

I closed my eyes against the pain that thought brought with it. I didn't want to be merely a convenience—I wanted a man who would choose me because of who I was, not because of some connection that was lost several hundred years before, and certainly not because of one random act of sex.

Oh, dear god, that was the single most erotic, most fulfilling experience of my life. But as the endorphins faded, the thought returned to me that I had had sex with a vampire. Jas would *never* let me live that down if she ever heard of it.

"Who is Jas?"

"Jacintha. My sister. And stop reading my mind."

"Stop projecting into my mind if you don't want me to read your thoughts. Jacintha, eh? The one who is a . . ." I felt the brush of his mind against mine for a moment. "A Beloved? Interesting. I do not know this Avery Scott, but I do not get to Britain much."

"I object to you just marching into my head whenever you like," I told him, my hands on my hips now that I was decent again. "I don't think it's polite at all."

"That fact that I've marked you isn't right, either, but that doesn't seem to concern you." He frowned at me. "Just who *are* you?"

"I've told you three times now!"

"Yes, I know your name, and I know that you're mortal, and that you hum when you orgasm, but who are you? Why are you here, and why did you revive me?"

"I felt sorry for you, more fool me," I said, pushing past him to glare at the gently rolling landscape of rocks, dirt, and more rocks. "I hum? Really?"

"Yes."

"How mortifying." It was, too. I had no idea I was a hummer.

He shrugged. "I don't see why you'd feel that way. I think it's charming."

I stared over my shoulder at him. "You're . . . you're a strange man."

"That's been said before. Is that why you came on to me, because you felt sorry for me?"

"I did not come on to you! You were the one thinking all sorts of smutty thoughts about me!"

"You thought them about me, too."

"Only because you put them in my mind! Besides, you manhandled me!"

He raised one glossy black eyebrow, looking me over from crown to toes. "If I had manhandled you, love, you wouldn't be standing right now. I will admit to responsibility for a certain amount of what just happened, but

I don't make a habit of engaging in sexual acts with women I've just met."

There was an odd sort of mental twitch, as if his words weren't quite the truth. I tried to peer into his mind to see just what it was he was shielding from me, but I lacked the ability to just go marching into his head as he did mine.

"Well, thank you so much for making me sound like a great big ho!" I slapped his arm. "For your information, I have never, ever had sex with a man who I knew less than six weeks. Minimum! So you can just stuff that in your 'I'm so incredibly sexy, women can't keep their paws off me' pipe and smoke it!"

He tipped his head to the side, a lock of his hair swinging over his brow. "*Can* you keep your hands off me?"

"Of course I can!" I pushed the lock of his hair back, my fingers trailing down his jaw. Just the touch of his stubble on my fingers restarted fires deep within me. "Look, we had sex, OK? It's no big deal. I admit that it's totally against my character to do that, and that I can't wholly blame you for what happened, but the bottom line is that it's never going to happen again. I don't like you. I don't like men who are prettier than me. And I especially don't like bloodsuckers!"

Is that so? His mind was filled with arrogance as he pulled me up against him, his mouth like fire on mine.

I put both hands on his chest and shoved him back, slapping him before I realized what I'd done.

"Oh!" I stared at him in horror, one hand over my mouth, the other reaching out to touch his cheek. "I'm so sorry! I've never hit anyone before. Did I hurt you?"

Ire flashed in his gorgeous eyes for a few seconds before it faded to amusement. "Unfortunately, I *have* been struck many times. No, you didn't hurt me, although I do not like to be slapped. Please refrain from doing so again."

"I'm sorry," I repeated, appalled at my behavior. "Really, I seem to be all discombobulated today. I think it's because of this whole weirdness of being in the Akasha."

"What did you do to end up here?" he asked, frowning again.

Even frowning, he was the sexiest thing I'd ever seen.

He smiled.

"Stop that!"

"You're projecting."

"I am not! I never project! And what did you mean, you marked me?"

He sighed. "Why won't you ever answer a question I ask?"

"Probably because I don't want to. Did you leave some sort of Dracula mark on my neck? I don't remember Avery doing that, although he sure gave Jas a whole lot of hickeys that she just thought were funny." I tried to look at my own neck, failing as I knew I would. "What sort of mark is it? Am I going to have to wear a scarf forever to keep the Van Helsings of the world from staking me so I won't become a female vamp?"

He rolled his eyes, and just walked away.

I stared after him for a minute, not believing what I was seeing.

"Where are you going?" I finally called once I realized he was really leaving.

Away.

"Away where?"

Does it matter?

"Yes, it matters! You can't just walk away! I gave you blood!"

Thank you for the blood. Good-bye.

I stared at his receding figure, stunned. He was going to leave me? Just leave me? After I'd given him blood and had the most erotic experience of my life, he was just going to leave?

"Hey!" I bellowed. "Alec? You're leaving me?"

He stopped, and I knew, just *knew*, he was sighing.

I apologized for taking more blood than I should. I didn't berate you for reviving me. I made you hum. What more do you want from me?

I bit back my pride and ran after him, trying to follow the same path he took around the rocks. "Well . . . geez, I don't know. I just think that you kind of owe me, you know?"

He turned, his expression dark with anger. "For bringing me back to awareness that I am doubly damned?" He made a low, sweeping bow, his mind filled with bitterness. "Thank you for tormenting me as no one else has done."

"I didn't mean to . . . you didn't want to be woken up?"

"No."

"Why not?"

He gestured around us. "If you had the opportunity of slipping into unawareness of this torment, would you not choose to do so?"

"No. I'd choose to leave."

The look he gave me was filled with scorn. "There is no way out."

"Of course there is. If there's a way in, there's a way out. Am I going to be a female vampire now because of your mark?"

He just stared at me for a couple of seconds, then took me by the wrist and pulled me after him as he headed to what I thought was the north. "If your sister is a Beloved, you must know that it doesn't work like that. The marking I referred to is the mental connection we have. It is one of the seven steps of Joining, which is wholly impossible given that my Beloved died six hundred years ago, but understandable given the amount of blood you gave me."

"Well, I don't know about this marking business," I said, carefully locking away the thought that reincarnation might very well mean his Beloved was alive and kicking, and damned close to jumping his bones again despite her desperate attempt to stay away from him, "but as for the other, I don't know that much about you guys. Jas went off to live with Avery, and . . . well, I'm not very comfortable around him. Or his brothers. Plus there's the fact that Jas has been trying to fix me up with Avery's youngest brother, Daniel, and I—"

The word Alec snarled wasn't at all polite, nor was the face he turned on me as he gripped me with both hands. But what was most intriguing was the hot spurt of jealousy that I could feel rip through him.

He was jealous? Of me? Why did that delight me so much?

I am not *jealous.*

No? So the thought of me having sex with Daniel does nothing—Alec!

His tongue was there in my mouth again, his thigh shoved between mine, his fingers working my zipper down again. *Mine!* he snarled into my head.

Oh, I am so not yours!

You are. You gave yourself to me.

We had sex, Alec. That's all. Get over yourself. Oh, holy mother, do that again first, though. Hooyeah!

Another shout from the distance, somewhat louder, brought sanity back to us. Alec removed his hand from my underwear, his eyes burning with passion as he rezipped my jeans.

"That 'mine!' crap? It's so not happening. I don't like possessive men," I told him.

"At this moment, love, I don't particularly care what you like," he snapped, grabbing me by the hand and hauling me after him.

Chapter Five

"Where, exactly, do you think you're taking me?"

"Away."

"Away where?"

"Just away. You didn't wish to be left behind, so you're coming with me."

"Why?"

Alec stopped and shot me a look that probably should have warned me he was at the end of his patience, but I decided that was less important than knowing where he was hauling me. "Do you ever stop asking questions?"

"Not really, no," I said after some thought. "There are so many things to be answered."

He grinned. My inner devil squealed and swooned at the sight of it. I told her to buck up, that he may be sexy as hell, but he was not for us. "I happen to agree with that philosophy, but now is not the time to discuss it. What did you do to get tossed in here?"

"Wrong place at the wrong time, as best I can figure it out," I said, following when he tugged on my wrist. Although the screaming in the distance had stopped, I had an uneasy feeling that something was back there that I'd rather not meet.

Something is. A wrath demon.

How did you hear about that? You were unconscious.

I know the sound of a wrath demon when I hear one. What wrong place?

I sighed. "You're really persistent, aren't you?"

"No more so than you. Why are you glowing?"

I looked down at myself. "I didn't know I was until Ulfur told me—"

He jerked me forward, spinning around. "Ulfur? You know Ulfur? A ghost about my height, with brown hair?"

"He has brown hair, yes, but he wasn't a ghost. He said he was a . . ." I bit my lower lip, trying to dig the word out of my memory.

Alec's gaze flickered to my mouth. *Stop that.*

Stop what, trying to remember?

No. Stop tempting me with your mouth.

I'm not.

You are. You're flaunting your lips at me. Stop it.

A little warm kernel of feminine pleasure glowed inside me at his mental growl. "I hardly think a bad habit like biting my lip is deliberately flaunting, but if it amuses you to think that, knock yourself out. Lich. That's the word. Ulfur is a lich."

"That's right." Alec looked beyond me, his eyes unfocused. He rubbed his chin with his thumb as he thought, the rasping noise sending little shivers down my back. "Pia said something about them trying to bring him back, but the Ilargi had him by that time."

I couldn't stop looking at him. I tried to look at his shoulder, or the rocks beyond him. I reminded myself that he was a man who didn't think twice about murdering people, not that I didn't feel sympathy with the fact that the ox lady had decapitated me with her cart and left him without his only salvation, but still, he admitted he'd murdered other people. He was bad to the bone, and I didn't give a damn what my swoony inner bad girl thought—I was going to tolerate him only until he got Diamond and me out of this hellhole.

Dear god, I wanted him again. He just stood there, his brain whirling away with some thought, all smoldering sensuality and raw male attraction that made my body hum with happiness.

"Stop that," I said, unable to stand it one minute longer.

He looked startled. "Stop what?"

I stared at his thumb. "Stop tempting me with your manly stubble. And chin. And jaw. But mostly your chin. Did I mention stubble?"

A little frown pulled his eyebrows together. Merciful heaven, even his eyebrows were sexy. I wanted to lick them. "What in the name of the saints are you going on about now?"

It was too much. It was all suddenly too much. "You're too damned handsome, OK? I don't like handsome men! They're always halfway in love with themselves, and they use their looks and their seductive bodies to sway women into doing whatever they want, and I won't have it, do you understand me! I will not have it! Stop being handsome!"

"Corazon—"

"Garrgh!" I yelled, and with both hands, mussed up his hair until it stood up in clumps.

He looked deliciously tousled, like he'd just been engaged in a wonderfully energetic romp between the sheets.

"I hate you!" I yelled, and stomped off, muttering to myself that I would not let him affect me. Sex, I told myself. We just had sex. Not even real sex, more a quickie, just a purely physical reaction to me giving him blood. What right did he have to go around looking all steamy hot and gorgeous?

"I sense that you're angry with me about something," he said drily, falling into step beside me. "But since I also sense it has to do with my hair and beard, I'm at a loss as to how to placate you. If you are through having a temper tantrum, would you mind telling me how you met Ulfur?"

"I might. But first, let's discuss this plan of yours to get us out of here. I assume the exit place is where you're taking me?"

Alec sighed, and stopped. "You're part of my punishment, aren't you? It's not bad enough the council banished me to the Akasha—they sent you here to drive me insane, didn't they?"

"What council? One that oversees the killing of innocent women?"

"No." He started forward again. I watched his back for a moment, absently noting that he had a very, *very* fine walk, before hurrying to catch up with him. My little devil had me taking his hand before I realized what she was doing, but I figured it would be rude to suddenly drop it like it was full of worms or something, so I pretended I didn't feel all warm and fuzzy when his fingers threaded through mine in a way that made my little devil happy. "I was sentenced to remain in the Akasha for crimes committed against Dark Ones."

"But you're one of them," I said, looking at him.

His jaw tightened. "Yes."

"What did you do?"

"How did you meet Ulfur?"

"How are you getting us out of here?" I countered.

"If you don't stop asking me questions instead of answering them, I'm going to make you stop," he threatened, his voice a low, sexy growl that I felt all the way to my toes.

"You're going to kill me, too?" I asked, surprise kicking in when I realized that I wasn't afraid of him. He was a murderer, yes, but somehow, I knew he didn't pose a threat to me. Not that sort of a threat, anyway . . . my peace of mind was another subject.

"Tempting as that thought is, no, I would simply kiss you until you couldn't think anymore."

My eyes widened as he thought about doing that, my breasts, suddenly becoming strumpets, demanding that I walk them right over to his chest, and let them have their way with him.

"Stop it," I said, looking down at my shirt. My nipples had hardened at the thought of Alec's chest, my breasts feeling heavy and very, very needy.

"Now what have I done?" he asked with a distinct note of exasperation.

"It's not you. I'm having some trouble with my breasts."

His gaze instantly dropped to my upper parts. "Problematic, are they?"

"Right now, yes. They want an introduction to your chest. I've told them no, that what happened before was simply a reaction to me feeding you, but they won't listen."

"Perhaps I can be of some assistance," he said in his polite, slightly accented English. "Would you like me to take up the discussion with them?"

"It wouldn't do any good," I said, shaking my head. "They wouldn't listen. They're headstrong."

"We won't know until we try, hmm?" he said, suddenly stopping, turning me around so I faced him. My breasts cheered as his gaze caressed their upper slopes visible through the lacy part of my top.

"Oh, I think I know . . . hooobah!"

Alec didn't bother to introduce himself properly—he just slid both hands underneath my shirt to cup my boobs, and did a cleavage dive. The sensation of his stubble on my now highly sensitized breasts left me clutching his head, my breath caught in my throat as he snaked his tongue between my breasts, his thumbs gently rubbing where my nipples were trying to burst free of my bra.

This is just the blood, I said somewhat desperately. *It's just because I gave you blood that my boobs want you so much.*

This isn't due to you feeding me, mi cielo, he answered, his voice rubbing against my brain in a way that threatened to tumble me into another pit of need and desire. *This is something else.*

What? I asked, shielding from him my secret.

I don't know, but I will enjoy myself fully finding out what. Do you want me to make love to you again?

You didn't make love to me before. We had a mutually desired quickie, brought on by bloodlust.

You just keep telling yourself that, love. He pulled his head from my chest, his grin downright cocky as he pulled down my shirt, giving my breasts one last caress before taking my hand again. "What's this nonsense about me getting you out of here?"

"We have a deal," I said when I was able to pry my tongue off the roof of my mouth.

"We do?"

"Yes. When you were lying there being roadkill, I told you that I would give you blood and you would get Diamond and me out of the Akasha."

"You made a deal with me while I was all but dead due to lack of blood?"

"Yes. You didn't say you wouldn't do it," I pointed out.

He shot me a look.

"All right, all right, I know, it wasn't a fair deal, but it was a deal nonetheless, and if you insist on walking around here looking like sex on two legs, then you can just honor the deal."

"My appearance again," he sighed. "I can't help the way I look, Corazon."

I narrowed my eyes on him. "You could *try* looking ugly, you know."

His green-eyed gaze cast upward for a few seconds in an obvious plea for patience. "If I covered myself in mud, would that help?"

I had a vision of him standing naked, his body slick with water, as I slowly, gently, carefully moved a soapy sponge over his flesh, cleaning him, leaving all that satiny, hot skin exposed, just waiting for me to touch it, taste it—

"You continue with that thought, and I *will* make love to you right here," he warned with a growl.

"Sorry. Mind got away from me. What was the question?"

"Akasha. Getting you out. Me. Someone evidently named Diamond."

"Oh, yes, well, as I said, I made this agreement with your unconscious self, and since you're a big, bad vampire, and everyone is scared to death of you, I figured you could get Diamond—she's the woman who stole my husband, not that I really mind because he's a total dill-wad, but still, there was a matter of pride for about five minutes—then I got over it and realized I should be grateful to her—anyway, she was in the house with me when Ulfur and the English Satan dude were arguing, and whammo! Here we are."

It took Alec a minute to work through all of that. "English Satan dude? A demon lord, you mean? Which one?"

"Um . . . Dean? No, Dale."

"Bael?"

"Yes, that's the guy."

"Christ," he swore.

"I gather he's the head bad guy."

"Very much so." He eyed me with speculation. "What did Ulfur do to bring down Bael's wrath on him, and by extension you and the husband-stealer?"

"He stole some gold thing. Oh, and this." I dug into my pocket and pulled out the broken bits of stone and twisted gold.

"Christ," he repeated, staring at it in horror. "That's one of the Tools."

"It's called the Oculus of Lucifer, I think."

"Occio di Lucifer . . ." His gaze snapped up to mine, a sense of disbelief and wonder and amazement all rolling around inside him. "The Tool has been destroyed."

"Yeah. I didn't do it, though, if that's what you're thinking."

He lifted up my hand that he still held. "You're glowing."

"Well, I can't see it on myself, but I did see Ulfur with a glow. How come you don't glow? I mean, shouldn't you, since you were sent here, too?"

He looked confused for a second before shaking his head. "Cora, you're not glowing because you were sent to the Akasha. You're glowing because somehow you've become infused with the power of the Occio di Lucifer. For all intents and purposes, you are the Tool now."

"Hey! I am not a tool!" I said before what he had said filtered through the dim recesses of my mind. I gasped and grabbed his arm. "Oh my god, you don't mean that! Tell me you don't mean what I think you mean! You do, don't you? You mean it! I'm Satan's eyeball! I'm evil!"

"Calm down, you're not evil. You're simply . . . well,

I don't know what you are. The personification of the Occio, assumedly, although I don't have a lot of experience in that sort of thing. Still, I would guess—"

I never did find out what he guessed, because at that moment he grabbed me around the waist and literally threw me aside. I smashed into a particularly pointy boulder the size of a small pony, cracking my head against it painfully.

"I am really not having a good day," I groaned as I rolled off the boulder to glare at Alec. Or started to glare, but when I realized that he hadn't just gone mad and thrown me aside because I was now the personification of evil, and had, instead, protected me, I snatched up a couple of rocks and got painfully to my feet.

The woman who had appeared before the English demon lord was now stalking toward Alec, a wicked-looking sword in her hand, pointed directly at his heart. "I have no quarrel with you, Dark One. Cease interfering and you will not be harmed."

Alec, who stood with his back to me, balanced to spring forward, gave a dry little laugh. "I've lived in perpetual torment for the last six hundred years. I have no soul, my Beloved was killed almost before my eyes, I tried to destroy my best friend, was banished to the Akasha by my own people, and the woman sent to drive me insane makes me hard just looking at her. There is nothing you can do that will make my existence any more miserable than it already is, demon."

I make you hard when you look at me?
Now is not the time for this discussion.

The woman smiled a particularly creepy smile. I moved closer to Alec.

Stay back, querida.
You're unarmed. And she has a herkin' big sword.
It's not me she wishes to harm. Stay behind me.

"Move, Dark One," the woman commanded.

I bent to pick up a couple more rocks. *OK, you get a little inner squeal for the "hard" comment, and more importantly bonus points for wanting to protect me, but I'm not some delicate little flower who can't protect herself.*

"Give it up, demon. You won't get her." *You're not up to battling a wrath demon. This woman is second-in-command to Bael. She wields more power than you know.*

And you think you're going to fight her unarmed?

I have no choice.

"Do you know who I am?" she snarled.

"I don't particularly care," Alec said, shifting his weight as if he were bored with the conversation. "You're wasting your time. Go back to Bael and tell him he will not have this woman."

Alec truly felt he had no choice but to fight the demon; that I knew. He carefully nursed anger inside him, using its strength to focus his attention on the woman, his intentions quite clear even to me—he would die trying to protect me.

I didn't ask myself why a man who a few minutes ago walked away from me, not to mention so callously killed others in the past, would risk his own life to protect me, a stranger; I just accepted that he felt that way, and started frantically looking around for something he could use as a weapon.

Thank you for not arguing with me.

Hey, I may not be comfortable with taking down Satan's BFF, but I'm not stupid. You have a whole lot more experience fighting people like that woman than I do.

"She is your Beloved?" the demon asked, speculation rife in her eyes as she tried to look around him to see me.

Alec hesitated for two heartbeats before answering, "Yes. Bael will not have her."

I held my breath for a moment, gently feeling around the edges of his mind, relaxing when I realized that he believed he was lying.

"That she is bound to you will make your destruction that much sweeter, but it means little else to Lord Bael. If you wish to amuse me for a few minutes before I take her, then I will indulge you."

Her blade flashed, causing Alec to leap back. I felt the sting of pain in his mind, and knew the demon's sword had slashed him. *How bad did she hurt you?*

Not badly. Stay back.

Alec, you can't fight her. You don't have a weapon. She'll just carve you up like a rotisserie chicken.

I would thank you for your faith in my abilities to protect you, but I'm a little busy at the moment.

I searched desperately for something that he could use for fighting her. *I'm sorry. All I can find are rocks.*

The demon laughed as her sword danced around Alec. He moved steadily backward as he dodged the worst of the sword cuts, shielding me with his body. I could feel the pain each time the sword struck true, driving my own level of frustration sky-high.

I don't need rocks. Just stay behind me, out of her reach.

Without warning, the woman suddenly lunged forward, the sword she wielded piercing clean through his body, popping out his back.

"No!" I screamed, flinging my handful of rocks at her head as I jumped forward.

"Stay back!" Alec yelled, twisting to catch me as I tried to fling myself on the woman.

She snarled words that hurt my insides, tearing away something within me. My inner devil screamed in agony, and as Alec's hands closed around my waist, reality seemed to shift and refocus itself, a buzzing sound like that of a thousand hissing voices filling my ears, and I froze, locked in position, as the buzzing grew louder and louder until it burst out of me.

A high, horrible scream tore through the air, followed by the metallic clang of an object hitting the ground. The buzzing in my head faded to nothing, leaving me reeling against Alec, staring in stupefaction at the sword lying on the rocky ground before us.

The woman was gone, a faint black whiff of smoke slowly curling around itself the only indicator of her presence.

"What . . . what happened?" I asked, instinctively clinging to Alec as he bent to pick up the sword. He looked at it curiously for a moment, then turned his head to consider me.

"I believe we just received confirmation of our suspicions. You destroyed Bael's wrath demon."

"I did? How? I was just standing here—"

"I think . . . I think I used you." He looked back at the sword in his hand. "Just as if you were a Tool of Bael, I used the power you harness to destroy the demon's form and send it back to Abaddon."

"Are you saying I've got some sort of demonic powers? Because I may be a lapsed Catholic, but that's going to definitely send me screaming to the nearest priest."

"No, you don't have the power itself," he said, now examining his stomach.

"Aieee!" I screamed at the blood that soaked the lower half of his shirt. "Oh my god! Lie down! No, don't move! I'll get a . . . a . . ." I spun around, searching for something I could use to stanch the flow of blood.

"Good lord, what sort of place is this that they don't have a first aid kit?"

"I'm all right. The bleeding has stopped."

"Don't be ridiculous," I said, coming to a swift decision. I took him by the arm and gently but firmly guided him over to the nearest butt-height rock. "You were skewered clean through. Those sorts of wounds simply do not stop bleeding. Now, you sit here, and I'll go find someone to help you. Try not to move around."

He dug in his heels midway to the rock, his expression alternating between incredulity and annoyance. "You don't want to listen to me, do you?"

"It's not that I don't want to," I said, tugging on him as gently as I could. "You're in shock. You don't know what you're saying. I'm simply doing what's best for you."

A little ripple of surprise claimed him. *You're . . . tending me?*

If you want to call it that.

No one has ever done that. No one has cared.

Well, sheesh, you're hurt, badly hurt, and although I may not want to have sex with you again—

You do, though. I can feel your interest in me just as you can feel mine in you.

—although I may not want to have sex with you again, I'm not so callous that I'll let you die here. Or come close to dying again.

Why not? You think I'm a murderer and abuser of women.

"I never said you abused a woman. I just said you killed one."

"One day we will discuss why you had a vision of my past, but for now, allow me to relieve your anxiety by showing you this." He pulled open his shirt.

Instinctively I flinched at the blood on his belly, but then I realized that, rather than looking at a great big gaping hole, I was seeing blood and nothing more.

"You . . . I saw the sword. What . . . ?" I touched the spot on his stomach where the sword had pierced him. There was an ugly red line there, hot to the touch, with dried blood flaking off around it, but no open wound.

"Dark Ones have regenerative powers."

I spread my fingers out over the wound, noticing that his eyes lightened a little in color from a dark forest green to jade. "You're hungry again."

"I lost blood. That happens."

"You should feed—"

"No. You've given me too much blood already."

"I feel fine now," I said, waving my arms around in the air as if that proved my point.

Querida, *as you found out, to a Dark One, the act of feeding can be highly arousing. Do you really wish for me to bury myself in your body again?*

The words, spoken with such intimacy, caused my body to go up in flames. For a few seconds, I was about to tell him to go ahead; then the good part of my brain, the smart part, shoved the inner devil aside and took over. "I'm happy to give you more blood if you need it, but there will be no more sex, Alec. That was an aberration, nothing more."

He said nothing, but I could feel him thinking plenty. He just didn't let me see what it was he was thinking.

I walked along beside him as he rebuttoned his shirt, heading once again to the north. "So, about this Tool thing. I don't like being evil. How do I make it stop?"

"You're not evil; you're simply a conduit to Bael's strength. That's all the Tools are—they have no abilities of their own; they simply allow others to tap into his power."

"So you used me to access the English dude's power to destroy his own demon?"

Alec's expression was bleak, surprisingly so, considering that he had just defeated someone who I assumed was going to make mincemeat of us both. "Yes."

"Why aren't you happy about this?" I asked, nudging him in the side. He wrapped an arm around me, pulling me up next to him. I ignored, for the moment, the fact that I felt extremely secure snuggled against him. "This is a good thing, isn't it? I'm not evil. You got rid of that mean chick, although why she wanted to hurt me is totally beyond me. Assuming she wanted to hurt me. Maybe she wanted to take me out of the Akasha?"

"She's Bael's right hand. I can assure you that for whatever reason Bael desires your presence—and I assume it's because he put two and two together, and realizes what happened to the Tools—it is not going to be something you want to experience."

I shivered at the dark images in his head. "That doesn't explain why you're not happy about taking down his evil henchman."

Alec sighed again. He seemed to be doing a lot of that.

"I can't help it. My life has suddenly become fraught with things to sigh over," he said, his grip around my waist tightening. "I'm not happy because if you are now effectively the Occio di Lucifer, it means every being with half a brain is going to want you."

I stopped and glared at him. "Just because we had sex half an hour after I first saw you doesn't mean I'm a raving nymphomaniac!"

"Want you to *use* you, Cora," he interrupted, pulling me back up against him. "Or, more properly, to use Bael's power."

Horror skittered along my flesh as I understood what

it was he meant. I had a vision of evil being after evil being lining up to use me as some sort of a demonic power source, blasting the world with innumerable cruelties. "Oh, shit."

"And lucky me," he added, his voice as grim as his expression. "It appears you have chosen me to protect you from them all."

Chapter Six

"You know, this doesn't look like hell."

"That's because it's not Abaddon. It's the Akasha."
Alec strolled beside me as we walked down a long hallway, our footsteps echoing slightly along the smooth
walls and stone floor.

"Yeah, but that greeter person told Diamond and me
that this was a place of perpetual torment, and that
sounds like hell to me. However, this"—I waved a hand
around at our surroundings—"this just looks like any
old office building. I don't see anything tormentish
about it."

"Try opening one of the doors," he said, nodding to
one as we passed it.

I paused. "Why? Is something ghoulish going on in
there? Are people being dismembered? Tortured?
Eaten by fire ants?"

He crossed his arms and nodded toward the nearest
door. "Open it and see."

"All right, but if it's something gross, I'm aiming at
you when I barf up my breakfast." I opened the door
and looked in, braced for the worst.

A group of a half-dozen people sat around a long

table, papers scattered across its surface, which was also littered with half-empty bottles of water, and a rainbow of highlighters. Crumpled paper spilled off the table onto the floor, leading in a trail to a whiteboard covered in several different styles of handwriting.

"We are agreed, then, are we not," said a man in a business suit at the head of the table, "that examining the cost savings that will accrue from our cutback on the performance-related functions will make good any and all productivity shortfalls we experience this quarter?"

A woman shook her head and tapped at the table with one of the highlighters. "I believe that if we realign our organizational aims to better benefit the enterprise, we can absolve our office of the clearly unsustainable redundancy of not only the expense claims, but of the external consultants, which I think we all agree will lead to the downfall of this and other management teams within the venture."

"No, no, no!" a third man said, hoisting his pants up over his beer belly as he rose to his feet. "If we form a task force to investigate the benefits of a mentor program—"

"Good god," I said softly, closing the door. "It's worse than I thought."

Alec nodded. "Middle-management committees. Still think this isn't a bad place?"

I shuddered. "We have to get out of here."

He slid me a look as he took my hand, making me hurry to keep up with his long-legged stride. "I'm glad you're including me in your escape plans, although I regret to inform you that there is no way to get out of the Akasha short of being summoned out."

"Then we'll just have to arrange for that," I said, feeling a bit mulish. I didn't plan on spending the rest of my life dodging committee meetings.

"And just how do you expect to pull that off when we're stuck in here with no way to communicate to the outside?"

"I don't know, but I'm sure as shooting not going to sit around here waiting for people to use me for who knows what bad—Diamond!"

A familiar face turned as I called out her name. She was standing with two other people, but smiled when I almost dragged Alec up to her, her eyes moving from me to him, widening when she took in all his manly glory.

You are making far too much of my appearance, querida.

Oh, don't tell me you don't like it, because I can feel just how much you enjoy overhearing my inadvertently and wholly insincere smutty thoughts about you. I bet you just love it when women go gaga over you, pandering to your insatiable ego, inflating your head until it's approximately the size of Montana. I'm equally sure you love it when women look at you like Diamond is looking at you, which honestly I have to say is way out of line, considering she has a husband she claims she loves, not to mention the fact that she stole him from me.

I thought you no longer wanted him?

I don't, but no woman likes to have a man stolen out from under her nose, and if Diamond thinks she's going to pull that again with you, she's going to be in a whole world of hurt.

Now who's jealous?

I transferred my glare from Diamond to Alec. "I really don't like you," I told him.

"And just when I was beginning to think otherwise of you," he almost purred into my ear.

A shiver of the purest pleasure rippled down my back.

"Cora! You missed a fascinating breakfast. There were some lovely speakers talking about the sorts of things that are available for us to pass the time here in the Akasha. But tell me, who is your friend?" Her gaze flickered from where my fingers were twined through his to his face.

"This is Alec Darwin. He's a vampire. He killed a woman several hundred years ago." I bit back the words that my inner devil was trying to force out, hiding them deep in my psyche so Alec wouldn't overhear them: *And he's not available.*

"Hello, Alec," Diamond said with a cheery smile.

He responded politely, then peered at her for a few seconds. *She's glowing.*

She is? I glanced at her, my eyes widening. *Oh, no, she is! Was she affected by me becoming the eyeball of Sauron?*

Occio di Lucifer, and no, I don't think it works that way. I could feel him turning the facts over in his mind. *Did you say that Ulfur glowed, as well?*

Yes.

And that he had stolen something from Bael?

Something gold, yes. It looked like a flattened disk when he showed it to me.

Before or after you were cast into the Akasha?

After.

Sins of the saints . . . Ulfur must have stolen all three Tools.

You think he's an Occio, too?

No, it sounds like he's the Anima di Lucifer. That used to be a dragon-shaped aquamanile. Which means that this woman must have been holding the third Tool.

"And you just met?" Diamond interrupted my thoughts with a pointed look at where I still held Alec's hand.

"Yes." I pushed away the spike of jealousy, focusing on what was important. "Diamond, when we were at the house and you were in the basement, what were you doing?"

"Taking pictures. You know that."

"No, I mean right at the moment when suddenly we were zapped here."

"Oh." She looked thoughtful. "I was examining a very pretty goblet I found that had rolled beneath the stairs. It looked valuable, and I was going to bring it up to show you, when poof!"

"Goblet?" I asked Alec.

He nodded. "The Voce di Lucifer. All three of you were holding a Tool when Bael banished Ulfur."

"Bael?" Diamond froze. "The demon lord Bael?"

"Yes." Alec looked at her with speculation that was mirrored in my mind. "Do you know him?"

"Me? Merciful sovereign, no! But I know of him, of course. Everyone does," she explained, her hands fluttering in the air as she spoke. "Are you saying Bael sent us here?"

"That's what we think," I said slowly. "Diamond, how come you know about the demon lord guy? Why didn't you see him at the house? Why aren't you freaking out about being here? And why were you so happy to go off to a breakfast of the damned without so much as wigging out one tiny little bit?"

"What is there to wig out about?" she asked with a bright smile shared between us. "It's the Akasha, not Abaddon, Cora. I've never seen a demon lord before, so I didn't know he was at the house, although it did feel as if there was a very old entrance to Abaddon somewhere on the premises. As for being here, well, I've always wanted to see the Akasha, and here we are! It's so very fascinating, don't you think? And the people here are so nice. Almost desperately pleased to have someone to talk to, if you know what I mean. Margaretta told me there were some informational meetings I could sit in on if I liked to see how things were done here, which sounds super fun, don't you think?"

She's deranged, I told Alec, staring at her in astonishment.

It's tempting to agree, but I don't think she is. I think she's . . . hmm.

She's what?

I'm not quite sure. She appears human, but that could be just a glamour. Whatever she is, I don't believe she's mundane.

Mundane?

Mortal.

I pinched his fingers. *Are you saying I'm mundane, buster?*

You are mortal, yes, he said with a mental leer. *But you're anything but mundane in every other sense of the word.*

Warmth washed through me, which I strove to keep him from feeling, but I knew by the smug smile in his mind that he felt it nonetheless.

I seriously needed to get out of here and away from this man before I lost all my wits and ended up like Jas. "I think that this is just about the worst place I've ever been in, Diamond. I've asked Alec to help us get out of here, in fact, and I think maybe you should help us think of a way out."

"Oh, that's no problem," she said, waving away

something so minor as permanent occupation in the Akasha. "My great-grandmother is very resourceful. I'm sure she'll figure out something to get us out of here."

Mentally, I shook my head at that comment, but so long as she wasn't worried about being stuck here, I wasn't going to push the point.

"In the meantime," she continued happily, "I intend on enjoying myself. I think I'll sit in on one of those meetings Margaretta told me about. Why don't you and Alec come with me, and we can brainstorm if it will make you feel better?"

"Pass," I told her, smiling to myself at Alec's mental shudder. "We'll just work on getting out of here. I'll give you a yell if we find a way."

"Suit yourself," she said, giving Alec another once-over that had me shifting closer to him, which just made my inner devil giggle. "Then again, perhaps you are doing exactly that. Ta-ta!"

"Don't say it," I told Alec as he was about to make a comment that I knew would make me blush. *Don't even think it.*

He laughed, and my stomach did a happy little quiver at the sound of it. Dammit, he had a wonderful laugh, warm and deep and filled with genuine amusement. "I won't, but only because I'm doomed to disappoint you by not finding a magic solution to the problem of you being here."

"All of us being here," I said, allowing him to lead me out to a courtyard. It was the same shade of dusty brown as everything else, the building an anachronism of modernity in an otherwise blighted landscape. "You'll have to come with us when we leave."

"I can't. I've been banished here by the Moravian

Council. If I was to manage to find a way out, they'd simply send me back."

I eyed him, leaning against yet another sharp, pointy rock. "What exactly did you do to piss off all the other vamps?"

His gaze skittered away as he gently, but firmly, closed his mind. "Seduced my best friend's Beloved, tried to have them both destroyed, and betrayed Dark Ones to those who would see us exterminated."

His face was a mask of indifference, but his eyes, oh, those lovely eyes, they revealed the emotions he kept from me. Pain was in them, both self-loathing and pain caused by others. His words confirmed what I believed about vampires—that their characters were reprehensible and unworthy of my concern—but just as I knew that not every vampire was created equal, so I knew that Alec wasn't truly any of those things.

"When you killed that woman, what were you thinking?" I couldn't stop myself from asking.

It took him a minute to respond. I had the feeling he was far away in his thoughts. "The one who killed my Beloved?"

I nodded.

His eyes closed for a few seconds as he struggled with the gut-searing agony that memory brought him. "I didn't think. I saw the corpse burned and mangled, and knew the reaper had deliberately killed her. I struck out of instinct. It wasn't until recently that I found out it had been an accident all along, and that the reaper hadn't specifically targeted my Beloved." He gave a short, bitter laugh. "All those centuries I spent convinced revenge would lessen the pain, all that wasted time . . ."

"I don't believe you," I told him, my emotions tangled up with one another, but his honor, at least, was something I didn't doubt.

His expression hardened. "That doesn't surprise me. No one else believes me; why should you?"

"I meant"—I slid my hand under his jacket, spreading my fingers out over where his heart beat true and strong—"I don't believe what you said about betraying your own people. You didn't."

His gaze searched my face for signs I was mocking him. I let him feel the strength of my conviction. "No, I didn't, but that didn't stop them from condemning me for acts I didn't commit."

"Why didn't you defend yourself?"

His lips twisted in a self-mocking smile. "Because I *did* betray my friend."

"And seduced his Beloved?"

He rubbed his thumb along my bottom lip, his eyes on my mouth. "That was before I knew she was his Beloved, actually. Once she made it clear her choice was him, not me, I left her alone. Other than trying to have them killed, but even that plan had lost its charm."

"So you're martyring yourself because you were a bad friend?"

His gaze flitted away again, his hand dropping. "It's a bit more complicated than that, but ultimately, I was responsible for trying to ruin Kris's life, and it's only right I should pay for that."

"Bullshit," I told him, causing his eyes to widen. "You're having a good old-fashioned wallow in self-pity is all. I don't say that you don't have it coming to you, because I think you've done some things that you shouldn't have done, but it seems to me that you've paid more than the price of your penance, and it's time to move on. And that's just what I intend to happen. We're going to get out of here, all three of us, and no, I'm not going to leave you behind—"

The words were ripped from my mouth as if a giant

hand had snatched me aside, and flung me down somewhere else entirely.

Which is basically what happened. I was aware of a
momentary dropping sensation, and landed on my
hands and knees on a wooden floor. I stared for a moment down at the grain of the wood, my brain stunned
into a complete lack of cognizant thought, before I
looked up to see a man and a woman standing before
me.

We were in a room that looked like a library of some
sort, all deep leather armchairs, and pretty bound
books in floor-to-ceiling bookcases. I glanced at the
people watching me.

The man was of middle height, with black hair and a
goatee. The woman, who edged away from him, had a
sunny face, curly red hair, and a friendly demeanor that
made me address her rather than her companion.
"What on earth just happened?"

"I summoned you," the woman said. She had an
English accent, and a nice smile as she gestured toward
the man, who stood with his arms crossed, his eyes narrowed on me. "You have Mr. de Marco to thank for
that, though, since he hired me. I'm a Guardian, you
see. My name is Noelle. Do you know that you're glowing?"

"So I've been told. Why . . . wait, de Marco?
You're—" A shadow moved behind the man, coming
forward and resolving itself. "Ulfur!"

"I am Alphonse de Marco, and you will give to me
the Occio di Lucifer," Ulfur's boss said in a no-nonsense
tone of voice that really just irritated me more than
frightened me.

"The . . . oh. That." I wondered how he'd feel if he
knew the Tool was broken, and that I was the desig-

nated hitter. I glanced at Ulfur, but his expression gave nothing away.

Ulfur hadn't told his boss what happened, I realized with a secret smile. Bless his heart, he used the fact that I had the Occio to convince his boss to pull me out of the Akasha.

Leaving Alec and Diamond behind.

"Do you have it?" de Marco asked, his expression darkening into anger.

"Yes." Hastily I assembled a plan that I hoped would rescue both Alec and Diamond. "I do."

"I have summoned you out of the Akasha. In gratitude, you will give it to me," he ordered, his bossy tone really starting to get under my skin.

I looked at the imperative hand he held out before me. "Well, you know, the Occio is a really big deal. It's one-third of the Tools of Dale."

"Bael," Noelle the Guardian corrected.

"Bael, sorry." De Marco's eyes narrowed on me suspiciously. I cleared my throat and said with what I hoped was convincing insouciance, "I call him Dale. It's a little thing we do."

Ulfur rubbed his hand over his eyes, but said nothing.

"But that's neither here nor there, and what *is* here is . . . well, actually, he's *there*, not *here*. If you know what I mean. Do you know what I mean?"

"No," de Marco growled.

"Oh. Well, it's Alec."

"Alec? Who is Alec?" De Marco was clearly getting angrier with each passing second.

Ulfur's eyes widened as he glanced between his boss and me. I had the feeling he was trying to tell me something, but I didn't know what it was.

"He's a friend," I said carefully, trying to suss what had Ulfur so agitated.

"I don't care about your friends. I just want the Occio, and I want it now. Hand over the payment for your removal from the Akasha, or I will have you returned there immediately."

"Hang on there, buster," I said, deciding that the best way to deal with people like him was to bluff my way through his demands. "I will make a deal with you—you spring my two friends from the Akasha, and I'll give you the Occio."

Ulfur's eyes just about bugged out of his head.

"You dare—" De Marco sucked in a huge amount of air just like he was inflatable or something. "You *dare* to defy me? Do you know who I am, mortal?"

"Yeah, you're Ulfur's boss, the guy who told him to steal the Tools from the frickin' king of hell!"

"Prince, not king," Noelle said, then looked away quickly, pretending interest in a picture on the wall.

"Dale likes me to call him king in our private moments," I lied, trying to look like someone who dated Satan. "So here's the thing, de Marco: You want Dale's Occio, you can have it . . . just as soon as you get Alec and Diamond out of the Akasha."

"I am not an Akashic removal service!" de Marco snarled, his black eyebrows pulled down to form a unibrow. I was tempted to tell him it wasn't a good look for him, but felt he wouldn't be receptive to such criticism. "You owe me, mortal, not the other way around. You will hand over the Occio now."

"Or what?" I said, buffing a fingernail on my jeans.

"Or I'll make you sorry you ever drew breath," he snarled.

"Hello? Who has the eyeball of Dale? That's right, I

do, and that means you can't hurt me." I fervently prayed that was true.

Ulfur weaved a little, like he might pass out. Noelle looked startled.

Maybe it *wasn't* true.

De Marco seemed to swell again, then let out a scream of sheer frustration. "One."

"Huh?" I stopped edging toward Noelle, who was in turn sliding covertly away from de Marco.

"One." His nostrils flared. "I will have the Guardian summon one more person, but that is it."

"But . . . I have two friends there."

"Then you will choose between them. Now!"

I swallowed back a little zing of fear at the look in his eyes. He didn't strike me as being too mentally stable. "Um . . ." I thought frantically. Diamond, I should tell him to get Diamond out. She was my friend . . . of a sort . . . and she didn't do anything to deserve being banished to the Akasha. I would get Diamond out.

Leaving Alec behind.

Alone.

With no one to feed him.

And worse, he would know I hadn't cared enough about him to rescue him, too.

But he was a murdering vampire and, by his own admission, had betrayed his friend. He had accepted the punishment meted out to him. He was resigned to being in the Akasha.

"All right," I said, sending a little prayer that Alec would understand why I had no choice but to pick Diamond. "I've decided."

"Give the name to the Guardian, and let us be through with this!" de Marco snapped.

"Noelle, would you please summon . . . ?" I looked at

her. She looked at me, waiting. I thought of Diamond. My inner devil wept and called me all sorts of names.

No one had ever tended Alec's wounds.

"Summon Alec Darwin, please," I heard someone say, and to my astonishment—and inner devil's joy—it was my mouth that spoke the words.

Chapter Seven

Alec stared at the spot where, seconds before, Corazon had stood. He narrowed his eyes. He put out a hand to touch nothing but empty air.

She wasn't there. Just like that, she was gone.

Someone must have summoned her.

"Good riddance," he said defiantly, not wishing to admit to the hurt that spiked through him as sharp as a dagger. It was annoyance, not pain, he told himself. She was simply someone put there to torment him, and he'd be damned if he gave her the power to hurt him.

She had left him, just left him, without so much as a backward glance, or one last jab at his appearance. She hadn't even called him a murdering bloodsucker before she left, dammit, and he was beginning to be fond of the way she caressed the words in her mind.

"Very well," he said aloud to no one, gritting his teeth and looking around for a new spot in which he could almost die. "So be it. She's gone. I'm here. That's all there is to it."

But it wasn't all there was to it. Cora was out in the mortal world with no one to protect her, no one to keep her safe from anyone who might want to use her.

"I don't care," he told the nearest rock, stomping off to find a new resting spot. "She's not my problem anymore. I don't mind at all never seeing her again, never smelling her, never watching those hips that know how to make me hard with just a little twitch, never letting her suck my tongue almost out of my head, never making her hum with ecstasy. I don't need her or her blood. I'm quite happy being miserable here on my own."

He kicked a rock, defying it to dispute his words, knowing he was a fool, but in too much pain to care.

She had left him.

He spotted a rock that he felt would suit as a spot where he could perch and be even more miserable than he already was by admitting that her defection had, in fact, hurt him as deeply as anything could, but just as he was approaching it, the world shifted, gathered itself up, and punched him in the gut.

"Alec!"

He was groggily aware of a voice that seemed to sing in his veins, a scent that wrapped itself around him, gentle hands that turned him over and touched his face.

"Sorry," another female voice said. "I told you it was harder to summon beings of a dark nature. I don't think I could have done it if you hadn't been here to provide a connection to him."

"Are you all right? Alec?"

He opened his eyes to find Cora's exotic, mysterious eyes filled with concern as they peered at him. "You didn't leave me?"

"No," she said, a smile curling those delicious lips.

He couldn't stop himself. He slid his fingers into her hair and pulled her down to him, his heart singing with the pleasure of tasting her again, of plunging into her sweetness, of feeling her respond to him with a little shiver of excitement.

"Well, well, well, what do we have here? A Dark One. How very interesting."

A man's voice interrupted his pleasant contemplation of just how quickly he could get Cora into bed so he could make her hum like she'd never hummed before.

"You did not tell me you were a Beloved, woman," the man continued.

There was something about his voice that had Alec leaping to his feet, a startled—and breathless, he was smugly pleased to note—Cora shoved behind him.

Two men stood watching him—one he recognized as being the lich who had ties to his friends Kristoff and Pia, but the other . . . "Who are you?"

"I am de Marco. You are known to me," the man answered, his eyes narrowed as he raked Alec over with a look that had him instantly annoyed. "I make it my business to know Dark Ones who cross my path, and you are friends with that irritating reaper, are you not?"

Do you know him? Cora asked.

No. But he seems to know me.

I don't think that's a good thing, Alec.

I suspect you're right.

"Yes, this is going to work out well," de Marco said with a fat smile. "Ulfur, take the Dark One to our guest rooms. You, Beloved, you will now give me the Occio."

Alec? Cora asked, pressing against his back.

Yes, we run. Right now.

She didn't want to debate the subject; she just turned on her heels and ran for the door. Alec anticipated the shouted order that the man de Marco gave, and, with a look of apology, slammed his fist into Ulfur's face as the latter attempted to stop them. He grabbed the hand of the other woman who stood there, hauling her after him with the assumption that she was not a part of what was going on.

"Who are you?" he asked as he shoved her through the door, slamming it shut on de Marco's face.

"Noelle. I'm a Guardian. Is Cora really your Beloved? I'm a Beloved, too, although the Dark One who I was supposed to save found someone else, and—"

Cora stood down the end of a hallway in an open door, sunlight spilling in around her as she yelled at him to come that way. He didn't hesitate, just shoved the chatty Guardian toward her, spinning around when de Marco burst into the hallway behind them, a gun in his hand.

"Run!" he shouted to the women, hefting a small half-moon table to hurl at de Marco.

"He's got a gun, Alec!" Cora yelled back, and he knew even without looking that she was coming back to save him.

Dammit, woman, I am the man! I will do the saving! You will run when I tell you to run!

You can stuff that macho crap where the sun don't shine. Besides, he's got a gun! He'll shoot you!

He can't hurt me. You, however, are still mortal.

Cora flung herself on him just as de Marco opened fire, sending them both to the floor. He twisted as they fell, rolling over on top of her to protect her, pulling her head down so it was tucked against the wall of his chest.

You fool! he growled into her mind. *You'll get yourself killed that way.*

Use me!

What?

Use me! Tool me! Like you did with the demon.

"There's always a price to pay when you use Bael's power," he warned, but did as she suggested, holding her tight. He felt her shudder; then power began to flow from her to him, which he channeled and threw in a mass toward the man just as the first couple of bullets hit his back.

Cora jerked, and he knew one of the bullets had gone through him to her. He ripped savagely at the power, slamming it into de Marco, sending the man flying backward into the wall, where he collapsed in a heap on the floor.

"How badly are you hurt?" he asked as he rolled off Cora, his gaze pouncing on the bloom of red along her upper leg.

"I don't think badly. Holy moly, we did that?" She stared at the crumpled heap that was Alphonse de Marco, horror skittering around her mind. "Is he . . ."

"Dead? I doubt it. He is not mortal. Let me see your leg." He tore at the bullet hole in her jeans, ripping it wide open to examine the wound.

"Thank you, that was my favorite pair of jeans!" She slapped at his hands as he found an exit hole on the underside of her thigh, the bullet buried in the floor beneath her.

"I'll buy you another. Dammit, it's bleeding heavily." With no other choice, he bent over her leg, hearing her gasp as he swirled his tongue around the upper wound, fighting the need to suck the blood from the wound.

You're feeding? Right now? Is this what they call bloodlust?

No, this is what they call stanching the flow of blood. Reluctantly, he gave one last lick to the wound before pulling her leg up and repeating it on the exit wound.

You can do that?

I'm a Dark One, love. If we weren't able to clot blood, our donors could bleed to death.

Oh. Well, thank you. I'm sorry I accused you of wanting to eat.

I do want to eat, but now is not the time or place. Put your arms around me.

I beg your pardon!

"I don't want you walking on that leg until you've seen a doctor. Put your arms around me. You there, Guardian, see if de Marco is harmed."

He got to his feet again, Cora in his arms, striding toward the open door at the end of the hall.

"Your back! You got shot, too! Put me down, Alec. I can walk."

My back is fine. The wounds are already healing over. Remember the attack by the demon? I heal very fast.

"Yeah, but bullets!"

"I'm fine."

Ulfur emerged from the room behind them, watching silently as Noelle squatted next to de Marco.

"He's out, but not hurt badly," she said, hurrying after them.

Alec stopped at the door, looking back at Ulfur. "Can you come with us?"

Ulfur shook his head, gesturing toward the fallen man.

"Has he bound you not to speak?"

Ulfur nodded, his expression one with which Alec had more than a passing familiarity—utter despair.

"I'll tell Kris and Pia where you are. They'll help."

Ulfur smiled, but it was a sad smile. Cora waved and he lifted his hand in response, watching with black eyes as they left the building.

"Have you a car?" he asked, hissing in pain as the sunlight caught him full in the face. He glanced around quickly, but the sun was full on the house, giving no shade.

"Oh man, you're turning red," Cora said, glancing toward the sky. "The thing about the sun is true?"

"Somewhat."

"I'll get my car," Noelle said, running down a long flagstone walkway toward steps leading down to a parking area. Scrubby desert plants and a few small cacti lined the path, the air around them hot, and filled with the dusty scent of warm, dry earth. A small gecko dashed out from the shade of a rock in front of him as he started down the path toward the driveway.

"Put me down, and go around the side of the house," Cora ordered. He gritted his teeth against the pain in his hands and face, ignoring her demand.

"Alec, stop! You're getting blisters!"

"I'll survive. I don't need you opening up those wounds again."

"Oh, for the love of the saints . . ." She squirmed in his arms for a moment, pulling off her shirt and wrapping it around his head.

Now I can't see.

"I'll tell you where to go. Forward five steps, then stop."

"I really don't need—"

"Stop being such a baby. Five steps."

They made it to the car, although Alec's hands were burning something fierce by the time he placed Cora in the backseat. He was going to sit up front next to Noelle in order to give Cora room to stretch out her leg, but she just grabbed him by his shirt and pulled him in after her.

"Go!" she ordered Noelle, and the Guardian, at least, didn't argue. Gravel kicked out behind them as the tires spun, finally getting a grip.

"Put your leg up on me," Alec ordered, trying to arrange Cora's leg, but she shook her head and pulled him toward her, plastering herself against the window.

"Get in the middle," she said in her delightfully bossy tone.

"I'm not—"

Get in the middle, you idiot. The sun won't reach you there.

I'm not going to let you hurt yourself—

"I'll sit on you, OK? Just sit there."

Have I mentioned that I don't like bossy women?

Have I mentioned that I don't like vampires?

Frequently.

Yeah, well, get over yourself. She waited until he moved to the middle of the seat before she scooted over and carefully sat across his legs. "There. Comfy?"

He closed his eyes for a second, the sting of his face and hands fading as her scent permeated his awareness, the feeling of her in his arms, warm and soft, one of her exquisite hips pressed against his penis, making it instantly come to life. He had an almost overwhelming urge to bite her, not just to feed, but simply because he wanted to mark her, to let every man know she was his, and his alone.

Cora turned to look at him, her eyes wide and somewhat hazy with passion. *I'm not yours, Alec. Although the biting thing really sounds . . . no. Never mind. I didn't just think that.*

He was surprised that she had overheard his thoughts, since she hadn't been able to previously.

Who's projecting now? she asked with a smug little smile into his mind.

He pinched her behind, caressing the sweet curves of her ass as he asked, "Where exactly are we, Noelle?"

"Arizona. Outside of Flagstaff, actually. How did you knock out Mr. de Marco? I didn't see you do anything."

Cora sagged against him, her fingers absently toying with the hair at his nape. He wondered how long he'd be able to stand that without having to make love to her.

Her fingers stilled for a moment as she glanced at him from the corners of her eyes before a wicked little smile curled her lips.

"Where are we going? I only have this rental car for another day, so if you're hoping to drive somewhere at a distance, I'm afraid—"

"Into the nearest town, then the airport," Alec said, warring with his need to claim Cora again—her mouth, her body, her soul—and common sense.

"Will do," Noelle said, turning onto a main highway.

"Airport?" Cora asked. "Where are we going?"

"Where do you live?" he countered.

"Outside of San Francisco."

"Then we'll have a doctor see you first, and fly into San Francisco, so we can pick up your passport and anything you want to bring with you."

"Bring with me where?" she asked, and by the way she held herself, he knew she was in increasing pain. He wished he could take it from her, and nuzzled her neck, hoping to distract her.

"Florence."

"Florence . . . Italy?" Cora asked, her voice a squeak as he nibbled on her earlobe. *Jesus wept! Do that sucky thing behind my ear again.*

He sucked. She moaned in his head.

Why Italy?

That's where my friend and his Beloved live.

The friend you betrayed?

Yes. Kristoff and Pia are tied up with de Marco and Ulfur. They'll help us.

Why on earth would they do that when you betrayed one and seduced the other?

He smiled at the jealousy she fought whenever she thought of Pia.

We didn't have sex, mi corazón. *Well, she touched*

me, I touched her, and that was it. I suppose you could call that sort of a minor form of sex. Regardless, you have nothing to be jealous of.

I am not . . . oh, move on. Why would they help us?

Because I'm not going to give them any other choice, he said, and gently pushed her out of his mind. He had some planning to do.

Two hours later Cora limped out to Noelle's car, glaring at him when he offered to carry her.

"The tetanus shot hurt more than the bullet. Stop hovering over me, Alec, I'm fine. It's just a smidgen pinchy now. Did you do something to me to make me heal faster than normal? Because that doctor said that it looked like the wound was several days old, and almost healed over."

He kept to the shadows of the medical building before sliding next to her into the backseat of the car. "I haven't done anything to you, no. It could be the Tool making you . . . more."

"More what?" Cora looked startled at the idea.

"More than mortal, I think," Noelle said, starting the car, pausing to glance back at him. "We Beloveds, even when not Joined, are kind of . . . oh, I like to think of us as 'woman plus.' We have extra bonus abilities, like healing faster, and being more resilient, things like that."

"We Beloveds?" Cora almost choked on the word.

She thinks you're my Beloved. Do not argue with her—it's easier if she believes it to be true.

Is it? She clearly wanted to say more, but withdrew from him mentally.

"Yes. Didn't Alec tell you? I'm a Beloved, too, although the Dark One I was supposed to save ended up liking my roommate more than me."

Cora cast him a curious look. "Beloveds can do that?"

"No," he answered.

"Sometimes they can, yes," Noelle contradicted him. "Sebastian—he was the Dark One—said it had something to do with fate, that sometimes it got messed up, and assigned the wrong Beloved to a Dark One. Airport?"

"Please," Alec answered.

"You got it. I should return home, anyway."

"So this vampire you were supposed to hook up with ran off with your roomie? The dog!" Cora said, shooting him irritated glances just as if he were at fault. "I hope you let them know how you feel."

"Oh, I did. At first I was hurt, but I realized that they really were meant for one another. Besides, Belle—she was my roomie—promised to help find me a Dark One who doesn't have a Beloved."

Noelle's gaze in the mirror flickered to him.

Cora put her hand on his leg and glared at the mirror. *You say one word, and I'll pop you on your incredibly gorgeous nose.*

He put his hand over hers and stroked the backs of her fingers. *I'm surprised you care enough to feel possessive,* querida.

I'm not being possessive. I'm just protecting you because you let de Marco shoot you in the back in order to save me. Noelle wouldn't be right for you at all. You can thank me later for getting her off your back. "And I take it she hasn't found one yet?"

"No, although I've met just about every unredeemed Dark One in Europe." Noelle sighed.

"You'd think one of them would be happy to have you swoop in and save him," Cora said, drumming her fingers on his leg.

"You'd think so, but I guess not. I wouldn't mind, except Belle is constantly after me to try to meet more Dark Ones, and to be honest, I'm perfectly happy the way I am. And besides, men are like stray cats, you know? When one needs you, they find you."

Cora laughed. Alec refrained from making any comment, focusing his attention on more important matters. He had to figure out how he was going to convince Kristoff to go against the Moravian Council. Kris wasn't going to like it, but Alec had too much at stake to tolerate any refusal of help.

He had to protect Cora, and it was beginning to look like there was only one way to do that.

Chapter Eight

I spent the entire flight to Florence pretending to sleep. I wasn't proud of that fact, and I did actually snooze a goodly part of the time, thanks to some pain pills, but I had just reached a point where my mind seemed to be completely out of my control.

"I am going to sleep," I told Alec an hour after the private jet he had chartered took off. The fact that he had the resources to think nothing about hiring private jets to send him rocketing around the world was one of the things my mind had a hard time dealing with.

"I don't know why," he said without looking up from his laptop.

"I'm tired. And that dinner you insisted I eat was huge, and it made me sleepy."

"I meant that I don't know why you feel that traveling in a private jet is in any way outstanding. I assure you that the company that hires out this jet flies their clients all over the world."

"It may be standard operating policy where vamps are concerned," I said, dropping my voice so the stewardess at the other end of the cabin couldn't hear us, "but in my social circle, it's a big deal. I'm going to curl up on the couch, if you don't mind, and try to sleep off all that food."

"You needed to eat. I had taken too much blood," he said, his gaze still on the laptop that sat before him. "Why don't you sleep in the bed?"

I looked over at the long brown suede couch that was tucked against one side of the cabin. The whole interior was done in a lovely latte and cream color scheme, the six leather chairs made with butter-soft leather that was so comfortable, I could have slept sitting upright in them. "It turns into a bed?" I asked, nodding toward the couch.

"No. There's a bedroom in the back." He looked up, his green cat's eyes dancing with amusement. "I could show it to you if you like."

I leaned forward over the glossy inlaid wood table that sat between our facing chairs, my voice a whisper as the stewardess tidied up the remains of our dinner— Alec's having been eaten by me, since he evidently didn't eat food that didn't come straight from the vein. "I said no sex, and I mean it, buster. If you so much as think of seducing me again—"

"I believe the seduction in the Akasha was a mutual endeavor."

"—like you tried at my apartment—"

He smiled, the handsome bastard. "Ah. That was due to the fact that I thought you were stripping for me rather than simply changing your clothes. I apologized for that."

"—and at the airport—"

He shrugged. "I was hungry. You offered to feed me. We were alone. Things got a little carried away. I apologized for that, too."

"—and five minutes ago, when I was in the bathroom."

His smile broadened. "That was simply a matter of wishing to make sure your wound had thoroughly healed, and being unable to resist the nearness of your naked flesh."

"Flattering as it is to be the object of lust by a blood-thirsty fiend in sexy men's clothes, I stand by what I said, Alec—no sex. I'll feed you because you helped me, and are continuing to help me, but I'm not interested in you in a male-female sort of way. Have I made myself perfectly clear?"

"Yes," he said, swiveling around in his chair to consider me, his gaze raking me from toes to nose. "You've made it extremely clear that you're in denial, because you know you're just as attracted to me as I am to you. Anger should be next, although perhaps you're at that stage simultaneously with denial. I can't wait for bargaining."

I glared at him. "I am not in the five stages of grief, and I am definitely not attracted to you!"

He splayed his fingers across one of my breasts. My breath caught in my throat, my heart beating wildly at the touch, and my nipples, those traitors to my better intentions, hardened visibly under the thin gauze dress I'd donned for the anticipated warmth of Italy.

Alec pursed his lips as his thumb swept over my nipple. I shivered, for a moment entertaining the idea that I could have my cake—hot, steamy lovemaking with Alec—and keep him at arm's length at the same time, but realized that was the sheerest of follies.

"Damn you," I snarled, stalking off toward the back of the cabin.

Sleep well, love.

You can go to hell!

Pleasant dreams, too. Hopefully ones about you and me being naked together.

I froze for a second at the images with which he filled my head, then ran the rest of the way to the bedroom, desperate to shut out both the images and the knowledge that he was right.

I was utterly, completely, wholly in denial, and determined to stay that way.

An hour later I was still tossing and turning on the bed, not totally comfortable with the idea of an airplane having a bedroom to begin with. What if there was turbulence? I looked, but there were no seat belts on the bed, so I contented myself with very carefully tucking myself in with the sheets pulled very tight over me. But mostly, I was sleepless because my body sang a sad little song of loss over the fact that it was confined to the bed, while Alec was sitting out in the main cabin, in glorious manliness.

Just what was he doing with that laptop?

Taking care of some business.

Stop eavesdropping! I ground my teeth at him for a few minutes, then unable to keep from asking, *What sort of business? Businessy business, or vampire business?*

I am involved in several mundane financial businesses, querida.

Really?

Yes, really. I have to have some way to fund trips in private jets, he answered, amusement rife in his mind.

Oh, I suppose . . . I thought you just . . . you know . . . had money.

I do have money. I've spent my life working for it.

I didn't know why, but that pleased me. I've always liked people who made their own fortunes, both literal and figurative.

As do I. I thought you were tired?

I was. I am. Don't you dare offer to have sex with me so I'll sleep. And don't tell me you're not going to offer that, because I can feel that you are.

His laughter echoed in my head as I snuggled into the pillow, willing myself to sleep.

I surfaced from a dream of being bathed in warm, golden honey to find myself facedown on the bed, the lights in the room dimmed, and a sexy vampire kissing his way up my spine, his hands caressing my behind. "You are wearing black lace. Have I told you how much black lace lingerie arouses me? Nothing is quite so sexy as it is against the flesh of a warm, willing woman."

I swear his hands were made of fire. I struggled against the need to purr, saying instead in a hoarse voice, "Have we landed?"

"Yes. We're in New York, refueling. We should be taking off again shortly."

"Oh. Alec, I said no sex, and I meant—"

Hush. I won't do anything you don't desire me to do. I simply can't resist you any longer.

I groaned to myself, both at the sensation of his tongue painting a line up my spine and at the knowledge that what I desired was him, pure and simple.

But not on the only terms he wanted me.

Oh, great, he was right—I was at the bargaining stage! Dammit!

Even that knowledge did nothing to stop me as his hands slid between my legs, stroking me through the black lace and satin underwear, teasing me until he slid them off, his magical fingers making sure to inflame me further. His fingers danced in my hidden depths, his mouth moving over to one hip. I shivered at the heat of it, moving restlessly on the sheets, my breasts aching for his touch. "You're hungry again."

"I'm always hungry for you." One finger sank into me, making my muscles quiver and grip him, my body tight and hot with need.

"Then you'd better go ahead and have a snack. I wouldn't want it getting around that I was a poor hostess. My mother would never let me live it down."

He licked a spot on my hip, his breath steaming it, hesitating to ask, "How do you feel?"

"Chock-full of blood."

His mind was full of concern. I smiled at it, letting him feel how aroused I was. *Truly, I'm fine. Go ahead, Alec. I can feel your hunger gnawing at you.*

The familiar sting of his teeth piercing the skin on my hip dissolved to pure pleasure as he drank from me, his finger joined by a second as they curled within me, making me squirm as they found sensitive spots that I had no idea existed.

His fingers flexed as I moved against him, driven wild by the combination of his touch and the sensation of him feeding, everything I ever wanted in that small room at the back of a narrow jet.

When a third finger joined the other two, I just about came off the bed with the orgasm that followed, my toes digging into the mattress as I tried desperately to get air into my lungs.

You are so responsive, he marveled, his fingers still inside me as my muscles quivered around them. *One touch and you go up like a powder keg. Do you want me to stop,* querida?

"No," I panted, amazed at the fact that my body was still keyed up . . . until I realized that what I was feeling was his arousal, bound so tightly to mine, I knew I would never be able to separate them again.

That thought scared me to my core, but before I

could address it, his fingers were gone, the hard length of him thrusting into me, drawing a moan of absolute rapture from deep in my chest.

Alec! I cried, not used to the position, wanting to wrap myself around him, needing to touch him even as he pounded into my body, my muscles welcoming his intrusion with happy little quivers.

Now, love, now, he moaned, his fingers sweeping across flesh that I had assumed would be too sensitive for touch, but his climax triggered another of my own, sending us both flying.

Literally, since a subdued comment from the pilot over the intercom warned we were cleared for takeoff.

He poured his pleasure into both my body and brain as the climax seemed to go on and on, suddenly biting hard on my shoulder, not a feeding bite, but one of possession, a way of marking me to warn all other males that I was taken.

I knew what he was doing, knew it wasn't what I should allow, but was helpless to stop him. *It's just sex,* I quietly told my inner devil. *I haven't had sex in forever, and he's really, really good at what he does, and it's confusing things. Besides, now that we're out of the Akasha, he'll have other people to feed from. He'll go off and dine on prettier, younger women, and I won't feel so guilty about him anymore.*

But how, my devil asked as Alec rolled off me, pulling me with him, *will he get along without his Beloved?*

I shushed her lest he hear the thoughts rolling around in the private part of my mind, guilt riding me hard nonetheless. It was getting harder and harder not to tell him the truth about what had happened in my past-life regression. I had no idea if Beloveds could be reincarnated, but I had a very bad feeling that I was going to have to broach that subject with him sooner rather than later.

The real question was, if I was his Beloved, did I want to spend the rest of my life with a vampire?

Alec murmured something about me getting some rest before we got to Italy, promptly falling asleep, his gentle snore ruffling my hair as he curled up behind me, one arm around me, holding me tight against his chest. The wonderful scent of him mingled with a slightly earthier note of our activities, causing me to relax against his warmth. I felt oddly protected despite the fact that the man holding me could be brutal when driven to it, and I was unwilling to look any closer at the warmer, softer feelings that had suddenly started to take over my mind.

I'd think about it later, when I could put a little distance between us. Then sanity would return to me. Wouldn't it?

My inner devil laughed until I fell asleep.

"OK, your friend has seriously good taste," I told Alec some ten hours later as he skirted the sun and stepped into the shade cast by a lemon tree that stood next to the front doorway of a beautiful cream-colored stone villa. The house itself was gorgeous—with a dark tile roof, green shutters, and elegant Gothic archways, not to mention extensively landscaped grounds—but situated on a hill overlooking Florence, it had a view that took my breath away. "Is the rest of the house as pretty as the outside?"

"Yes. Ring the bell, would you?"

I pressed a discreet bell that lay flush against the stone wall, warmed by the morning sun. "You did tell them we were coming, didn't you?"

Before he could answer, the door opened, and a

plump blond woman smiled expectantly and said something in Italian.

"Hi," I said. "Are you Pia?"

"Yes, I'm Pia. Er . . . have we met?"

"No, but Alec described you as being very pretty and having a lovely smile, so I guessed it must be you."

"Alec?" She looked startled. "You're a friend of Alec's?"

"Yes. Um . . ." I slid a glance over to where Alec stood in the shade of the tree, leaning against the trunk, obviously waiting for me to give him the go-ahead to dash through the sunlight. "You're not still mad about him seducing you, are you? Because if you are, you don't have to help us. Not that I mean that to sound ungrateful or jealous or anything like that. I mean, what happened in the past is no business of mine, obviously. But he seemed to think that you guys weren't still angry with him. . . ." A tall man with dark curly hair and brilliant blue eyes loomed up behind her. His eyes narrowed on me, raking me from head to foot. I sighed. "You are still angry, aren't you?"

"Who is this?" A second man pushed his way out past Pia. He was shorter than the first, very thin, with a narrow face and pinched expression, as if he smelled something nasty. He gave me a once-over that made me faintly uncomfortable.

"My name is Corazon Ferreira," I answered, embarrassed as hell. *Dammit, Alec, your friends are still pissed at you!*

They are?

"She's a friend of Alec," Pia told the tall man, who I assumed was her vampire. The two of them gave me a strange look. "This is Brother Ailwin. He's . . . uh . . . he's going to help us out with a little problem we have concerning a friend."

I murmured a polite nothing, feeling horribly in the way.

"Perhaps you wish to conduct this business another time?" the skinny man asked, turning his sour face on Pia.

"No, no, we want it done as soon as possible. Er . . ." She shot me a hesitant look. "I'm sure we can come to some arrangement regarding the terms of your summoning a lich for us."

"I will, naturally, be obligated to charge more since the lich in question belongs to an Ilargi." The man gave me a considering look, his eyes filled with speculation.

"I'm sorry," I apologized. "I'm interrupting. I'll come back—"

"No, please, don't leave, we'd love to talk to you about Alec, wouldn't we?" She turned to the large man behind her.

"Yes, we would. We are finished here. We will expect the ceremony to take place this evening, Brother Ailwin," Kristoff said.

What is taking so long? Who is that man who keeps looking at you?

Some priest, I think, and we're in the way. Just so you know.

We are not. And that is no priest.

"That is too short of notice," the man said, biting off the words as if he was reluctant to let them go. "But assuming you will pay for my time, I will make the arrangements."

Maybe he's a monk? I asked as the man, with one last look at me, got into a small car and drove off. *He seems kind of ascetic to me. Although he's wearing jeans and a shirt like anyone else. Do monks still wear robes?*

That is no monk, either, querida. *I do not like the way he kept looking at you.*

Jealous? I asked with a smile.

Not in this case.

The grim tone to his words had my mental smile melting away to nothing. I had to admit that Brother Ailwin was making me more than a little nervous.

"So, you're Alec's friend," Pia said as both she and Kristoff examined me again.

"Was a friend," I growled, "if he keeps up pulling this sort of stunt on me. Look, I'm sorry to have bothered you and interrupted your meeting. We'll just be on our way."

I started to turn from the door but stopped when Kristoff said, "We?"

You didn't tell them we were coming, did you?

Why would I do that?

"Oh my god," I said, mortified to the tips of my toes. "He didn't tell you we were coming. I'm so sorry. I'll yell at him later on your behalf, all right?"

"He who?" Pia asked, stopping me when I would have marched away to give a certain vampire a very large piece of my mind.

You are in so much trouble, buster!

I'm well aware of that. The Moravian Council is not going to be happy.

Not with them, with me! I could die of embarrassment! These people think I'm a pushy interloper! And I am! "Alec."

"Alec is in the Akasha," she said slowly, as if I were a nutball.

Great, and now they think I'm crazy, too! "No, he's not. He's right there." I waved a hand toward the tree.

Pia moved out of the doorway to look, her hand shading her eyes against the sun before she gave a whoop of happiness and ran toward the tree.

"Er . . ." I looked from where Pia had flung herself on

Alec, who was spinning her around in the shade, to the vampire standing very close behind me. Alec had told me a little of his history with Kristoff, including the fact that he was the one responsible for Kristoff being a vampire in the first place. "Your . . . um . . . Beloved seems to be happy to see him. I'm confused."

"No more so than am I," he said, his voice rich with an Italian accent. He pushed past me and strolled toward the tree, not running through the sunlight as I assumed he would. I stood in the doorway and watched as he and Alec sized each other up for a moment, then embraced in a bear hug that looked like it should have broken at least one rib.

OK, I guess I was wrong.

About many things, love, but I try not to point them out too frequently.

Stop being smug. I thought they were pissed! How come your friend isn't affected by sunshine?

He is, but Dark Ones who are Joined have more of a tolerance to the sun. I'm sure Kristoff still avoids it when possible.

"This is . . . oh, my. We never expected you to get yourself out. That's why we . . . oh, dear. Is Cora . . . um . . . Kristoff, maybe you could . . . ?"

Something was wrong with Pia. She looked uncomfortable, and slightly distressed, and she kept shooting little glances past me toward the house.

"Come into the house," Kristoff said with a dark look. "There is much we have to . . . explain."

What's up? I asked Alec as Pia bustled past me, her gaze curious as she sized me up.

I have no idea, but it can't be too bad. Despite your concerns, they are happy to see us.

I said nothing to that, but the uneasy feeling continued.

"Who was that man?" Alec asked Kristoff.

"Brother Ailwin? He's a lichmaster. We've been negotiating with him to steal Ulfur from whoever the Ilargi is who has him."

"Alphonse de Marco," Alec said, nodding.

Pia and Kristoff stopped and stared as Alec pulled me into the house after him.

The inside of the house was even more attractive than the outside, long, cool rooms with stone floors and arched entryways giving way to a columned loggia. Through a large set of French doors, I could see outside to where a small tiered garden rose into the hillside.

"You know who the Ilargi is? Alphonse de . . ." Pia sucked in a huge breath. "Al! Al from the tour! Oh my god, he is the Ilargi? Holy cow!"

"Interesting, but not, I think, of utmost importance at this moment," Kristoff said, his hand on Pia's back as they escorted us into the house proper. "Alec, we need to talk."

"This is so lovely," I couldn't help but say, wondering how many people it took to keep up a house and grounds of this size. The room we were in was clearly a favorite, the walls a dappled oatmeal color, bearing a number of small, brilliantly colored, but obviously quite old paintings of the Renaissance style. Antiques mingled with more comfortable furniture, a blue and cream rug on the floor mimicking a mosaic. Outside, the garden was dotted with red and amber flowers, along with a thousand different shades of green. "And the views are outstanding."

"Perhaps you and I should have our discussion in the library," Kristoff said slowly, his speculative gaze on me.

"There's nothing you can say to me that you can't say in front of Cora," Alec said in an even tone. "For lack of a better phrase, we are bound together."

"Temporarily," I said quickly, giving him a look that

should have melted his hair right off his head. "We're *temporarily* bound together."

"Cora is in denial," he told the two of them. "There's nothing temporary about our bond."

"Er . . . bound together how?" Pia asked, her face rigid with some strong emotion.

"It's a long story. What did you have to say to me?" Alec asked.

Pia swallowed nervously, glancing over at Kristoff.

"Maybe I should leave," I murmured, moving toward the door. "I think I'm in the way."

"You're not—" Alec started to say at the same moment that a shadow moved in front of me, and a woman stood in the doorway, pinning me back with a glare.

"Yes, you should leave. You're most definitely in the way, and I, for one, don't appreciate you trying to steal my man."

Alec spun around to stare at the woman, a stupefied expression on his face. "Eleanor?" he said, looking as if he had just taken a kick to the gut. "It can't . . . Eleanor?"

"Who exactly are you?" I couldn't keep from asking, the hairs on the back of my neck rising.

"I'm Eleanor of Riger," she said with a venomous look and toss of her head. "And I'm Alec's Beloved."

Chapter Nine

I stared at the woman, stunned beyond anything in my experience. She was shorter than me, barely over five feet, with dishwater blond hair, shrewd black eyes, and a sharp, angular chin that was raised as she looked down her nose at me. This was me? The past me? But how could that possibly be? I shook my head, so confused I just wanted to walk out and leave it all behind me.

"Eleanor," Alec repeated, finally pulling himself together as the woman—I couldn't think of her as me, since she was nothing like me—walked over to him, and without a glance at anyone wrapped her arms around him and damned near sucked his face off.

"Yes, my darling, it's me. I'm back."

"But . . ." My fingernails dug into the flesh of my palms as I struggled to keep from yanking her off Alec. "But I . . . er . . . Alec's Beloved is dead. She was run over by an oxcart several hundred years ago."

"How do you know that?" Kristoff asked, giving me a long once-over.

"I . . . uh . . . I had a vision of the event."

"Ah." He didn't look convinced, but let the matter

drop as Eleanor came up for breath. I noticed Alec didn't seem to be fighting her very much, although his expression was anything but overjoyed to see his long-lost Beloved. Or, rather, the original version of her.

Jesus wept, what had I gotten myself into? I should be happy she was back. Now I could wash my hands of him and be through with vampires forever.

My inner devil delighted in the feelings of intense unhappiness that thought triggered.

"I was dead," Eleanor said, kissing Alec's chin before turning to face me. I ground off a good layer of enamel trying to keep from yelling at her for doing so. "But they had me brought back."

"We know a necromancer," Pia said, her gaze flicking between Alec, Eleanor, and me. "We thought if we brought her back, the council would be forced to get you out of the Akasha, Alec. We didn't know that you . . . that Cora . . . oh, man, what a mess."

"One that I'm sure we can figure out," Kristoff said, gesturing toward a couple of couches. "Please sit, Cora."

"Where are my manners? Yes, please, sit down, all of you. We have so much to talk about." Pia shook off her stunned expression and smiled as she moved over with me to one of two couches.

"It's a lovely room," I said, standing awkwardly by the door, miserable but refusing to acknowledge that when Eleanor, with one hand on Alec, tugged him down next to her on a love seat. "And a lovely house."

"It is pretty, isn't it? It's built on a twelfth-century tower that was later part of a monastery. There's a cloister and everything. But I can show you around the house later—there are so many questions that Kristoff and I have. Like how did you meet the Ilargi who stole Ulfur? And how did you get out of the Akasha, Alec?"

Alec had been watching me with an avidity that evidently didn't make Eleanor happy at all, for she put a proprietary hand on his thigh and gave me a cool look as he answered. "I have Cora to thank for that."

"Do you indeed?" Eleanor said softly.

"Are you a . . . what do they call them . . . ?" Pia turned to Kristoff.

"Guardian," he said, eyeing me. "She does not appear to be one."

"I'm not. I'm a secretary. I got zapped into the Akasha myself, and when I was de-zapped, I arranged for Alec to be brought out, as well."

"Why?" Eleanor asked.

I swallowed back the urge to shout at her that I was his Beloved, not her, and I had saved him because he needed me, chastising myself for such stupidity. I had an out in the form of Eleanor—I would be an idiot not to take that.

And leave Alec, never to see him again.

My heart shattered as everyone looked at me, curiosity almost palpable.

"It seemed like the thing to do," I said lamely, avoiding Alec's gaze, but all too aware of the swift lance of pain that shot through him at my words.

Both Pia and Kristoff looked at me as if I had turned into a giant dancing panda bear.

"I think Kristoff's right, and you're going to have to tell us what happened from the beginning," Pia said, gesturing toward a pale blue brocade couch.

As I passed Kristoff, he froze, an odd look on his face as I could have sworn he sniffed the air.

"Cora, why don't you—*what*?"

Pia turned a shocked expression first on her Dark One, then on me.

"*What* what?" I asked, wondering if I had somehow offended them.

"You're . . . you're a Beloved? *Alec's* Beloved? But Eleanor . . . Kristoff, are you sure?"

It was my turn to freeze. "Uh . . ."

"Cora can't be my Beloved," Alec said, rising from the love seat, much to Eleanor's dissatisfaction. His face was a mask, absolutely devoid of emotions, but I could feel them all twisting around inside him. "I don't say that we don't have a blood bond, but . . ." His voice trailed off as he glanced toward Eleanor.

"What sort of a blood bond?" she asked, her eyes narrow with suspicion.

Alec ignored her as Pia spoke hesitantly.

"But . . . but Kristoff said . . . he said she smelled . . ." Pia blinked at me.

"I smell?" My voice came out close to a shriek, because honestly, if being told you stink by people whom you were going to ask for help isn't a moment to shriek over, I don't know what is. "I don't know what . . . I mean, I took a shower. . . . Did I step in something? . . . Jesus wept, Alec! Why didn't you tell me I stink?"

"Kristoff is wrong," Eleanor said, her voice as hard as granite. "I am Alec's Beloved. He said I was, the first day he saw me. He was courting me, had asked my father for my hand, and I was going to agree to it, except that stupid woman with her stupid oxen came down that hill and ran me over."

Sympathy welled up inside me. I knew just how bitter she felt about those oxen and that woman. I was just as annoyed when they had run me over. . . . What was I thinking?

I put my hands to my head, hoping to shake some sense into it.

"No, no, you don't smell at all, Corazon," Pia said soothingly, reaching out to pat my arm. I backed away, worried that I might have some sort of hideous Akasha-based body odor that had escaped my notice. *Why the hell didn't you tell me I stink? I could just die!*

You don't stink. You smell wonderful, like sun-warmed wildflowers.

Your nose is clearly out of whack because the others certainly think I smell. I realized that I was talking to Alec, something I hadn't done since we'd come into the house, and immediately was swamped with emotion. *Can you . . . er . . . can you talk with her, too?*

It took him several seconds to answer. *Yes.*

"I don't think I am wrong," Kristoff said slowly, his eyes filled with speculation as he looked at me. I was too busy battling a sense of nausea that followed Alec's admittance. That he could talk to Eleanor confirmed she was truly his Beloved, and made my path clear. I had to leave. He no longer needed me, and if I stayed, I'd just end up confusing myself with the desire I had for him.

"Explain it to Cora," Pia growled at Kristoff, pinching the back of his hand.

He shot Alec a look. "He can explain."

"Cora, before you run off to bathe yourself in perfume, please sit down," Pia said, shooting both men annoyed looks.

"I'd like to know just why he thinks that woman is my Alec's Beloved," Eleanor said with an injured sniff. "When it's clear I was, and am."

"Yes, but you don't smell. At least I don't think she does. Does she, Kristoff?" Pia asked.

Kristoff lifted his chin and sniffed. "Not really, no."

"Your nose is wrong," Eleanor told him.

"I don't understand this smell thing," I said, wrapping my arms around myself. "But I'm sorry if I've offended anyone."

"You haven't offended anyone, Cora." Alec moved over toward me, but stopped when Eleanor grabbed his arm and held him back. His face twisted in anguish for a second, his eyes burning into mine.

Stop it, I told him. *Stop looking guilty. You found your Beloved. You should be happy.*

My Beloved is dead, he answered, shaking off Eleanor's hand to move over next to the couch.

That was true enough. *And she's been brought back. As a lich.*

So?

His gaze wavered. *Something is not right here, Cora, the least of which is the pain I feel in you.*

I gently pushed him out of my mind, uneasy that he could read my emotions so effortlessly.

Pia sighed. "Since Alec never bothered to explain this to you—honestly, men!—I will. There's this weird thing about Beloveds. I know I freaked out when I heard about it, but Kristoff assures me it's no big deal, and it can vary, so don't think you're walking around smelling like a big ole manure factory to all Dark Ones."

"Mother Mary," I gasped, staggering to the couch, drawn against my will toward Alec. If I was going to stink, he could just be inflicted with it. "I smell like manure?"

You do not stink. Just the scent of you makes me hard.

Damn the man! How did he get into my head so easily?

"No, of course you don't," Pia said soothingly. "Beloveds, to Dark Ones who are not theirs, have this . . . odor. Supposedly it alerts them that they are taken or some such thing, and that their blood is basically poison to anyone but the designated Dark One. So I suppose I can see that there should some marker to indicate that someone shouldn't be munched on, although really, I think they could have come up with a better method than smelling."

Does Pia smell bad to you? I couldn't help but ask.

Not bad so much as . . . mildly unpleasant.

I looked at Kristoff in horror. He laughed, and wrapped an arm around Pia. "Pia is making too much of nothing. Beloveds in the process of Joining smell a little different, that's all. Once Joined, it's a bit stronger, but even then I've never found it repellent. We are used to it, I assure you. What I'm curious about is how you came about to be."

"My mother and father fell in love," I said somewhat indignantly.

"Boy, you're really Mr. Put Your Foot in Your Mouth today, aren't you?" Pia asked him, her hand doing a little possessive leg touch. "I think he means how you can be Alec's Beloved when Eleanor was killed several hundred years ago."

"And brought back, just to save him," Eleanor added, glaring at me. "I do not like this woman, Alec. I don't know who she is, or why you all seem to feel she's as good as me, but she's not. I am your Beloved. I am the one you begged to Join with you all those centuries ago. And it is I who will redeem you now."

My gut tightened as my inner voice nagged me to spill the truth, urging me to explain my connection to Alec, but that way would only cause more pain, for both of us. He would just feel even more guilty than he did already, and I didn't want to spend my life with a vampire.

Liar, my inner self snarled.

I rubbed my head, my emotions as confused as my brain.

"You were, at one time, my Beloved, as Kristoff knows," Alec admitted slowly, the pain from inside him spilling out onto me. "But be that as it may, there is a bond between Cora and me that we cannot deny. I do not believe such a bond exists between us anymore, Eleanor."

She's your Beloved, Alec. Stop fighting it.

Do you dislike me so much that you are so happy to be rid of me? he asked.

Tell him! my little devil demanded. *He's hurting because he thinks you don't want him.*

I tried to argue that I didn't want him, but even I didn't believe that anymore.

It just figured that the one man in the world I wanted was the one I should never have. Way to go, life.

"How does Kristoff know?" I asked the room in general, trying to drown out my conscience. "How did you know about Eleanor?"

"It was his wife who killed my Beloved," Alec answered, his eyes a pale jade. "His first wife."

My eyes widened as I stared at Kristoff. "Your wife was the one with the oxcart? The one who cut off my head?"

The second the words left my mouth, I cursed myself. My devil cheered.

"*Your* head?"

Slowly, I turned to look at Alec.

Your head? he asked again.

Um . . .

"What do you mean, *your* head?" Pia asked, leaning into Kristoff when he sat next to her.

"Yes!" Eleanor said, leaping to her feet, her face red with anger. "What exactly do you mean, *your* head? It was *my* head that was cut off, not yours! You're trying to steal him, aren't you?"

Cora?

"You're trying to steal Alec from me!"

Alec's pain lashed him so hard, I crumpled into a little ball, hugging my knees, unable to look at him.

"You bitch! She's using you, Alec, nothing more. She had some sort of a vision about the day I was killed—she said so herself—and now she's trying to use that to confuse you. I'm your Beloved, not her. I don't care what Kristoff says—it's me who has the bond with you."

"Corazon?" The word was spoken softly, with a world of warmth behind it. Alec knelt next to me, his hand lightly touching my head as I rubbed my cheek against my knees, torn with the need to tell him the truth, and the knowledge of what such an action would mean to us both. And to Eleanor. Could I do that to an innocent woman?

That innocent woman is you! my inner self yelled. *She is a past version of yourself!*

"Do you remember that I told you I'd seen a vision of the time when I . . . when your Beloved was killed?" I asked, unable to bear Alec's pain any longer.

"Of Kristoff's first wife killing my Beloved? Yes."

I lifted my head to look at him, needing his warmth, needing his strength. His eyes searched my face, and I could feel him gently prodding my mind. I kept him out of my head, unwilling to say what needed to be said, but having enough pride to do it the honorable way, rather than just letting him pick the facts out of my brain.

"Well, it wasn't really a vision. It was a . . ." I swallowed, casting a nervous glance at the others. "It was more of a past-life regression."

"A past-life regression," he repeated, looking confused.

"Yes. I was the woman whose head was lopped off by the crazy lady with the oxcart. Oh, sorry, Kristoff. I didn't mean she was nutso crazy, just a little . . . well . . ."

"No!" Eleanor shrieked, leaping to her feet. "She lies!"

"Oh, my god, you really are Alec's Beloved," Pia

said, obviously astonished. "You're . . . what? Reborn? How can that be? And how could we have raised Eleanor if you're here now? Kristoff?"

"I don't know," he said, his gaze first on me, then on Alec. "But I'm happy for Alec nonetheless. One way or another, it would appear he has a Beloved again."

My gaze shifted back to Alec, as well. His expression was impossible to read, his eyes burning with a light . . . but what sort of a light?

"This is ridiculous, nothing but a tissue of lies," Eleanor said, marching over to clutch Alec. "And I resent the fact that any of you could be so foolish as to believe any of it. I was his Beloved, not her. You summoned me back from death. She is nothing to us, nothing!"

"I'm sorry," I told Alec, ignoring Eleanor's ranting.

"For what?" he asked.

I made a wordless gesture of confusion. "For . . . for making things more complicated."

"'Complicated' is an understatement. I just don't understand how you can both be here if you're really . . . what, the same person?" Pia asked.

"We can't. That is proof that she is the false one," Eleanor said, trying to force Alec to look at her. "Feed from me, my darling. Then you will know the truth."

To my dismay, Alec turned his attention on her, looking very much like he was going to accept her offer and feed. He gazed into her face, his eyes glittering jade. "You have no soul," he said finally.

She jerked back out of his grip, her own eyes blazing with fury as she jabbed a finger toward Kristoff and Pia. "That is not my fault! It is because they had me brought back as a lich!"

"Liches have souls," Kristoff said slowly as we all looked at Eleanor. "They get them back when they are raised by a necromancer."

"Then the necromancer who you hired to raise me did it incorrectly," Eleanor snapped.

Alec looked at me with speculation. "Kris, what do you know about reincarnation?"

"Not a lot," he said with a shrug, then raised his eyebrows. "I've heard that only a certain type of mortal can be reincarnated, that the mortal being dies, is judged on their purity of heart, and accordingly granted life again based on that purity. Oh, you mean—"

"Yes," Alec said, his sudden smile so brilliant, it made me clutch the couch to keep from flinging myself on him. "I think Cora is one of those beings. She was born as Eleanor, was killed, and reincarnated into her current form, soul and all."

I stared at him, caught in the green snare of his gaze, wanting to believe the joy he felt was due to the fact that there might be a future for us rather than I was merely a form of salvation.

"That would explain why Eleanor doesn't have a soul?" Pia asked.

"No, it wouldn't. It doesn't," Eleanor insisted. "If she and I are the same person—and really, the idea is ludicrous; just look at her! She's completely unlike me. If we were the same person, we couldn't exist together in the same time and place."

"But you don't, not really," Kristoff said gently. "You're a lich. Your existence is beyond the mortal world. Cora is mortal. You aren't."

I dragged my gaze off Alec to look at Eleanor, wondering if I had really ever been her. *What a pain in the ass I was.*

Alec laughed in my head. *I wouldn't say that, but I admit that I had only just met you when you were killed.*

"Even admitting that was possible—and I don't admit that for one minute. But let's say it is. Then all that means is that she's a knockoff of me, and I'm the original Beloved, and she has my soul." Eleanor's eyes narrowed on me. "And she can just give it back!"

"Oh, that is not going to happen," I told her, amused despite the unpleasant situation. "Finders keepers, and all that."

"Faugh!" she yelled at me, and spent the next five minutes arguing that Alec owed his allegiance to her.

"It seems to me that you're just going to have to decide," Kristoff told Alec when Eleanor wound down long enough for someone else to get in a word. "Cora or Eleanor. Which Beloved do you want?"

Instantly, my eyes went to Alec's, my heart beating with sudden urgency.

"That is the question, isn't it?" he said softly, smiling at Eleanor. She beamed back at him until he lifted her hand and kissed it. "I can't tell you how grateful I am that you agreed to the plan to save me. You will have my eternal appreciation for such a noble act."

"No," Eleanor snarled, jerking her hand from his and backing away, her face black with rage. "You can't mean that! You can't pick her over me. I was brought back to save you!"

"I know you were, and I regret greatly—"

"Nooo!" she wailed, and bolted from the room.

An uncomfortable, highly charged silence fell upon us all as the sound of her footsteps racing up a flight of stairs, followed by the slamming of a door, drifted down to us.

"Oh, Alec," Pia said, her shoulders slumping. "I'm so sorry. We thought we were helping you—"

"And I appreciate that you would do so," Alec interrupted before turning to me. I struggled to keep my face placid, and not express any of the pleasure that I couldn't deny when he obviously chose me over Eleanor.

He said nothing for a minute, simply looking at me.

"You knew that you were my Beloved, but you didn't tell me," he finally said, his voice as carefully neutral as his expression.

Where were his expressions of undying devotion? Where was his declaration that he had picked me? Where was his arrogant statement that I was his Beloved, and he would fill my nights with endless passion, and my days with expressions of utmost gratitude?

Rather than any of that, I got a sense of carefully masked anger.

"Yes." I lifted my chin a little. "I knew. I don't like vampires. I never have."

"And yet you fed me."

"I didn't realize who you were then," I pointed out.

"You don't like vampires, but you fed me."

Kristoff and Pia sat opposite, their gazes shifting from Alec to me and back again, just as if they were watching a tennis match.

"I explained to you about that. I thought you could help Diamond and me get out of the Akasha."

"You fed me multiple times."

"Well, you were hungry!" I said, slapping my hands on my legs, wanting desperately to know what he was thinking and feeling, needing the reassurance that he wanted me. "What was I supposed to do, let you starve?"

"You didn't leave me behind. You were worried about my wounds."

"Are you going to catalog every single one of my actions with regards to you? Because if you are, you should include me slapping you for trying to kiss me."

His eyes narrowed. "You gave yourself to me. Repeatedly."

I glanced at the others. "OK, really, I'm sure they don't need to hear about that."

Pia giggled.

"You're my Beloved."

"Well . . . yeah, I guess I am. I wasn't quite sure about whether a reincarnated Beloved can be the same as the original one, but I guess that's been proven."

"You're my Beloved," he repeated, and without another word walked out of the room.

"Well, hell," I said, now thoroughly miserable. "He hates me!"

"I don't think . . ." Pia looked at Kristoff. "I don't think that's possible, is it? Can you hate your own Beloved?"

"No." Kristoff got up, waving Pia back when she rose, as well. "He's just a bit stunned is all, what with Eleanor, and now . . . this. I'll go talk to him."

Alec? I asked, wanting desperately for him to reassure me.

No, he said, and closed me out of his mind.

No what? No, he didn't want to talk to me? No, he didn't hate me? No, he never wanted to see me again? If that was the case, why had he more or less dumped Eleanor?

"I could just cry," I said, pleating the material of my pants in an effort to keep from doing exactly that.

"Don't, it'll just make your eyes puffy," Pia said, moving over to sit next to me. "Alec's a man, and you know how they are—some of them don't cope well with emotional things, and you have to admit, going from no Beloved to two in the space of a day could make the calmest vampire go a little bit nuts. I'm just a bit curious, though. You said you don't like vampires?"

"No, I don't. I saw Alec kill that woman who beheaded me. It was . . . he just bit her and drained her dry. It was horrible. And then my sister married one, and although she seems to be really happy with Avery, it seems so wrong, somehow. He drinks her blood!"

"Just as Kristoff drinks mine, and Alec feeds from you. Do you think that's wrong?"

"No," I admitted, pleating and repleating the material of my jeans on my leg. "It's very enjoyable, actually."

She smiled a slow smile that let me know that I wasn't the only one who found the act of feeding erotic.

"It's just that—I never wanted to be with Alec. I wanted him out of the Akasha, because that was only fair—he saved my butt in there from a wrath demon, and Diamond was having a good time, so when the de Marco guy said pick one, I picked him."

"Of course you did," Pia agreed. "I would have done the same. Not that I understand how you came to know the Ilargi, but we'll get to that, I'm sure."

"But I didn't want a permanent relationship with Alec. He's . . . a vampire!"

"You know, I think you're going to have to move past that point," she said gently.

I sighed and slumped against the back of the couch. "I know. And to be honest, I think I have. I was going to tell him about the past-life thing, I really was. I just was waiting for the right moment, and then . . . then . . ."

"Then we went and screwed it all up by having Eleanor brought back. Nothing like having your hand forced," she said, nodding. "I'm sure that, given a little time to get over the shock of today, he'll be right back in your hair, driving you crazy."

"Now probably wouldn't be the best time to say that I'm not sure I want him in my hair," I muttered, wishing I could rewind my life a few days.

That would mean I never met Alec again. My heart

grew sad at that thought. Oh, dear heavens, was I already past hope? Had I started giving in to all that charm and magnetism and smoldering sexuality that had every woman within a five-mile radius ready to rip off her clothing and throw herself at him?

I looked at the woman next to me with a hard expression.

She blinked at it. "What?"

"You let Alec seduce you!"

To my surprise, she laughed. "I was wondering if you were going to come back to that. I did, yes. Well, not really. It's a little complicated. We didn't actually have sex, you know. That is to say, he didn't . . . we didn't . . . it was more just some mutual groping. I mean, we were naked, but that was really all we did. And he didn't even stay the whole night with me."

I stared at her, trying to sort through all of that.

"I didn't make it any better, did I?" she asked, still laughing.

"No." The word dropped like a lead weight.

"Honestly, I think he was just lonely. The fact that he couldn't have real sex should have warned me that he wasn't the man for me, but I didn't see it at that time. It wasn't until Kristoff and I got together, and I thought he was still in love with . . . well, our rocky start is neither here nor there."

"You had a rocky start?" I asked, momentarily distracted from the painful thought of her touching a naked Alec.

"Yeah, just about as rocky as they can get. I'll tell you about it when you have an hour or two sometime. But first, you have to tell me about Alphonse de Marco, which means we need the boys. I think Alec has had enough time to get over himself. Let me run and check on Eleanor to make sure she's all right—then we'll go remind Alec how lucky he is to have you."

She rose and left through one of the arched doorways. My own feelings aside, I wondered if Alec truly wanted me for his Beloved, or whether he had just picked me out of gratitude for saving his life and springing him from the Akasha.

And what would happen to Eleanor? Would guilt over her eventually taint his feelings for me? Was he even now blaming me for putting him in a position where he had to hurt one of us?

"You really know how to screw up your life," I told myself as I got slowly to my feet, and tottered off to find Pia.

Chapter Ten

Guilt pricked Alec. He didn't like the sensation. "Dammit, Kris, she didn't tell me. I thought the marking was due to the amount of blood she'd fed me. I almost drained her dry when she brought me back. I didn't know. . . . She didn't tell me."

"You've been around long enough to know how women are," his friend answered, standing next to him as they both stared out into the shadowed garden. What Kristoff saw, Alec had no idea—all he could see was the look on Cora's face when she made the verbal slip, and realized she would have to tell him the truth. "There are times when I give up trying to understand Pia. I just accept that some things are important to her that don't mean a damn to me, and let it go at that. What matters to me is that she's happy. I find it interesting, however, that your first concern is for Cora, not Eleanor."

"Eleanor . . ." Alec rubbed his nose as he thought about what to do with the extra Beloved. "She's . . . not needed."

Kristoff gave him a rueful look. "I'm sorry we brought her back. We thought it was the only way that the council would sanction your removal from the Akasha. We should have just let matters lie."

"And left me there? I'd much rather be facing the problem of one too many Beloveds than that. It wasn't at all pleasant."

"No, but I imagine you're none too happy right now, either, faced with both your original Beloved and her reincarnation. What are you going to do about Eleanor?"

"I have no idea," he said, his shoulders slumping. "I assume since I never even fed from her that she'll be fine picking up a new life as a lich. Our bond, such as it is, is tenuous, and she shouldn't be affected by it being severed. It's Cora who concerns me. She has an aversion to Dark Ones. She saw me kill the reaper." Alec cast his mind back to that horrible day. Odd, though, that the memory now carried with it no pain. After centuries of it causing him the utmost agony, emotion had been drained from the memory, just as if Cora's admission had wiped it all clean. "Sorry, she saw me kill your wife."

Kristoff made a half-shrugging gesture. "Ruth was a reaper. She just didn't mean to run down and decapitate Eleanor."

"No." He knew that now. He hadn't for centuries, but after the last time he tried to kill Kristoff, they had finally worked out what had really happened, and moved past it. "Did I ever apologize for killing her?"

"No, but I never apologized on her behalf for killing your Beloved."

"I never apologized for turning you, either," Alec said moodily, feeling that so long as he was going to lash himself with guilt, he might as well get all of it out at the same time.

"If you hadn't, I wouldn't have found Pia, and she was worth all those centuries I had to wait for her," Kristoff allowed. "I could have done without you planning on destroying her, but since you couldn't see it through, it's all a moot point."

Alec couldn't help but smile at that. "She smote me with that damned reaper light of hers. That was no fun, I can tell you. My chest hair hasn't been the same since."

Kristoff laughed and punched him in the arm. "You had it coming. If Eleanor goes off without giving you any grief, what will you do about Corazon?"

He sighed. "She's my Beloved. What do you think I'm going to do with her? Bind myself to her and spend the rest of our lives convincing her I'm not a murdering bloodsucker. Assuming, that is, no one gets to her first."

Kristoff slid him a curious look. "Gets to her how?"

"I'd tell you, but I believe we're about to have company, and it's probably easier to explain it once rather than twice."

"Have you gentlemen worked through Alec's issues?" Pia asked, appearing in the doorway, her gaze drawn, as ever, to Kristoff. He held out his hand for her, and she moved immediately to his side, snuggling against him with a private smile meant only for him.

Alec watched them, wondering if Cora would ever cleave to him the way Pia did with Kristoff. "I have no issues. I was just . . . surprised." And hurt, but it wouldn't do to admit that.

I'm sorry. I didn't mean to hurt you.

He turned to find Cora in the door, her eyes wary. *Eavesdropping,* querida?

No, she said, startled, and he realized she hadn't picked up his thoughts. *I just . . . I figured I must have hurt you when you left like that, and then didn't want to talk to me. You've been put in a bad place, and part of that was due to the fact that I hadn't told you the truth about me. I wanted to tell you about it. I think I probably would have, but then Eleanor was there, and she was your real Beloved, and I figured you'd want her.*

I don't.

No, I gathered that. But it didn't seem fair to you to have to choose. I thought I might just make it easier on you by letting Eleanor serve her purpose.

He studied her face for a few seconds, then decided to see what path his life would take. He held out his hand for her, just as Kristoff had done with Pia.

Cora looked at his hand, hesitating. His heart contracted with the pain that accompanied the knowledge that she didn't want him, truly did not want to be his Beloved. He was a convenient end to a means, that was all.

Her hand was warm in his as she moved next to him, one delicious hip pressing against him. Hope flared deep in the empty space where his soul was meant to be, the hope that, after more than five hundred years, he might not be alone any longer.

Pia murmured something about getting some refreshments before they got caught up on all the news, taking Kristoff with her as she left the room. Alec barely noticed them leave, so caught was he in the beauty of Cora's eyes. *"Mi corazón,"* he said, rubbing his thumb down her silky cheek to that lush lower lip that begged to be tasted. "My heart."

"Alec, we need to talk. Eleanor—"

"We will talk to her. I do not want her hurt any more than you do, but she must come to the realization that you are my Beloved, not her."

"I don't know. It seems so heartless, somehow."

"Is your hesitation due to the situation with Eleanor, or that which is between us?" he asked, suddenly worried again. Was he misreading her emotions? She felt guilt with regard to him—that he knew—but whether it was about hiding the fact that she was his Beloved, or for the fact that Eleanor had been upset, was beyond his understanding.

"It's . . . it might be both. I feel like I stole you from Eleanor somehow, even though I know I really didn't. She's me, for heaven's sake. Or a past version of me. So I couldn't steal from myself, could I? And yet it feels like I did, and, Alec, I've never been the 'steal someone else's man' sort of person."

"You didn't steal me, love," he said, amused despite the fact that she was obviously distressed. He wanted to kiss the worry right out of her mind, but knew she had to work things out for herself, or she would never be content to bind herself to him. "We were meant to be together. There's no other explanation for the fact that you saved me in the Akasha."

"You were *supposed* to help me get out," she said with a dark look. "That's the only reason why I saved you."

"There were others you could have approached for help. That you didn't abandon me after you knew who and what I was tells me that deep down you know we are meant to be, as well."

She sighed, and leaned her head against his shoulder. "Do you have any idea how annoying it is to have your inner devil saying, 'I told you so'? It's almost more than I can bear."

"Inner devil?"

She smiled into his neck. "It's what I call my conscience. She seems more of a little troublemaker than an angelic bit of righteousness meant to keep me on the straight and narrow. She liked you from the start, for one."

He laughed, delighted with the sudden quirky turn of her mind. "Then she has my full approval. Do not distress yourself, Cora. I won't ask anything more from you than what you want to give me."

Her gaze dropped. "What if I don't want to give you anything?"

"Then I will continue on as I have." Only he wouldn't. Thinking over the past few days, he realized they were one short step away from Joining. Although it was physically possible for him to still feed from others, he knew he wouldn't. Somehow, without his being aware of it, this woman had found her way into his heart and bound him to her. But he wouldn't let Cora know that; despite her protests and rather odd ideas about Dark Ones, she had a large heart, and he knew with absolute conviction that she would allow guilt to sway her into Joining rather than a true desire to do so.

"I . . . do I have to make a decision right now?" She wrung her hands.

He smiled, and gave her a quick kiss just because he couldn't resist that delectable mouth, and then gave her a second one because there was no way one was going to be enough. "No. We have all the time in the—"

The door opened. Pia stuck her head in, her face tight with concern. "We have company, and they're looking for you. Kristoff has them in the sitting room, but we need to hide you. Can you find your way to the cellar? There's a hidden door behind some casks of wine. I have to run upstairs and warn Eleanor to keep mum about you, so I don't have time to show you where it is."

Alec nodded. "I know where the hidden room is. I helped Kris clean it out."

"Good. We'll give you the all clear when Julian and his buddy are gone."

"Julian? The messenger?"

"Yes." She said nothing more, leaving them silently.

"Who's the messenger?" Cora asked, prodding him when he opened the door enough to peer out of it.

"He's part of the Moravian Council. Which means they know I'm out, and either know or suspect I've come to Kris for help. Quickly, they've gone into the other room, but I doubt if they'll stay there for long."

He hustled her through the sunlight, ignoring the pain as they headed through the kitchen to a small door, down a rickety flight of stairs, and through a series of musty, dark, close rooms that smelled greatly of the earth. He pulled out a small penlight, flicking it around the rooms to avoid the stacks of old furniture, barrels of wine the previous owner had left, and the usual detritus found in a house a few centuries old.

Cora said nothing as he counted down a line of oak wine casks, handing her the penlight as he gripped a cask with both hands, throwing all his weight against it, willing it to move. It shuddered and groaned for a few seconds before giving way, sliding to the side, revealing a cobwebbed entrance cut low into the stone wall.

"In," he said, kicking the remains of a wooden crate out to cover the marks on the ground where the cask had moved.

"Are there mice? I have a thing about mice," Cora said, her fear palpable.

"If there are, I won't let them near you," he promised.

She gave him a long look. "Do I have to go in there with you? Would the Julian guy know who I am? With regards to you, that is?"

Pain laced him at her words, although he understood her reticence. If it weren't for her, he'd say to hell with the council and face down the messenger. But he no longer had only his own future to consider. "No, he wouldn't. You don't have to go with me if you don't want to. Pia will claim you as a visiting friend, I'm sure."

She looked at him for the count of five before she nodded and ducked down to enter the room.

He smiled at her ass. He couldn't help himself—she was just so contrary at times, it was all he could do to keep from pouncing on her and claiming her right then and there.

The hidden room was more a hole scraped out of the side of the mountain than anything else, the smell in it particularly earthy when he pulled the door closed behind them. Cora scooted to his side, clutching the back of his shirt and peering around suspiciously as he shone the narrow light around the tiny room. There was no sign of rodent life, but his nose told him otherwise.

"Do you see anything?" Cora asked, pressing herself into him.

No. Surely you cannot be scared of a tiny little animal.

"You're kidding, right? Because if there is anything more frightening than little mousy feet and tails and those twitching noses, I don't know what it is. Well, OK, rats are icky, too, but I count them in the mouse category."

"I see nothing," he lied, meeting the beady-eyed, but mildly curious, gaze of a large brown rat that scampered onto a broken chair across the small room.

"OK, but if you do, I'm out of here. It's no reflection on HOLY JESUS!"

Cora screamed and pointed in a direction forty-five degrees from the rat, and proceeded to climb him like he was a ladder.

"You know," he said conversationally, her heaving breasts pressed against his face as she struggled to climb even higher up his body, her heels digging into his hips, "that mouse is probably far more terrified of great big you than you are of it, mousy feet and twitching nose aside."

"Don't let it get near me!" she shrieked.

If you keep doing that, love, Julian will hear you.

Sorry. MOUSE! Can we leave yet? Please?

I don't know, he said, rubbing his cheeks against the thin linen shirt, the scent of her and the feel of her breasts waking his appetite . . . both appetites. *I'm rather enjoying this. Except the way your heels are poking into my flesh. Could you . . . thank you.*

Sorry. It's just that I really do not like mice.

I've ascertained that fact for myself. Much as I appreciate having my face buried in your breasts, at some point, I'm going to need oxygen.

She pulled back slightly, just enough for him to get some air into his lungs. "Sorry," she repeated softly. "Can you see the mouse?"

He glanced over to the rat. It was cleaning its face, one eye on them. "No, I don't see a mouse. It probably ran when you screamed, and went back into its home."

"You think so?" She shifted, obviously trying to peer into the darkness. "Maybe. Why are you hiding something from me? I've admitted I'm your Beloved—aren't you supposed to let me have a lifetime membership pass into your brain?"

He leaned back against the wall, his hands on her wonderful ass as she tightened her legs around his hips. "Are you giving me complete access to your thoughts and feelings, as well?"

That stopped her. He could feel how disgruntled she was over the thought that he could keep things from her, but knew she couldn't demand he allow her into his mind willy-nilly unless she honored those same terms.

He frowned at that thought. Just what, exactly, did she have to hide from him? "A Beloved should never keep things from her Dark One," he said primly.

"I'll be sure to pass that along to the next Beloved I see. Is your back getting tired?"

"No, although if you slid down a bit, I could at least kiss you. Unless you wish to take off your shirt so I can kiss your bare breasts?"

He felt her thinking that over, but she sighed, instead and cautiously unlocked her legs from their death grip on his hips, slowly lowering herself to the ground.

"Do you mind?" she asked, squeezing between him and the door.

"Not at all. The rat doesn't live who will make it past me to you," he said.

She froze. "RAT? You think there are rats in here?"

Cielito, you're going to pass out if you hyperventilate, and then I'll have to stop guarding you to resuscitate you, and that will leave the path open to the mouse to touch you with its feet.

She screamed into his mind at that thought, but made an effort to breathe. He couldn't help but smile into the darkness at the fact that she thought nothing about facing down one of Bael's wrath demons, but was almost prostrate with terror at the thought of a few rodents.

"Distract me," she ordered his back.

He started to turn, intending on taking her into his arms.

"No, not that way! You have to stand guard. Distract me while you watch for attacking beasts. I suppose we should talk about Eleanor."

"I'd prefer not to."

"I hate to say it, but I'd rather not, as well. What a chicken I am. Tell me . . . tell me about your past. Jas told me that vampires are either born that way or made. Which were you?"

"My father was an unredeemed Dark One; thus I was born that way, as well. What do you want to know about my past?"

"Well . . . how old are you? You look like you're my age, but I have a feeling you're older than you look."

"I was born in 1336 in what is now Dachau, Germany."

"The place where the concentration camp was?"

"Yes. It is a lovely area, despite that blot on its history. I have a summer home there that I think you'll like."

"Do you have any brothers or sisters?"

"None left living. My mother had several children before my father seduced her."

"Sounds like Daddy had some issues."

"Several, not the least of which was an inability to remain with any woman longer than a few weeks. He died in a fire in the eighteenth century."

"Really? I didn't think you guys could die."

"We can be killed, yes. We don't die of natural causes, however, and it's not easy to end our lives, but in my father's case, the building he was in collapsed on him, trapping him in the fire. Even a Dark One cannot stand up to that sort of thing."

"I'm sorry," she said, and he knew she honestly was sorry about the loss of his father.

"Thank you. I was not close to him, but he was my only living family member. I felt his loss." He didn't say more, but she read it in his mind nonetheless.

Her arms went around him, her cheek pressed

against his back. *After you'd already lost your Beloved. I'm sorry, Alec. Sorry that I wasn't around for you when I should have been.*

It wasn't your fault, querida. *It was just one of those cruel accidents that fate deals us sometimes.* He wanted to add that it would be worth it if he knew he had found his Beloved at last, but he kept his thoughts to himself, wanting her to make the decision for herself and not be swayed by his need.

"What's a lichmaster?"

"Hmm?" Cora's question interrupted his contemplation of how much time they had, and whether he could convince her that the room was mouse-free enough to make love to her. "It's someone who controls liches."

"Like Ulfur?"

"Yes. In fact, it's Ulfur that Kris and Pia are trying to save."

"Ah, is that how you knew who he was?" she asked, snuggling up against his back.

He might be hungry, object to being hidden like he was a criminal, and dislike the closed-in feeling of the small room, but he'd happily stand there to the end of his days to protect Cora, if she continued to rub herself against his back that way. She was so obviously his Beloved, the one woman put on the earth to be with him, he was surprised he hadn't recognized her from the first. "Yes. He was in Pia's charge before de Marco stole his soul and used it to have him resurrected as a lich bound to him."

"Poor guy. Do you think that monk can summon Diamond, too?"

"From the Akasha? No. That would take a Guardian, and unless he has one on call, he wouldn't be able to organize a rescue for your friend."

"Well, I'm going to have to do something about her soon, Alec. She's been in there for some time now, and if nothing else, my ex-husband will be worried about her."

"Time passes differently in the Akasha than here," he said, not liking the feeling of obligation she felt toward the other woman, but aware that it was now his problem, as well. "We will contact the Guardian who summoned us to have her do the same for Diamond."

She pressed her face against the back of his neck, her breath warm on his flesh, sending little rivulets of fire into his veins. "That's got to be expensive."

"It is."

"You'd do that for me?" Her hands slid around his sides, her fingers spreading wide on his belly.

"Of course. You're my—" He stopped, but she knew what he was going to say.

"That's still nice of you. Alec, do you think we could go to a mouse-free room? You're driving me wild with all those thoughts of licking me, and tasting me, and biting me, and oh my god, yes, I really like that one! Can we do that? Right now?"

He laughed, turning to face her, about to say that he would be happy to indulge her every fantasy, but at that moment, the door behind her started to move with a low grating sound.

"It's just me," Kristoff said, heaving the door aside before waving them out. "Julian's gone. You can come out."

"Oh, thank god. There's a mouse in there!" Cora said, giving a visible shudder before hurrying out of the room.

Kristoff looked past Alec to the shadows, where the rat stopped cleaning itself to consider them. "Indeed," was all he said before Alec helped him push the door back into place.

"I assume, since you're not escorting me out in handcuffs, that the messenger didn't convince you to turn me over to them?" Alec asked as they trooped back upstairs.

"Did you think I would?" Kris asked, a smile on his lips.

"It would have been sweet revenge."

"We don't want revenge," Pia said as they entered the same sitting room they had been in earlier. She held out a cup to Cora, plying her with food as the two women sat opposite each other. "We never have. That's why we had Eleanor's remains found and brought back to life. Even before that, we didn't want it. Kristoff spoke on your behalf after the council had you banished, but those new vampires who took Rowan's and Andreas's places on the council are bastards. Well, and that Sebastian guy, who I have never liked."

"He's had a hard time of it. He's still recovering from being tortured by a demon lord," Alec said with a little smile at Cora as he sat next to her on the couch. She ate three ginger cookies rapidly. *I'm sorry, love, I didn't know you were hungry, or I would have asked Pia to feed you.*

It just kind of hit me when I saw all the goodies. Is that lemon pound cake? It is! I love lemon pound cake!

Alec pushed the plate of cake closer to Cora, who murmured something to Pia before taking two slices.

"Oh, Kristoff told me why Sebastian's such a big pain in the butt, but that doesn't make him any easier to take. Cora, if you like the pound cake, you have to try the cream cheese pinwheels. I get them from a little bakery in town, and they are to die for. I've always said that if you're going to eat for two, you might as well eat what you like. And by 'eat for two' I don't mean I'm having a baby, so you can just put your eyeballs back in, Alec. I meant being responsible for feeding a vamp gives you a bit more license to indulge."

"My eyeballs were in no danger of popping out, thank you," he said drily, leaning back, one arm draped over Cora's shoulders as she and Pia consumed just about every last bit of food. "Where is Eleanor?"

"Still pouting in her bedroom. She had some not very nice things to say about you, which I'm afraid I encouraged."

Cora looked surprised. "Why did you encourage that?"

Pia smiled at them both. "Because she didn't know that Alec wasn't down here, so she was more than happy to stay upstairs and nurse her grudge in private. Which meant she didn't see the messenger."

"What did Julian say?" Alec asked, needing to know the worst. He had to protect Cora from whatever penalty the council would mete out on him.

"The council knows you're out, of course," Kristoff answered, sitting next to Pia on the love seat. "They assume you'll come here. I told them I would tell them if I saw you."

Alec's eyebrows rose. "You lied?"

"Of course. But that's not going to fool them for long, Alec. Julian didn't outright accuse me of having you hidden away, but he did notice your car, and he's not stupid. He'll be back. And when he does . . ." Kristoff's gaze shifted to Cora.

"Why do I have a feeling that what you're not saying is something I'm really going to dislike?" she asked him.

Alec tangled his fingers in her hair, idly stroking her

neck as he mulled over the possibilities. "I will have to leave."

"Yes, but that's not the answer," Kristoff said, meeting his gaze with one that spoke volumes. "They'll simply follow you."

"Do they have some sort of special vampire tracking ability?" Cora asked, worry uppermost in her mind. "Will they be able to find you quickly, I mean?"

"Not if I don't wish to be found, no. But Kristoff is correct that they won't give up—they'll continue to track me until they find me and return me to the Akasha."

"Well, don't let them," she said, sounding indignant at the thought. "I went to a lot of trouble to have that Guardian pull you out of there. Maybe if you talked to them—"

Pia and Kristoff were shaking their heads right along with him. "We tried that," Pia said, wiping her fingers on a linen napkin before sitting back. "We talked ourselves blue in the face, but they absolutely would not listen. They maintain that Alec's actions have indirectly caused the deaths of Dark Ones, and that he should pay for that. That's why we resurrected Eleanor."

Cora's shoulders dropped as she leaned into him, delighting his senses with her warm, feminine feel and scent. "Maybe you could hide, then, somewhere that they won't find you."

"It's possible," he said, wondering if she'd consent to shut herself away with him.

"Possible, but not reasonable," Kristoff said, frowning. "They'll find you, Alec."

"There is one solution," Pia said, her hand on Kristoff's leg. She glanced at him before continuing.

"What's that?" Cora asked, and in a flash she knew what Pia would say.

Pia took a deep breath and pinned Cora back with an intense look. "Someone has to Join with Alec. I know you said you didn't want to, but there's really no other way to save him from the Akasha. I'm afraid you're going to have to make a decision, Cora; it's either you or Eleanor. One of you is Alec's only salvation."

Chapter Eleven

What, I ask you, do you say to a statement that you are someone's only means of salvation?

Oh, yes, I completely disregarded the part about Eleanor also filling that role, because Alec obviously didn't want her. That thought kept me smugly content for about thirty seconds, until I realized that if I didn't do the job, Alec wouldn't have the choice—he'd have to Join with Eleanor just to save himself.

An image rose in my mind of him feeding from her, bound to her for the rest of his life. It was not a good image.

On the other hand, that whole "for the rest of his life" part had me a bit skittish. "You're kidding, right? Because I did the saving thing, already. Twice, if you count having Alec yanked out of the Akasha."

"Third time's the charm," Pia said with a smile, but judging by the look she slid the vampire next to her, she didn't really believe what she was saying.

"Yes, you did already save me, twice, as you point out," Alec said smoothly, his fingers withdrawing from where they'd slipped down between my back and the couch. "And for that, I will be eternally grateful. It is enough. This problem with the council is not yours, Cora. I will find a solution."

Alec's words disturbed me almost as much as the fact that his friends clearly agreed with him. It rankled that no one there believed that I would exert myself to save Alec. Oh, I was no fool—I knew I'd brought this on myself with my reticence to become involved with anything vampirish, but dammit, I *was* involved now, and I wasn't so closed-minded that I couldn't adapt to a situation.

My inner devil rejoiced, and made plans for what dress she'd wear to the Joining party. I told her to go jump in a lake.

You are distressed, Alec said, the words as soft as his touch on my mind. *Do not let yourself be,* cielito. *I will find a way out of this situation.*

I didn't answer him, too busy fuming over my growing sense of injustice to bother pointing out the obvious.

It took a half hour, but we explained the happenings of the last two days to a rapt Pia and Kristoff. By the end of it, Eleanor had evidently worked out the worst of her temper tantrum, and rejoined us, sullen and prone to shooting me nasty looks, but she appeared to have accepted the fact that she wasn't going to end up with Alec as her boy toy.

Unless, of course, I didn't want him . . .

"So your friend is still there?" Pia asked when Alec finished by detailing our arrival at their house. "In the Akasha, I mean?"

"Yes. And even though Alec says time operates differently there, I can't help but think that at some point Diamond is going to get tired of all those managerial meetings and want to leave. Not to mention what my ex is going to think about her disappearance. I left a voice message for the office when I picked up my passport, saying that I was going to take a little time off, and Diamond was going to fly out to Hawaii to join Dermott at his real estate conference, but it's been two days now. If anyone from the office calls Dermott, he'll be bound to notice that his wife isn't there with him."

"Hmm," Pia said, looking thoughtful. "As I see it, we have two problems to tackle: saving Alec and rescuing Diamond. Well, the latter, at least, should be easy enough. You simply contact that Guardian who got you out."

"Alec has offered to finance that, yes," I said with a grateful glance at him. He was looking particularly gorgeous, his hair slightly mussed from our sojourn in the mouse-infested room, a rich brown manly stubble on his chin and cheeks that left me feeling shivery inside, as if he were rubbing his cheeks along my skin. His leg was warm next to mine, making me want to just curl up against him and forget everything else.

Eleanor glared at me as I leaned into him just a little. "How very generous of him."

"So that just leaves Alec to save," Pia said, ignoring the sarcasm in Eleanor's voice.

"I can save myself," he answered, his hand sliding down my back again, his fingers gently stroking the curve of my hip.

Eleanor snorted.

"And if you get sent back to the Akasha, what's going to happen to Cora?" Kristoff asked.

Alec's fingers stilled.

I frowned. "What do you mean, what will happen to me?"

"Alec is acting as your protector. Who will assume that role if he's banished to the Akasha?" Kristoff's eyes were a pale blue as he watched me.

"That's right," Eleanor said, considering me with

something other than hostility, a speculative glint to her eyes. "She is a . . . what did you call it? Earwax of Lucifer?"

"Eyeball!" I corrected her. "I'm the eyeball of Lucifer, not the earwax!"

"Eye of Lucifer, actually," Alec corrected.

"Hmm," Eleanor said softly, looking pleased with herself.

She's totally going to try to use me to blast you to smithereens, I warned Alec.

He laughed. *Perhaps, but we will not allow that.*

Hrmph. He might not be concerned, but I made a mental note to keep a close watch on Eleanor for signs she would try to use me against him.

"That's a good question. Is there anyone else who can protect Cora if Alec is banished?"

"Like Alec," I said, straightening up from where I was slumped against him, "I can take care of myself."

"Can you?" Kristoff asked. "Can you protect yourself against a wrath demon?"

"Well . . ."

"Leave it, Kris," Alec said, his fingers once again stroking gently down my side.

"Can you protect yourself against the Ilargi who captured Ulfur?"

"If I had to, I might," I said hesitantly, thinking about the gun de Marco had wielded. My leg had healed, but even so . . .

"Kristoff," Alec said with a distinct note of warning in his voice.

"What about Bael himself? He makes frequent appearances in the mortal world," Kristoff said, pounding home the point. "How will you protect yourself against him?"

"Bael . . . he's . . ." I stopped, knowing it would do no good to lie to myself and the others. "He's pretty bad."

"That's an understatement," Kristoff said drily.

"Stop trying to pressure her," Alec told his friend, a frown between his brows.

"Yes, god forbid someone should actually *want* to save you. It's far better to force that on a person, instead," Eleanor said acidly.

Kristoff ignored the comment. "I'm simply trying to point out the obvious. Her life is tied to yours now. You need each other."

I was about to protest, but Kristoff's words resonated in my head in a way that made a warm glow kindle. Alec *did* need me. I'd never before been vital to anyone's life, and yet here was the answer to everything I'd ever wanted—someone who truly did need me.

He's a vampire, my devil pointed out, just to see what I would say to that.

But he's not a bad vampire! I answered her. I knew now that the pain that had driven him almost past sanity would have been enough to excuse all his actions, but despite that, he still carried guilt about it. He had committed sins, but had paid his penance a thousand-fold.

He *needed* me.

Do not let Kristoff make you feel you must do something that is personally repugnant.

You *need me.*

I want you, yes. I desire you above all women. But I could not live with making you feel as if you had no choice. I will find the means to hide you away, with a protector other than me to guard you.

You need me.

He sighed into my head, the words coming reluctantly. *Yes, I need you.*

"I think—" I started to say, but a bell pealed from the courtyard.

"Hold that thought," Pia said, hurrying to see who was at the door. "I won't be but a—ack!"

Pia backed into the room as Kristoff, with a growl that sounded downright feral, leaped across the room, skidding to a halt when a man lunged forward, grabbed Pia, and pressed a wickedly long, slightly curved dagger against her neck.

"Do not make a move, or your Beloved will be without a head."

Isn't that the monk guy who was here a little bit ago? I asked as Alec slowly rose, reminding me of a panther on the prowl.

I told you that he was no monk.

"Brother Ailwin," Kristoff said, his voice filled with threat as he stood about eight feet from Pia, his hands at his sides, but anyone would have to be a fool not to read Kristoff's body language.

"Hello again!" Eleanor said brightly. "Interesting things have happened since you were last here. Would you like to hear about them? I'm thinking about detailing my experiences on a blog. And maybe a Facebook page. I wonder how much the domain 'alecisajackass. com' would cost?"

"I have come for the Tool!" Brother Ailwin announced after giving Eleanor a disbelieving look.

"OK, that is really going to get old fast," I muttered, glaring at him.

"Release my Beloved," Kristoff demanded.

"I have no argument with you, Dark One," Brother Ailwin told him in a dramatic tone, pausing to add in a much less aggressive voice, "and will, in fact, be able to summon that lich for you later, since the bank transfer went through. Would you prefer I summon him here, or in town?"

I think Kristoff may crack a tooth or two if he doesn't

stop grinding his teeth like that, I told Alec. I had gotten
to my feet, as well, intending on moving to Alec so he
could use me to blast the bad monk, but Alec had moved
very slowly behind the couch, obviously getting into a
flanking position to help Kristoff.

Move to the windows, Cora.

Why?

You'll be out of harm's way.

*I may be afraid of mice, and I may not be up to tack-
ling Bael, but I am not such a coward or a wimp that I
have to be kept out of the way,* I said indignantly.

"Release my Beloved," Kristoff said again.

That is not what I am worried about.

"I will if you give me the Tool of Bael." Brother Ailwin shot me a look that had me upping the wattage in
my glare. "It is her I have come for."

"Oh, sure. Everyone wants her and the soul she stole
from me. Not to mention my man. But let someone res-
urrect you into lich form, and you can't get so much as
the time of day," Eleanor snarked.

"Look, I'm sorry that you were resurrected after I
was born, and thus my soul is stuck to me, but I did not
steal Alec. He said I didn't. So you can just knock off
the guilt trip, because it's not going to work!" I told her.

She sniffed and looked away.

Brother Ailwin clapped his hands together. "Brother
Godwin! Brother Esmund!"

Two men appeared out of nothing, both clad in long
brown monk's robes, ropes bound around their middles.
Their hair wasn't tonsured, but other than that, they
looked straight out of a medieval fair. One had a short
beard, while the other had a bad case of acne.

"Now, see, those are monks," I told Alec. *Are they
ghosts or something?*

Liches, like Eleanor. Brother Ailwin is a lichmaster.

"Take the Tool," Ailwin ordered the two liches, who started toward me, but Alec leaped in front of me.

"Like hell you will," he growled.

"Halt!" Brother Ailwin cried, spinning Pia around so we could see her face. The point of the dagger slid a tiny bit into her neck, making her eyes open wide. She stared at Kristoff, who obviously was only barely restraining himself from smashing Brother Ailwin into monk pulp. "One move from either of you, and I'll remove her head. You, woman. Come here."

"How do you know I'm a Tool?" I asked, then closed my eyes for a moment. "I cannot believe I just said that sentence."

"I can," Eleanor said.

I took a deep breath and asked, "How do you know that I'm a Tool of Bael?"

"You are glowing," he said simply, and added as an afterthought, "And I heard that one of my rivals had a lich who stole the Tools, but they were later imbued into three individuals. You are obviously one of those individuals, and with you at my side, I will have no difficulty in destroying the other lichmasters."

"What an excellent idea, one I heartily approve of. Please keep her in chains, too," Eleanor requested, but by now, no one was paying her comments any attention.

I put my hands on my hips as I faced Brother Ailwin. "You seriously think I'm going to let you use me to hurt other people? You're nutso. Hey, now!"

The two robed liches moved fast, both grabbing one of my arms and pulling me forward, past Kristoff.

Cora—

If I can knock them down, do you think you can use me against him?

You will not risk yourself in such a manner.

Yeah, well, I'm not going to let him use me to hurt

*other people, either. Especially Pia. She's nice. I like
her. Eleanor is starting to get on my nerves, but I suppose it would be wrong to hope she's knocked out or
something.*

*It would be wrong, although I understand your senti-
ment. And I like Pia, as well, but I will not allow you to
come to harm. He will become distracted in a moment.
When that happens, I want you to run toward me.*

How do you know he's going to be distracted?

Because Kristoff is about to strike.

I glanced at Kristoff. He looked furious, but I didn't
see any signs he was about to leap forward.

*I have a better plan. One that won't put anyone at
risk.*

Cora—

"Right, here I am," I said, shaking off the two monks,
striding forward until I stood next to Pia. "Let her go."

"Gladly," he said, releasing Pia and giving her a
shove toward her vampire.

Less than a second later, he grabbed me by my hair,
spinning me around, the knife now at my throat as he
started to pull me backward through the door, the two
monks on either side of him. "Now we leave."

Oh, yes, that was a better plan, Alec said in a disgusted tone.

*O ye of little faith. Get ready. You're about to wield a
bona fide Tool of Bael.*

"No," I said, digging in my feet, wincing when the
knife cut into my flesh.

"Come, woman," Brother Ailwin said, jerking my
hair backward.

Here we go. Ready?

Corazon!

Rather than fight Brother Ailwin, as he clearly expected me to do, I threw myself backward against him,

relieving the tension of the blade against my neck enough to allow me to spin around and face my abductor. I slammed my knee into his groin at the same time I jammed a thumb into his nearest eyeball, sending him to his knees screaming bloody murder.

Before I could do more, an Alec-shaped blur flashed by me, and I was thrown across the room, narrowly missing a table to career first into Eleanor before rebounding onto Kristoff, who shoved me toward a chair and leaped forward to help Alec. Brother Ailwin had stopped screaming as Alec lifted him off the ground by his throat.

"Now, lichmaster, let me tell you how I deal with those who would use my Beloved," Alec growled, his voice so menacing it made me pause for a moment. It was the voice of the man who had seen his salvation cut down before him, the man who had murdered a woman, the same man who was filled with so much agony, it would have driven anyone else insane long, long ago.

"Dear god, I think my back is broken." I helped Eleanor to her feet from where she lay smashed against the wall, her arms and legs moving feebly. "Seriously, man-stealer, you need to go on a diet. Ouch. Double ouch."

I pushed Eleanor gently onto the couch, and spun around to help Alec.

The spotty monk, who had been sent flying when Alec attacked Brother Ailwin, suddenly yelled and tackled me, throwing me to the floor. "Harm him, and I will use the Tool against you, Dark One!" he cried, one hand clutching my hair, his knees on my back as he pinned me to the ground.

"The hell you will!" I snarled. "I refuse to be used!"

"You cannot refuse. You are a Tool," Brother Ailwin

said, his face turning bright red as Alec's stranglehold eased up.

The spotty monk yanked me up to my feet, holding me in front of him like a shield.

"Yeah? Well, maybe I'll just use myself, then!" *Can I do that?*

No.

Damn! "Fine, then. I won't use myself. But I refuse to let you use me!"

"You cannot refuse," Brother Ailwin repeated, his color fading as Alec released his death grip on the lich-master's neck. "You are a Tool; the power flows from Bael through you."

"Well, maybe I just won't let that power out of me. Did you ever think of that?"

"Oh, let him use you," Eleanor said, passing a hand over her forehead. "I've got a hell of a headache and want to get out of here. I just want to go home."

"Home?" I asked, distracted. "You were dead!"

"Even the dead have homes," she said primly, brushing her blouse. "I had a very nice little cottage in the seventh hour of the Underworld. My roses were about to bloom when I was yanked out of there. Since Alec has so plainly lost his mind, I will go back to my cottage and roses and Gregory, the handsome soldier who lived next door."

"You have a boyfriend in the Underworld and you're yelling at me for stealing Alec?" I asked, aghast at her nerve.

"Gregory isn't a boyfriend. He's more a friend with benefits." She considered Alec for a moment before she sighed. "He's not as handsome as Alec, but he's not a bastard like him, either."

"Lich!" Brother Ailwin told Eleanor in a haughty

tone of voice. "You will be silent while your betters speak!"

"Oh, that's going to go over well," Pia muttered.

By the time Eleanor got done chewing out Brother Ailwin, everyone was snappish.

"Right, we got off track," I said, trying to look as badass as Alec. "But the fact remains that I will not let Bael's power pass through me, so you might as well just give it up."

Unhappily for my plan, Ailwin looked anything but worried. In fact, he shrugged and, with a petulant look at Alec, smoothed out the collar of his shirt. "You would destroy yourself if you were to try that."

Alec—

No! I forbid you to even try that. Now we will do this my way. "Let go of my Beloved and I will not destroy you," he said in a conversational voice to the monk holding me.

"Brother Godwin would not be so foolish as to do that," Brother Ailwin said, nodding to the spotty man who held me. "Perhaps a little demonstration of how serious I am to possess the Tool is in order. You may use her to destroy the Dark One, Brother."

"Jesus wept!" I swore at the same moment Alec lunged toward me.

The same sense of standing in a river swept over me, and I knew the monk was pulling on the power of Bael. I also know that it was directed at Alec, and that I absolutely could not allow.

You will not sacrifice yourself for me! he yelled into my head.

I'm not going to let you suffer any more, Alec. You've done enough of that. I wrapped my arms around myself as the power built and built within me, wanting to escape me, wanting to flow out of me and nail Alec in the chest. I fought it, spinning it around and around inside me, trying to contain it, but knowing in my heart that I hadn't the strength to do so for long.

Brother Godwin dropped me as I curled up on myself in an attempt to hold back the power, and sneered, "You will only destroy yourself, Tool. Release the power!"

"Never!" I panted, writhing on the ground with the agony of the still-building power. Alec reached me just as the second monk threw himself on his back, sending both men to the floor. Kristoff started forward to help, but Brother Ailwin screamed something about Pia, his dagger glinting as he jumped over the ottoman toward her.

Eleanor yelled god alone knew what, dancing around on the fringe, waving a vase and threatening pretty much all of us.

Inside me, the pressure continued to grow, pain lacing every breath as I struggled to hold it back. I felt like a stuffed potato in a pressure cooker, my entire body twisting upon itself as I screamed in anguish.

Corazon! We must Join! Now!

This is not really the moment for this!

If we don't, you'll die!

Jesus wept! It hurts, Alec! I don't know how long I'm going to be able to hold it. Get out of here! If I lose control, it'll destroy you!

Alec, whom I could barely see through the tears that blurred my eyes, was fighting like a madman with the monk. In the middle of clawing desperately at the floor to reach me despite the monk trying to bash his head on the floor, he did something that boggled what was left of my mind—rather than biting the monk and draining him of his blood, he bit his own thumb, then with a tremendous effort dragged himself and the monk toward me. *Take my blood, Cora. You must take it to complete the Joining.*

I didn't argue the point. I didn't question my need to obey his command. I didn't even debate with myself the wisdom of taking a step that I knew would change the course of my life forever. I'd already made that choice. I rolled over toward Alec, kicking out at Brother Godwin as I did so, every last atom of my body in torment with the need to fight the power. My control started to slip just as Alec's hand loomed before my blurred eyes. I opened my mouth, praying the few drops of blood on his thumb would be enough.

As the blood touched my tongue, the power surged within me, spelling certain death to Alec. I screamed an oath of vengeance as I made one last, desperate attempt to turn it back onto myself. "Hide!" I yelled at Alec. *For the love of the saints, hide from it!*

My back arched as the power broke free, pouring out of me, slamming into the man in front of me before sucking me down into an ebony pool of oblivion.

Chapter Twelve

The words came through to me as if through a dense fog.

"—think we should get a doctor. She's been out for two hours now. Maybe she's seriously hurt."

"I'm not hurt," I said, amazed that my mouth was working even before my brain was. I opened up my eyes, even more amazed that I was still alive. My last cognizant thought before my brain had shut down had been that Bael's power must surely have burned me up and left me nothing but a crispy shell of my former self.

Former self . . . for some reason those words wiggled around in my mind until I sat up, clawing at the blankets that covered me, gasping, "Alec!"

"Is out with Kristoff dumping Brother Ailwin in the river. At least that's what they said they were going to do. I don't think they really would, but there are times when I just don't want to know, and this is one of them," Pia said, smiling at me. "How do you feel?"

"Groggy." I put my hand to my head, surprised to find it intact. *Alec?*

You're awake? Good. Are you sitting down?

Yes, I'm awake, and why on earth would you want to know if I'm sitting?

Because I intend on lecturing you for a very long time, and it would be better for my peace of mind if I knew you were comfortable during it. For the love of the saints, Beloved, do not ever do that to me again! If I had been mortal, you would have stripped at least twenty-five years from my life span!

I giggled. Pia raised an eyebrow. "Is he giving you hell?"

"Yes, I think he's about to." I laughed again.

"It's probably best if you let him work it out of his system. I've found that the vampires may look all urbane and in control and stuff like that, but they get grumpy if you don't let them have their drama queen moments. I'll be downstairs when he's through. I should probably check that Eleanor hasn't gone on a rampage while I've been waiting for you to wake up."

All right, I told Alec, sitting on the edge of the bed. *What happened? How come you escaped being fried to a crisp, or blasted into kingdom come, or whatever would have happened to you if Bael's power had hit you?*

You told me to hide. As soon as I realized we had been Joined, I threw myself out of the window.

But I saw someone get nailed.

It was the other lich the dark power struck. He is no more.

Poor guy. Should have been his boss. Hey, you went into the sunlight? Oh Alec! How badly are you burned?

I'm not now. I wasn't much burned then, either, because the Joining was complete. How are you feeling?

I took stock of myself. *Arms and legs seem to be moving OK. I've got a bit of a headache, though. What happened to Brother Ailwin, and are you really dumping his body into the river?*

He's not dead, although that thought is very tempting. When you collapsed and he realized that he couldn't use you again until you were conscious, he tried to carry you out to his car. I stopped him.

There was a distinct tone of satisfaction in his voice that I knew I should protest against, but honestly, I felt Brother Ailwin had it coming to him. *You beat the tar out of him?*

That's one way of putting it, yes. Kris helped a little because he threatened Pia. But he let me have most of the fun.

So now you . . . I stopped, feeling awkward and suddenly a bit shy. After all that protesting I had made about Alec being a vampire, it was a bit too much like eating crow to admit that I was willing to bind myself to him for the rest of our lives.

Yes, now I have my soul back. Thank you, Corazon. I know you did not want to do this. I know you did not want to share my life.

You know, if you were anyone else, I'd say you were fishing for a compliment, I said somewhat testily. *And if you were any sort of a gentleman, you wouldn't make me eat my hat.*

He laughed.

Fine, have it your way, you obnoxious man, you. I did it because I wanted to, not because I felt I had to. And I know you're not really a murderous bloodsucker. Happy now?

With regards to you? Beyond your imagining.

His words, and the emotions behind them, warmed me for the next hour as Pia and I waited for the two men to return.

"Well, if this doesn't just take the rat's ass and make it into a hat!" Eleanor snarled, stomping into the room with Pia's cell phone in hand. "I just called the lord in charge of the hour where I live, and he says I can't come back. He says liches are not allowed into the Underworld."

"Uh . . ." Pia blinked a couple of times at Eleanor.

"So now what am I supposed to do?" Eleanor demanded. "Alec would rather shack up with her than me, and I can't go back home, where at least I had a life and a friend with benefits, and roses who loved me, not to mention the class I was thinking about starting on how to spin yarn using a drop spindle and dog hair, and now I can't!"

"Er . . ." I said, at a loss. "What's an hour? And there really is an Underworld?"

Eleanor sighed and slumped into a chair. "The Underworld is divided into twelve hours, each ruled by a lord. I live in the seventh hour. It is very pleasant. The lord there is English, so the hour looks like a quaint little English village with thatched cottages and digital cable TV and high-speed Wi-Fi Internet access. I won't tell you how many of my favorite shows I'm missing on the Home and Garden TV channel, but you can rest assured that I am not happy about it!"

"Since Kristoff and I were responsible for bringing you here, we'll be responsible for getting you back," Pia said after a moment's thought. "I'm not sure how we'll do it, but there must be a way."

"No, Alec and I will do it," I said, turning back to Pia's laptop, where I had been trying to find a phone number for the Guardian Noelle. "Ultimately, she's our responsibility."

"I really dislike being spoken of as if I'm not here," Eleanor said with a surly look to both of us. "And I really don't care who fixes things, I just want them fixed."

"Want what fixed?" Alec asked as he and Kristoff entered the room.

I quickly explained the situation with Eleanor before she could unload yet another tirade.

"Ah. Yes, we'll find some way to get you home if that is what you desire," Alec reassured her.

She gave him an injured sniff, and kicked her heel idly against the chair.

"I won't ask you how it went because I can tell by the looks on your faces that you got rid of Brothers Ailwin and Godwin. You didn't do anything really bad to them, did you?" Pia asked, immediately moving over to her vampire, her hands all over him as if to check he was OK.

Kristoff looked cranky. "Alec only let me have a couple of shots at Ailwin, so no, I didn't."

"I owed him more than you," Alec replied, cracking his knuckles and looking very pleased with himself as he came over to see what I was doing, his fingers trailing across the back of my neck in a caress that had me shivering with arousal. "All we did was rough them up and hand them over to the watch with a complaint of assault, Pia. I don't expect them to be held for long, however, so we will have to be on our way soon."

"You'd have to leave anyway with Julian hanging around," Pia said.

I slanted a look up at Alec, warmed to my toenails by the passion in his eyes. *You can't possibly want to—I almost killed you, Alec! How can you want to make love to me when I could be used to destroy you?*

Pia is a Zorya, and wields the power to destroy Kristoff—and every other Dark One, for that matter— but it doesn't stop him from indulging himself every opportunity he gets. Why would you being a Tool of Bael mean I should do likewise?

I shivered again at the things he was thinking. "What's a Zorya?"

"Huh?" Pia, who had been gazing into Kristoff's eyes, blinked at me a few times. "Oh, Alec told you about me? I'm a reaper."

"You're a *former* reaper," Kristoff said.

"Zoryas are a group of women who have the power to call down the light of the moon. They're next in line to the Zenith. I'm also a Zenith."

"A *former* Zenith." Kristoff was back to looking cranky as he allowed Pia to lead him over to the love seat.

"It's all part of a wacky religion called the Brotherhood of the Blessed Light," she said, cuddling up to him. "Better known as the reapers. They booted me from the group a month ago, which I have to admit was a bit of a bummer, because I seriously enjoyed light binding people. But all in all, it's better that I not be the Dark Ones' most hated enemy."

"Merciful Mary," I said, wondering how on earth she had ended up that way.

It's a long story. I shall tell it to you sometime when you have exhausted me with your lustful demands.

I'll hold you to that. Both the story and fulfilling all my lustful demands, that is.

He smiled, a long, slow, sultry smile full of much promise.

"Oh, for the love of the saints . . . if you four are going to sit there making googly eyes at each other, I'm going to go see what passes for the Home and Garden channel in Italy," Eleanor said, stalking off to another room. "Call me when I can go back home."

"So if Brother Ailwin is in jail—and stop looking at me like I'm insane, Kristoff, because I wasn't going to suggest that we have him summon Ulfur after the events of this afternoon—but since he's out of it, how are we going to get Ulfur?" Pia asked.

"We'll find another lichmaster," Kristoff told her, looking toward where I sat.

"I'm almost done. I found a Web site for something called the Guardians' Guild that lists a contact number." I scribbled down a phone number and relinquished the laptop. "Evidently you can hire Guardians through them. I wish I knew Noelle's last name."

"It wouldn't do you any good if you did," a tired voice came from the doorway.

Kristoff was across the room before I could blink, Alec right there with him. Kristoff pinned a slight, balding man with dark hair and dark eyes to the wall, Alec leaning in with a wicked intent.

"Who are you?" Kristoff snarled.

"My apologies," the man said in a choked voice. Literally choked, since Kristoff held him up by the neck just as Alec had done with Brother Ailwin. "I should have known better than to startle Dark Ones with Beloveds in the same room."

"Yes, you should have," Alec said. "Answer the question."

"I'm not sure he can," Pia said, tapping Kristoff on the arm. "His face is turning red, Boo. You should probably let him down before he passes out."

Boo?

It's Pia's love name for Kristoff. She said he scared the hell out of her when she first met us.

That's fitting. You scared the crap out of me, too.

Your first sight of me was when I killed the woman who decapitated you. That hardly counts.

"Who are you?" Kristoff repeated, releasing the man. He was a good foot shorter than Alec and Kristoff, balding, dressed in a brown suit, but with a pleasant face despite the fact that he'd just been throttled. "And how did you get in here?"

"What did you mean about it being of no use to call the Guardian?" Alec added.

I moved over to where he stood, telling my inner devil to stop attempting a new career as a matchmaker. Unattached Beloveds were not my problem. "Just out of curiosity, do you know Noelle?" the devil forced me to ask nonetheless.

"My name is Terrin," he said, answering Kristoff first. "I walked in. Mortal doors have never been a problem for me. It's of no use to contact the Guardian— who I do not personally know, by the way—because she couldn't get Diamond out of the Akasha."

Mortal doors? So this guy is one of you?

He's not a Dark One, no. But he is immortal. Alec considered him with interest. *The name seems familiar to me, but I can't place it, or him.*

"Why couldn't Noelle spring Diamond?" I asked at the same time that Kristoff, in a growl, asked Terrin what he was doing there.

"I would be happy to explain both if you would allow me a glass of water?" Terrin rubbed his throat, grimacing when he hit a tender spot.

Pia gestured toward the couch. "Of course. Please come in and sit down. Do you drink tea? The water's fairly hot still, I think."

"Tea of any temperature would be most welcome, thank you. I have had a long journey to get here." Terrin held up a hand, giving Kristoff a watered-down smile. "I see you're about to object to such civilities. Would it relieve your mind if I told you that I am a member of the Court of Divine Blood?"

The who of what, now? I asked Alec, moving over to the couch to sit with Pia opposite Terrin.

"It might," Kristoff allowed.

It is what the mortals think of as heaven. Or rather,

the mortals based their notion of heaven upon the Court.

So he's a good guy?

Presumably so.

"Heaven?" Pia said aloud, looking startled. I had a feeling she'd been asking the very same thing of Kristoff. "You're from heaven? Are you an angel or something?"

"The Court is not heaven, although we are frequently confused for it, and there are no angels there, simply employees. Thank you, I'll take it black if you don't mind." Terrin gratefully accepted a cup of tea from Pia, who gestured at me with the teapot, setting it down when I shook my head. "In answer to both questions, I am here because I have been sent by the mares to seek the help of Corazon. You don't mind me calling you that, do you?" he asked me.

"No, I don't. You don't work for Bael, by any chance?" I asked, suddenly suspicious. Why would someone want me to help them if not to use my Toolness? "And how do you know about Diamond?"

"Who are the mares?" Pia asked at the same time. "More importantly, just how did you know where to find Cora?"

"So many questions," he said, sipping his tea. "And so little time to answer them. I will explain as quickly as I can. I am unarmed," he added to Kristoff, who lurked next to him, watching him with a suspicious expression. "And I intend no one here any harm."

"You just admitted you wish to use Cora," Alec said, in a mild voice that didn't at all disguise his hostility.

"Not in the sense you mean," Terrin said, suddenly looking exhausted. "It has been a very long day. Let me start at the beginning, and see if we can't get through this quickly, so that my visit will not have been in vain.

I am a seneschal at the Court, which basically makes me a middle-level bureaucrat. One of the three mares—they are second-in-command to the Sovereign, who rules the Court—has sent me to seek the aid of Corazon Ferreira, mortal, who was imbued two days previously with the Occio di Lucifer."

"Former mortal. She is now my Beloved," Alec corrected him.

I really am immortal now?

Yes.

Wow. I thought about that for a few minutes. *That's kind of mind-blowing. At least now Jas can stop fretting that she's going to live forever, and I'll be an old lady who looks like her grandma rather than her sister.*

"So I see. You have my felicitations."

Alec bowed his head in acknowledgment.

Are you guys always so formal and old-fashioned?

It is the way of the bureaucrats, yes. I prefer to live in the here and now, but many beings in the Otherworld honor the old ways.

Gotcha. "What sort of aid?"

"I believe our goals are the same," Terrin said, setting down his teacup. "The mare in question—Mare Disin—desires to free her great-granddaughter from the Akasha, namely, one Diamond Reed."

I gawked at him despite the fact that I was gawking far too much ever since I'd met Alec. "Diamond has a grandma who is in heaven?" I shook my head. "That came out wrong. She's got a grandma who is a big-time angel? Boy, that still doesn't sound right."

"Diamond has a great-grandmother who is one of the three individuals who wields great power in the Court of Divine Blood, yes," Terrin said, glancing at his watch. "And we are running out of time to effect a rescue."

"I have heard of the mares," Alec said, rubbing his chin thoughtfully. "If they wield as much power as is reputed, why does not this mare simply remove her descendant from the Akasha?"

"The mares' powers are confined to the Court; they have none outside of it, much less so in the Akasha."

"But they do control the Hashmallim," Kristoff interrupted.

"I was just going to point that out," Alec agreed, turning to me to add, since he knew I was going to ask, "The Hashmallim are the beings who act as the police force of the Court of Divine Blood. They also serve to guard the Akasha. It is because of them that we could not simply leave it."

"I remember the greeter saying something about them," I murmured, wondering what Diamond was doing at that moment. Was she worried? Afraid? Guilt swamped me at being so caught up with Alec that I had been ready to let her happily putter on her own in the Akasha. Despite her reassurance that she was looking forward to seeing all the Akasha had to offer, it was still a place of punishment, and she had done nothing to deserve being trapped there.

"They do indeed direct the Hashmallim," Terrin acknowledged, smiling his thanks when Pia poured him more tea. Already the bruise marks on his throat had almost faded to nothing. "And if Her Grace Disin had asked the Hashmallim to take her great-granddaughter to the Akasha, she would most certainly be able to demand a release. But Diamond was banished by Bael himself, and combined with the fact that she is a vessel, it makes for difficulties in gaining her release without extraordinary measures."

"I understood, like, one word in five in that," I told Pia. "How about you?"

"One in four," she said, patting my knee. "But I've been around these guys longer than you. What's a vessel?"

"A member of the Court of Divine Blood. In the hierarchy of the Court, they are the lowest member, and justly serve mortals. They answer to—"

"Whoa, wait just a second, here," I interrupted, shaking my head. "You're saying that Diamond is an angel, too? Diamond who stole my husband away from me?"

Alec made an abortive gesture.

"Not that I wanted him anymore, and I'm much happier without him," I said quickly, flashing a quick smile at Alec. "But still, she stole him from me! Angels don't do that!"

"She is a vessel," Terrin said, his warm brown eyes doing a little twinkle thing at me. "She serves mortals."

I thought about that for a moment. "You're saying she took Dermott from me because . . ." My gaze shifted to Alec, enlightenment dawning in the dusty hallways of my mind. "Because I was going to meet Alec?"

"Because you are a Beloved, and you have a moral code that would not allow you to fulfill that role if you were bound to another man," Terrin said, hiding his smile in the cup of tea.

"I can't help but be a little annoyed with the fact that she thought she'd just come along and manipulate my life like that," I said, feeling disgruntled and somewhat betrayed. "I thought she really loved him. I thought he was better off with her. I thought I was doing the right thing by giving them my blessing."

Terrin shrugged. "She most likely does love him. Her job would not have required her to marry him, so I assume she felt they had a future together. And just for the record, no member of the Court takes it upon themselves to manipulate mortals. We may guide now and again, but in the end, the choice of what path your life takes is entirely yours."

My gaze went again to Alec, whose mouth was tilted up on either end in the very faintest of smiles.

You look smug.

I do not feel smug. I feel grateful.

Grateful that I let my inner devil have her way and hook up with you?

Grateful that Diamond had the foresight to separate you from your ex-husband. Did you love him?

When we were first married, yes. But it wasn't the sort of love that had much depth to it, and before six months were up, I knew I'd made a mistake.

"That's all and well, not that I mean to make light of your relationship with your ex-husband, Cora, but what, exactly, do you expect Cora to do to get her friend out of the Akasha?" Pia asked Terrin. "Are you going to . . . for lack of a better word . . . use her?"

"Would that I could," Terrin said, looking even more tired. "But although one Tool by itself is powerful enough to pull most people from the Akasha, a member of the Court is beyond its power. Two Tools, however, should do the trick."

"Are you saying that the Tools can work together?" I asked. "That they can . . . what, chain power or something?"

"That is a very apt way of phrasing it."

"So if two of the Tools together are enough to yank Diamond from the Akasha, what would all three be like?" Pia asked.

Terrin shuddered and closed his eyes. "The three Tools wielded by one person would rock the mortal world. They could cause irreparable damage to any being, mortal or immortal. It would, in short, have a devastating effect the likes of which have not been seen by this world since the creation of Abaddon."

Pia looked at me as if I were a walking time bomb. I knew just how she felt. I looked down at my hands, panic and fear swamping me.

I will let no harm befall you, mi querida. *No one will use you in such a way—that, I swear.*

But they could, Alec. I could be part of something seriously, unimaginably bad.

I would not allow it, he reassured me, but there was a shadow in his mind that made me feel sick to my stomach.

"So you need us to summon Ulfur in order to get Diamond out, yes?" Pia asked as I was trying to come to grips with my emotions. She glanced at Kristoff. "We'll have to find another lichmaster."

"There is one in France. We will contact her," he answered.

"Won't it be dangerous for Ulfur and me to be together?" I said slowly, leaning into Alec when he sat on the arm of the couch next to me.

"Normally I would agree that it would not be in any way ideal for you to be within close proximity of another Tool, but this is an extraordinary situation." Terrin glanced at his watch again. "The time of acclimation is almost upon her, and that would be most tragic."

What's an acclimation?

I have no idea.

I hate to always be the one asking questions. Your turn.

"What is the time of acclimation?" Alec asked just as Kristoff did the same thing.

"The Akasha was created by the Sovereign as a place of punishment for members of the Court who deserved such treatment. Later, others were allowed to be banished to its confines, but since it was created to hold former members of the Court, it deals with them particularly harshly. There is a period of time during which the individual sent there may be resummoned to the Sovereign's presence if it should so desire, but after that period is over, the individual loses his or her powers and becomes mortal."

Did he just call God an it?

The Sovereign is not God, and it is commonly referred to by a gender-neutral pronoun, yes.

"What's wrong with being mortal?" I asked, letting that point go for the moment.

"Nothing," Terrin said, getting slowly to his feet. "For one used to such a thing. But for a member of the Court to be stripped of his or her powers in the Akasha is a life sentence. Not even the Sovereign itself could change that."

"A life sentence? But nothing can die in the Akasha," I argued.

"Exactly," he said, his eyes suddenly serious.

"But why couldn't she simply be summoned later, even if she was mortal?"

He shook his head. "I wish she could, but Diamond is immortal. If she loses that quality, she ceases to exist in any plane mortals touch. She would exist in the Akasha, but"—he spread his hands—"nowhere else."

"Oh, my god." I looked at Alec as I realized what he was saying. "She'll be trapped in the Akasha forever."

"How long do we have?" Alec asked as Kristoff pulled out a cell phone.

Terrin gave us all a long look. "Two hours and thirty-three minutes."

Alec swore as Pia leaped to her feet, exclaiming loudly, "There's no way we can have Ulfur summoned in that time!"

Alec? What are we going to do?

Be patient, love. Let Kris determine if the lichmaster will help us before you think about panicking.

Kristoff turned his back on us, speaking rapidly in French into his cell phone.

"I'm afraid there is no other choice," Terrin apologized.

"But the lichmaster is in France! There's no way we could fly there in time," Pia wailed, moving over to her vampire.

Could a private jet—

No. Do not worry, mi corazón. *If Kristoff can locate a lichmaster, we will be there in time,* he said, obviously listening to Kristoff.

How?

We will take a portal.

To where?

To wherever we need. Ah. This sounds hopeful. Alec moved over to Kristoff, asking a question in French that Kristoff repeated.

I looked at Terrin, whom I was unnerved to find watching me. "You couldn't have told us this earlier?" blurted out of my mouth, making me blush at the rudeness. "I'm sorry, I didn't mean for it to come out that way, but really, a little more time would have been nice. Not that I've been proactive about getting Diamond out, so I'm just as guilty as you, but still. You, at least, knew the truth about her."

"I began tracing your whereabouts as soon as Mare Disin realized what happened to her descendant," he said gently. "You appeared to have traveled quite a bit in what is a very short amount of your time."

"Yeah, but you're some sort of an angelic bureaucrat, aren't you? Couldn't you just tune in your magic TV screen or whatever you guys have up in heaven, and see where I was?"

He gave a soft, but genuine, laugh. "I would give much to have a magic TV screen. Alas, the Court does not work that way. I traced you by means of bribery and several acts that I would prefer not bandied about."

"Thank god," Pia said, smiling at Kristoff. "We got the lichmaster, Cora. Very nice work, Boo."

He rolled his eyes as Alec held out his hand for me. I expected him to look a bit happier, but he looked worried.

Is there something wrong with the lichmaster that Kristoff found? I asked as Pia and Kristoff dashed upstairs to toss a few things into a bag, and alert Eleanor to our change in plans.

No.

Then why do you look so worried? If the lichmaster will summon Ulfur, we can get Diamond out. Oh, do you think he will do the same thing that Brother Ailwin will do, and try to use us?

No.

I moved around to his front, examining his expression. His eyes were a pale, seawater green, his brows pulled together. *Then what?* I asked as I put my hand over his heart.

It's what comes after, he said after a few minutes' silence.

After?

Yes. His gaze slid over to where Terrin was examining the pictures on one wall. *But I believe I see a way through it.*

Chapter Thirteen

Cora was uncharacteristically calm about the idea of taking a portal to Avignon, surprising Alec when, as she landed on the foam padding set up on the receiving end, she whooped and said she wanted to do it again.

"You are the strangest woman I have ever met," he said as he helped her to her feet, guiding her out of the way as the air sparked a few times, indicating another body was about to emerge through the permanent tear in the fabric of space that the portalling company maintained for the use of its customers.

"You told me that already," she answered, applauding when Pia appeared out of nothing and hit the padding with a *whomp*. "And the judges go wild!"

"Thank you. I think," Pia said, accepting the hand he held out to her. "I did try for a reverse gainer, but I'm not sure if I pulled it off or not."

"Seriously, tens across the judges," Cora assured her before turning to him. "Screw private jets—I want to portal everywhere from now on."

"Most people only use portals when they have no other choice," he warned her.

Eleanor appeared, screaming as she hit the padding. "Goddess above, I never want to do that again. Urgh."

He helped her to her feet, as well.

"Why don't they use portals?" Cora asked him.

He gave a little shrug. "Some beings don't like it. Dragons and elemental beings will do just about anything to avoid using a portal. Some of the Fae are opposed to it on the grounds that it desecrates their beyond. Others, like some spirits, cannot use it unless they are in corporeal form."

"I completely understand their feelings," Eleanor muttered, brushing off her pants.

Cora stared at him for a moment before turning to Pia just as Kristoff materialized and hit the padding. "One in ten words, maybe."

Pia laughed. "Believe it or not, I understood all of it. Give it time, and you will, as well."

"Uh-huh." Cora's mysteriously dark eyes considered him. "You're not any of those things that you mentioned, though. Are you?"

"No, I'm not, and I don't have an issue with using a portal per se, but it is also expensive."

"Really?" She moved aside as Terrin appeared about ten feet off the ground, arms and legs flailing as he dropped to the pad. "How expensive?"

He told her the price for all six of them to be transported from Florence to Avignon.

"Jesus wept! I could buy a house for that! A *nice* house!" she gasped.

"Am I here? All of me?" Terrin asked.

Alec hauled him to his feet, brushing him off, since the seneschal appeared to be somewhat disoriented by the portal. "You're here. Where to, Kris?"

"The lichmaster said she'd be waiting for us at the Chauvet caves."

"Caves? I love caves!" Cora said, her eyes bright with excitement as she took his hand. The fact that she did so automatically warmed him like nothing else had in . . . well, since his beloved mother had died. She had been the only person who touched him with genuine love . . . until Cora. He wondered if she loved him. He wondered if she knew he was quickly falling into that state.

"Caves? That ought to be interesting," Eleanor said.

"Do we have to meet there?" Alec asked Kristoff.

The latter gave him a sympathetic look. "She wouldn't budge from there. Evidently that is where her headquarters are."

"I've heard of that cave," Pia said as they exited the portalling company's building, and emerged into the soft darkness of the evening. "Isn't it where they found those pretty cave paintings?"

"I believe so," Kristoff answered, shooting him another look before he hurried off with Pia to rent a car.

"Caves," he muttered, disgusted with the turn of events.

"What's wrong with caves? They're awesome fun. I love the ones with the stalactites dripping limewater, making all sorts of creepy shapes. Kinda reminds me of ectoplasm, really, not that I've ever seen it, because I don't believe in ghosts. . . . Oh." She blinked at him, a wry smile making him want to kiss her senseless. "I guess I need to change that, huh?"

"There are many types of spirits," the seneschal said, consulting his watch. "But none, I believe, take on the form of wet stalactites. We have slightly over two hours left."

Avignon at night was enchanting, and Alec was possessed with the urge to watch Cora's face as she explored all the delights contained within it, but that would have to wait until after she was safe.

He became aware that Cora was watching him closely. He kissed her just to take that speculative look off her face, then kissed her again because once again he couldn't get enough of her sweetness, ignoring a rude comment by Eleanor as he did so.

You don't like caves?

No.

Claustrophobic?

He didn't answer.

I'm sorry. That's got to be the pits. You don't have to go into the cave if you don't want to.

"You're being silly," he said, releasing her lower lip when Terrin made a polite little cough. "I don't know what you're talking about. I am a Dark One. I fear nothing."

"Big talk," she said, but, with a glance toward Terrin, did nothing more than smile and take his hand, sending him wave after wave of reassurance and comfort. *It'll be all right. You'll see.*

"Well, as long as I'm here, I might as well window-shop," Eleanor said, moving across the street to browse in a store window.

"The mare you mentioned—she is anxious to have her grandchild out," he told Terrin, amused by Cora's attempt to soothe him, but not willing to hurt her feelings.

Terrin looked faintly surprised. "Of course. Wouldn't you?"

"It seems to me that she is in a very difficult spot. In a matter of two hours, she will lose her descendant forever to the Akasha."

"Yeees," Terrin drawled, his gaze sharpening upon Alec.

What are you doing?

Trying to solve two problems at once.

"It also seems to me that without Cora's help Diamond cannot be saved in time."

"What do you want?" Terrin asked baldly.

Yes, what do you want? Do you think he can help you with the vampire council thing?

No. Alec smiled. "And the Sovereign . . . surely the Sovereign must be aware of the situation? I assume the mares keep it informed of all that goes on?"

Terrin's suspicious expression tightened. "I am told they do. What reward is it that you expect? I can reassure you that the mare Disin will be most grateful—"

"It's not the *mare's* help I seek," he interrupted smoothly.

Terrin's eyes opened wide at the same moment that Cora probed his mind, gasping into his head. *Jesus wept, Alec! You can't blackmail God!*

The Sovereign is not God, and I'm not blackmailing it. I'm simply ensuring we receive its help.

"The Sovereign does not take kindly to being used," Terrin said, scorn dripping from his voice. "If that is your intention, and I see by the expression on your Beloved's face that it is. I don't know what it is that you want the Sovereign to do, but it won't do it, I can assure you that."

"Then Diamond will remain in the Akasha," he said blithely, brushing off a bit of nothing from Cora's arm. "Love, I believe we have time to do some sightseeing after all."

Cora gaped at him, her mouth open just enough that he gently pressed his fingers under her chin to close it. "Alec, you're nuts."

"So I've frequently been told."

"You can't blackmail God!" she repeated.

"The Sovereign is not God per se," Terrin said tiredly. "Why do I have to keep telling you that? It's an easy concept to understand, after all. It's not like trying to plumb the unfathomable depths of a woman's mind."

"That sort of a crack isn't going to do you any good," Cora said with a sharp look at the little seneschal.

He apologized, glancing at Alec. "Just out of curiosity, not that it will happen in even the most bizarre imaginings, but let us say the Sovereign was feeling gracious. What is it you wish for it to do?"

Yeah, what? Cora asked, evidently not having probed far enough to see his plans.

"My Beloved is a Tool of Bael," Alec said, gesturing toward her.

"She is," Terrin agreed.

"There is nothing I can do that will relieve her from that burden."

Terrin eyed first Cora, then him. "No," he said at last. "Such a thing is beyond your power. Or indeed mine, for what that's worth."

"Every low sort of being in the Otherworld and mortal world will desire to use her for their own gain," Alec continued.

"Where exactly are you going with this?" Cora asked, looking a bit disgruntled. "Because so far, all it's doing is depressing me."

"Patience, *mi querida*."

"I imagine that is so, yes," Terrin agreed. "If you expect the Sovereign to strip the Tool from Cora, however, I'm afraid you're doomed to disappointment. Such a thing is not within the bounds of even the Sovereign. For all intents and purposes, the Occio di Lucifer and Corazon are now perfectly joined, and will never be able to be separated again."

"Exactly," Alec said, smiling.

"What am I missing?" Cora asked him.

He turned to her, taking her hands in his, kissing

each one of her fingers before answering. "We must eliminate the biggest threat to you."

"The Tool? But Terrin just said—"

"That is the cause, but not the threat itself." He kissed her wrist, the hunger within him roaring to immediate life, twisting his gut with a need so great it almost made him dizzy.

She thought. "You mean the people who would use me to access Bael's power?" She shook her head. "You can't possibly eliminate all of them, Alec. That must be hundreds of people."

"Thousands, and they are just interested in the effect of you being the Tool. We must go after the source, the true danger that threatens you."

"But . . ." Her face twisted as she tried to reason it out. "The Tool gets its power from Bael. So . . . oh!" Her eyes grew round as Terrin sucked in his breath.

"You cannot think—" the little man started to say.

"You want to take down Bael?" Cora asked, her eyes searching his. "The devil? You want to destroy Satan?"

He sighed. "Cora, why do you persist—"

"All right, all right," she said quickly. "I know he's not Satan, but he's as close as dammit. Alec, you're bonkers. You can't just go after the head prince dude of hell!"

"Why not?" He gave her a reassuring smile. Really, she was the most alluring woman. Even as she was standing there fully flabbergasted, he desired her. He wanted to sink into her heat, to absorb her warmth, to let all those dark corners of his mind be lit up by the glow of her being. "Normally the princes have a battle each millennium to name a new premier prince. For some reason, Bael did not allow that, and has remained on the throne, so to speak, for well past his time. I simply seek the Sovereign's help in removing him."

Terrin's jaw worked up and down a couple of times before he could speak. "The Sovereign does not concern itself with the doings of Abaddon."

"No?" Alec pulled Cora into his arms, his mind preoccupied with the lush curves of her body, with her scent, with the beat of her heart. He let her see just how much he wanted her, needed her, at that moment. Awareness flared in her eyes, and she swayed against him, wordlessly offering herself.

"It is out of the question. Wholly out of the question."

"It would be a worthy cause," Alec murmured against Cora's temple as he breathed deeply.

"The Sovereign does not get involved with mortal concerns. It leaves that to the vessels."

"Ah, but this is not a concern that deals solely with mortals." He kissed the line of her jaw, leashing the overwhelming hunger that rode him so hard. "You yourself said that if the three Tools were brought together, they could be used to devastate the mortal world."

"*Mortal* world," Terrin emphasized.

"And what—" He paused just long enough to claim Cora's sweet, sweet mouth. "What is to stop someone from using the combined Tools against the Court? Or, for that matter, the Sovereign itself?"

Cora giggled into his mind. *You're devious, do you know that? It's a good thing that he can't read your mind like I can, or he'd never believe this bluff. The idea of you threatening to destroy heaven—honestly, Alec, how can you even say what you're saying to poor Terrin with a straight face?*

I'm not bluffing, mi corazón.

He caught her gasp in his mouth before lifting his head to meet the gaze of the seneschal.

"Down that path would lie destruction for many," Terrin said slowly, his gaze calculating.

"It would be preferable to the alternative."

Alec, you're . . . you're . . .

Insane, yes, I know. But it's the only way to save you, Cora. You can't stop being a Tool of Bael, and although I can protect you to a certain extent now that we're Joined, we will live our lives looking over our shoulders. Do you want that?

No, but—

We must eliminate the source of the threat. We must destroy Bael. We have no choice. And since I can't do that by myself, we're going to need help. The only being powerful enough to do so is the Sovereign.

"But . . . why don't you just wait until we get Diamond out, and then you can use all three of us against Bael?" she asked, stroking his chest in a way that left him growling with desire. "Surely that would be easier than trying to blackmail the Sovereign-who-isn't-God?"

"I would if it was possible, but I am a Dark One. By my very existence I have a tie to Abaddon. It's impossible for me to destroy that to which I owe my existence."

"Well, then, someone else will have to do it," she said, obviously distressed. His heart swelled with love at the thought that she was worried the Sovereign would be angry at him. No one—not in all the long centuries of his life—no one had ever worried about him. "Kristoff . . . oh, I suppose he can't, either. Pia, then."

"Pia does not have the knowledge to defeat a premier prince. She would not be able to control the power of the combined Tools. No, my love, there is only one being who can topple a premier prince, and we must simply point out that it must do so, or risk its own existence."

"You're threatening to use the Tools against heaven,

but you couldn't against Abaddon? How can you do that?" Cora touched his face in such a gentle expression of love, it almost unmanned him.

"I have no ties to the Court," he said with a grim smile, fighting the need to feed from her, to make love to her, to hide her away where no one but him could ever feast their eyes on her. She was his, and he would do whatever it took to keep her safe.

She would have argued more, but Kristoff and Pia arrived at that moment, in possession of a sleek black car.

"As you do not need me for the summons, I will go and speak to the mare Disin regarding your request," Terrin said with a long look at Alec. "I will return here in an hour. That should leave us time to rescue the vessel."

Terrin disappeared into the evening just as Eleanor, bored with window-shopping, wandered up.

"OK, what did we miss?" Pia asked some minutes later as they were driving out of town, heading for the caves. "And don't ask me how I know we missed something, because Cora looks stunned, Terrin looked sick to his stomach, and you, Alec, you look like the cat who's gotten into the cream. Spill."

"I look charming," Eleanor added with thinned lips at Pia.

"Yes, you do, very charming," she hurriedly added.

Should we tell them? Cora asked as she leaned into Alec.

Yes, but not until we are private.

She looked surprised for a moment; then her gaze slid over to where Eleanor sat on his other side. *Oh, you don't want her knowing?*

I'd prefer not, no.

Gotcha. And I agree. I think we need to watch out for

Eleanor, Cora told him, as Eleanor had looked oddly interested during the discussion concerning the Tools. *I swear she intends on paying us back.*

Perhaps. She seems sincere in her desire to return to the Underworld.

Yeah, but what's to stop her from wanting a little payback before she goes?

We shall see. Do not worry about the situation, Beloved. I will not let her harm you.

Fortunately for Cora's friend, it took a short time to reach the cave area.

"That sign says that the cave is closed to the public," Pia said, pointing at a sign headed with GROTTE CHAUVET-PONT-D'ARC.

"It is," Kristoff agreed, stepping off the path and pushing his way through the undergrowth.

"Then how are we going to meet the . . . oh. Side door, huh?"

A metal door set into the wall of rock was unlocked, by arrangement with the lichmaster. Alec allowed Kristoff to go ahead while he took up the rearguard position.

"Do we need a rear guard?" Cora murmured as he gestured for her to go in front of him.

He couldn't help but glance at her ass. "Yours will if you keep wiggling it at me like that."

She giggled, but stopped him, her eyes warm with concern. *Now, Alec, I don't want you to feel like you can't tell me if you get panicky inside. I'm not claustrophobic, myself, but my mother is, and I remember how she used to have panic attacks whenever she had to go into our tiny little basement. There's no shame in feeling nervous in a cave, you know.*

He debated telling her that he wasn't the least bit

claustrophobic, that he was more concerned with walking into a situation where he couldn't defend her properly, but decided he enjoyed the feeling of being coddled. *I assure you that you'll be the first to know if I panic.*

Good. She gave him a bright smile and a pat on the hand, which she changed into a quick kiss before hurrying off the metal walkway after the others. Lights had been strung in this part of the cave, along with long black cables that snaked across the floor, no doubt there to bring electricity and air down to the lower depths, where the cave art was located.

The low echo of voices reached them as they followed the walkway, emerging in a small, low-ceilinged room. A half-dozen wooden crates were stacked tidily along one side of the room, lighting equipment leaning drunkenly against them.

Cora took his hand, her fingers gently stroking his as a tall, thin black woman clad in an orange down vest and hard hat popped up out of an inky hole on the far side of the room.

"Oh, good, you're on time. I can't tell you how annoyed I get with groups who don't understand that my time is very valuable these days. If you think it's easy to convince people that a union is really for their benefit, well, you're wrong. You must be Christopher."

"Kristoff. I take it you're the lichmaster?" Kristoff asked, eyeing the woman with open disbelief. If anyone looked less like the sort of person who controlled liches for her own end, it was the woman before them. She had close-cropped hair and wore a faded blue T-shirt that read *Liches Are People, Too.* "Erm . . . did you say union?"

"Yes, I'm Jane Woodway, the head of the Liches International Union. The union encompasses the first liches to organize themselves into a group dedicated to the preservation and betterment of their members. I am not a lich myself, but I am wholly dedicated to their cause. We also fight for higher wages—well, actually, any wages, since liches seldom receive compensation for their services—health benefits, education, and job placement. It's our goal that one day all liches will stand in such a way that members will no longer be used and abused. We will reign victorious over those who would subjugate our lich brothers and sisters!"

Jane's voice rang out with fervor, echoing off the low stone ceiling.

"Er . . . yes." Kristoff pursed his lips for a moment while they all considered the lichmaster.

"I like you," Eleanor told her.

Jane eyed her. "You are an unbound lich, yes? Would you like to join the union? We have need for many helping hands."

"I would, but I'm expecting to go back to my hour soonish," Eleanor answered. "Although it does seem like a worthy cause. What sort of work do you need done?"

"You wouldn't happen to know anything about Web sites, would you? We're trying to start a social network for liches called Lichbook, but our Web person got sucked up by that fiendish Brother Ailwin, and we haven't had time to replace her."

"Lichbook, hmm? I might be able to lend a hand with that," Eleanor allowed before turning to Alec. "I still expect you to find a way to send me home, if I do stay for a bit to help out this nice woman."

He bowed. "I will do all that I can to make you happy, Eleanor."

She snorted in derision, but said nothing more, leaving him hopeful that they might be able to have a little respite to take care of more troublesome problems before tackling hers.

She's not what I expected, Cora told him, squeezing his hand. *You're not panicking, are you?*

Not yet, no. Thank you for asking, though.

OK, good. Just let me know if you need me.

He thought the day would never dawn when he wouldn't need her, but luckily, she was too involved in watching the union lichmaster to chase his thoughts.

"Now, if you're quite ready, I'd like to get the summoning done, so I can get back to my members. We're planning a rally to be held in Monte Carlo next month, and you wouldn't believe how far off track the planning committee has gotten. Liches," Jane confined to Cora, who stood nearest her, "are absolutely horrible when it comes to organization."

"Are they?" Cora asked. "Then it's good they have you."

"Yes." Jane beamed at her. "It is. Shall we get started?"

Alec had seen a few ceremonies over the centuries, but never one to effectively steal a lich from one master to another. He assumed there would be a certain amount of ritual, however, and he wasn't mistaken.

Jane began the ceremony by asking Pia for some personal belonging of Ulfur's.

"I'm afraid the only thing we have is this," Pia answered, pulling out a small wad of yarn.

"Yarn?" the lichmaster asked, looking askance.

"No, it's Ulfur's horse. A very nice Summoner taught me how to bind spirits to things, so we bound the horse to this so we could bring him here. Ragnor, we need you now."

Cora scooted closer to him as the ghostly horse appeared out of nothing, bobbing its head up and down a couple of times before it tried to take a bite out of Kristoff.

"Don't even think about it," the latter told the horse, who just laid back his ears and snorted.

Is that what I think it is?

It is.

Cora whistled to herself. *A ghost horse. OK. Horses can be ghosts. Don't you think I'm handling this really well, Alec?*

I think you're acclimatizing yourself to the Otherworld very well, yes. Are you, by any chance, the one who is freaking out?

No! Not over a ghost horse. Cora looked at Ragnor as the horse snuffled her front. She put out a wary hand to pat it, but her hand passed right through its neck. *OK, maybe a little.*

He put an arm around her, kissing the top of her head. *You have nothing to fear, love. I will not allow anything, mortal or immortal, to harm you.*

You know, that sort of an attitude could be cloying and very annoying.

But you understand my need to protect you and cherish you, he said, making it a statement and not a question.

Something like that.

Jane the lichmaster seemed to be suffering the same sort of surprise as Cora. "A horse. Yes. Well. Can it take a corporeal form?"

"For short periods, yes," Pia answered. "Ragnor?"

The horse's form solidified. Cora pressed against Alec. *Not because I'm afraid,* she told him.

Of course not.

She snorted, then smiled when everyone looked at her. "A ghost horse. So . . . yeah. Um. Do I need to do anything for this ceremony?"

Jane eyed her. "Are you related to the summonee?"

"No. Well, not unless you consider the fact that we're now both—"

"She is not related," Alec said quickly. *Beloved, this woman is a lichmaster. I don't think we need to tell her that in a few moments she'll have two of the three Tools of Bael in her presence.*

Oh! I didn't think of that. She seems so nice. But you're probably right. I'll just keep my lips zipped on that subject around lichy people. How come she doesn't recognize what I am, like Brother Ailwin?

Probably he's much older than her, and has either seen a Tool or knows what signs to look for.

"'Now both' what?" Jane asked Cora, obviously curious.

"Both . . . having had contact with his boss. Alphonse de Marco, that is," Cora said with a toothy smile.

"Ah. Shall we proceed?" Jane drew a circle in the dirt floor, chanting as she did so. She directed Ragnor to stand in the middle of the circle, which the horse did, then held out a small silver dagger to Pia. "The lich is to be bound to you, yes? He will initially be bound to me when I summon him, but directly after that, we'll transfer him to you. This blood bond should help that transfer. If you would prick yourself with the dagger and squeeze six drops of blood into the circle, following with six strands of your hair. Then blow on the horse six times. I shall do the same."

"They have to blow on the horse?" Cora asked Alec.

"Blood, hair, and breath. They are the three common elements in summoning spells."

He could feel her turning that over in her mind, one part of her warning her to run as fast as she could from the concept of magic, the other part of her, the curious part, fascinated with the whole proceeding.

It took longer than he hoped it would take, requiring three separate summonses and an hour and a quarter before the air in the circle shimmered, pulled itself together, and resolved into the form of the former ghost.

"Ulfur!" Pia squealed, starting forward toward him. Kristoff pulled her back before she reached the circle at the same time that Jane called out a warning.

"Do not touch him yet! We must first bind him to me quickly before his master can summon him back, and then we will transfer him to you. By my blood I bind you, by my body, I bind you, by my breath, I bind you." Jane slapped her hands together, the sound reverberating with the intensity of a small bomb.

Too late. Cora clapped her hands over her ears. *Jesus wept, what was that?*

The sound of a lich being bound. It is done at last, and by my reckoning, we have less than an hour to summon your friend.

But won't de Marco just summon him back?

He can't, Alec answered.

Why not? Cora nodded toward Jane. *She just did.*

Jane summoned Ulfur because Pia had a connection to him in the form of his horse, who he was bound to in death. De Marco has no such link; thus he has no way to summon Ulfur from Pia.

Well, that's a relief.

The transfer to Pia went quickly after that, and in no time Kristoff was writing out a very large check while Pia repeatedly hugged a teary-eyed Ulfur.

"I will never be able to thank you for what you've done," he said, holding Pia's hands before turning and making a formal bow to Kristoff. "For what you've both done. I will be eternally grateful that you released me from my bondage to de Marco. But I must tell you—"

"I think we'd better be leaving," Alec interrupted with a telling glance to Kristoff, who nodded and shooed Pia toward the side door. "Beloved?"

"Right here. Nice to see you again, Ulfur. We have a lot to talk about, but I'm sure Jane is anxious to get Eleanor up to speed on her Web project, so we'll catch up back at the hotel, OK?"

Ulfur opened his mouth to say something, but evidently caught the undercurrent of tension, and simply nodded.

They made their good-byes to both Eleanor and Jane, using the time spent traveling back to the hotel at which they'd agreed to meet Terrin to fill in Ulfur on the recent happenings.

"I never thought other lichmasters would want to use us in that way," he said after hearing about Brother Ailwin's failed attempt to take Cora. "Oh, god, we're going to have to live with that forever, aren't we? Not to mention the fact that every lichmaster and necromancer who knows what we are will summon me away from you, Pia."

"Well, as to that, Alec has a plan," Cora said, giving him a worried look. "I won't say it's not crazy as a coonhound, but it's the only thing we can think of to fix the situation."

"A plan?" Ulfur asked, looking slightly worried.

"What plan?" Kristoff demanded to know.

"Crazy as a coonhound? Oh, it sounds completely up our alley," Pia added, patting Kristoff's arm. "Dish!"

"It's quite simple, really," Cora said as she leaned into him, her scent teasing him, as it always did. "Alec is going to destroy Bael."

The silence that met that statement wasn't particularly flattering to his ego, nor was the "He what? 'Crazy as a coonhound' is the understatement of the year" comment as issued by Kristoff. But Alec was a man driven, and he knew that if he wanted to have any sort of future with Cora, he'd have to do the impossible.

It was just a matter of organization, and if there was one thing he was good at, it was making plans.

Chapter Fourteen

"Cora . . . this isn't going to hurt, is it?"

I gave Ulfur a reassuring smile. "Of course not. It just makes you kind of tingle, like you're almost touching an electric fence wire. Why would you think it hurts?"

His lips twisted. "Everything else does. Why should being the Tool of Bael be any different?"

I stared at him for a few seconds as Pia cooed over him. *Another one who is in pain. What is with you guys?*

Alec was startled for a moment. *Another one? You can feel my pain?*

I did before we Joined, yes. Shouldn't I have?

No. Once I realized we had a sympathetic link, I made sure to keep those emotions from you.

I thought of the anguish, the endless well of torment, that bound him so tightly it would have driven anyone else stark raving mad, and said nothing.

"Are we all here? Excellent. I've taken rooms for the summoning," Terrin said as he bustled out of the elevator of the hotel at which we'd arranged to meet. He shooed us toward it, glancing at his watch to add, "We have slightly less than twenty minutes, so we really should get started."

"What exactly does a summoning consist of?" Pia asked as we all squished together in the elevator. "I've never seen a Tool being used before. Is there something we should do? Do I have to order Ulfur to do anything now that I'm officially his lich . . . er . . . mistress?"

"Yes. You should be running far, far away," Kristoff muttered under his breath, shooting Alec a crabby look. Kristoff hadn't taken very well to Alec's plan to overthrow Bael. None of them had, really, although in the end, they all agreed that if Ulfur, Diamond, and I wanted to live any sort of normal lives, Bael had to go.

That didn't mean that Kristoff hadn't pulled Alec aside as soon as we got to the hotel, and had what appeared to be a heated discussion in German.

"Do you speak German?" I had asked Pia, watching the two of them as they stood in a corner of the hotel's lobby, Alec standing with an implacable expression, while Kristoff, gesturing wildly, evidently vented his spleen.

"No. Which, I have to say, right now I'm really happy about, because I have a feeling Kristoff isn't being very nice to Alec, and I really would hate to have to yell at him for that, since he was so sweet about paying for Ulfur."

We watched for another minute, Ulfur joining us. "Are they angry at me?" he asked.

"No. Kristoff doesn't seem to like Alec's plan, and I don't think Alec likes being yelled at. . . . Oh, now that was just uncalled for." Kristoff had, with an angry word, turned away from Alec, who put out a hand to stop him. Kristoff shoved Alec back.

"Ouch," Pia winced as Alec returned the favor, shoving Kristoff, who stumbled backward over an ottoman, smacking his head on a table. She sighed. "I suppose we should intervene. On the other hand, maybe they just need to work things out between themselves."

"Probably." *Are you all right?*

Yes.

His answer was as terse as his mood, so I didn't push him, simply waited for Kristoff, who had leaped to his feet and was now yelling in Italian at Alec, to get done so we could continue on. By the time they had done so, and Ulfur inquired worriedly about the level of pain involved with being one of Bael's little playthings, the two men had worked out most of their animosity without, thankfully, any blood having been drawn.

Terrin eyed Alec as we rode up in the elevator. "I spoke to the Sovereign on your behalf."

"And?" Alec asked, one eyebrow rising in question.

Terrin sighed. "The Sovereign wishes it to be known that it does not involve itself in situations not of its making, or which lack a direct impact on its purview, which, despite your threat, this does not fall under."

Alec swore under his breath. My stomach clenched with worry, causing Alec to pull me up next to him, his arm around me.

"That's all it had to say? It doesn't get involved in situations like ours?" I asked, alternately wanting to cry and to yell at the head of heaven that it had to help us because we were the good guys.

"No, that's not all that was said. It made mention of a few other things, one in particular which I think you might find pertinent." Terrin's eyes twinkled with amusement.

"What's that?" I asked.

"It was in the form of a personal addition to Alec."

"And that would be?" Alec asked.

Terrin smiled. "Bring it on."

Alec snorted in derision.

"Bring it on?" I asked, astonished.

"That's what it said, yes."

"Bring it on!" Fury roared through me at the words. "What the hell sort of thing is that to say? *Bring it on? I* don't think I like this Sovereign at all. Just wait until we get Diamond out. We'll see who's got the attitude then!"

"Cora, I don't think—" Pia started to say, but I interrupted her.

"Your precious Sovereign wants us to bring it on? Well, we'll just do that!"

Terrin looked shocked as Alec pulled me tighter against him, saying in a weary voice, *"Mi corazón—"*

"I will not stand here and let some jerkwad flip us that kind of crap, Alec!"

"Jerkwad?" Terrin asked on a gasp.

"Oooh," Pia said, her eyes big.

Alec's eyebrows rose as he considered me. "I had no idea you were so aggressive."

"I'm not aggressive, not overly so," I said, pushing up my sleeves, just as if I were going to battle that moment. "But I don't tolerate being pushed around by anyone, not you, not Bael, and not some half-assed leader of a group of pansy angels and cherubs and . . . and . . . and whatever else they have in this lame version of heaven!"

Terrin blinked.

"Why don't you tell us what you really think, Cora?" Kristoff suggested with a hint of a smile.

Before I could do just that, we arrived at the floor where Terrin had taken a suite. I marched into the room feeling as if I were a dog with my hackles up, annoyed beyond anything that our sole hope for help had dismissed us without so much as batting a heavenly eyelash.

"Bring it on," I growled to myself, and added a few more thoughts as Terrin arranged Ulfur and me on either side of him.

Beloved, muttering curses to yourself is not going to help our cause.

Perhaps not, but it sure makes me feel a whole lot better. Besides, our cause is lost at this point. At least it is until we show the Sovereign that we mean business.

Not lost, no. We have yet to hear what the Sovereign will do to help us, although if you continue invoking curses upon its head, you risk losing that help.

I stared at Alec as Terrin put one hand on my shoulder, and one on Ulfur's, closing his eyes to chant softly to himself. *Didn't you hear Terrin? He said the Sovereign refused to help.*

He stated the Sovereign's policy toward mortal involvement, yes. He also mentioned that wasn't all that was said. I imagine Terrin is waiting until your friend is safe before revealing what form the aid we seek will take.

I really hate it when you are smarter than me, I groused, giving him a quick glare that melted instantly at the burning heat shimmering in his forest green eyes.

I'm not smarter, love. I simply have more experience with Otherworld officials like this one. And if you keep looking at me like that, I will take you off to the nearest bed and ravish you exactly as you are imagining at this moment.

Oh, that would be lovely. . . . My attention, unfortunately, was demanded by Terrin at that moment, so it was with reluctance that I gave up imagining licking every inch of Alec's body, and focused on the task at hand.

The summoning was much briefer than that conducted by the Guardian Noelle, presumably because

Ulfur and I were there to give Terrin's summons a bit of an oomph. Whatever the reason, no sooner had he spoken the few words of summoning than the air shimmered and gathered itself up into the form of a woman holding a bright pink marker in one hand, and who was saying over her shoulder, "Now, if you restructure the focus group to include participants who haven't been strung up by their toes, you'd have a better idea of what torments really work, and what sort of a bias the group has. . . . Why, hello, Cora!"

Terrin's shoulders sagged in relief as he released his hold on our shoulders. "Thank the stars. Welcome back, Diamond."

"Terrin! It's been forever since I've seen you. You look marvelous, as ever." Diamond smiled happily at him, her smile growing when she spotted Alec. "Oh, and it's that nice Dark One of yours, Cora. But I wish you hadn't summoned me out just as I was presenting my workshop on better torture methodology."

She gave me a hug, then stepped back, her head tipped to the side as she gave me a once-over. "Something is different about you. You look . . . changed."

"Yes, well, we found out we're—you, Ulfur, and me, that is—now officially Tools of Bael. You're the Voice of Lucifer, I think, and something like that is bound to have an impact on appearance."

She looked startled for a moment at that statement. "I'm the Voce di Lucifer? How . . . oh, that chalice, the pretty one in the basement? How very curious." She gave Pia and Kristoff a wary look. "I hope you know those two people very well, Cora, because if what you say is so—and really, I have no reason to doubt it, since no one would joke about being a Tool of Bael—then all three Tools are present in one spot, and that could be a very bad thing if those two people are not at all trust-worthy."

"They are," I said with a smile, and made the intro-ductions, briefly explaining the relationship between Ulfur and Pia.

"Mercy, a Zorya?" Diamond said, looking thrilled to her toes. "I've never met one of you, but I've always wanted to. Is it true you control the light of the moon?"

"Former Zorya," Kristoff growled as Pia answered, "Yes, although I can't anymore, now that I've been stripped of my Zoryaness."

"Too bad," Diamond sighed.

Terrin, obviously drained by the summoning, straightened himself up and announced that he would return to the Court to notify Disin that Diamond was once again in the mortal world.

"Thank you, although I really was having the most interesting time in the Akasha," she said, giving him a hug, as well. "Tell Great-grandma that I'll pop in to visit her one of these days, just as soon as I can. Oh, I sup-pose I should call Dee and let him know I'm all right. He's probably beside himself with worry." Diamond pulled out a cell phone and wandered into a bedroom, humming softly to herself.

"She has no idea how close she came to being stuck there permanently, does she?" I asked, looking after her.

"She does; she just assumed we'd get her out in time," Terrin said, his dark gaze slipping from me to Alec, who stood watching the little man with his arms crossed over his chest.

"Sounds like her. So, are we going to have to beat down the gates of heaven, or is your Sovereign dude going to do something to help us?" I said, giving Terrin a firm look that should have warned him I was going to brook no nonsense. "Alec says you're keeping something from us, that your boss will help us, but frankly, I don't think so. I think we're going to have to show your precious Sovereign that we are a force to be feared."

Terrin sighed, making a tired gesture toward Alec. "I don't know how I can stand in the face of such a threat. As it is, your Dark One is correct. The Sovereign, while unable to violate the protocols of the Court of Divine Blood, is nonetheless sympathetic to mortal causes, and for that reason, has ordered me to contact, on your respective behalves, someone who has experience with both Bael and Abaddon."

"Who's that?" Pia asked, looking as curious as I felt.

"Me," a feminine voice said from the doorway.

We all turned to see a pretty woman with fluffy blond hair and a candy-apple red wool power suit standing at the door. "Ooh, two Dark Ones and their Beloveds! How exciting! I never get to see Dark Ones anymore. Terrin, my dear, you look positively ancient in that suit! What have I told you? You're a summer; you should be wearing lovely peaches and grays and creams, not those dreary browns that you insist on wearing all the time. Have you used that microbead skin care kit I gave you for your birthday? You haven't, have you? I can see you haven't. Honestly, why do I go to the trouble of trying to help you if you are just going to resist all of my advice?"

"This is Sally," Terrin said, a look of martyrdom coming over his face.

"That's Prince Sally to you," she said with a little laugh as he grimaced. "Or 'Your Infernal Highness, Lord Sally of the twenty-seven legions.' Or even, 'Sally the *magnifique*.' French makes everything better, don't you think? Not that it's an official title, you understand," she told us in a confiding tone, "but I think it has a snazzy ring to it, and it annoys the other demon lords, so I like to use it. I understand you have a little issue with Bael you'd like taken care of?"

"Prince Sally?" I asked, wondering if the day would come when I wasn't confused by things everyone said.

"Dio," Kristoff swore, rubbing his face. "That's all we need."

"What do we need?" Pia asked, turning to him.

"Um. I hate to sound like the stupid one here, but why are you a prince and not a princess?" I asked. "Unless . . . oh. You're a transvestite?"

"Me?" Sally said with a tinkling laugh. "A transvestite? Oh, my, I'm going to have to remember that joke to tell everyone. Me! Hee hee hee."

Terrin rolled his eyes heavenward. "Now that Sally—who, I assure you, is not a transvestite—is here, I will take my leave of you all. The mare is awaiting my return."

"Ah, gotcha. You two are . . . together?" I said, nodding at Sally.

She smiled at Terrin and blew him a kiss. "We are indeed together, aren't we, sweetness?"

"Alas, that is the truth." He sighed, and toddled out of the room.

"He's so cute when he's in Saint Terrin the Martyred mode, isn't he?"

"I heard that," he protested as the door closed behind him.

Sally took the opportunity to give me a very thorough visual examination. "You look quite charming in that dress. The color goes well with your skin tone," she said at long last, not at all what I expected. I looked down at the amber-colored short lace dress, brushing a hand down the beading at the neckline, becoming aware of Alec staring at my legs.

Stop it. You've seen my legs before.

Yes, but I hadn't realized until this moment just how much of them your dress exposes. In the future, I would prefer that you get them made so they fall below your knees, not above.

That's seriously control freak, and going to do nothing but make me walk around in a bikini.

"However," Sally said, interrupting the lecture that I could feel Alec about to deliver, "your hair! My dear, when I was at the Carrie Fae Academy of Good Looks and Perky Bosoms, we had one rule, and that was that bad-hair days should be abolished from this earth. You are not doing your part to achieve that goal."

I touched my hair, an indignant retort on my lips, but she gave me a smile that had an awful lot of teeth in it, and added, "I'm a prince because the rules of Abaddon say that all demon lords are princes, regardless of gender."

"Good lord, you're a demon lord?" Pia asked, just as shocked as I was.

I pressed up against Alec. "Jesus wept!" *Alec, we have to get out of here! She's a demon lord!*

"Ulfur!" Pia said, reaching for him. "Kristoff, don't just stand there! Do something!"

One that the Sovereign of the Court of Divine Blood has recommended to help us.

"Do what, exactly?" Kristoff asked Pia.

But all three of us are here! Together! She could use us!

"She's a demon lord!" Pia said, waving at Sally, obviously having the same thought that I was. "That's bad, isn't it?"

Yes, Alec said slowly, his mind turning over all sorts of possibilities. *That's exactly what I think the Sovereign intended.*

"I am not an it, and I am not bad," Sally said with another toothy smile, this time shared between all of us. "Well, sometimes I am, but most of the time, I'm just naughty, if you get my drift."

You mean this woman is supposed to boot Bael from power and take over his position? But what's to stop her from using us then?

Bael will be destroyed. So will his power. You will no longer be able to channel it; thus, no one could use you.

"Oh," I said aloud, understanding at last why Alec wasn't in the least bit panicking. "You're going to take Bael's position, aren't you?" I asked Sally.

"Well . . ." She brushed at nothing on her wool power suit. "I admit to having a tiny little urge, a very tiny desire, to be the premier prince of Abaddon, but really, I'm doing it because the Sovereign feels it is important that you get some help."

"I don't understand," Pia said, releasing Ulfur from the death grip she held on his arm.

"I don't, either," Ulfur said, giving Sally a doubtful look. "If you're a demon lord, why does the Sovereign trust you?"

"Yeah," I said, wanting to know that very thing.

She shrugged. "You'd have to ask the Sovereign that. Right now, I have work to do. And I think we should start now."

The door to the hall opened, and two people strolled into the room, one of whom was a familiar-looking woman bearing a long, black sword.

"Wrath demons!" Ulfur said, stumbling backward, but not fast enough. Sally grabbed him, sending him flying toward the door, before turning to me. I thought at first she was simply getting him out of the way of the demons, but one look at her face told me otherwise.

"Alec—" was all I had time to say. The two demons, one of which we'd seen in the Akasha, leaped forward, heading straight for Alec and Kristoff. I screamed and kicked at Sally as she jerked me out the door with her, shoving Ulfur before us.

Chapter Fifteen

You'd think that two people with reasonable intelligence and in a good state of health would be able to overpower one tiny little poufy-haired woman, but if that tiny woman was also a demon lord, you'd be very, very wrong.

"Ouch!" I yelled, trying to punch Sally when she slammed me against the back of the elevator, throwing Ulfur in after me. "You son of a bitch! I'll get you for this!"

I lunged at her, unable to get up with Ulfur lying across my legs, but I did try to bite her. She waved a hand and I hit the floor again.

"Oh, please," she said, making a gesture that had me frozen to the floor, Ulfur lying half on top of me.

She stepped across our bodies, pressing a button and humming softly along with the elevator music as we began to descend.

"I knew it! I knew a demon lord couldn't be good!" *Alec!*

Beloved, are you all right? Where are you?

In an elevator, lying on the floor. Alec, the wrath demons . . . Sally is evil! I knew she was evil! She took us all in!

Why are you—sins of the saints!

What's wrong?

Other than the fact that Kristoff and I are trying to keep from being beheaded by two wrath demons, you mean?

Oh. Am I distracting you?

Are you harmed?

No.

Then you are distracting me. I will come to you as soon as we destroy these demons' forms.

"Good, bad . . . that's so black-and-white when there are so many shades of gray that are far more interesting," Sally said complacently.

"Oh, you think you're so smart," I growled. "Just you wait until Alec takes care of your demon minions! Then we'll show you what's what. Right, Ulfur?"

"Urgh," he groaned.

"Exactly. You'll be one sorry chickie, and I just can't wait to tell your boyfriend about you."

Sally continued humming for a few seconds as a horrible thought occurred to me.

"Merciful Mary! He's in it with you, isn't he? Oh! And to think I believed him when he said the Sovereign recommended you. What bull! Well, I can tell you, we will be having a little chat with this Sovereign dude, and telling him . . . it . . . all about you and Terrin!"

Sally was about to reply when the elevator opened to reveal a couple with a small child in hand. "I'm sorry, but would you mind waiting? My friends here are about to threaten me with untold torments, and I'm very curious to see what exactly those will be. I hope they include thumbscrews. I love thumbscrews. They look so innocuous, and yet can give you such marvelous results, don't you think?"

The couple fled toward the stairs, the small child in the man's arms.

"That's just one more thing I'm going to mention to the Sovereign," I told Sally's ankle.

"Tattletales never end up good," was all she said as we descended again.

"What are you going to do with us?" I tried very hard not to let even so much as a hint of a quaver taint my voice.

"A friend has badly wanted to see you, and I am obliging him."

"Friend? You have a friend? I thought people like you just used others."

"Such ingratitude," Sally said, buffing a nail with absolute lack of concern about anything I said. "And to think I've gone to so much trouble about you. Ah, here we are."

We hadn't descended to the basement, or some dank lower floor that only hotel employees used; no, the doors slid open to reveal another cream-and-gold-colored hallway, and three pairs of legs. Men's legs, two pairs in black pants, one in jeans. I couldn't move my head to look up and see who they were, but I knew without a single shred of doubt that Sally was about to hand Ulfur and me over to Bael.

"I'll get you, too," I told the pair of feet nearest me. His shoes were expensive-looking, the kind you see on billionaire businessmen as they step out of their limos. "And if I don't, I know a vamp who will!"

"Why is it mortals insist on believing they have the least amount of power against me?" a plummy English voice asked as the expensive shoes stepped to the side. "What did you do to them, Sally?"

I wondered if I should let Alec know that Sally had grabbed Ulfur and me, but decided that distracting him with that information now could have deadly consequences. I'd wait until he gave me the all clear; then I'd tattle on Sally like she'd never been tattled on before.

"Damn you!" I snarled at the shoes, struggling to force my body upright. It was no use—whatever Sally had done to us held me to the floor like I was nailed there.

"Just a simple immobility spell, my prince. She was getting a bit difficult. Well, you know how mortals are—they can raise such a fuss over the most trivial of things."

"Trivial like betraying us when we trusted you?" I gasped, outraged at her callousness.

"Bring both the woman and the lich. It will be my pleasure to show them both what my wrath truly consists of."

I did not like the sound of that. Maybe now would be a good time to tell Alec what was going on. Then again, if he was still battling with Bael's wrath demons, it might make things worse.

Much worse.

"Be careful," Sally advised. "The female bites."

No, I had better take care of this myself, at least until Alec was free to help Ulfur and me.

"Damned straight I do!" I glared at the pair of shoes nearest me as two hands hefted me up, slinging me face-down across a man's shoulder. I growled as my face was buried in his suit coat, blinding me to everything but a narrow slice of floor visible when I rolled my eyes to the top of my head. "I swear by all that's holy, you'll pay for this! You all will!"

"She's also fairly antagonistic, although that probably is to be expected," I heard Sally say as she followed behind us.

"Where are you taking us?" I demanded to know of the man's back.

Bael wasn't hauling me around, but it was he who answered . . . in a bland voice that nonetheless left my skin crawling. "I do not recall giving you leave to speak, woman."

"And I don't recall giving you the right to make me your Tool, and yet here I am!" I snapped in return.

"Cora, Cora, Cora," Sally said in a disapproving tone. "Dear one, I realize you are not versed in the etiquette of Abaddon, but surely even you must realize that one simply does not snarl at Lord Bael without suffering the consequences."

I had a horrible feeling that the word "suffering" was going to take on a very real meaning, one I was pretty darned desperate to avoid, so despite my desire to do otherwise, I kept the string of abuse I wished to hurl at everyone's heads behind my teeth.

"Silence the woman if she continues," Bael said in an offhand voice as a door was opened and I was tossed onto a bed, Ulfur dumped next to me. We were still immobile, so I couldn't even roll over or shove Ulfur's torso off my legs, but I could see Sally as she faced Bael near the doorway of the hotel room.

"Oh, I will, naturally, because you know, life is just too short to put up with people lipping off to you. Well, not *my* life," Sally said with a giggle. I ground my teeth and wished I could fire some of Bael's power right at her. "But you know what I mean—life in general. In fact, I had better silence her now, because she's sure to scream and beg and plead and generally carry on, and I wouldn't want to disturb you."

"The day will never come when begging and pleading disturbs me," Bael said with a gesture that had his two companions dissolving into nothing. "But you may silence the woman if you desire. She will not need to have a mouth in order to be unmade."

"Hey!" I said, my skin crawling again at the casual way they both talked about what could only be torture. "I am right here! And I like my mouth! Sally, for the love of all that's holy . . . er . . . for the love of . . . crap!

All I can think of are appeals to your goodness, and you're so utterly not good, the comparison would be obscene. I don't know why you're doing this, but I should point out that Alec will not tolerate you abusing me in any way, shape, or form. And I know Pia won't let you do anything to Ulfur, either. What . . . er . . . what did you mean we would be unmade?" The last bit was directed at Bael, who ignored me to consult his cell phone.

"Do you know," Sally said slowly, looking particularly thoughtful as she sat on my feet, making me bite back an exclamation of pain, "I believe Cora might have a point? That brings to mind something I should tell you, my lord."

An unearthly wail rose high into the night, like the sound of a thousand souls in torment all crying out at once.

"Jesus wept, what was that?" I gasped, the hairs on my arms standing on end.

"Oh, dear, that would be just exactly what I was going to mention," Sally said, *tsk*ing softly to herself. "That was one of Bael's sweet wrath demons, Cora. Evidently the Dark Ones destroyed it. And although I would never presume to speak for the Lord Bael, I believe he's referring to the fact that his Tools cannot be destroyed. Otherwise"—she gave a delighted little giggle—"he would simply kill you and be done with it."

"You are the meanest person I have ever met, and I grew up in the San Fernando Valley—you haven't seen mean until you've been deemed too lacking to join the popular girls' clique," I told Sally, even though I couldn't see her where she sat crushing my feet.

"Flattery, my little dumpling of delight, will get you everywhere. Now, what was I saying? Oh, yes, about the unmaking. You can't be destroyed, you see? Otherwise Lord Bael would simply squash you into a Cora-shaped smear on the carpet. But I imagine he doesn't want you to be left sitting around annoying him, either."

"I do not," Bael agreed, obviously in the middle of texting something. My inner devil gave a little deranged giggle at the idea of Satan addicted to his smart phone. I wondered if he did Facebook. "The entrance the lich used to gain access to my palace in Abaddon in order to steal my Tools has been sealed up, so no others will be able to use it." He glanced up, his gaze on Ulfur for a moment. "The lich will, of course, be suitably punished for his part in wasting my valuable time, but once I am satisfied that my vengeance has been wrought, it is better that the Tools be unmade so that they will pose no further threat."

Fear on Ulfur's behalf gripped my guts at his intentions about punishment. I heard Ulfur gasp in horror, but he said nothing, evidently feeling the less attention that was focused on him, the better.

I agreed and, in an attempt to draw Bael's attention to me, asked, "But what's this unmaking stuff? I thought Terrin said there was no way to separate the Tools from us?"

"There isn't, sugar, there isn't," Sally said, rising and patting my squashed ankles. "I'm afraid when Lord Bael unmakes the Tool inside you—and he needs to find the Agrippa who made the Tools in order to unmake them—then you'll be unmade, as well. Sad, of course, but what can you do? We can't have you Tools running around where anyone can take advantage of Lord Bael. That would be unthinkable."

"Oh, completely," I said with acid sarcasm. "Sally, you amaze me, you really do. You look so nice, but you truly don't have a heart, do you? It doesn't bother you one single damned infinitesimally small bit that you've betrayed Ulfur and me, does it? You honestly do not have one single iota of sympathy for us, or even care that he, that man who is essentially the devil, is going to torture and destroy us. It just doesn't matter a fig to you, right?"

"Dear one, I am a demon lord," she said with a gentle smile. "Heartless is what we do best. Besides, Lord Bael would never tolerate someone who had compassion as a prince of Abaddon. It's just not done."

I closed my eyes for a moment, my heart sick. I had to figure out a way to get Ulfur and me away from them . . . or at least survive long enough for Alec to finish off the second wrath demon so he could come save us. I've never been a big fan of women needing a man to save them, but I was willing to recognize there was a time and place for it, and if ever I saw one, this was it.

"To get back to this unmaking business," I said, trying to stall for time. "What exactly is an Agrippa, and—"

Bael had no issue with cutting me off. "My time is valuable, Sally. What is it you wish to say to me?" he asked, putting away his phone and making a slight gesture of annoyance.

"As Cora mentioned, she's a Beloved." Sally pointed to me. "And he's a lich, and his lichmaster is the Beloved of another Dark One."

Bael frowned. "That is of little concern to me."

"Not in the sense of it being a threat to you, of course not," Sally said soothingly, undulating her way over to him, smiling her perky, tooth-filled smile. I wondered how she—even as evil as she obviously was—could stand doing so to a man who more or less exuded terror. "No one can threaten you, you're so very powerful."

I couldn't swear from where I was lying, but she may very well have batted her eyelashes at him.

"If you have a point, make it. I have much work to do

to locate the Agrippa who made the Tools," Bael said, looking anything but impressed.

"Now, you know me, sugar—my poor little brain simply cannot cut to the chase the way yours does," Sally said, and this time I was sure she was flirting with Bael. She touched his hand as she all but cooed up to him. "However, I know you're a busy, busy man, so I will simply point out that where there are Beloveds, there are bound to be angry Dark Ones, and where there are angry Dark Ones, there is the Moravian Council. And I know that, given the nature of the relationship between you and the council, you do not want to antagonize them."

What was this? Did the vamps have some sort of a hold over Bael? If so, why had Alec not mentioned it before? I wanted badly to ask him. *Alec? How are things going?*

Argh!

That well, huh?

We destroyed the form of one of the demons, but the other . . .

I felt his pain as a blade slashed his arm. I winced, feeling guilty for distracting him when he needed to be focused.

Sorry. Radio silence until you're done there.

Bael said nothing for a moment, his gaze turned inward before he finally said, "I will see to them, myself. One of my lieutenants is still with them, so I will simply ensure that they understand their minions are beyond their help. You will take these two to my palace, and await the arrival of the Agrippa."

Sally bowed her head. "As you desire, my lord. I live, as you know, to do your bidding."

I waited until Bael closed the door as he left before I hissed to Sally, "You are going to be so sorry when Alec gets through with you. And I am *not* Alec's minion!"

Sally rolled her eyes and headed for the bathroom. "Must powder my nose. Be back in a mo."

Alec, I hate to distract you, but you have incoming. You have to get out—now.

Incoming in what form?

Bael.

He swore profanely. *Are you and Ulfur away from here?*

I wanted badly to tell him that he needed to come rescue me, but knew he had enough on his plate with the remaining wrath demon. *We're . . . fine,* I lied. *Where's Diamond? Is she OK?*

She hasn't left the bedroom. Christ!

What?

Just as I thought the words, another unearthly howl tore through the night.

That was close, Alec said, and even several floors away, I could feel his exhaustion.

You killed the demon? Good. Now get the hell out of there before Bael finds you.

I will come to you. Where are you? Are you with Sally?

Yeees, I said slowly. *About that—*

Stay with her. We will escape with Diamond. Christ, I think he's here. I will find you as soon as I have Diamond safe.

He shut off communication before I could warn him that Sally wasn't as benign as he believed. I hesitated to do so with Bael right there about to pounce. "I think we're on our own for a little bit, Ulfur, while everyone gets away from Bael. You doing all right?"

"Yes," he answered, his voice pained.

"I don't suppose you can move?"

"No. I wish I could."

"You and me both."

"Cora—"

"Yes?"

He hesitated a few seconds. "I'm sorry that I got you involved in this. With Bael, and being made a Tool. I had no idea there were others outside the exit from Bael's palace."

"Well, it's not like you had a choice in the matter, is it? I mean, didn't de Marco force you to steal the Tools?"

"Yes," he said, his voice filled with misery. "But I'm still sorry."

"And I appreciate that. Don't be so quick to give up, though. We'll get through this. First things first—we have to get away from Sally. There's got to be some way we can knock her out, or blast her with Bael's power or something. If I could just put my hand on you, I might be able to channel the power through you. . . ."

"There, so much better. I just feel absolutely stark naked if I go out without lipstick," Sally said as she emerged from the bathroom, fresh as could be. "Now, shall we get going? Lord Bael wants you to be taken to his palace, but the nearest entrance to that is in Paris, and that is a nightmare trip I just don't even want to think about. My palace, however, has a presence in the form of a lovely little Louis the Fourteenth villa in the town of Privas, which isn't too far from here. I'll take you there first, and then we shall proceed to Bael's Black Palace."

"We're going to your villa?" I asked, hope blossoming. "You can't possibly carry us all that way."

"Of course not," she said, laughing.

She'd have to remove the immobility spell. She'd have to let us up to walk, and then . . . I sighed with relief. Then we'd escape. "Well, I have to say, as much fun as it has been being a human blob, I really do welcome the chance to move around. I'm starting to get a cramp in my calf."

"Oh, I'm not going to be able to take the spell off you," she told us, making a face that looked as sincere as hell. "You'd try to escape, and Lord Bael would be most angry with me if I let you do that."

"You just said you couldn't carry us," I protested.

"And so I won't."

My hopes plummeted. "But then . . . how are you going to get us to your villa? Do you have henchmen like Bael?"

"Thousands of them, but they're busy wreaking havoc and destruction, so I'll just have to do this myself."

To my astonishment, she reached out into the air, and with a jerking motion tore . . . well, tore what I assumed was the fabric of space. It gaped open like the wall of the hotel room was a photograph on a sheet that had been ripped apart, a swirling blackness beyond it.

"Madre de Dios," I swore, shrieking as Sally, with a strength that belied her tiny little form, grabbed me with both hands and flung me through the rip in space.

Chapter Sixteen

Alec absently wiped the blood that dripped down his arm and off his fingers onto the material of his pants, very aware of the heat building in his left arm as the shoulder-to-elbow slash made by the wrath demon's claws slowly healed itself. "This way," he said, holding up his uninjured hand to help Diamond down the last few yards from the balcony where they'd made their escape. "I think this alley leads to . . . you can't possibly be serious."

"Oh, I am, I assure you. You wouldn't believe how cutthroat the real estate business is in northern California! You think the demon lords are bad? They don't have anything on—"

"Hush," Alec said, lifting his hand in warning as he turned his head, straining to catch the words of the two men who ran past the entrance of the alley.

". . . Sally, said she . . . Corazon . . ."

"I think Alec's comment referred to those two men, not your experience in real estate, Diamond," Kristoff said as he leaped to the ground, holding up his arms for Pia, who followed him with a whomp.

"Nice catch, Boo," she told Kristoff with a kiss as he

held her in his arms. He smiled and looked like he
wanted to kiss her with much more thoroughness, but
obviously realized in time that the back alley of the
hotel, with the premier prince of Abaddon on their
heels, was not the ideal place for romance.

"What two men?" Diamond asked, brushing off her
legs. "Dratted hotel. Don't they dust their drainpipes?"

"Why would they mention Cora and Sally, unless . . .
bloody hell." Alec stopped talking and started running,
fear snatching at his breath as he ran.

"Where is he going?" he heard Diamond call. "Ow!
I can't run in these shoes! Hey, you don't have to shove
me!"

"They have Cora," Kristoff growled, obviously trying to hurry the women. Alec didn't wait for them to
catch up to him; he shot out of the alley. Down the street
a few blocks, a black sedan pulled out and sped off into
the night. Alec swore under his breath, spinning around
to head for the car park next to the hotel. Kristoff and
the two women emerged from the alley as he passed. He
didn't pause, just grabbed Diamond and slung her over
his shoulder. "They're heading west, to the highway," he
called as he ran, ignoring Diamond's protests that she
could walk. "Be quiet, woman—you're too slow. I won't
risk Cora for the sake of your shoes. Kristoff, keys?"

Alec knew it didn't take much time at all for them to
reach the car and set off after the two Dark Ones, but
he felt every passing second as if it were an hour. How
the hell had the bastards found Cora? And why hadn't
she told him they were around?

Mi querida, are you safe? he asked as he slammed on
the brakes to avoid plowing down a couple who weaved
into the street, obviously a bit too flushed with the fruit
of the grape. He spun the wheel and drove around them,
partially on the sidewalk, until he reached the highway

that ran to the north out of town. He had no idea which way the two councilmen had gone, but was betting on the more populated north than the south. *Corazon?*

"I don't understand what's going on," Diamond complained, righting herself from where Alec had tossed her into the car. "Who has Alec seen that has him so upset?"

Cora, you will speak to me right now.

"The two men from the Moravian Council," Pia answered her.

"But . . . Alec and Kristoff are Dark Ones. Is it bad to see the members of the group that rules your people?" Diamond asked.

Beloved, this silence worries me. I need to hear from you.

"It is when they want to imprison you in the Akasha. Alec?" Kristoff, playing navigator, pointed to the right as the highway curved around a hill. "Junction with another highway coming up. They could be taking that and we wouldn't know."

Alec swore. "Sins of the saints, why doesn't she talk to me?"

"She's not answering?"

"No." Alec ground off a few layers of enamel, jerking the car's steering wheel as he pulled off the road, sliding on the gravel that littered the shoulder. Ahead of them was a sign announcing the exit for the highway that ran roughly east to west. He had no idea whether the two councilmen had taken that road or the one they were on. Hell, for all he knew, they could be going in the opposite direction.

"Well, they're with Sally, aren't they?" Diamond said, giving a little shrug. "They probably went to her house."

Alec ripped off the seat belt in order to turn around

and face Diamond. "Sally has a house in France? Here, in the south?"

"Yes," Diamond answered, looking startled. "In Privas, not too far from us, from what I can remember. She held a big barbecue here last summer, when she became a demon lord, and invited everyone from the Court to see her new palace. Well, the extension of her palace into the mortal world, because naturally we couldn't go into the Abaddon part. I mean, what would the Sovereign say if it found us all frolicking around Abaddon enjoying steak and cedar-planked salmon?"

Alec stared at her for the count of four. "Why would the messenger wish to go to Sally's house?"

Diamond gave a little shrug. "It's handy? If they're trying to lure you into a trap, which I assume is what you mean by the reference to banishing you to the Akasha, then that seems like the most private place to do so. Unless the Moravian Council has buildings in this area?"

"No," Kristoff answered as Alec turned around and gunned the motor, ignoring the merging traffic behind him as he drove over the shoulder and verge and onto the highway going to the east. "They don't. They must be holding Sally and Ulfur, too. Cora still not answering?"

I am coming to save you, Beloved. Do not fear for your safety; I won't let anyone hurt you. "No, she isn't." His voice was raw as he thought of Corazon being treated roughly. The messenger, he knew, wouldn't kill Cora, but she would no doubt fight him, and he might use more force than necessary to subdue her.

That thought made him grind his teeth even more, a desperate need to be with her, to protect her, riding him hard until it caused the hunger within him to awaken.

The drive to Privas was the longest event he'd ever

suffered, filled with all too many horrible visions of Cora being harmed, and he swore that if the messenger or his partner so much as bent one single hair on her adorable head, he would have his vengeance.

"Is Alec growling?" Diamond asked Pia.

"Yes, yes, he is. And swearing," she answered.

"In Latin," Kristoff added. Alec shot his friend a look. Kristoff grinned, and added in Italian, "She'll be all right. They have no reason to hurt her."

"Cora is a fighter. She won't tolerate being used as bait to trap me. She'll fight them."

"She's also your Beloved now, and won't take injury like a mortal would. I know you're worried, but just remember that it's you they want, not her. She's just a means to an end."

"What are you guys saying?" Pia said, flicking a finger at the back of Kristoff's head. "You know how I hate it when you talk in languages I don't understand, which really is all of them because I'm horrible with languages. So stop it and tell me what you're saying."

Alec ignored the chatter of the women as they discussed what the council could or could not do to his Beloved, and focused his attention on getting them to Sally's residence as quickly as possible without killing any mortals in his way. Kristoff, knowing what emotions he was feeling, was blissfully silent with the exception of pointing out turns, a map of the area spread across his lap.

Periodically Alec tried to get Cora to respond to him, but all was silence. Worse, and far more worrisome, he had no feeling of her presence. The messenger might have silenced her by means of threat or drugs, but he would still be able to feel her being, bound as it was with his. But now . . . he felt empty, as if she had left, and taken his soul with her.

"If they've harmed her," he said in German to Krist-off.

"Don't torture yourself with that," Kris answered him, pointing to a wrought iron gate. "Christian Dante may be many things, but he wouldn't condone a Beloved being harmed. His own would never let him hear the end of it."

Alec growled to himself, not waiting for the door of the gate to open—he simply jammed his foot on the accelerator, and crashed through the double gates in best action-movie-hero style, crumpling the front of the car in the process.

Kristoff sighed. "There goes the damage deposit."

"Whoa!" Pia gasped, clutching the back of Kristoff's seat. "You almost gave me a heart attack! Next time warn us when you're going to—holy moly, will you look at that place? It looks like a palace."

"It is," Diamond said without looking up from where she was texting on her cell phone. "One of the Louis, I believe, gave it to a mistress. Louis the thirteenth? Fourteenth? I lose track of them. Sally said she got it cheap from a mage who was unloading some property to buy a quintessence."

Alec was out of the car almost before it had come to a complete halt, his hands fisted as he glared for a moment at the car that the members of the council had driven. He swore vengeance again as he marched toward the door. One hair, if they so much as touched one single hair on her delightful head . . .

"Would it do any good if I asked you to stay here?" he heard Kristoff ask.

"None whatsoever," Pia answered.

Alec tried the front door, found it locked, and stepped back a few paces to assess the building. It was rather blocky, but built in a warm cream-colored stone, with tall windows divided into numerous small panes, encased in a darker marble. Formal gardens made wings on either side of the main building, with well-kept gravel paths winding through the greenery. Alec didn't wait to see if anyone would respond to the bell that Kristoff rang—he ran to the left, skirting a small koi pond, and leaping over a low stone balustrade to stride up to large French doors flanking a gigantic stone urn. "Corazon!" he bellowed as he jerked open one of the doors, luckily unlocked. "You will answer me now!"

"I'm afraid she can't," a woman's voice answered him. "Oh, you're all here? Goodness. I'll have to have one of my minions rustle up more orange cinnamon rolls. I wasn't expecting everyone. Why, Diamond, I haven't seen you in . . . oh, it must be a century or two. You look so mortal now."

Alec spun around to find Sally beaming at them from a doorway that clearly led into the main hall.

"I try to fit in," Diamond said, breathing a little fast from the run around the house. "You look as fabulous as ever. Is that a Chanel suit?"

"You like?" Sally did a little spin to show off the cherry red suit with short skirt. "I prefer simple lines, myself, not all those fussy bits that so many designers seem to want to put into clothes these days."

"Where's my Beloved?" Alec demanded, his patience at an end.

"Cora?" Sally clucked her tongue and moved forward until she could put a hand on Alec's arm. "I am the last person to criticize, as anyone will tell you, but really, Cora needs to take in an anger management class or two. You would not believe the things she said to me! She threatened me with the most heinous, the most cruel . . . well, let us draw a veil over exactly what she said, and instead acknowledge that should she ever wish to become a demon lord, she'd fit right in."

Alec stared at the woman in utter disbelief. "*Cora* threatened you? Why would she threaten you?"

"Oh, you know how it is," Sally said with a wide smile as the others gathered around them. "Misunderstandings, misconceptions, a little binding spell or two . . . these things get blown out of proportion, and then poof! Someone threatens someone else with drawing and quartering, and it all goes downhill from there."

He rubbed his forehead. Either he was going insane, or the world was. "Cora threatened you with drawing and quartering?"

"Well . . . no, perhaps that was me, but she definitely said unkind things to me when I called the Dark Ones to take her and the lich away. *Uncalled-for* unkind things."

Alec's blood froze solid in his veins. "The messenger has her?" As he was about to demand to know more, her words filtered through the fury and fear for Cora that held him in such a tight grip. "*You* called them?"

Sally tried to step back, but he was too fast. His roar of rage made her wince as he lifted her off the floor to shake her. "Where the hell is my Beloved?"

"Abaddon," she corrected him, her eyes wide with surprise as he snarled a few threats of his own into her face. "Oh, my! I see where Corazon gets her ideas! That was . . . really? With Popsicle sticks? I never thought about that, but I suppose if you sharpen them first . . ."

"Alec, stop," Kristoff said as Alec wrapped his hands around the woman's neck. "You won't achieve anything attempting to throttle her to death, so it's not worth wasting your time. Where is Cora now, Sally?"

"I told you," Sally answered as Alec released her. "Abaddon. Well, the part of the house that's in Abaddon. Technically only the north side is in the mortal world, although I was thinking about reclaiming the west garden—"

Alec was off before she finished the sentence, Kristoff on his heels.

"Stay here!" Kristoff bellowed to Pia, who answered with a terse, "In your dreams!"

"I'm going to stay here," Diamond told them. "My great-grandma would have kittens if she knew I went to Abaddon."

The house was filled with antiques, a showcase that should by rights be on a historical register, but Alec appreciated none of that as he tore through the large entrance hall, heading for the opposite side. The hall itself was divided down the middle by what looked like a curtain of dark light, delineating the part of the house that projected into the mortal world from that which resided in Abaddon. He passed through the ebony field, stumbling over the twisted tiles of the floor as he entered the hellish side.

The antiques here were grotesque parodies of furniture, all the angles skewed, odd little legs and arms projecting, twisted, into space, snaring the unwary passerby. The light was different, as well, feeble streams of light from the other side of the hall dying a quick death in the murkiness inherent in Abaddon. "Corazon!" Alec bellowed, jerking his jacket from the grasp of what was once an armchair. *Where are you?*

Alec? What the . . . run, Alec, run! The vampires are here!

I know, he answered grimly, starting off down a side hallway just as Kristoff and Pia entered the Abaddon side of the building.

"Good god," Pia gasped, clutching Kristoff. "This is horrible! Look at that couch. It looks like it's been tortured. Who in their right mind would torture furniture?"

"A demon lord," Kristoff answered.

"I had to practice my persuasion techniques on *something*," Sally said, her voice reaching Alec as he ripped open door after door searching for Cora.

"Sally, really, I must insist you unhand me. What's my great-grandma going to say?" Diamond objected.

"Don't be such a sissy," Sally answered. "Where's your sense of adventure? Where's your gumption? Where's your desire to see the seamy underbelly of life?"

Are you harmed, Beloved?

No, but, Alec, you have to leave. Sally is evil! She's working with Bael, and she called up the vamps to tell them that you were going to be here, and as if that wasn't bad enough, she did something to Ulfur's horse that made him not a ghost anymore, so now he can't go invisible.

"It's back on the non-Abaddon side of the house," Diamond grumbled.

Alec jerked open one of a set of double doors that led into a grand ballroom, once obviously the pride of a bourgeois heart, and now a horrible battleground made up of black and mildew-stained parquet tile that erupted upward in sharp spikes, as if the ground itself couldn't bear its unholy existence. The walls were likewise stained, tatters of once beautiful flocked wallpaper hanging in despondent strips, a broken and twisted chandelier drooping almost to the ground. But it was the group of people at the far end that caught and held Alec's attention. Two men crouched behind an upturned broken sofa, its wooden claw feet clutching at nothing as an enraged horse snorted and pawed the ground, clearly protecting the two people behind it.

"Alec!" Cora screeched, then clapped her hands over her mouth. *Oh, my god, I'm sorry. Now they know you're here.*

The two men, the messenger Julian and a Dark One Alec didn't recognize, both turned to look at him.

"It's all right, Beloved," Alec said with dark intent as he stalked forward toward the two men, who hastily—but with one eye on the horse Ragnor—got to their feet. "We have nothing to fear from them. They, however, should be extremely worried."

"You threaten us, Alec Darwin?" the messenger asked.

"You took my Beloved," he answered, the thought of anyone touching her fueling a rage unlike anything he'd known.

Alec, I'm all right. They didn't hurt me. In fact, they haven't been near us since Sally zapped Ragnor.

They took you. They will die for that.

"You can*not* be serious," Cora said, moving around the horse and heading straight for him. "It's not really their fault, anyway. Well, part of it is, because we wouldn't be here if Sally hadn't told them that you were going to show up, but really, it's all Sally's fault."

"Did I hear my name being taken in vain?" Sally entered the room with a still-protesting Diamond. "I do hope so, because really, how can one call oneself an effective demon lord unless one's name is taken in vain all over the place? Oh, good, you found the Dark Ones."

"Smite her!" Cora commanded, pointing at Sally, a furious look on her face. "She's pure evil!"

Smite her?

"Oh, not pure, surely," Sally said with a little giggle. "And, you know, I did say I was naughty, not truly evil."

You can't smite?

"That's right, she is," Diamond said, giving Sally a

gimlet look. "Although I am willing to bet that Great-grandma Disin is going to have a thing or two to say about you dragging me here. You know how she gets."

Not that I'm aware.

Sally shuddered, her smile dissolving as she muttered, "She wouldn't know anything if you didn't tell her."

Well, hell. It sounded so dramatic, too.

Alec moved quickly, pushing Cora behind him as he faced the messenger. "You will say what you have to say to me, Julian. Then I will destroy you."

"Alec—" Kristoff said, sighing as he stepped forward between the two men. "You can't do that."

"No, he can't," Cora agreed, shoving Alec on the back before moving around to his side.

He wrapped an arm around her, holding her close, needing her warmth, needing her light to banish the darkness that threatened to claim him again. "It is a crime for one Dark One to threaten the life of another's Beloved—"

"We made no threats against her, nor did we harm her," Julian protested. "Give us a little credit, Alec. We simply wished to talk to her . . . and you."

"Oh, sure you do!" Cora flung herself in front of him, her arms held wide as if to protect him.

He would have found the idea laughable, but he felt in her a determination to save him.

You already have, love.

Saved you? Your soul, maybe, but there's more to you than that.

"You wish to talk, messenger? What do you have to say to me that doesn't include a command of punishment?" Alec demanded to know, gently but firmly moving Cora back to his side. *Now is not the time for relationship talk,* mi querida.

I'm a woman—there's always time to talk about relationships, she answered, digging an elbow into his side when he spent a few moments wishing he had a sword. *No decapitating, Alec. It's not nice, and besides, they really aren't to blame.*

"I'm thinking that if you've got something to say, you'd better hold on to it," Sally suddenly interjected, strolling over to the mangled remains of a table, leaning one hip on them. Diamond, looking vaguely uncomfortable, trailed after her.

"Why's that?" Cora asked. "Are you going to do something else 'naughty' to us? Maybe bring Bael in to torture us a bit? Burn down hell? Destroy the entire planet?"

"You see?" Sally whispered to Alec with a little nod toward Cora. "Anger management counseling would do her a world of good."

Cora sputtered something extremely rude under her breath, and started toward Sally. Alec caught her and held her tight against his body. "Beloved, I know you are enraged at her—as am I—but as Kristoff pointed out, it can do no good to think about beating her with a two-by-four. Nor dropping her in the La Brea tar pits. No, not even feeding her to a tank of hungry sharks."

Sally gasped in horror, her eyes huge. "Sharks! Cora!"

"It was just a thought," Cora muttered, crossing her arms over her chest. "A damned good one, too, if you ask me."

"No one did," Sally said, looking decidedly disgruntled.

"Why should we be quick?" Kristoff asked, clearly curious as to Sally's warning.

"And tar pits? Do you have any idea how difficult it is to clean tar off of wool—what? Oh, we're about to have company."

"Who?" Alec asked, his eyes narrowing on the woman.

"Some liches," Sally answered, gesturing to Ulfur. "Other than you, dear boy. Come over here so I can pet your nice horse."

"Don't do it, Ulfur!" Pia warned. "It's some sort of a trap!"

"Honestly, I wouldn't have your mind for all of the minions in Abaddon," Sally said, giving Pia a look. "Such suspicions!"

Ulfur moved slowly toward her, the horse, now perfectly solid and not in the least bit ghostly, at his side.

"What liches?" Alec asked. "The lichmaster who lives in the caves nearby?"

"I expect she'll be here, too," Sally said, giving Ragnor a pat on the neck. "She's smart, Jane is. She'll see Brother Ailwin sniffing around, and know he's up to no good, so no doubt she'll follow him here."

"Brother Ailwin!" Pia clutched Kristoff. "He'll use Cora and Ulfur! We have to get out of here!"

"Too late," Sally said, waving. "Welcome to Abaddon, Brother Ailwin. Oh, I see you brought your monks with you. Mercy, a whole army of them. Welcome, gentlemen."

Chapter Seventeen

"You ever have one of those days when everything just keeps getting worse?" I asked Pia from where we stood huddled together behind the solid wall made up of two large, angry vampires.

"I think I'm having one now," she answered, casting a worried look over to the table where Sally sat with composed grace, her eyes bright with excitement as she watched Brother Ailwin and about twenty men in monk outfits pour into the room.

"How come Brother Ailwin gets to wear modern clothes while they have to wear the brown robes?" I asked Pia in a whisper.

"Dunno. But they have swords and he doesn't, so that balances things out, don't you think?"

"Hmm." I slid a glance to the side. The two vamps from the Moravian Council stood leaning against the wall, watching everything, but making no attempt to grab either Alec or me.

"At last I have found where you cower and attempt to hide from me," Brother Ailwin announced in a bossy voice as he marched into the room, trailed by two lines of sword-bearing monks. "The two Dark Ones will not keep me from you this time, Tool."

"I *really* hate being called that," I said to no one in particular.

"You will be mine, and with you, I will—" Brother Ailwin's eyes, which had been on me, widened as he glanced toward Sally. Both Ulfur and Diamond were next to her, and I knew the moment he realized that they were the other two Tools. His jaw dropped down a good couple of inches for the count of ten; then he gave a triumphant crow and pointed at them. "The three Tools of Bael! Together! God has indeed cast his blessings upon me, for with the three Tools, I will rule the mortal and immortal worlds! Brothers, you are witnessing an historic event! With the joining of the three Tools of Bael, I will become the most powerful being to ever exist! A new age is dawning, the age of the lich, and as its leader—"

"Christ, don't you ever shut up?" Alec interrupted, and, to my utter amazement, pulled out a gun and shot Brother Ailwin.

Alec! I yelled.

Hmm?

You shot him!

Brother Ailwin looked down at his chest in surprise. As he was clad in a navy suit and pale blue shirt, the dark red stain that blossomed across his middle was clearly visible. He touched a hand to it, his expression full of disbelief as he examined the red on his fingers. "I've been shot."

Yes, I did.

My mind spun around like a hamster wheel for a few seconds. *Oh. Well done. Although where did you get the gun?*

Kristoff gave it to me. He thought we might need it.

"That is a gun. I've been shot. With a bullet," Brother Ailwin said, turning to show the blood on his fingers to his mini-army. The monks looked back at him in confusion. "The Dark One shot me."

"Liches," Sally said in an aside to Diamond.

"They *always* state the obvious," Diamond added, and nodded.

How come you didn't shoot the vamps?

It wouldn't have done anything but make them angry.

Brother Ailwin evidently got over his stupefaction, for he straightened up and glared at Alec. "You will die for that—"

Alec shot him again, this time in the leg. Brother Ailwin lurched to the side, his leg buckling.

"You can't kill a lichmaster, can you?" I asked, watching as Brother Ailwin stared for a moment at his leg.

"No, but I can put him out of commission for a bit," Alec answered, his mind filled with grim determination to keep me safe. "Kristoff?"

Love swelled within me. I couldn't deny it any longer—it was love that I felt for him, this bloodsucking fiend, this nightwalker, this utterly adorable, sexier-than-sin man who I knew would literally give up his life to keep me safe.

With a sigh, Kristoff pulled out a small gun.

"This is intolerable!" Brother Ailwin yelled. "I will not be—"

Kristoff shot him in the other leg.

"Stop that!" Ailwin screamed as he fell to the ground. "Stop shooting me! I will not be treated in this manner! I am a powerful lichmaster, and the wielder of the three Tools of Bael, and—oh, bloody hell, I've lost the feeling in my left leg. Brother Anton, assist me to a chair so that I might destroy those two Dark Ones."

"This is almost as good as watching the Black Knight scene from *Monty Python and the Holy Grail*, but I think we should probably not wait around until he's nothing but a torso," I suggested with a wary look at the two vampires lounging against the wall, watching the scene with identical expressions of polite interest.

"'Tis but a flesh wound," Pia quoted, nodding.

"Get them!" Brother Ailwin said, waving toward us as one of the monks hefted him up and set him less than gently down on a mangled remains of what was once probably a quite pretty dining chair.

The other nineteen monks started toward us, but paused when Alec and Kristoff leveled their guns. "We have enough bullets to shatter the bones in all your legs," Alec told the monk army. "You won't make it ten feet."

The monks looked at the two vampires holding guns, down at their swords, then over to Brother Ailwin before turning back to our little group.

Alec smiled.

The monks, as a group, turned and in perfect formation marched out of the door.

"Wait!" Brother Ailwin screeched, glaring furiously at them. "I did not order—you cannot leave now, not when I'm about to claim the greatest victory known to lichkind! I demand that you come back here! I demand that you destroy the Dark Ones! What's a few shattered thighbones when it comes to . . . damnation! You cowards! *Come back here!*"

"I told you that a lich army was a bad idea, if you recall," Sally said, getting to her feet as two women burst into the room. "They just have no backbone, any of them, and collectively, they're sponges. But I'm sure you see the wisdom of my advice now, don't you, Ailwin? Oh dear, your blood is going to stain the floor if it keeps up like that. You really should stanch the flow of it. Jane, my dear, how lovely to see you again. Is that the new T-shirt design? You must send me a gross or two, and I'll order my minions to wear them."

"You!" Brother Ailwin spit, glaring up at Jane as she stopped next to him, giving him a confused look. "I might have known you'd find out about the Tools. No, no, Brother Anton, not that leg, you fool, this one. The one that's bleeding all over the place. Wrap it tight so I can stand up long enough to wield the Tools."

"What . . . the Tools?" Jane looked even more confused as she glanced around the room. "Hello, everyone. Er . . . is this a Dark One convention or something?"

"Tools as in plural?" asked Eleanor, who stood with Jane in matching *Liches rule, others drool, especially revenants* T-shirts. She frowned at me for a moment before narrowing her eyes on Sally. "I could swear I know you."

Sally batted her lashes and gave a little smile and shrug, but said nothing.

Great, just what we need, Brother Ailwin clueing in Jane as to what we are, and how to use us. Can you shoot him again? I asked Alec.

I would gladly, but it would serve no purpose. I simply wanted to frighten away his monks and disable him, albeit temporarily. Jane, I believe, will pose us no threat.

I caught the whisper of a thought that Eleanor might be an entirely different subject, but wasn't sure if that was just my inner devil being snarky, or something he was truly worried about.

"You have the Tools of Bael?" Jane asked Brother Ailwin.

He looked furious with himself, and shoved away the

poor monk who was trying to bind up his left leg. "I do. You may bow down before me now, before the rush to curry my favor."

"Oh, for the love of—no one has the Tools," I couldn't help but say, moving around to Alec's side.

Beloved, please stand behind me, so that I can protect you.

Pfft. I'm a frickin' Tool. I can protect you, I answered with bravado.

He sighed into his mind, and pulled me up against him, which I had to admit was what I wanted all along. Just the feel of him, so warm and solid, and bristling with indignation, made my inner self sigh with happiness.

Dammit, Alec, I've gone and fallen in love with you, I told him.

He almost fell over. *You what?*

You heard me.

His eyes glittered with a combination of ire and desire, so green they almost glowed. "And you pick now to tell me? This exact moment?" He waved his gun toward the liches. "You couldn't wait until we were alone?"

"Tell you what?" Pia asked.

Kristoff shot her a look.

"Oh. That." She giggled and gave me a thumbs-up. "I'm so happy for you both. You'll have to invite us to the wedding. Kristoff didn't want to marry me, because he said it was a human thing, and meaningless to Dark Ones, but in the end, he gave in, because my family would have gutted him if he didn't."

Kristoff rolled his eyes, and murmured something in her ear. She giggled again.

I eyed Alec.

"I will be happy to marry you in a mortal ceremony," he answered the look.

"In a church?" I asked. "My family is like Pia's—they're big on weddings."

"In a church," he agreed solemnly, but his lips twitched.

"A wedding!" Sally said, clapping her hands excitedly. "Oh, I love weddings! You have to let me do your hair and makeup, though. When May—she's a doppelganger and the sweetest wyvern's mate you ever did meet—when she was becoming the consort to a demon lord, which really is the same thing as a wedding, you know, I did her makeup and hair, and she looked absolutely gorgeous. Well, except for the little nothing that Magoth made her wear as a wedding outfit, but you know how men are—if a few leather straps and bit of fur covering the naughty bits aren't included in the ceremony, they just lose interest."

If you even think of asking me to wear—

Don't worry, my tastes are quite different from those of a demon lord, he answered, adding after a moment's thought, *Although if you wanted to wear a little nothing made up of leather straps and fur, I wouldn't object.*

I pinched his hand and twined my fingers through his.

"I'm so confused," Jane told Eleanor.

"I'm not, unfortunately," the latter answered, shooting both Alec and me a testy look. "Although I don't understand why all of the Tools have been brought together. That seems foolhardy to me."

Jane leaned to the side and whispered in her ear. Eleanor shrugged her off with a harsh word.

"I demand that you leave this instant!" Brother Ailwin shouted. "They are my Tools, and I don't intend to have any upstart lichmaster get her grubby hands on them! Brother Anton, smite the two women, and then bring the Tools to me."

The poor monk glanced hesitantly at Jane. "Er . . ."

"Must I do everything?" Brother Ailwin looked mean enough to do as he threatened.

Maybe you should shoot him a few more times. He looks like he's recovering.

That's not a bad idea, Alec answered, raising the gun.

"Really, you know, you're such a disturbing force here, I just can't take it any longer," Sally said wearily. "Normally I like disturbing, but now . . . no. It's intolerable. Sable, please return them to the mortal world."

At the name, a thickly muscled man appeared out of nothing, obviously one of Sally's minions. He had absolutely no neck, and muscles on his muscles, all clearly evident because he was clad only in a leopard-print G-string.

We all gawked as Sable picked up a now-swearing Brother Ailwin under one beefy arm, and Brother Anton under the other, before he did that fabric-of-being tearing thing, and stepped through the tear, taking the two men with him.

"Ailwin can be delightfully entertaining sometimes, but other times . . . well, I'm sure no one here will complain at him being removed. Now, where were we? Oh, yes. As delightful as it is to chat with all of you—and, Cora, I'm quite, quite serious about my offer to do your hair and makeup for your wedding—I do have other things to attend to, and would like to wrap up this business now. So if you don't mind, please join the other two Tools of Bael, and we'll be out of here in a few minutes."

I stared at Sally in abject disbelief. "You have got to be out of your ever-lovin' mind!"

"Not really, no, although sometimes I admit it's a tempting thought. Come here, Cora," she answered with a little gesture.

"There is no way in hell that I'm going to let you use me after what you did!"

She gave me a look that was filled with disappointment.

"No!" I said again, pressing into Alec. "And that's an 'over my dead body' sort of no!"

"Really? That's an awfully definite statement."

"Yes, it is. I'm *definite* that I'm not going to let you use me to destroy everyone."

"Oh, I won't destroy *everyone*," she said with an airy wave of her hand. "Just the people who annoy me most."

I clung to Alec's arm. "I don't think so! Diamond, you really should move away from Sally. She's clearly a nutball."

Sally sighed. "Such abuse from you, when really I'm just trying to help."

"Yeah, but the question is, who are you trying to help?" I snarled. "It's certainly not us!"

"Beloved, this is not doing any good. Cease baiting Sally," Alec said with a little squeeze. "The seneschal promised us that she would assist us with our plans, and despite the recent events, I expect she will do so."

Sally giggled. "Well, as for that—"

"Right. I think I've had just about enough of this," Eleanor interrupted as she strolled forward to Sally. "I know I've had enough of your inane comments, and as for you . . ." She turned to face Alec and me, her eyes narrowed slits. "I've definitely had all I intend to take from you two. Wedding, indeed. Not with my Dark One, you don't. It sounds cliché to say this, but I'm going to nonetheless: If I can't have him, no one will."

I screamed as Alec shoved me away from him, not so much because of the fact that I stumbled over a bit of twisted floor tile and ended up careening into the tangled legs of a piano that lay upside down, but because

Eleanor grabbed Diamond and, holding her in front of her, directed a massive blast of black-edged light from Diamond directly at Alec.

"Nooo!" I shrieked as Alec was thrown backward a good forty feet, blood flying in an arc, splattering against the wall as he hit it before sliding down to slump into a pile on the floor. My heart stopped dead in my chest as I stared at Alec, the dark power channeled by Diamond having torn open his chest and shoulder, and ripped away half his throat.

Kristoff and Pia ran to him as I slowly turned to look at Eleanor, my heart, my blood, everything in me, frozen in horror as I realized she had just killed the man I loved.

I started toward her, my movements at first jerky, but by the time I took three steps, I was running, bent on nothing more than her utter and complete destruction. She killed Alec! My Alec!

Kristoff ripped off a strip of his shirt and bound it around the remains of Alec's neck. It would do no good, I knew. Alec couldn't possibly survive such devastating damage. He was dead, and with him had died my heart.

"Vengeance, you know, can be either a satisfying thing or one that lacks satisfaction," Sally said absently, polishing one of the rings she wore.

I stopped as Eleanor, who had been watching Kristoff look up and shake his head at Pia, smiled.

"Diamond," I said softly.

She glanced at me, her face ashen as she watched Kristoff bow his head over his friend. Pia dropped to her knees, sobbing. The two other vampires moved over to examine Alec's body.

Rage filled me, consumed me, gave me strength when I wanted to do nothing more than scream the agony that I knew was just on the edge of my awareness, waiting to suffocate me.

Alec was dead, and I would destroy Eleanor if it was the last thing I did.

"Go to Sally," I said, my gaze on Eleanor.

Diamond moved quickly, sliding out of Eleanor's reach to stand on Ulfur's far side.

"Um . . ." Jane backed up a couple of steps. "I think maybe we should go."

"I'm not going anywhere," Eleanor said, a brittle smile on her lips as she eyed Sally. "I have five hundred years of revenge to dole out, and I intend to enjoy every moment of it. I don't know who you are, missy, but I do know that you have annoyed me, and I don't intend to put up with anyone annoying me ever again. First you'll go, then I'll use that blond strumpet to take down the one who stole my soul, and then I may just clean up the room before I head out to bring order to the chaos that is the world. You, Jane, you may live, but you're no longer in charge—I am."

Sally, oddly enough, wasn't paying Eleanor any attention. Her gaze was on me, speculation evident in her eyes, and just the merest hint of a smile softening her mouth. "Do I take it you've had a change of heart?"

I met her gaze, allowing her to see the full measure of my fury. "I have no heart left."

"Very well." Sally inclined her head in acknowledgment, turning to face Eleanor as I moved over the few yards to Sally's side.

This would be my last act, I knew. I would go out in a blaze of righteousness, though, claiming vengeance for Alec's death. . . . A sob caught in my throat, threatening to choke me. I swallowed it down, fighting to focus on the woman before me. There was no time to grieve for Alec, to mourn the loss of our future; there was only time for me to do what needed to be done, and then I would allow Bael's power to consume me.

"Just what do you think you're going to do?" Eleanor asked suspiciously, shooting a nervous glance at Jane as the lichmaster began to back up toward the door. "You don't . . . no, you couldn't. Jane, she doesn't have the power to use the woman, does she?"

Sally's smile grew.

"She's a demon lord," Jane almost stammered—the words tumbled out so fast. "She can do anything she wants. I think I hear some members calling. I'd better go see what they want—"

She was out of the door before Eleanor could do so much as blink.

"Such a smart woman, Jane. I've always liked her. Caring, too. And so good with the liches," Sally told me. "She has endless patience with their fussy ways."

"A demon lord? Oh . . ." Eleanor's demeanor changed from aggressive to subservient. "I . . . uh . . . I didn't mean any offense, if you took it. It's just that she took both my soul and my Dark One." Eleanor pointed at me.

Sally considered me with newfound interest. "Mercy. I had no idea you had all that in you. Did you threaten her with untold torments, as well?"

I stared at Eleanor, my throat tight with pain. I couldn't speak, so great was the agony that threatened to claim me. Tears burned in my eyes, but I blinked them away, wanting to see Eleanor's face when she realized that I would give up my life to ensure she was utterly and completely destroyed.

Sally touched my shoulder. "I can see we'd better begin before emotions run too high. If you three would join hands, please."

Eleanor's eyes widened as she, too, started to back up. "I'm sure Jane needs me. I promised to help her. . . . What the devil?"

Sally made a gesture at Eleanor, evidently one of

those binding things that she'd mentioned earlier. "Ward," I think, was the word. I started to reach out to Alec's mind to ask him if that was the correct term, my inner devil collapsing in anguish when I realized that I would never again feel the brush of his mind against mine.

Never is such a very long time, came the softest of whispers.

"Look, I know I said a few things that probably were unwise, but really, I think they're perfectly understandable given the situation," Eleanor said, struggling to make her feet move. "What on earth did you do to me?"

Diamond took my hand as I half turned to the side to look at Alec's body.

"Oh, dear, and you looked like you had so much potential, too," Sally said, *tsk*ing at Eleanor. "But you don't even know about a common, ordinary binding ward. . . . Such a shame. You could have gone places."

I ignored Sally, peering intently at the scene on the other side of the ballroom. Kristoff was holding a weeping Pia to his chest, his head bent to hers. Beyond them, the two vampires stood in consultation. Alec's body remained where it had slumped, his head at an unnatural angle, blood everywhere, soaking his shirt and jacket, seeping out to form a thick pool around him.

Alec? I asked, half-convinced I had conjured up his voice out of desperation.

"All right, I'm willing to admit I made some mistakes, just a couple of tiny ones, and assuming you were all show was one of them," Eleanor told Sally. "But that doesn't mean you have to do anything rash. Why don't you unbind me, and we can talk about this like civilized people."

Silence answered my mental plea.

"Ah, but who ever told you I was civilized?" Sally

asked with one of her toothy smiles. She placed two fingers on my shoulder, and two on Ulfur's, standing behind the three of us now locked together by Diamond's firm grip. "Besides, I think you'll want to stay for this. It should be very exciting."

Hope, which had lifted up its head, curled up into a ball and withered away again. There *was* no hope. Without Alec, there could be nothing.

You've come a long way from wanting to stake me every chance that presented itself.

Alec, you are *alive!* My heart, formerly shattered into a million pieces, miraculously re-formed itself, my skin tingling with electricity as Sally started chanting.

Barely. What happened?

Eleanor used Diamond against you. Oh my god, Alec, you're alive! I thought you were dead. I was going to destroy Eleanor for killing you, then die, myself.

The tingling ramped up to that familiar sense of power flowing through me, but my heart and mind were concerned with one thing only—Alec.

As flattering as it is to know you'd kill yourself because I was dead, such a thing doesn't please me at all. You could survive me, Beloved. I would want you to continue to live, to find happiness should I be destroyed.

Alec?

Yes?

Shut up and heal yourself. . . . Jesus wept! The power flowing through and around me suddenly turned back on itself, moving from an explosion of power to an inversion . . . straight through me to Sally.

Her chanting stopped abruptly as she said in a loud, clear voice, "Bael, lord of Abaddon, ruler of seven hundred legions, by that which makes thee, I summon thee to my hand."

What is it?

Sally!

I tried to stop the flow of power going straight to her, but it was no use and I knew it—I was merely a Tool, a channel through which the power moved.

What about her?

She's gone rogue! "What the hell, Sally? You're supposed to be destroying Eleanor, not summoning Bael!"

"I thought that was the plan?" Diamond asked, her voice breathy as she, too, obviously felt the effects of the power now pouring into Sally. "Aren't we supposed to destroy Bael?"

That makes no sense, love. She's here to help us.

You poor, deluded man. You just don't understand—she's not one of us, she's a bad guy. Very bad!

"That's what Corazon said she wanted," Sally said, and began the summoning again. "Bael, lord of Abaddon, ruler of seven hundred legions—"

"Yes, but she won't do it!" I told Diamond. "We can't trust her to actually do away with him. She'll just bring him here and wipe us all out! Don't you see? They're buddies!"

Diamond shot me an astonished look. Beyond her, Ulfur looked confused, and distressed. His horse bore a similar expression. "Sally is what?" Diamond asked.

"Bael's friend, and I use that word with air quotes around it."

"His *friend*?"

"Air-quotes friend," I corrected. "More like she was rubbing herself all over him in the hotel room, and sold us out to him."

"I did no such thing," Sally interrupted a third repetition of her summons to protest. "I never sell out. I may opt to do things that perhaps are open to differing interpretations than that of which I'd prefer, but sell out? *Pfft*. There's no material object I desire enough to do that."

"I notice you didn't dispute the rubbing-yourself-all-over-him statement," I snapped.

She smiled demurely. "Well, some of his mortal forms are really quite handsome, and you know, I've always had a passion for bad boys. You don't get badder than Bael. There were times when it was just too delicious an opportunity to let pass by."

"See?" I told Diamond. "She's turned on by Satan. Only someone extremely evil would get the hots around Bael."

"Cora, my dear, you're wrong. You don't understand about Sally—"

Sally giggled and cut her off with another summons. "Bael, lord of Abaddon, ruler of seven hundred legions, by that which makes thee, I summon thee to my hand."

I heard Pia cry out Alec's name, and glanced toward them to see Alec attempting—but failing—to pull himself up into a sitting position. *You try to move before I get there to see how badly you're hurt, and you'll be one hurtin' cowpoke. Er . . . more hurtin' than you are.*

"Bael, lord of Abaddon, ruler of seven hundred legions, by that which makes thee, I summon thee to my hand."

I love you too, Corazon.

Happiness filled me at the gentle brush of his mind against mine. Even if Sally didn't sell us down the river, I knew the future wasn't going to be easy, but somehow, none of that mattered anymore. *Stay still, Alec. I'll be right there, and then we'll find you a doctor.*

A doctor wouldn't know what to make of me. Kristoff will find a healer, I'm sure, but it's you I really need.

"Cora!" Pia called, gesturing to me. "Alec's alive! He's *alive*!"

"I'll be there in a second," I yelled back, then turned to pin back Sally with a look that should have scared her witless.

She was watching me, which startled me right out of my antagonism. "Well?" she said.

"Well?"

"Shall we do this, or not?"

"Do which—take out Bael, or grind Eleanor into lich dust?"

"I *beg* your pardon!" Eleanor said in an outraged tone. We ignored her.

Sally's eyebrows rose. "Which would you prefer?"

I glanced at Eleanor. She was my past self, a previous version of me. It wasn't her fault that she'd been killed, or brought back after our soul was in use by me.

But she almost killed Alec. Willfully, deliberately, and with more malice than I could understand. "Will you do what I want?" I asked Sally, hesitating to commit myself.

She thought for a moment, then nodded. "Yes. I will agree to abide by your desires."

"You've been summoning Bael. He doesn't seem to be here," I pointed out.

"Hey!" Eleanor said, waving her hands to get Sally's attention. "She's got a chip on her shoulder about me. She also has my soul and my man, although I don't quite understand how he survived when he should have been blown to kingdom come. I think if there is any grinding into dust to be done, it should be her and not me who's destroyed."

"The summons hasn't worked because you have not allowed it to do so," Sally told me.

"I can do that?"

Sally nodded.

"How come I couldn't stop the power when Brother Ailwin used me?" I asked, exasperated.

She gave a little shrug. "He does not have the ability to truly master the Tools. In the hands of amateurs, your control will lessen just as theirs will. But I am different."

"Yes," I said slowly, eyeing her before turning my attention to Alec. Kristoff was wrapping torn bits of his shirt around Alec's neck while Pia was doing likewise to what remained of his shoulder. Once again I was overcome by the sight of so much blood, and the destruction that Eleanor had wrought. *Are you going to be all right?* I asked.

He smiled into my brain. *Yes. The damage is too extensive for me to fully repair by myself, but I am not dead. That is something.*

It's not something; it's everything to me. We'll get you a healer to fix you up.

Kristoff has already called for one. Finish with Sally, Beloved. Only then will you truly be safe.

He was talking about Bael, I knew, but the same thing could be said of Eleanor. I eyed her. *Will you rest now? You sound tired.*

I will rest, he agreed, and just the fact that he did so told me how much it was costing him to remain in contact with me.

"What if I want both?" I asked Sally. "What if I want both Bael and Eleanor pounded into pulp? Would you do that?"

"Of course," she said promptly, taking me by surprise for some reason. I guess it was because I was expecting her to hinder me every step of the way. Heaven knew she'd done a good job of doing that ever since she popped onto the scene.

"I protest this wanton abuse of power," Eleanor shouted. "She has an agenda concerning me."

"Oh, please." I may have snorted a little as I curled a lip at her. The two vampires from the vamp council headed toward me with a look in their eyes that did not bode well.

"I don't think I like you," Diamond told Eleanor, who just looked shocked in response.

"How about them?" I asked, pointing at the two approaching men. "Can I wipe out them, too?"

"I just love someone who thinks like I do!" Sally said, clapping her hands with pleasure. "Is there anyone else you'd like destroyed?"

The two vamps froze, their eyes big as they looked from me to Sally.

Beloved . . .

I know, I know. It's no answer to our problems. But awfully darned tempting, you have to admit. Go back to sleep, or whatever it is you're doing to fix the fact that half of your neck is missing.

"I suppose I shouldn't," I said with a sigh, giving the two vampires a meaningful look.

Sally shook her head. "You just have no follow-through. You'd never make a demon lord if you can't follow through with such interesting ideas."

"I don't want to be a demon lord," I protested as the vampires started toward me again, and added in a rush, "But I don't want them here, either. Can you zap them away?"

"Of course," Sally said, and with a blinding smile at them called for Sable again.

"Now, wait—" one of the vamps started to say as

Sable appeared and bowed to Sally, obviously waiting for her orders. "We have no quarrel with you, Beloved. Our business is with the Dark One."

"Cora?" Sally asked, nodding toward the vampires. "Death or just a little relocation, and please don't say the latter because that always makes Sable pout."

I hesitated for just a second. "Just get them out of here."

"You do not know who we are—" the first one said, strangling to a stop when the demon grabbed him by the throat. The second vampire squawked as Sable hauled them both through the opening torn into the fabric of space, presumably out of Abaddon itself.

"Nicely done, although it's not you who will have to put up with a petulant wrath demon," Sally said. "I've always said that having the least amount of witnesses possible when you are conducting heinous acts is the best policy. Now, as to your former self . . ." She inclined her head in question toward Eleanor. "Kill, dismiss, or banish?"

"That's it!" Eleanor snapped, struggling to free herself from the binding ward. "I'm done being nice! Release me this instant so that I can go back to the caves and Jane!"

"Can she get back to the Underworld?" I asked Sally.

"Of course. Mind you, it would mean having a Summoner, and we don't have one, so the only other way will be to kill her, and I, naturally, couldn't do such a thing. I'm a very hands-on sort of person, and it would completely ruin my manicure were I to do so, but you could."

"What?" Eleanor screamed. "Don't encourage her!"
Alec?

No, mi corazón. *You do not wish to stain your soul with her death.*

I sighed again. "Then I guess it's back to the cave with her. Jane can deal with her."

"I protest this high-handed . . . wait, you're sending me back to Jane?"

"Do you agree to be bound to her union?" Sally asked.

"Yes!" Eleanor said quickly, blinking a couple of times as Sally snapped out a command, Sable appearing out of nothing for the third time. "You're not going to punish me for killing Alec?"

"Oh, I haven't forgotten what you did, or the intention behind it," I told her, and hoped she accurately read the depth of my fury visible in my eyes. "But we'll settle our differences later, once we've taken care of more pressing issues."

Eleanor started to smile, but was yanked through the tear before she could do more than say, "I can't believe you're so—"

"I just hope the word that follows that is 'generous' and not 'gullible,' but I get a feeling it isn't," I said softly.

"Possibly not," Diamond agreed, then looked over her shoulder at Sally. "Are we going to continue? I really should get back to my husband, and my great-grandma is sure to be demanding I see her to explain everything that's been going on."

"That's up to Cora," Sally said, nodding toward me, one eyebrow cocked in question.

I glanced over to where Kristoff and Pia worked at binding Alec's wounds. *You hanging in there?*

I am mending myself as quickly as possible, but am somewhat hindered by loss of blood.

Help is forthcoming—just let me take care of this and I'll open up the diner. "Let's do this," I said, taking a deep breath.

"At last," Sally said with a slow, satisfied smile. "Now we begin."

Chapter Eighteen

Alec had heard the phrase about senses "swimming" in the past, but he never truly understood just what it meant until he woke from insensibility to find not just the room spinning around him but apparently the entire world.

He knew he was gravely wounded by the fact that he didn't have the strength to reach out mentally to make sure Cora was not harmed in any way. The fact that he felt as drained of life as when he had given up in the Akasha told him the rest of what he needed to know—that damned Eleanor had killed him.

Well, *almost* killed him. The bitch. And to think he'd spent centuries mourning her death.

After a few minutes of thinking indignantly about that fact, and dwelling, with much pleasure, on the thought of how Cora would fuss over him once he was recovered enough to tell her that he had almost died, the distant nagging of a familiar heat warned him that his body was making a tremendous effort to repair itself.

He stopped struggling to reach Cora, and relaxed, letting what remained of his energy focus on healing the damage. It wasn't until a sense of her despair reached him that he tried again to reach her mind, reassured by the joy evident in her thoughts that she really did love him as she claimed.

He smiled to himself as Cora ranted to him about Eleanor, aware now of the faint sounds of Pia and Kristoff speaking over him as they bound his wounds. With that awareness came pain, intense pain, an agony that seared through his body and left him breathless with the need to scream, but he knew that would be a wasted effort.

Instead, he pushed the pain down, fighting to keep his mind clear of the agony that threatened to consume him. Only when he was in control of it did he open his eyes and look up at Kristoff as his arm was bound to his chest.

"Thanks," he said, his voice coming out cracked and rough with pain.

Kristoff gave him a smile, but was immediately pushed out of the way by Pia, who bent over him, her face wet with tears, as she said, "Alec! Don't speak!"

"Hello, Pia," he said, summoning up a little smile for her.

"Hush! And stop trying to move. Kristoff has bound up your neck and shoulder, but you shouldn't try to move anything until after the healer comes to take care of you."

He was touched by the evidence of Pia's tears, but his thoughts, inevitably, turned to Cora. What had she thought when she first believed he was dead? Was she angry? Sad? Relieved?

Try devastated beyond human belief, and if you don't do what Pia says and relax so you can heal, you'll find out just how cranky feelings of devastation make me.

Alec relaxed, smiling once again to himself at the

gentle caress of her mind, ignoring both the hunger that gnawed deep inside him and the pain that lingered even as his body struggled to make whole once again that which had been destroyed.

He drifted for a bit, jerking back to awareness only when some vague sense of danger finally permeated his dulled senses.

With tremendous strength, he shoved himself away from where he was slumped against the wall, staring with growing fury at the scene before him. "You would do this now?" he snarled in a rough, almost unrecognizable voice as he struggled to his feet, one arm still bound to his chest. "Kris, you should have stopped Sally."

"Oh, for the love of god," Pia muttered, hurrying over to him. "Don't distract Cora! Sally said it's very important that no one disrupt the process, or she'll lose control of Bael."

Beloved, what the hell do you think you're doing?

Cora shot him a startled glance before facing the monstrosity that snarled and screamed in front of her. *I'm helping get rid of Bael. You're the one who said that's what needs to be done. Why are you up? How do you feel? Are you in pain? You are, aren't you? I can feel you hiding something from me. Lay back down, you silly man, and I'll feed you as soon as I'm done here.*

"I am not a child that you must order me around," he answered, trying to wrap his dignity around him, but it was difficult to do so while listing heavily to one side.

Cora must have noticed the list. "Sit down before you hurt your owies."

"I am a Dark One!" he said, managing to stand upright at last, ignoring the pain and tearing feeling on his left side. "We do not have owies! We have grievous, nearly fatal injuries!"

The entity that was Bael in his true form writhed and twisted upon itself as it cursed in Latin.

"Seriously?" Sally said, *tsk*ing and shaking her head at the horrible sight. "I don't think you're in any position to make threats like that."

"Pia," Cora said, not taking her eyes from the now-constantly morphing figure of Bael, his form changing from human to demonic and all variations in between. "Would you please get Alec a chair before he does more damage to, or topples over from, his grievous, nearly fatal injuries?"

Bael shifted his form from that of a horned, pustulated, slimy demonlike being to the form he wore previously. "You will suffer as no one has ever suffered," he told Sally, his eyes literally glowing red. "Do not think that my generosity with you in the past will affect my punishment of this insurrection."

"It's mutiny, I think. Isn't it?" Sally asked Diamond.

Alec lurched over to Cora's side, wrapping one arm around her protectively. *Do not fear, Beloved. I am here to protect you.*

My fear is for you, not me, silly, she answered, but with her words came a warm rush of love so great it almost brought him to his knees in profound gratitude. *You idiot man, you.*

"Death will seem like heaven by the time I'm done with you," Bael snarled at Sally, impotent to act, clearly bound by his own power that Sally was using against him. The three Tools stood in a semicircle before her, their hands touching, providing an arc through which the power was focused directly at Bael, bathing the demon lord in a blue-black light.

"Here, Alec, sit in this." Pia dragged the mangled remains of a chair over toward him. He didn't spare it so much as a glance.

"Your death, when it pleases me to end your torment, will be my most exquisite act yet," Bael promised her, his voice stretched thin as he fought the bonds of his own power. "I will make you wish that no woman had ever pushed you from her body!"

Diamond giggled.

"Oh, Bael, and I hoped we could do this without threats and name-calling," Sally said, sadly shaking her head.

"Hope has deserted you," Bael growled in a voice that made Alec want to push Cora behind him.

"You think?" Sally tipped her head to the side, and smiled. "You know, for one of the most powerful beings on the planet, you're awfully careless about what goes on in Abaddon, specifically . . . but no, you probably aren't interested."

"Careless? I am never careless. Every action, every detail, has been part of my master plan." Bael looked almost insulted at such an accusation. "Do not allow your ignorance to confuse lack of attention with in-depth schemes the like of which you will never understand."

"Really?" Sally gave a one-shouldered shrug. "So then you knew all along who I am?"

Alec heard something in her voice that had him (painfully and with much stiffness) turning to look at her. Kristoff's eyebrows were raised, indicating that he, too, had picked up on it. He glanced at Cora. She seemed perfectly in control, her expression serene.

Bael's eyes narrowed until they were little black slits. "Your role in my plan has always been minor, and thus, your origins concern me not."

"Oh, you say things like that and I just can't resist showing you," she responded with a light, tinkling laugh, and for an infinitesimally small fraction of a second, a golden flash of light blinded Alec. It was gone before he could even blink, but he knew by the expression of profound disbelief on Bael's face that he hadn't imagined it.

"You . . . that can't . . . how . . ." Bael got a grip on himself and took a deep breath, obviously in preparation for what was likely to be a group-wide curse. Alec couldn't risk Cora being injured, and lurched toward the demon lord to stop him.

"Silence!" Sally commanded, her voice a whipcrack that was almost painful to hear. Alec hesitated, glancing at her. "As delightful as it would be to chitchat more, Diamond has things to do, and Cora's Dark One appears to be under the misimpression that he is well enough to stand, so I'll cut this short and simply say that Bael, known also as Beelzebub, premiere prince of Abaddon, ruler of seven hundred legions, by this light, by my virtue, by my being, I do banish thee."

Bael's scream of pure hate was a horrible thing to behold, the rage in it so great, it slammed through the room with the impact of a small bomb. Alec staggered backward, doing his best to protect Cora from it despite the pain that seared through his still damaged body. He gritted his teeth, fighting to keep from losing consciousness, determined with every atom of his being to protect her or die trying.

So melodramatic. Are you going to be like this when you get a cold? Because my ex-husband used to be the biggest baby in the world whenever he got sick or hurt, but he has nothing on the sort of thing you're thinking right now. As if I'd let you die.

You seem to be confused about our roles, he answered, slowly straightening up as the last echo of Bael's scream faded. He helped Cora over a small table that had been sent flying toward them. *I am the Dark One;*

you are the Beloved. I protect you. That is my role in life.

And here I was hoping it was to provide me with never-ending highly erotic nights, she said with a faux sigh, her arm sliding around his waist as she leaned into him, the scent of her making his head spin with need and happiness and hunger.

"That's . . . that's it?" Pia asked as she and Kristoff slowly picked their way across the furniture that had been toppled in Bael's wake. "You just say a few things and he's gone?"

"Well . . . I could have made it a big production if it would have been more satisfying," Sally said, getting down from the piece of rock that had thrust itself up through the floor. "I just assumed everyone had better things to do."

"But . . ." Pia looked around the room as if seeking an answer. "But that was so easy. Why didn't you do that before?"

"Easy? Oh, lawks a-mercy, no, it wasn't easy." Sally shook her head. "Bael was the premier prince, sugar. You don't get to be the premier prince unless you're packing a whole lot of wallop, if you know what I mean. And Bael had more wallop than anyone I'd ever met, which is curious, really, when you think about it. . . ." Sally looked thoughtful as her voice trailed off.

"I'm still confused," Pia complained.

"I think it was us, Pia," Ulfur told her, relief evident in every line in his body. "I think we made the difference. Being Tools, that is."

"If Bael's gone, does that mean no one can call me a Tool again?" Cora asked Alec, her hands gently caressing his arm and chest as she checked his injuries. *Do you still hurt?*

Not when you are near. "Yes, that is exactly what it

means. Thank you, Sally," he said, giving the petite woman a formal bow.

Sally, who had just resummoned Sable and was giving orders in a low tone, waved her hand in acknowledgment.

"But . . . they're just three people. I mean, I understand they're conduits and all. . . ." Pia shook her head. "I guess I'm missing something."

Kristoff bent his head to whisper in her ear.

"I think it's just that we're awesome when joined together," Cora said with a little laugh, licking the tip of Alec's nose. His heart warmed at the silly gesture. He wanted to sing and dance, to shout from the highest peak that Cora loved him.

"Say it again," he demanded of her.

She smiled a secret smile that delighted him to the tips of his toes, her dark eyes glowing with love. *"Te amo."*

"Speaking of that, Cora, sugar, if you're going to molest your Dark One, why don't you do it somewhere private rather than jumping his bones right here where any of the demon lords coming to pay me homage can see? If you're worried about Alec's injuries, you can use one of the rooms on the human side of the house if you like." Sally, having dismissed Sable once again, brushed past them, straightening the little red wool jacket and patting her hair. "Now, should my first act as premier prince be to restructure the hierarchy, or to install highspeed wireless Internet in Abaddon? I'm thinking the latter. I'm just a grouchy ole thing if I have to go a day without my LOLcats."

"LOLcats? Right, that's it!" Cora said, turning in his arms to frown at Sally. "One minute you're being all nice, and apparently perfectly normal, if slightly obsessed about hair and makeup, and the next you're the evil demon lord who wants to conduct the most horrible tortures upon us, and hand us over to Bael so he can destroy us."

"Are you destroyed?" Sally asked her sweetly, and Alec could feel the frustration and genuine confusion that gripped his Beloved.

"No, of course not," Cora said with a glance over her shoulder to him.

"Then I didn't want to hand you over to Bael."

You're not in the least bit concerned about Sally despite the fact that she is the source of all our troubles, are you? Cora asked.

She isn't, you know. For some reason, she just likes to make it look that way.

Cora sighed into his mind. *I'm missing something, aren't I?*

You didn't happen to see a flash of light a few minutes ago, did you?

Huh?

I'll explain it later, if Sally doesn't do the job herself.

Cora rubbed her temple as if she had a headache forming. "You didn't want to hand us over to Bael, and yet you told him you were doing just that. How is bringing us to Abaddon not handing us over to him?"

"Cora, Cora, Cora. I don't know where you get your ideas about dear Sally, but I can assure you that you really are not being quite fair to her. Oh dear, is that the time? Dee will be absolutely furious with me. I must go reassure him that all is well." Diamond bustled over to them, patting Cora's hand and kissing her cheek before turning her eyes to Alec. "You take care of her, now."

"I intend to," he said gravely, amused that anyone could imagine he would do anything but worship the woman who made him whole again.

Diamond took her leave, greeting a man as he strolled into the twisted remains of a ballroom.

"Somehow, I knew you'd be here," Cora said to Terrin as he made a bow in their direction.

"Indeed? I take it all is well?" He looked around the room with curious eyes before turning back to Sally. "I thought you said the room was full of liches and Dark Ones?"

"It was, darling, it was positively teeming with them! You couldn't put so much as an iron maiden down without hitting one or the other of them."

"Iron maiden!" Cora said, straightening from where she had been leaning against him. "You're back to that, are you?"

Sally giggled. "I just put that in to see if you were listening, sugar. I would never use an iron maiden."

Cora glared at her with suspicion.

"Now, a Catherine wheel is a whole other matter. One of the demon lords—you wouldn't know him; Bael had him expulsed because of his dragon consort, and oh, there's ever such an interesting story to be told about them, but far too long to go into here since I am a busy person now that I'm the premier prince . . . where was I?"

"One of the demon lords?" Terrin prompted, propping one hip on an edge of the table.

"Oh, yes, one of the demon lords had such interesting ideas about ways to use a Catherine wheel, given to him, he says, by a Spanish wyvern's mate who was very inventive when it came to matters of bondage and such. But I digress. How are things at home?"

The last question was directed to Terrin.

"Fine, although the mares are a bit distressed that—"

"What is this?" A man's roar interrupted him, ripping through the room with the force of a bulldozer. Instantly, Alec moved to guard Cora, aware of her mingled annoyance and appreciation over that fact, amused when she grumbled to herself about men who had to learn a thing or two about women.

Terrin turned in surprise to look at the slight, small dark-haired man who strode into the room, a piece of paper clasped in his hands.

"Who are you?" Alec demanded, Kristoff moving Pia to stand next to Cora, the two men presenting a solid, protective front. Alec knew full well the newcomer was a demon lord, and thus not likely to bother them, but Cora had been through a lot, and he wanted nothing more than to get her away from all this business so he could seduce her as she deserved to be seduced.

She pinched his back and ignored his demand to stay behind him, her arm around his waist as she stood next to him.

"I am Asmodeus," the man answered, dismissing them with a curl of his lip as he shoved the paper at Sally. "What does this mean?"

"You got the e-mail already?" Sally gave a little shake of her head. "I told Sable to wait until the others were gone. Oh, well, I suppose you're here to make a scene about the fact that I've banished Bael to the Akasha."

"No," Asmodeus said, his expression closed. "That act can only gain my approval. I am here to claim the position of premier prince."

Are you sure I can't be used as a Tool anymore? That guy looks mean enough to use me against Sally. Or, heaven forbid, you, if you keep thinking those things about what you'll do to him if he so much as looks my way. Really, Alec, I'm a big girl.

Unbidden, his hand slid up to cup her ass, just the thought of it and her hips and breasts, and all the rest of her, making him hard. *A fact for which I'm prepared to get down on my knees and thank whatever fates, gods, or circumstances sent you into my life, but that is really not the important point at this moment, Beloved, so you can cease trying to seduce me with your hips and long, long legs that wrap so nicely around me when I thrust into your heat.*

"Of course you are," Sally said in a soothing voice. "But you see, I've taken that position. I believe that traditionally the position of a banished demon lord goes to the banishee, and that would be me."

Cora moaned into his head, giving herself a little shake. *You are so going to get pounced on when you're healed up. Can I still be used, or not?*

No. Bael's power is no more.

Then why are you so concerned about protecting me from this guy?

"You cannot be premier prince," Asmodeus said in a flat, emotionless voice.

It is my nature. I explained that earlier.

Yeah, yeah, all that macho stuff that doesn't cut squat with me. Is he a danger to us?

"Um . . . I think I *am* the premier prince. Aren't I?" Sally looked down at herself. "Yes, yes I am. Asmo, dumplin', we've never really seen eye to eye ever since that holiday party that I threw last year, when you insisted that Bael remove me from Abaddon because I may have spiked the eggnog, and subsequently your wrath demons got a bit tipsy and thought it would be a hoot and a half to drug and put you in a vat of Jell-O so all of your legions could have their pictures taken indulging in nude Jell-O wrestling with you—which, I have to admit, *was* a hoot and a half—but I can see you're still holding that bit of festive frolicking against me. My advice is just to get over it, and move on. I'm boss now."

I don't see how he could be a threat. That is the reason Kristoff and I have allowed him to continue.

Cora smothered a laugh at Sally's conversation. *He looks like he's going to explode. Maybe we should move back? I wouldn't want your owies to hurt again.*

They have healed, and I have to admit to wanting to stay a few more minutes, despite the temptation you pose.

"You are not," Asmodeus insisted.

Why?

Because I think Sally is about to explain something important.

"Look, this is how it works—I banish Bael, and that makes me the boss," Sally started to say, but Asmodeus cut her explanation short.

"You cannot be the premier prince of Abaddon because it is not allowed." Asmodeus gestured toward Terrin. "I had my suspicions before, but this proves it."

"Oh, dear," Terrin said, getting to his feet and moving over to stand next to Sally, who didn't look in the least bit concerned by what Asmodeus was saying. "Sally, my sweet, perhaps now would be a good time to dismiss the others."

She glanced toward them, a twinkle visible in her eye. "Oh, I think they've earned the right to see this to the end, don't you? Cora and Ulfur certainly have, and since the Dark Ones helped, they deserve to stay, as well."

"Thank you," Alec said politely as Kristoff bowed, and said, "We are all gratitude."

"It doesn't matter who is here—the news will be made public throughout the Otherworld so that everyone will know of your perfidy," Asmodeus said, looking almost bored now.

"I'm still confused," Pia murmured. "Why can't Sally

be the head boss if she took down Bael? Doesn't that make her the strongest?"

"That's a very good question," Cora said, then addressed Asmodeus. "What perfidy? Other than, you know, kidnapping us and all that jazz, which Alec swears wasn't bad, but I still have my doubts."

Sally blew her a little kiss. Cora grimaced.

"She can't be the premier prince for the reason that the Sovereign is not allowed to rule Abaddon as well as the Court of Divine Blood."

Alec smiled, glad his suspicion was confirmed, aware at the same time of Cora's gasp of surprise and jerk to the side.

"The . . . the . . . you mean . . . no!" she stammered, taking a step toward Sally. "You can't be God! You're all wrong for God! Not the fact that you're a woman, although all of those plagues and wiping out of innocents sounds like the act of a man rather than a woman, but no, I just refuse to accept that you're God."

"I'm not," Sally said, giving her a sympathetic pat on the arm. "For one, the Sovereign isn't the same as the mortal concept of a Christian God. For another . . ." She slid a glance toward Terrin.

"Jesus wept!" Cora exclaimed, clearly missing the irony of her words, running her hands through her hair. "God is married?"

Sally's eyebrows rose. "You mean Terrin? Oh, we're not married."

Alec thought Cora was going to explode with frustration. Her hair stuck out at odd angles as she all but screamed, "God is living in sin? What the hell?"

"Abaddon—" Terrin started to correct, but stopped at a look from Alec.

"Terrin isn't my lover," Sally said with an irrepressible giggle. "He's my . . . well . . . my other half."

Enlightenment flooded Alec at that moment, the explanation of Terrin's role sliding together like the last piece of a jigsaw puzzle.

"But—you said you were together. Earlier today you said that," Pia said, looking almost as confused as Cora.

"We are. He's my other half."

"We couldn't exist without each other," Terrin explained, obviously taking pity on them. "Think of it as a symbiotic relationship. A platonic one—I'm dating a power, as a matter of fact, and I believe before Sally took over the demon lord Magoth's position, she was seeing one of the cherubs who was responsible for the Internet."

"LOLcats," Sally said, nodding her head. "He's awesome about things like that."

"I'm so lost," Cora said, spinning around to look at him. "Alec? Is she God or not?"

"Not," he said, taking her in his arms and giving her a little kiss just to stop her from pulling out all her hair. "Together, Terrin and Sally are the Sovereign. They aren't a god, but they are good, so you can stop worrying that she's going to harm us."

"But she talked about torturing Ulfur and me," she protested. "Surely go—er . . . the Sovereign wouldn't do that? Surely he or she—"

"We're commonly referred to as it," Sally said with a little smile at Terrin.

"—surely *it* couldn't be a demon lord, could it?"

"Evidently she can." Alec wrapped both arms around her, providing her with the comfort he knew she needed.

"But wouldn't someone have recognized her?" Pia asked.

"I was wondering the same thing," Kristoff said, nodding as he glanced at Asmodeus. "Why would you not tell the other demon lords who she was?"

"I didn't know. It wasn't until I saw the two of them together that I could see her for what she is."

"Separate, we're nothing, just . . . well, just people," Sally explained. "I made sure that Terrin never came for a visit while I was in my palace here, just in case someone saw us together."

"Until now," Cora pointed out.

"Yes, well." Sally made a vague gesture. "It was inevitable that sooner or later someone would figure it out and take the premier princedom from me. I'm just sorry it was sooner; I was really looking forward to being the head demon lord. I don't suppose—"

"No," Asmodeus snapped. "Make me the premier prince now, and I will allow the others to go unscathed."

Sally sighed. "You just have no idea what you're missing not having me as a boss. Fine, you can have the job. I'll just spend all the energy I would have had to reorganizing Abaddon into thwarting your every move. Happy now?"

Asmodeus just looked at her with an expressionless mask, before turning to face toward Alec and the others. "You have three minutes to leave Abaddon. If you are here beyond that time, I will take you prisoner."

"The agreement between Abaddon and the Moravian Council—" Kristoff started to say, but was interrupted.

"The agreement is null and void as of this moment. You have two minutes and forty seconds remaining."

Before Alec could do so much as protest the cavalier overturning of an agreement that had stood between Abaddon and the Dark Ones for centuries, Asmodeus disappeared in a cloud of oily black smoke.

Chapter Nineteen

"Are you sure this is a good idea? There's a whole bunch of people after us, and they're bound to know we're here." I turned the lock on the door, just to make sure no one could get into our room.

"What people?" Alec asked.

"Eleanor, for one. That lichmaster dude for another."

"Bah." He waved them away, moving toward me with a familiar glint to his eye.

"Maybe I should feed you again. You only got enough blood to get your engine running before Pia and Kristoff left to take Ulfur back to Italy with them. I know you're still hungry."

"I'll feed in a bit."

I hesitated, worry riding uppermost in my mind. "Not only are those vamps still out there, and likely to come back and drag you off to the Akasha, but more importantly, you were literally almost ripped in half. Perhaps we need a bit of caution here. The healer did say that your injuries might take a bit longer to fully heal."

Alec gave me a sloe-eyed look, and before I could so much as rip off my clothing and fling myself on him, he had me naked and on the bed in one of Sally's non-Abaddon spare rooms.

"I'm fine," he answered, rubbing his hips against me, the bulging nature of his fly more than enough proof that he was just as anticipatory as I was. But still, I had to be sure.

"No, seriously, I think we should wait." It was a feeble protest at best, but I couldn't in all good conscience give in to the hunger that claimed us both.

"You want me as much as I want you," he murmured in my ear, his breath hot on my neck, his hands tormenting and teasing me with sensual little touches that immediately aroused my deepest passion. "I know you do. I can feel that you do."

"I think the fact that I can't keep my hands off you is a dead giveaway to that little fact," I said, grabbing his hands to keep them from further investigating my chest.

He stopped nibbling my neck and pulled back enough to frown at me, his beautiful green eyes narrowed slightly. "Why do you reject me?"

"I'm not rejecting, just delaying, and I'm doing that because I want to make sure that you're OK."

"I'm fine," he repeated, his hands diving back into breast central.

I squirmed out of his hold, rolled off the bed, snatched up his shirt, pulling it on quickly lest my own needs and desire drive me back into his arms. Luckily for my good intentions, the stark, horrifying memory of Alec lying torn apart and bleeding against the ballroom wall was more than enough to sober me up. "So you say, but I'm a doubting kind of person until I can see things for myself."

"The best way for me to prove to you that I have healed is to make love to you," he said, gliding toward me with a look that a panther probably gave a particularly succulent bunny in his path.

"No, the best way to prove it is to strip and let me see your—"

He was naked before the words had left my lips.

It took me a few minutes of allowing my gaze to caress the long, mouthwatering stretches of muscle lying so sleekly under skin that I knew was warm and satiny and tasted so very good. . . . With an effort, I stopped the path down which my brain was heading, and reminded myself that just a short time earlier he had been almost killed. "Nice try, but I refuse to allow you to distract me that way. Now, let me see. . . ."

The blast of power hadn't acted on Alec with the precision of a bladed instrument, meaning the thick scar that ran from the center of his chest to the top of his shoulder was jagged and uneven. It was also thick, and still red, and when I laid my hand on it, I could feel the heat as the flesh continued to repair itself. I let my fingers move upward to his neck, gently touching the twisting, angry-looking red seam that stretched from his collarbone around the side to the back of his neck. It, too, was hot to the touch.

Alec was clearly in no condition for the acts he so obviously desired, but if I told him that outright, he'd just scorn my concern and do what he wanted—giving me the most profound, intense pleasure without a single thought of whether it would harm him. I couldn't let him stress himself, obviously, but how was I to stop him? It was useless to tell myself to just ignore the lure he posed, because that just wasn't possible, and we both knew it.

No, I'd have to tell him he was going to take a new, much more passive role for the afternoon's activities.

"Are you finished touching me?" Alec inquired politely. "If you are, it's my turn."

"No," I said with a laugh as I pointed to the bed. "Lie down."

His frown returned. "You are being dominant. Evidently you are under the impression I like that in my Beloved. While it's true that I'm prepared to explore new things with you, I have never been one to take enjoyment from being passive."

"Alec, less than an hour ago I thought you were dead. I know you think you're perfectly fit for lovemaking, but I don't think you are, not really. However"—I held up a hand to interrupt his protest—"I am willing to admit that you're absolutely right in that I want you more than anything I can think of, so I'm willing to indulge us both, providing you let me do things my way."

"What way is that?"

"For one, you let me seduce you. I know that you don't normally like that, but—" I blinked as Alec, after staring at me for a moment, ripped the blankets from the bed standing across the room, and flung himself down on his back, his hands clasped behind his head, his feet wiggling in anticipation. I couldn't help but laugh.

"Come and seduce me, Beloved," he said in an arrogant, demanding voice. "I am willing to let you take the lead this once, so long as you do it now, and don't waste any more time in telling me I'm not healed enough to pleasure you as you deserve."

I laughed again, and slowly, so as to tease just a little, unbuttoned his shirt that I still wore. His eyes lit with faux outrage as I deliberately took my time working my way down the line of buttons, making sure I stroked my hands over my hips (which seemed to hold some fascination for him) all the way up to my breasts.

"Take off the shirt," he demanded, his breathing erratic as I stood, considering him for a moment.

"You're the only man I know who can be simultaneously demanding and submissive." I started to take off the shirt, pausing at the heat shining so brightly in his gorgeous green eyes. *You're going to seize me the minute I get within range, aren't you?*

Absolutely.

That's what I thought.

His eyes widened as I grabbed my jeans and jerked them on before turning on my heel and marching out of the room.

Corazon! Where are you going?

Stay there. Alec, I mean it, stay there! Don't think I don't know you're putting your clothes back on and going to come after me, because I know you are, and you can just stop it. I'm going to get something . . . fun. Just get back into bed, and consider how lucky you are to have a Beloved who plans on making you wild with delight.

You make me wild with delight without fetching anything else. And what is it you're getting? His tone was grumpy, but I knew he could feel the sincerity in my intentions, and was doing as I asked even though it wasn't what he wanted.

You get extra bonus points for that, I told him. *And you'll see.*

He spent the next ten minutes alternating between ranting at the way he would punish me if I didn't return to him that exact moment and telling me exactly how he wanted to make love to me. The former I ignored, but the latter made it extremely hard to carry on a coherent conversation with Sally, whom I found sitting in a sunny bow-fronted room with Terrin, sipping tea and eating petits fours.

Alec was scowling when I returned to the room Sally had given to us, his glare a truly magnificent thing to behold. "You have been gone exactly twelve min—what the hell do you think you're going to do with those?"

I twirled the red silk braided rope in one hand, while draping the matching scarf over my shoulder. "Sally gave them to me. I'm going to use them, my sexy vampire, to keep you from doing everything you want to do. You're still healing, so it's important you don't put too much stress on your wounds. The rope will ensure you don't."

"You don't seriously believe you can tie me down."

"Oh, yes, yes I do."

He rolled his eyes and tried to hide a smug thought that he would indulge me for a few minutes before simply ripping his hands free from the restraint. I smiled a secret smile to myself, and peeled off my jeans and shirt.

"You're not happy anymore," I said, gesturing toward his penis, now in a dormant state.

"You were gone for twelve minutes," he said, giving me a tolerant look as I slipped one of his hands through the adjustable loop in one end of the rope, snaking it through a couple of bars on the metal headboard before repeating the process with his remaining hand.

He tried to catch the nipple of my breast nearest him in his mouth as I leaned over him, but I shifted to the side, saying, "I would have thought you might have entertained yourself with thoughts of how you wanted me to pleasure you."

"I didn't, although I did spend some time on various punishment methods that will be meted out to you if you don't stop stalling and let me make love to you."

I smiled as he tested the bonds, distracted for a moment with the way the muscles in his arms and chest moved as he did so. The silk rope gave a little, but not so much that he could reach past his ears.

"What a delicious picture this is," I said, leaning forward to nip his lower lip. "A handsome-as-sin vampire all tied up, just like a smorgasbord for me to taste. But I think . . . yes, I think we can improve on this experience."

"I hope so, because I'm fast losing patience with you."

He tried to sound stern and unhappy, but I could feel that his interest and curiosity had been piqued.

Has no woman ever taken the lead with you in love-making?

Not like this, no. What are you doing with that scarf?

"It's a blindfold. Oooh, tricky!" As I leaned over him to tie the silken scarf over his eyes, he twisted and caught me with his legs, the powerful muscles in his thighs almost spelling an end to my plan. Just stroking my hand up their hard lengths was enough to have me giving in to all the wicked thoughts Alec was currently transmitting to me, especially when he added a sense of how much pleasure he received from me touching him. "But it will do you no good."

I pried myself out of the leg vise, and quickly tied the scarf over his eyes, making sure his nose was free for breathing. "Would you like a safe word?"

"Hell, no."

He was still smugly of the belief that he was in control of the situation. I let him continue thinking it as I cooed softly, stroking a hand down his chest from the jagged scar at his breastbone down to his penis. "Sooo hot, Alec. Your skin burns, but in a good way. I want to lick every inch of you. And since you are at my mercy and unable to distract me with your hands and mouth, I think I will."

I hummed a jaunty little song to myself as I bent over his chest, swirling a tongue around first one nipple, hidden in the soft curls of hair, before turning my attention to the other, allowing my fingers to stroke the ridged muscles of his abdomen. *I don't think I've ever slept with a man who had an actual six-pack, Alec. Do you work out?*

Sometimes, when I'm not doing anything else.

I mentally damned his genes for allowing him to be in such good shape without working at it, while lesser folks like me were at the mercy of sadistic personal trainers.

Do not pretend that your body does anything but please me, he chastised me. *You know it does, and it would not matter what shape it was.*

"OK, that right there would make just about every woman on the planet your love slave for life." I moved my kisses down his chest to his belly, swirling my tongue around his belly button as his hips jerked upward, his breath hissing when I bit the lovely indentation below his hips. "Luckily, no one but me is going to know you're so wonderful. Why, what do we have here? It looks like a penis."

"You love toying with me this way, don't you?" he asked in a voice tinged with amused exasperation. "You truly think you have me in your power?"

"I know I do." I let my fingers go wild on his groin, stroking and gently pulling, and generally just getting to know the scenery. I bent down and gently bit his inner thigh, enjoying the sheer spurt of pleasure that coiled through him as a result. His hunger was riding him hotly now, but I knew part of it was triggered by sexual need, and I couldn't help but want to push that just a bit higher before giving in to him. I looked up and gave him a saucy grin. "You don't know where I'm going to touch next, do you? You're wholly in my power, Alec. I can touch you here, or here, or even nibble you here . . ."

He groaned deep in his chest.

". . . and there's not a darned thing you can do about it. I have to say, I really enjoy having you spread out before me like this. Let's see, are you ticklish here?"

"Dammit, woman, you are deliberately baiting me!"

"Mmm." I looked up from where I was nipping gently at his inner thighs. "Isn't it wonderful?"

"Yes, but that's beside the point. Cease your teasing."

"Or what?" I asked sweetly, gently squeezing his testicles. "Oh, didn't I mention that Sally said those ropes are magic? You can't break them, you can't slip your hands out, and you can't untie them from the bed. In other words, my sexy vampire, you are well and truly bound until such time as I want you free."

"Is that so?" I couldn't see them beneath the scarf, but I knew his eyes were filled with heat and passion and hunger, promising retribution for both my tone and actions. I allowed my grin to grow before dipping my head and taking him into my mouth.

He swore in Latin, his hips thrusting upward as I tasted, and swirled, and generally drove us both close to the breaking point.

"Yes," I said somewhat breathlessly a short time later, admittedly smirking to myself.

He whipped the scarf off to give me a heated look that came close to making my blood boil . . . until I realized just what that meant.

"Hey—" I started to say, but suddenly, I was on my belly at the bottom of the bed, Alec hard and hot behind me, the scarf twisted around underneath me. Alec used it to pull my hips up, parting my legs with his knees as he bent over me. "Alec! How did you get out of the magic ropes?"

"They weren't magic, *mi corazón*."

"Damn that Sally! She lied to me!"

"I'm sure she would think of it simply as being naughty," he said, kissing a path from my spine over to one hip before giving in to the hunger that threatened to swamp us both. Pain flared for a fraction of a second before melting into the most exquisite pleasure as he drank, my body aching with need for him.

"God shouldn't . . . oh Mother Mary, that is so good. . . . God shouldn't lie."

Alec's tongue swiped across the spot he'd been drinking from before he pulled my hips up with the scarf. "Now we shall see who is the one in power, and who is helpless."

"What are you doing?" I asked, every atom of my body quivering with anticipation and desire. "Are we doing it doggy-style?"

"You wanted bondage. Now you shall have it," he said, pulling up on the scarf as he thrust inside my body.

I had been about to protest that I had never done bondage, even bondage light, as I suspected this would be classified, but the sensation of the scarf pulling up on my pubic bone as he entered me was enough to push everything from my mind but that of the rapture he was giving me just by flexing his hips.

What's that, Corazon? Not going to protest that you are now my helpless captive?

I moaned in his mind as he slackened the scarf when he withdrew before pulling me upward again as he stroked back in.

Not going to deny that you can't escape my touch?

The angle was different than if I'd just been on my

hands and knees, allowing him to plunge into depths that had not been reached before, waves of pleasure rippling outward with increasing intensity.

Not even going to demand I stop dominating you?

Oh, god, no! For the love of all that's holy, dominate me some more!

My approaching orgasm mingled with his sensations, tangling together until we were both poised on the brink.

Corazon?

Nnrng?

I love you, he said as he jerked upward on the scarf, sliding deeper and harder into me than he had before, his mouth hot on my shoulder as he bit.

It was too much for me, far too much. The orgasm, the sense of profound satisfaction he felt when drinking from me, and the knowledge that his love would burn eternally was all just too much. My body and soul seemed to explode simultaneously in rapture, a bright supernova of love and ecstasy that shone so brightly, I was surprised it didn't consume us both.

When I stopped being a brilliant, glittering ball of orgasmic wonder, I found myself lying panting on Alec's still-heaving chest, his arms holding tight to me.

I lifted my head. He opened one eye and rolled it down to meet my gaze. "Still think I haven't healed?"

"Oh, you've healed," I said, gasping for breath. "You're definitely cleared for duty. Jesus wept, Alec! That was . . . hoo! I'm totally a go on bondage from here on out. Do you think Sally will notice if we run out with the rope and scarf? Because frankly, I would give her just about anything to keep them."

He laughed and hugged me despite the fact that he was also struggling to catch his breath. *Ah, my heart, what would I do without you?*

"Luckily, my studmuffin extraordinaire—really, where did you learn to do that thing with the scarf?— you won't have to find out. Although I suppose we should get moving soon. Sally never did say where she sent the vampires, and Eleanor, not to mention Brother Ailwin, although I doubt if he cares about us anymore now that Bael is gone. But still, we should be moving on just in case people show up to nab you."

Alec closed his eye again. "Women. I'll never understand how they can talk after sex. I need sleep."

"Don't be silly, you're immortal," I said, pulling up the sheet and snuggling into him nonetheless.

"Immortal doesn't mean we don't need sleep. And stop worrying, Cora; I won't allow anyone to interfere with us any longer."

"Oh really? What do you plan on doing?" I looked up when he didn't answer, but he was telling the truth—he really did need sleep. His face was relaxed as I felt him drift off on a cloud of sated male satisfaction. I spent a long, long time holding him, wondering how we were going to untangle all the threads that seemed to weave around us into a knot. Uppermost in my mind were the vampires and their council who were still obviously intent on punishing Alec, but also niggling at the back of my mind was a concern that we weren't through seeing Eleanor. And then there was the lichmaster de Marco; he seemed to be overly interested in vampires. I made a mental note to ask Alec about it later. Last on my list was Brother Ailwin—would he decide to get revenge against us, or would he give up now that I couldn't be used?

I fell asleep worrying about it all, secure, at least, in the knowledge that Alec returned my love. If nothing else, that made the world seem infinitely more wonderful.

It was night again when I woke up to find the bed empty, and Alec gone.

"What do you mean, he left?" I asked ten minutes later, catching myself wanting to yell at Sally. She might not be God, but she was awfully close to that. More importantly, I had a feeling if I gave in to my frustration and vented my spleen upon her, she'd just get "naughty" again with me. "Left for where?"

She started to give me one of her smiles that I knew prefaced some outrageous comment or other, but with a glance at Terrin, who was glaring at a laptop as he punched angrily at the keys, she sighed and shook her head. "You make it too easy, you really do, sugar. You take all the fun out of it. And much though I should like tormenting you just a bit, just a tiny little smidgen, you know, to keep my hand in should I ever get the chance to be a demon lord again, even though I'd like to indulge in a bit of teasing, I won't."

I eyed her. "Asmodeus finally kicked you out of Abaddon, did he?"

Terrin said something rude under his breath. Sally sighed again. "Yes. Asmo really is very single-minded. He simply did not see the benefit in having one-half of the Sovereign being a prince of Abaddon. Such narrow-minded thinking has never been to my taste, but it takes all kinds, doesn't it? Alec went to see the vampires."

"The council?" My blood froze in my veins. *Alec?* There was no answer. I couldn't tell if he just couldn't hear me, or if he didn't want to. Damn him. "He went to see them without me? Mother of God! He's gone to sacrifice himself so they don't put me in the Akasha with him! You have to do something, Sally!"

"I do?"

"Yes, you do! You can't just sit there doing nothing!" My hands waved in the air as my inner devil prompted

me to snatch the glossy magazine from her hands and
beat her over the head with it.

"I'm doing something, sweetness. I'm reading a very
informative article about cuticle health." She glanced at
my hands. "One that is sorely needed in some people's
lives."

I took a deep breath. "Alec is a good guy. You are the
head honcho of good guys. That means you have to do
something when he needs help."

She looked puzzled as she consulted Terrin, who was
now swearing under his breath as he plugged in an iPod.
"Do I have to do something, punkin?"

"I swear, I know what projects that Guardian who
was proscribed used her minions on. . . . Hmm? Do you
have to do what?"

"Do I have to help Cora?"

Terrin looked from Sally to me. "I thought you already did? Surely you offered them sanctuary so the
Dark One could heal his wounds in safety?"

"Well, I thought that's what I'd done, but evidently
Cora here is feeling slighted." Sally plucked a sugar
cube from a bowl sitting on the table next to her, and
sucked it thoughtfully. "And then there was the matter
of the rope and scarf. They were my favorites, but I gave
them to her willingly, because I could see that she
wanted to indulge herself in a little nooky but was afraid
he'd hurt himself. I thought that was quite generous and
beneficent on my part, but evidently it wasn't enough."

I slumped against the wall, running my hand through
my hair. *Alec, please answer me. Please. I'm worried
about you. Just tell me you're OK.*

Silence was the only thing that filled my head. I
slumped even more. He might not want to discuss the
fact that he ran off without me, but he wouldn't let me
worry unduly. That meant that either he was physically

unable to talk to me, or something else was prohibiting communication. Either boded ill.

"I'm sorry, Sally, it was generous and beneficent, as was giving us a room overnight so Alec could rest and heal. Although . . . if you're no longer a demon lord, why do you still have this house?"

She crunched the remainder of the sugar cube with very white teeth. "Oh, the palace part that was in Abaddon is gone. All that's left is the original house, here in the mortal plane."

"Gotcha. Where exactly did Alec go to meet the vampires, do you know?" I straightened up, wondering where my wallet had gotten to. So much had happened since we arrived in France, I had lost track of my belongings.

"Vienna, I believe. Why? Oh, you wish to go and rescue him, do you?" Sally tipped her head to the side and gave me a once-over, a definite twinkle in her eyes. "Yes, I can see that's exactly what you intend to do. Good luck."

"Thanks," I said grimly, disappointed that she hadn't offered to fix everything with a wave of her omnipotent hand. Tempted though I was to beg them both to do just that, it was quite clear that Sally felt no further obligation to do anything for us, and really, I couldn't blame her. She had done what we asked—toppled Bael from power, ending my Tooldom. She had given us a place for Alec to rest after removing from the immediate location everyone who threatened us. She had even given us that lovely silk rope and scarf. "I'll just gather up what things I have here and be on my way."

"Ta-ta," she said, returning to her magazine.

I returned to the bedroom we'd occupied, but found no luggage, no purse, and certainly no wallet or passport. How on earth was I supposed to get to Vienna?

"I'll get there if I have to hitchhike the entire way," I growled as I wrapped the scarf around my waist like a sash, tying the rope on top of it. "Pia and Kristoff will loan me some money for one of those portals, I bet. And maybe I could call—" As I stepped out the door, I had a mental image of Terrin chastising Sally, who gave a little laugh in response before suddenly the floor was yanked out from underneath my feet, and I went tumbling into a black void of nothing.

"Hruh?" The black void was filled with a sharp pain. "Wha'?"

"You did not keep your arms and legs inside the portal at all times," a brusque male German voice chided me.

I opened my eyes to find myself on a mat in a small room filled with pale sunshine. A spot on my head hurt—obviously I'd conked it on the floor when I . . . memory returned at that moment. "Jesus wept!"

"You were warned to do so. If you are unkempt now, it is not the fault of Portals Elite, Ltd. Please to move off the receiving cushion."

I got somewhat painfully to my feet, dusting myself off as I limped out of the portal room, saying under my breath, "Thank you, Sally. I don't know how you did it, but zapping me to Vienna was a very nice thing to do."

Fifteen minutes later I was navigating the process of making an international collect call to Pia and Kristoff, who were unhappy, but not surprised, to find that Alec had abandoned me in order to take care of the vampires on his own.

"He wishes to protect you from the council, that is all," Kristoff said at the same time Pia said, "Stupid man. Doesn't he realize you guys are stronger together than apart?"

I agreed with both statements, and would have moved on to asking for the address of the Moravian Council's headquarters, when Kristoff's words struck me.

"What do you mean, Alec wants to protect me from the council? I haven't done anything to them. They're mad at Alec, not me. Aren't they?"

"You had Sally remove them from her palace," Kristoff said with a pronounced note of regret in his voice. "I'm afraid that means they consider you have directly opposed them in the act of completing their duty."

"So what?" I snarled into the pay phone, startling an elderly woman standing at a bus stop next to me. I turned my back on her and lowered my voice. "You did the same thing. Defied them, that is."

"Yes, but the difference is that they don't know for a fact that we had Alec in our house," Pia pointed out. "They suspect it, but have no proof beyond seeing us together in France, and I told them that was because of Ulfur."

I sighed yet again and rubbed my forehead. "Great, so that's why Alec ran off without me? To keep them from punishing me?"

"It's what I would do," Kristoff allowed.

"Well, screw that! I'm not going to sit around and let some damned holier-than-thou group punish Alec or me! Do you hear me? I won't stand for it!"

"You go, girl," Pia said with approval. "Boo, maybe we should go to Vienna—"

"No," he said quickly. "Alec does not wish for our interference. Cora, you must have faith that he will do what is best for you both."

Faith I had in buckets. It was the man of my dreams— literally—who was missing from my life, and I didn't intend on letting him martyr himself to save me. "Why won't he talk to me? Have they done something to him? Something heinous? Oh dear lord, did they already send him back to the Akasha?"

"No, they wouldn't banish him, not with you still here," Kristoff answered. "Most likely he has closed you from his mind so he can deal with the situation. It is, again, what I would do."

"Men!" Pia snorted.

"Agreed. What's the address of the council?"

Reluctantly, he gave it to me, along with the phone number I requested.

"Cora—"

"I know. Let Alec handle it. The only problem is that's the man I love in there with all those judgmental vampires, and I'm not going to let them touch so much as one hair on his adorable if sometimes far too stubborn head. Thank you for the information and advice. We'll give you a call when the dust has settled."

"Dust? What—"

I hung up the phone, dug around in my pockets to see what sort of change I had there, and resigned myself to making another collect call.

A half hour later I retraced my steps to the portal shop where Sally had dumped me, and greeted the first batch of arrivals.

"You're sure you want to do this?" Jane asked as she pulled out a cell phone. "It'll be very expensive having the entire union portalled here."

"Do it. Alec will just have to foot the bill."

She took one look at the grim expression on my face, and called her lieutenant to instruct the union members to begin the process of transporting them all from France to Vienna.

"And now the time has come for you to do penance

for your attempt at killing Alec," I said a short time later, grabbing the body that plummeted out of nothing to whomp hard on the receiving-end mats. I jerked Eleanor to her feet before she could even suck in her breath, twisting one of her arms up behind her back. "You're going to be at the front of the group that storms the vampires' castle."

Eleanor sputtered something rude. I jerked her arm upward, causing her to squawk. "You're going to do this, and then you're going to get the hell out of our lives forever. You got that?"

"You are not the boss of me—"

"No, but Jane, as the head of the union, is. Jane?"

"I'm sorry," Jane said, spreading her hands and moving out of the way as the union members started arriving with frequency now, one barely rolling out of the way before another appeared to drop onto the mats. "The donation Cora is offering the union is just too great to ignore, so I am forced to issue you with a direct command to obey Cora in all things."

"I'm not bound to you," Eleanor protested. "You can't command me like that!"

"You are not bound to me personally, but you are bound to the union, and as its leader, you are obligated to follow the rules I put into place. This is one of the rules."

Eleanor argued, as I knew she would, but I didn't have the time or patience to put up with it. "Either you agree to do this, or I get hold of Sally and have you sent to the Akasha," I bluffed, holding up my hand to stop her when she would have protested. "And don't think I can't do it, because Sally and I see eye to eye, and besides, I think she's aching to send someone to the Akasha."

Eleanor's lips tightened. "Very well," she finally said. "But I'm only doing this so I can wash my hands of the pair of you forever."

It took another thirty-five minutes before the entire union, all 112 members, were assembled. We spilled out of the building into the street, and Jane had to resort to the use of a megaphone before she finally got everyone organized in a long line of liches, three abreast, that snaked around the block and across a pedestrian mall. The walk to the Moravian Council house took another half hour, but at last we had the tall, elegant house in our sights.

"Charge!" I yelled, not waiting for Jane to give the command. To my surprise, the liches did exactly as I ordered—they ran forward, streaming into the house once the door was battered down.

I was at the head of the group as it entered the elegantly furnished hall, and leaped onto a couch to scream, "Alec!"

Noise drifted down the stairs as the liches poured into the house. I pushed past them on the stairs, ignoring a scuffle that had broken out between a couple of vampires and the liches on the landing. "This way!" I yelled, urging them up after me as I ran to two double doors that the vampires had obviously been guarding. I flung open the door, dashing inside, the liches swarming behind me.

"Aha!" I yelled, pausing to point a dramatic finger at the scene before me. "I knew it! I knew you people had Alec!"

There were four men at a long table. Facing them, seated in a chair, was Alec, flanked on either side by the messenger and his buddy.

All seven heads swiveled to look at us, identical expressions of surprise on all their faces.

Are you OK? I asked Alec. *Did they hurt you? Have they tortured you yet? And just what the hell do you think you're doing leaving me to go off and be Mr. Brave on your own, huh?*

What are you doing here? Alec answered, looking annoyed rather than relieved I'd come to save him from being St. Alec the vampire martyr. *And what the hell have you brought all of them for?*

"To save you, you idiot man!" I stomped forward, waving at the occupants of the room. "Liches, attack!"

"No!" Alec bellowed, leaping to his feet as the other vamps did likewise. "Stand down!"

"Who is this woman? The rest of you will not take one more step into this room!" commanded one of the vamps at the table, a dark-haired man with a pissed-off expression. To my surprise, the liches seemed to heed him as well as Alec, since all of them came to an awkward halt just inside the doorway. "Is this the Beloved of whom you spoke?"

Cora, you can't attack the Moravian Council.

Want to bet?

I am in no danger, love. "Yes. This is Corazon, my Beloved, and the one you have to thank for the actions of the day."

"And just so you know, Mr. Whoever You Are, I'm not going to let you send Alec to the Akasha or anywhere else evil like that," I said, swaggering toward him, my words dripping with implied threat that I prayed I could actually back up. "I know you guys are conducting some sort of a vendetta against him, but that ends now, do you hear?"

"Very well," the spokesman said, inclining his head, his expression now somewhat blank, although I could have sworn I saw his lips twitch once or twice like he was trying to hold back laughter.

Just the thought that he could laugh at something so heinous as Alec's life freedom being threatened made my blood boil. I would sic the liches on him, first, I swore to myself.

Cora, you're not listening to me.

"Who are you?" I asked, ignoring Alec as he tried to stop me from marching forward to the vampire. "Are you the head guy?"

"I am Christian Dante," the man said, giving me a little bow. I had to admit, as bows went, it was a pretty nice one, almost as smooth as Alec's. "And yes, I do lead the Moravian Council. Now, you will please remove your liches from the building before I have them removed for you."

Corazon! Alec all but yelled in my brain. *Will you stop?*

Alec, I know you're peeved at me for being here, but you're just going to have to deal with the fact that we're a couple now. I take that very seriously, and it does not mean that I'm going to expect you to solve all our problems by yourself.

To my utter surprise, he started laughing.

"Oh, they're not Cora's servants," Jane said, rushing forward to stand next to me before Christian. She bobbed a little awkward curtsy, gesturing toward her chest. "We're a union, you see. Technically the liches are under my control—"

Alec, are you insane?

"Oh, for the love of Pete," Eleanor said, pushing her way through the mob of slowly retreating liches. She gave Alec a sour look before running her gaze over the remainder of the vampires present.

No, just amused.

"—most of them are under my control, technically, as I said, but we are a cooperative, and under most circumstances function along the lines of a self-policing commune rather than a dictatorship. I'm Jane, by the way."

Amused because I expect you to give me the respect due to your partner in life? I asked, outraged and ready to punch him in the arm.

No, I'm grateful beyond human understanding for that, mi querida.

Christian made a bow at Jane before turning to give Eleanor his attention. "And you are?"

"She is my Beloved," Alec said, finally giving in to my glares enough that he stopped laughing, and, taking my hand in his, kissed my fingers.

Christian raised one eyebrow. The other vampires looked vaguely scandalized. "You have two, as well?"

"I do. Eleanor was my first Beloved, the one who was killed by Kristoff's first wife some five hundred years ago. Corazon is her reincarnation, and thus it is she who is now my true Beloved."

"You know," Eleanor said to the vampire nearest her, the one everyone called the messenger, "I'm really getting tired of being referred to as the disposable Beloved."

The vampire just stared at her.

"I don't suppose you'd like me for your own?" she asked him.

"Er . . ."

"That's it," Eleanor said, shoving the vamp aside. "I've had more rejection than is right for any one woman to have. Send me back to the Underworld. Right now. You can all go to hell for all I care—I just want to go back to my adorable little house, and garden, and friend with benefits who never, ever rejects me."

"Er . . ." I leaned into Alec. *Do you know how to send someone to the Underworld?*

Yes. You kill them.

My eyes widened as I looked at Eleanor standing angrily in front of us. "Uh . . ." *Is there no other way?*

Yes.

"Well?" Eleanor asked.

I looked at Alec. He looked back at me. *Well?* I asked him in turn.

Well, what? Are you trying to imply that you'd like me to take over this matter, rather than let you deal with it as you obviously prefer to do with problems?

I jabbed him in the side with my elbow. "You are so incredibly funny. Get over yourself already, would you? You know full well what I mean."

He laughed again, wrapped an arm around me, and addressed Christian. "Is your Beloved available for a Release ceremony?"

Christian pursed his lips slightly as he glanced at Eleanor's angry expression. "I have no doubt she would be happy to do so, although she has not yet conducted such ceremonies on the living. Allegra is nothing if not dedicated, however, and I'm sure she would be delighted to tackle the situation. Madame, if you would please follow August, he will take you to my Beloved."

The messenger's companion gestured toward the doorway, still filled with liches who were watching the proceedings with unabashed interest. They parted to allow Eleanor and the vampire through.

"You're welcome," I yelled after Eleanor when she turned on her heel and marched off without anything but an annoyed sniff in our direction. "I hope you stay there this time," I added in a much softer tone.

Alec's arm tightened around my waist, no doubt in warning to behave myself. That reminded me of just why I was there with Jane's lich army. I turned back to the four council members, who were now clustered around the messenger, who was gesturing at Alec and me as he spoke in a low tone.

"I am not going to let you send Alec anywhere," I announced in a firm, no-nonsense voice. "Or me, if that's what Mr. Nosy there is telling you that you should do. I know you guys are angry at Alec about some mix-up in the past, but that was then, and this is now, and although I may not be a lichmaster like Jane, I think you can see that Alec and I mean business."

Thank you for including me in that statement.

I told you, we're a couple now. That means we do important things together. I glanced at him, suddenly worried that he didn't really want to be part of a team.

He leaned to the side and kissed me, very gently. *There is nothing I want more than to be a team with you, Beloved.*

I smiled, all warm and fuzzy inside at the emotion behind the words.

"Yes, we can see that you mean business," Christian said, taking his own sweet time to finish his conversation before turning back to us. He made a dismissive gesture. "You're free to go."

I gawked at him for a minute. "Both of us?" I asked, just to make sure I was understanding him correctly.

"Both of you." He gave a pointed look toward the mass of people at the door. "I'd be appreciative if you took your lich army with you."

"We're not really an army," Jane said quickly. "We're fully unionized, so that each member can feel he or she is an important part of our family."

"Wait. . . . You're letting us go?" Alec laughed again as I shook my head. "You're really that worried about the liches?"

"On the contrary, with all due respect to the lich union, they are nothing more than an annoyance."

I thought for a moment. "Is it because Sally is helping us? Did she threaten you guys?"

"Sally?" Christian frowned. "Do I know of a Sally?"

"I mentioned her earlier," the messenger said with a dark look toward me.

"Ah, her." Christian's eyes widened for a moment. "No, it is not the threat of the—" He bit off the word with a look toward the liches. "It is not due to her that we have released Alec."

I looked at the love of my life. "Did they just come to their senses?"

"Something like that," he said, kissing me again.

"I didn't need to rouse the liches?"

"No. If you'd stayed put, I would have been back there by now, and it all would have been taken care of."

I smacked him on the chest. "Dammit, I hate being left out of things. What did you do to get them to let up on you?"

"He helped rid the mortal world of Bael," Christian answered. "That, along with continued petitions by Kristoff and Pia, have been deemed as suitable punishment for the acts of the past."

"But . . . I thought you guys didn't mind Bael? I mean, wasn't there some sort of a pact you had with him?"

"One he honored only when he felt like it," Christian said with a wry twist to his lips. "Bael was a danger to us, as well as mortals."

"Oh. So we really can go?"

"Yes." This time he did smile. "Although Allegra would like to meet you. She enjoys meeting other Beloveds. If you decide to stay in Vienna, I would be happy to introduce you to her, perhaps over dinner."

I looked from him to Alec. "The man who put you in the Akasha to die wants to do dinner."

"We would be delighted," Alec said politely, pinching my behind as I tried to wrap my brain around this sudden change in the situation.

Dammit, Alec, I was all prepared to fight for you!

I know you were, and I appreciate that. But there is no need. I had a feeling that once the council realized that you were instrumental in ridding the mortal and immortal worlds of Bael, they would look kindly upon my case, since they could not damn you to any punishment they wished to mete out upon me.

If you thought that, I said as Alec bowed his goodbyes and gently herded me toward the doorway full of liches, *then why did you not take me with you?*

Ah, he said, somewhat abashed, *there was the issue of you having the messenger removed from Abaddon. I simply wished to ensure that they weren't going to make a case out of that before I brought you here.*

"From now on, we tackle trouble together, OK?" I told him as we stopped in front of the mass of liches. "It's what couples do."

"So long as it doesn't endanger you, yes," he said as Jane shooed her liches out the door ahead of her. We followed behind her.

"Not acceptable. Oh, by the way, we owe Jane a whole ton of money for portalling everyone here to save your butt."

"You portalled all the liches?" he asked, looking horrified as his eyes roamed over the stream of bodies moving their way down the stairs and out of the house.

"You said you were rich, and I had to do something to save you," I muttered to him.

"Comfortable, *mi corazón.* I'm *comfortable,* not rich."

I shot him a look.

"All right, I'm relatively wealthy. But still, you couldn't have had them take the train?"

"A lich army doesn't ride a train," I scoffed, my heart

singing a song of lightness and happiness, one that would be suitable for the end of a Disney movie, the kind where birds sing, squirrels dance with chipmunks, and the hero and heroine gaze swooningly at each other.

The squirrels and chipmunks have gone to bed, Alec said, his eyes alight with a familiar glint. *But I will tell you how much I love you if it makes you look swoonily at me.*

I would, but there's still that one concern. That de Marco guy—why did he want Ulfur to lock you away? Do you think he had some evil plans for you?

Possibly.

And what about Brother Ailwin? He seemed pretty pissed at us. I wouldn't put it past him to try to get revenge for the fact that I'm no longer a Tool. Man, I have got to stop saying that!

He laughed into my brain and, as we reached the street, pulled me up tight against his body, his breath mingling with mine just as our souls seemed to do. *My love, my heart, all will be well. Let go of those concerns, and give yourself up to your happy ending with your prince.*

"You are *so* not a prince," I said, punching him in the shoulder as he scooped me up and carried me down the street to where one of those horse-drawn carriages that drove tourists around Vienna was slowly making its way. He yelled something in German at the driver, who obligingly stopped. "You're an annoyingly arrogant bloodsucker who thinks he's going to get his way in everything, and you're dead wrong there, Alec. I mean it. Stop thinking that you're going to let me believe I can have my way but you'll secretly have yours anyway. Alec! You just did it again! Oooh, with the silk rope? Really? That sounds . . . oooh! All right, maybe you can have your way about that, although the feathers and leg restraints are just downright kinky. . . ."

Enjoy Katie MacAlister's
bonus short story
"My Heart Will Go On and On"
featuring Cora and Alec!

"What do you see, Corazon?"

"Um. Mud." I sensed the hypnotherapist's disapproval of my answer, and qualified it. "Well, mud and grass and stuff like that. But mostly just mud."

"Are you sure she's under?" Patsy asked, her voice sounding dubious. "She doesn't look hypnotized to me. CORA! Can you hear me?"

"I'd have to be five miles away not to hear you," I said, cracking open an eye and peering at her from where I lay prone on the couch. "I'm hypnotized, you idiot, not deaf."

"Is she supposed to know she's hypnotized?" Terri asked, sitting on the floor across from me, watching with bright, interested eyes. "That doesn't negate the regression, does it?"

"Hypnotism isn't a magical state of unknowing," Barbara the hypnotherapist answered. "She is simply relaxed, in touch with her true inner spirit, and has opened up her mind to the many memories of lifetimes past. I assure you that she is properly hypnotized."

"Let me get a pin and poke her with it," Patsy said, bustling over to a bookcase crammed full of books and various other items. "If she reacts, we'll know she's faking it."

"No one is poking me with anything!" I shot my friend a quelling look.

"Please, ladies," Barbara said with a glance at her watch. Poor woman. I felt for her doing personal regressions at Patsy's yearly "Girls' Night In" party. Luckily, there were only three of us this year. "We have limited time. Corazon is in a light trance, also referred to as an alpha state. Through that, she has tapped into her higher self, her true Infinite Being, a state in which she is free to bypass the boundaries of time."

"Yeah. Bypassing all that stuff," I said, giving my friend a smirk. "So sit back and watch the show. What do I do now, Barbara?"

"Look around you. Examine your surroundings. Tell us what you see, what you feel."

"I see mud. I feel mud."

"There has to be more to her past life than mud, surely," Terri said, reaching for the bowl of popcorn.

"Are there any buildings or other structures around to give you an idea of what year you are reliving?" Barbara asked.

"Um . . . nothing on the left side other than a bunch of forest. I seem to be standing on a dirt path of some sort. Let me walk to the top of this little hill—oh! Wow! There's a town down below. And it looks like there's a castle way up on a tall cliff in the distance. Lots of tiny little people are running around in some fields outside of the town. Cool! It's like a medieval village or something. Think I'll go down to say hi."

"Excellent," Barbara said, adjusting the video camera she was using to record the session. "Now tell me, how do you feel?"

"Well . . ." I examined the scene my mind had created; whether it was from a past life or just a fertile imagination, I had no way of knowing. "I'm kind of hungry. No, really hungry. Kind of an intense hunger, throbbing inside me. Oh great, I'm a peasant, aren't I? I'm a poor starving peasant who stands around in mud. Lovely."

"We are not here to make judgments on our past selves," Barbara said primly.

"Geesh, Cora," Patsy said, looking disgusted. "Terri turned out to be Cleopatra's personal maid, and I was one of Caesar's concubines. You're letting down the team, here. The least you could do is be a medieval princess in a big hat or something."

I looked closer at my mind-self. "I have shoes on. Peasants didn't wear shoes, did they?"

"Some did, I'm sure," Terri said, stuffing a handful of popcorn into her mouth as she watched my past-life regression.

"Can you walk to the town?" Barbara asked, moving a light slightly so it was off my face. "Perhaps we can find out who you are."

"Yeah. I'm going down the hill now. Hey, watch where you're—oh my god. Oh my god! OMIGOD!"

"What? What's happened?" Barbara asked, looking worried.

"A woman with an oxcart just ran me over."

"What?" Patsy shrieked.

"She ran me over. Her oxen were running amok or something. They just came barreling down the hill behind me and ran right over the top of me. Holy Swiss on rye! Now the oxen are trampling me, and the lady in the cart is screaming and—Jehoshaphat! My head just came off! It just came right off! Ack!"

Terri sat staring at me, her eyes huge, a handful of popcorn frozen just beyond her mouth as she gawked.

"Oh, my. I don't—I've never had anyone die during a regression," Barbara said, looking more worried. "I'm not quite sure how to proceed."

"You're . . . decapitated?" Patsy asked, looking as stunned as I felt, staring down at the gruesome scene. "Are you sure?"

"I'm sure, Pats. My head's separated from my body, which is covered in ox hoofprints. A wheel went over my neck, I think. It . . . urgh. That's just really gross. Why the hell do I get the reincarnations where I'm killed by two bulls and a cart? Why can't I be Cleopatra's concubine?"

"Personal maid, not concubine," Terri corrected, stuffing the popcorn into her mouth and chewing frantically. "Are you absolutely certain you're dead? Maybe it looks worse than it is."

I shot her a look before relaxing back on the pillow. "My head is three feet away from my body. I think that's a pretty good indicator of death—good god! Now what's she doing?"

"The ox?" Patsy asked.

"No, the driver. She's not doing what I think she's doing, is she?"

"I don't know," Terri said, scooting closer, as if that would let her peer into my mind.

"This is very unusual," Barbara muttered to herself, checking her digital camera. "We should document it. Yes. Documentation is good."

"What's the lady doing?" Patsy said, sitting on the couch next to my feet.

"She's trying to stick my head back onto my body.

Lady, that's not going to do any good. No, you can't tie it on, either. Ha. Told you so. Oh, don't drop me in the mud! Sheesh! Like I wasn't muddy enough? What a butterfingers. Now she's chasing the oxen, who just bolted for a field. Oh, no, she's coming back. Her arms are waving around like she's yelling, only I can't hear anything. It must be the shock of having my head severed by a cart wheel."

"This is just too surreal," Terri said. "Do you think she purposely ran you down?"

"I don't think so. She seems kind of goofy. She just tripped over my leg and fell onto my head. Oh man! I think she broke my nose! God almighty, this is like some sort of horrible Marx Brothers meets Leatherface sort of movie. Holy runaway oxen, Batman!"

"What?" Terri and Patsy asked at the same time.

"She's doing something. Something weird."

"Oh my god—is she making love to your lifeless corpse?" Terri asked. "I saw a show on HBO about that!"

"No, she's not molesting me. She's standing above me waving her hands around and chanting or something. What the—she's like—hoo!"

"Don't get upset," Barbara said, taking copious notes. "You are in no personal danger. Just describe what you're seeing calmly, and in detail."

"I don't know about you, but I consider a decapitation and barbecue as some sort of personal danger," I said, watching the scene in my mind's eye with stunned disbelief.

"Barbecue?" Patsy asked. "Someone's roasting a pig or something?"

"No. The ox lady waved her hands around, and all of a sudden this silver light was there, all over my body, singeing it around the edges. Oh great. Here comes someone. Hey, you, mister, would you stop the lady from doing the light thing? She's burnt off half of my hair."

"This is the most bizarre thing I've ever heard," Terri told Patsy. "You have the best parties!"

"It's all in the planning," Patsy said modestly. "What's going on now, Cora?"

"The guy just saw me. He did a little stagger to the side. I think it's because the lady tried to hide my head behind her, and my ear flew off and landed at his feet. Now he's picking it up. He's yelling at her. She's pointing to the oxen in the field, but he looks really pissed. Yeah, you tell her, mister. She has no right driving if she can't handle her cows."

"This would make a great film," Patsy said, looking thoughtful. "I wonder if we could write a screenplay. We could make millions."

"Well, now the guy has my head, and he's shaking it at the lady, still yelling at her. Whoops. Chunk of hair came loose. My head is bouncing down the hill. Guy and lady are chasing it. Hee hee hee. OK, that's really funny in a horrible sort of way. Ah. Good for you, sir. He caught me again, and now he's taking me back to my body, hauling the ox lady with him. Whoa! Whoa, whoa, whoa!"

"Did he drop your head again?" Terri asked, offering me the bowl of popcorn. I shook my head.

"No, he just . . . holy shit! I want out of here! Take me out of this dream or whatever it is! Wake me up!"

"Remain calm," Barbara said in a soothing voice. "The images you see are in the past, and cannot harm you now."

"What's going on? What did the guy do?" Terri askcd.

"I want to wake up! Right now!" I said, clawing the couch to sit up.

"Very well. I'm going to count backwards to one, and when I reach that number, you will awaken feeling refreshed and quite serene. Five, four, three, two, one. Welcome back, Corazon."

"You OK?" Patsy asked as I sat up, gasping, my blood all but curdling at the memory of what I'd witnessed.

"Yeah. I think so."

"What happened at the end?" Terri asked. "You looked scared to death."

"You'd be scared, too, if you saw a vampire kill someone!" I rubbed my arms. Goose bumps ran up and down them.

"A vampire! You're kidding!" Patsy gasped.

"I wish I was. He just kind of pounced on the woman, fangs flashing, and blood everywhere, and then she collapsed and he had blood all over his mouth. It was horrible. I never, ever want to see anything like that again. Man alive! I need a drink!"

A half hour later, Barbara the hypnotherapist left, but only after giving me her card and telling me she wanted to interview me at length about my regression session.

I said nothing, just nodded, not wanting to remember the horrible scene.

"What really gets me is that the whole bit with me being run down and killed didn't bother me," I told my friends as we sat over a couple of bottles of wine. "But that man, that vampire . . . brrr. I'll never forget the look on his face as long as I live. It was like he was in hell. I've never seen such anguish before, and then he was just on her, biting her. Urgh. It was terrible."

"What did he look like?"

I thought, trying to separate the last images of him from the earlier ones. "Tall. Muscular. Dark hair. Green eyes. Squarish chin. Handsome, really. The kind of guy if you saw him in a mall, you'd do a double take."

"Sounds like my neighbor," Patsy said, getting to her feet.

"You have a handsome neighbor you've been keeping from us?" I asked her.

"Well, I don't see him very often. He works at night or something—I never see him during the day. But he's gorgeous, really gorgeous. He likes to swim in the nude."

"We're your oldest friends," Terri said. "You owe it to us to share gorgeous men who swim naked."

"How," I said, my mind slightly muddled because of the wine, "do you know he swims naked?"

Patsy hiccuped. "If you happen to be at the east side of my fence pruning the hedge, there's a bare spot where you can see into his backyard, and the pool."

"I wanna see," Terri said, tipping over.

"You have had way too mush wine, misshy," I said, pulling her upright. "But I agree. I want to see the naked gorgeous neighbor."

Patsy glanced at the clock. "Normally I don't see him until closer to midnight, but a little fresh air will do us good. Tallyho, ladies!"

"We're off to get a fox," Terri said, giggling as we clutched each other and staggered after Patsy, who carried a bottle of wine with her, pointing it toward the backyard.

It took a good ten minutes to get to the spot Patsy had mentioned, but only because we all had to troop back into the house, one by one, to use the facilities.

"Sucks having a tiny bladder," Terri said, wobbling slightly as she returned to where Patsy and I were lying on the grass, sharing the last bottle of wine. "C'mon, let's go find that neighbor."

There was no one in the pool.

"Dammit," I said, clutching a tree that stood next to the neighbor's house.

"Well, that's disappointing," Patsy said. "Maybe he'll be out later."

"Antimacassar," Terri said, taking a swig off the bottle.

"Huh?" I asked.

"I think she means anticlimactical," Patsy said with great precision.

"Ah. Gotcha. Well, hell. I'm all keyed up to see a gorgeous guy."

"I know!" Terri said, heading for the house. "Let'sh peek in the windows to see him."

"Ter!" Patsy said, her voice hushed as she ran after Terri. "That's illegal."

"No it isn't," she insisted. "He's your neighbor, right? That'sh not illegal to look in a neighbor's house. You ever hear of Neighborhood Watch? We do it all the time. It'sh good. C'mon. Let's peek."

"Somehow, that makes sense," I said, following the pair. "I think it's because I'm drunk."

By the time we found a window that wasn't curtained, and which looked in on what appeared to be a living room done in shades of cream and white, Patsy had to pee again, and was urging us to return to her house.

"What'sh the big deal?" Terri asked, having some difficulty navigating the one step that led up to the doors.

"He's my neighbor! I don't want him pissed at me."

"It's not like he's going to know we were here," I pointed out, admiring the intricate tile laid in the entryway.

"He's going to know I was here if I leave a big puddle

of wee," she said, her legs crossed as she did a little hopping dance. "Let's go back home. I really have to go!"

"OK. I don't see him anyw—hoo! I see him!" Terri plastered herself to the glass on either side of the double front doors, loudly jabbing the glass with her finger. "Look! Do you see? Oh, baby, you're right. He is gorgeous, although he's not naked. Hey, he's looking this way. I wonder if he can see us."

"It's night outside," I said, waving my arms around to show her the night. "See? Black. Night. No one can see us. We're like ninjas. Except for the wee puddles."

The door opened, light spilling out from inside, the silhouette of a man clearly visible. "Can I help you?" he asked, his voice deep and alluring with a slight German accent.

"I have to wee!" Patsy wailed, clutching at herself. She shoved the bottle at me and pushed past the neighbor into his house.

"Second door on the left," he directed her. She ran in the direction he was pointing.

He turned back to us, but I couldn't see him clearly, what with the light behind him. "Is there something I can do for you ladies?"

"Pats said you like to swim in the altogether," Terri said, looking hopeful.

"Ah. Well, I've had my swim for the day. Is there anything else?"

He stepped out of the doorway and onto the entryway, straight into the light cast by a standing yard lamp a few feet away.

I dropped the bottle of wine, pointing at him as my skin tried to crawl away.

"What's wrong, Cora?" Terri asked, weaving slightly. "You look like you're going to barf."

"Vampire," I said, the word coming out as a croak.

The man, who had been reaching out to steady Terri, suddenly whirled around to look at me.

"What?" Terri asked, wobbling her way down the lone step.

"Vampire," I repeated.

The man narrowed his green eyes at me. "Who the hell are you?"

"VAMPIRE!" I screamed, and suddenly, the world started to spin, and a great big black hole opened up at my feet, and I fell into it.

The last sound I heard was that of Patsy. "Oh, thank you, Alec. I really didn't want to wee on your lovely tile work. What's Cora doing on the ground?"

Dear Readers,

Lest you be freaked out by the excerpt that follows—and I know right now some of you are looking worried at even the mention of doing such a thing—let me reassure you that even though the excerpt from *It's All Greek to Me* is (gasp!) a contemporary romantic comedy, there are more Dark Ones and dragon books coming.

Why, then, you might be asking yourself, did I suddenly run amok and write a contemporary? I can answer that in two words: my muse. Or, rather, three words: my *pesky* muse. She had an idea for a book that would poke a little gentle fun at some romance novel stereotypes, and I learned long ago to listen to her when she insists we write a book.

While I'm on the subject of upcoming books, let me add a note about the Dark Ones in particular. I know many of you are hoping for another Ben and Fran book, and I want to reassure you that they have a significant part to play regarding the situations brought to light via the previous Dark Ones book, *In the Company of Vampires*. They may have to adopt secondary roles for the next book, but they will, indeed, be present and looking for some answers.

Katie MacAlister

The man in front of her was crazy. That, or he was having some sort of an attack—one that involved dancing up and down and gesturing wildly, all the while talking a mile a minute, his words tumbling out with such speed, they all ran together into one dense, unintelligible stream.

Not that Harry could have understood the words even if he had been speaking slower. She stood up from where she'd been seated on a wooden lounge, enjoying the peace of the balmy Mediterranean night. "The temptation to say 'I'm sorry, but it's all Greek to me,' is almost overwhelming—you do realize that, right?" she asked the man.

He continued his dancing-gesturing-babbling routine, this time adding a peculiar plucking motion with the hem of her linen tunic.

She glanced around, wondering if she'd misunderstood. "Am I not supposed to be here? Is this garden off limits to us? Derek said it was the garden area on the other side of the house that was for guests only. Did I get that wrong?"

The little man—and he was little, at least a good ten

inches shorter than her solid six feet—evidently grew distressed at her inability to understand, and grabbed her wrist, hauling her toward the massive bulk of the house.

"Is Timmy in the well?" she asked, a little smile curling her lips before her gaze moved from what must surely have been one of the servants to the house itself. "Only *house* doesn't quite cut it as a description, does it? It's more like a palace. Houses don't have wings— palaces do. And I defy you to find a house sitting by its lonesome on its very own Greek island. No, sir, this is a palace pure and simple, and although I'm sure you have a good reason for dragging me to it, I should point out that the only people who are staying in its palatial confines are guests, and I'm with the band. We have the little bungalow on the servant end of the island. Hello? You really don't speak a word of English, do you?" Harry sighed.

The man continued to drag her through a very pleasant garden, filled with sweet-scented flowering Mediterranean shrubs unfamiliar to her, attractive hedges, and pretty neoclassical statues. The night air was balmy, the heavy scent from some flower mingling with the sharper and, to her mind, more pleasing tang of the sea. It was everything she imagined a rich man's private island paradise should be. Well, with the exception of the wizened little man attached to her wrist.

"I couldn't just sit quietly somewhere?" she asked the man, whose fingers were locked like steel around her wrist. "I promise that I won't bother anyone. I don't think I could—I'm so jet-lagged, I can't even think straight. Look, that's a nice little bench right over there in the corner next to the statue of the guy with a really big winky. I won't be in anyone's way. I'll just go sit and contemplate his gigantic genitals, and all will be well."

"Harry!" A man appeared suddenly at a window, hanging out of it and waving frantically. "There you are! Hurry!"

"Derek, *what* are you doing in the house?" Harry thinned her lips at the sight of the young man. "You said we weren't supposed to go near it while the guests were here."

"That doesn't matter now! Hurry up!"

"If you think I don't have anything better to do than to fly halfway around the world to bail your butt out of trouble because you can't follow a few simple rules—"

"No, it's not me." He pulled back inside the window. "It's Cyn! She's been attacked!"

"What!" The fury in her bellow took the little man still attached to her wrist by surprise, for he dropped her hand as if it was suddenly made of fire. Adrenaline shot through her with a painful spike—adrenaline and a fury that almost consumed her. She leaped forward, easily hurdling the low stone balustrade of a patio area as she bolted for the nearest entrance to the house, wrenching open a pair of French doors. She didn't stop to apologize to the small group of people standing around a pool table, racing around the men and women in elegant evening clothes, making a beeline for the door that was bound to lead to a central area of the house.

The little servant trailed her as far as a marble-tiled corridor, where he veered off to who knew where. Harry didn't care—her mind was blank except for the horror of the words that kept repeating in her head. *It's Cyn! She's been attacked!*

"Harry, thank God—" Terry emerged from a side hall, gesturing toward a curving staircase, his face tight with worry. "We didn't know where you were. She's up here."

Harry ground off a good layer or two of enamel as the pair of them leaped up the seemingly endless stairs, one distracted part of her mind finding it ironic that now, of all times, she should be thankful for her height and long legs. "What happened?" she managed to get out as they crested the stairs, and Terry pointed to the left.

He cast her a worried look, but said nothing. Derek almost collided with her as he burst out of a room. "In here! Harry, you have to do something! The bastard . . . he . . . he . . . !"

"I'll kill whoever it is," she ground out, her blood running icy at the thought of whatever atrocity had occurred. She shoved Derek aside and entered the room, her breath ragged, her heart about ready to leap from her chest. She'd heard the phrase "seeing red" before, but had never thought it could be taken as literal. For a few seconds, though, she swore everything in the room had an ugly red tint to it. It was obviously a bedroom; a quick glance took in the usual occasional chairs, a large bureau with matching wardrobe, and a big bed swathed in some sort of filmy draperies that fluttered in the breeze drifting in through open French doors. Her attention narrowed to the bed as she dashed to it, immediately taking into her arms one of the two huddled, sobbing figures there.

Dimly, she was aware that there was another person in the room, but his identity faded to insignificance. "It's all right, Cyndi. I'm here now," she said, her fury rising as the younger woman sobbed onto her shoulder. "You'll be OK. We'll make whoever did this pay."

"He's evil! He's horrible!" Cyndi pulled back, tears spilling over already red and bloodshot eyes. She was naked, a sheet clutched to her bare breasts, her face unmarked but blotchy from the tears. There were some nasty-looking raw marks on her neck and chest, but it was the petulant purse of her lips that suddenly chimed a warning bell in Harry's brain.

"What happened? Did someone attack you?"

Cyndi drew in a long, trembling breath and glanced over Harry's shoulder. "Yes. Well . . . more or less. He dumped me, Harry. *Dumped* me!"

Harry blinked for a few seconds. "He what?"

"Dumped me, cruelly and . . . and . . . viciously. I came up to his room, and I thought we were going to hook up, and everything was going along very nicely, and before we could get down to, you know, really doing it, he told me to leave. Just like that!"

Harry passed a shaking hand over her eyes. Slowly, her heart rate dropped back to reasonable levels "So you weren't attacked?"

"Verbally I was. He told me that he didn't want to have sex with me, and that I should leave because he wanted to sleep." Cyndi gestured at the bed. "If it's not verbal abuse to entice someone to your bed, and get them naked, and then kiss them all over before telling them to leave, I don't know what is!"

"He enticed you?"

"Yes! Not so much in words, but he looked at me several times tonight, and a woman knows what that look means," Cyndi said with a peculiar lofty coyness. "He *wanted* me. So I came up here, and then everything was really nice until he went totally crazy and told me to leave. That's just not right, Harry. It's traumatizing! You have no idea how traumatizing it is to have fabulous sex and then be told to leave because someone wants to sleep. I'm not a slut! I should sleep here, too!"

Harry took a deep, deep breath to keep from strangling the young, self-centered girl in front of her, reminding herself that her whole purpose in being there was to watch over the kids and see that they came to no harm. Her eyes lit on the red marks on Cyndi's chest, and a little spurt of anger burned in her stomach.

She turned, moving aside the hovering forms of Terry and Derek. Amy had moved to cling to the latter, her eyes huge and wary. A man leaned drunkenly against the wall, dressed only in a pair of obviously hastily donned pants, the waistband undone, his face slack and devoid of emotion as he watched her walk toward him. He was a little taller than she was, obviously of Greek ethnicity, with dark eyes and hair, and what in any other circumstance would have been a classical sort of beauty that she would have to have been dead not to appreciate.

"I don't know what the hell you did to her to leave those marks, but I feel it's important to point out that she's only eighteen years old. Couldn't you have gotten her out of the room without touching her?" she asked, fighting with the need to yell at both Cyndi and the randy stallion before her. He had to have been a guest at the party for which the band had been brought out at great expense to entertain, but at that moment, Harry couldn't have cared less if he was the owner of this vast palace of sin—she just wanted to get Cyndi out of there without any further drama.

"I—" The man blinked at her, swallowed visibly, and shoved himself away from the wall to take a step forward. "The little bint threw herself at me. She was in my bed, waiting for me. I didn't screw her, if that's what you're all hot and bothered about."

"Bint!" Cyndi roared, and would have lunged at the man but for the sheet in which she was still tangled. "You bastard! I'm not a bint. Terry, what's a bint?"

"I don't care who tried to seduce whom—you should have known she's too young. You're just lucky she's legal. And obviously you were playing a bit too rough if you left those sorts of marks."

"I'm wounded!" Cyndi cried, grasping at that thought. "He hurt me! He's a beastly, horrible man who hurt me and abused me! I think I may faint."

"You're not hurt, you little—" The man wisely bit off the word as Harry frowned. "I didn't hurt her."

"Oh my God, I'm bleeding!" Cyndi cried in a dramatic voice, and clutched at Terry. "I need to go to the hospital!"

"Look, this has gone far enough. I just want you to promise to stay away from Cyndi for the rest of the weekend, OK?" Harry said with an attempt to take control of the situation.

The man scowled at her. "Who the hell are you to tell me what to do? I bet you planned all of this with that little bint, didn't you? What a setup you had, getting your friend there to screw me and then pretend she's been attacked. What's next, blackmail? You can just drop that idea, because there's no way I'm going to fall for your little scheme."

With every word, anger built in Harry. Oh, she knew full well that Cyndi was milking the situation for everything it was worth, just as she knew that Cyndi had pursued him and not vice versa, but his slander left her itching to punch him in the nose. Behind her she heard the whispered hush of the door opening, but she ignored it, saying simply, "Who am I? I'll tell you who I am. I'm your worst nightmare."

"I don't know." He leered in that sloppy way drunks had. "I'm willing to give you a try. Bet you know a few things that your little friend doesn't."

The man reached out and grabbed her breast. Harry saw red again before she knocked his hand away, stomped as hard as she could on his bare foot, swiftly bringing up her knee into his groin, and, when he doubled over with a scream, punched him as hard as she could in the eye. Still doubled over, he snapped his head back, his face frozen in shock and pain for a moment before he fell over backward.

"What the hell is going on here?" a voice roared from behind Harry.

She spun around to behold an absolutely furious man coming toward her. She blinked at the sight of him, amazed for a moment that such a glorious specimen of male beauty existed outside the pages of glossy fashion magazines. He was taller even than the man she'd just knocked out, a good six inches taller than her, with a broad expanse of chest that wasn't at all disguised by a black silk shirt open at the neck, revealing a bronzed stretch of skin that she suddenly wanted to lick. The little indentation where his neck met his collarbone beckoned to her with an unholy fascination, and she stared bemused for a moment, wondering what on earth her mind was doing demanding that she taste this strange—if terribly beautiful—man.

"Who are you?" he demanded, his black eyes blazing with a fury that looked familiar somehow. "What the hell did you do to my brother?"

"Your brother?" Suddenly, all the rage and anger and fury filled her again with righteousness. "I was seriously considering beating him to a bloody pulp. You're a big guy—I'll let you help if you like."

His ebony gaze raked her over in a manner that left her both hot and cold at the same time, instantly dismissing her as not being worth his consideration. He shoved her aside and marched over to where the other man moved groggily against the wall. "I believe the phrase is 'over my dead body.' Get up, Theo."

"You want on my list, too? Fine," Harry snarled, and

would have rolled up her sleeves except the fawn-colored linen tunic she wore was sleeveless. "You can be second. Go ahead, Theo. Get up so I can knock your block off."

The big, incredibly handsome man hoisted his brother to his feet, one of his lips curling. "You're drunk."

"Not drunk," Theo protested, his eyes glazed. "Barely had anything. That little bitch—"

Harry moved faster than she had ever moved, intent on slapping the word right off his lips, but the other man caught her as she lunged toward his brother.

"Who the hell are you?" he snarled, his arm like steel around her waist.

"I already used the 'your worst nightmare' line," she yelled at him, her fingers curling into a fist. "But you'd better believe I am!"

He stopped her fist just as she was about to punch him in the nose, shoving her backward into the small clutch of people next to the bed. His black-eyed gaze crawled over all of them. "You're not on the guest list. What are you doing here?"

"They're the band," Harry said, jerking her thumb toward where the four of them, Cyndi now standing in the sheet, pressed together in silent amazement. "The one your sister hired for her eighteenth birthday, assuming you are the owner of this house of debauchery."

The man's eyes returned to her, scorn just about dripping from his voice as he said, "You look a little old to be in a teenage band."

"I'm not old," she said, straightening up. Behind the man, Theo collapsed into a chair, slumping over to rest his head in his hands with a pathetic groan. She narrowed her eyes on him, wondering if she could distract his brother long enough get in a really good punch. "I'm only thirty-three, and I'm their manager. Kind of. By proxy. I'm a writer, really, but I'm acting as their manager because Timothy's appendix burst, and Jill had to stay with him because she's about due to pop any minute with their first child, and there was no one else to watch over the kids, so she asked if I would do it for just this one gig. And idiot that I was, I thought, How hard could it be to watch over things while they played for some obscenely rich oil billionaire's party? No one told me your brother was a drunkard who doesn't have the common sense God gave a potato bug!"

Harry glared at the man as he glanced from his brother to the huddled girl, now thankfully silent, taking in her disheveled appearance, before his eyes narrowed on Harry. "I made my money in real estate development, not oil."

She stared at him for a second. "Does that matter?"

"It does if you're going to consider the source of my wealth as material for an insult. As for this situation—" He gestured with distaste at Cyndi. "Theo has never had to force a woman into his bed. Usually, it's the other way around."

"Of course he asked me," Cyndi said with a sniff and jerk of her chin. "He smiled at me twice, and winked once, and then he brushed my arm when I walked by him. I'm not dense, you know! I can tell when a man wants me! So I came up here to wait for him, because it's clear he thinks I'm steaming hot."

Harry closed her eyes for a moment, then took Cyndi by the arms, fighting to keep from shaking her. "I don't even know where to start, Cyndi."

"Start with what? I'm not the one who's wrong here. Theo is!" Cyndi answered with yet another righteous sniff.

"I thought so. This wouldn't be the first time some

enterprising young lady has tried to, shall we say, benefit financially from Theo's lack of common sense," the
irritating man said.

"Bullshit!" Harry snapped, releasing Cyndi to march
over to the man. His eyebrows rose at the obscenity. She
couldn't remember what his name was—it was one of
those long names with a seeming abundance of vowels—
but she vaguely remembered hearing Jill mention something about him being on some world's-most-eligible-
bachelor list. If his appearance was anything to go by,
she could certainly believe that. "I'm willing to admit
that Cyndi has shown a huge lack of intelligence this
evening—"

Cyndi gasped, outraged.

"But neither of us is trying to blackmail your precious brother. It was just a case of a young girl—a very
young girl who is just barely legal, I might point out—
obviously being dazzled by the situation and making
some bad judgment calls."

"I'm not dazzled," Cyndi protested. "I'm hurt! I'm
bleeding all over!"

The man made a disgusted noise and looked like he
wanted to roll his eyes.

"There's no actual blood, Cyndi," Harry pointed
out. "Although I will admit that your playmate was far
too rough with you. And although that's not a crime, it's
certainly not a pleasant little roll in the sack!"

"No *crime* has been committed, other than that of
poor judgment," the man snapped at her implication,
his scowl shifting for a moment to one of surprise as
Harry poked him in the chest when she spoke.

"She's got marks all over her upper chest! Just look
at her! What sort of a man does that?"

Iakovos Papaioannou couldn't believe the Amazon
in front of him had had the nerve to poke him in the

chest, just as if she had the right to chastise him. For a moment, he was speechless at her utter and complete disregard for his consequence as she continued to lambaste him, throwing the most absurd accusations at his head.

He allowed her to continue just for the pleasure of watching her, admitting to himself that although his preference for women seldom extended to anything but slim, elegant, cool blondes, this woman, this earth goddess, with her abundant curves and wild brown hair spilling down her back, stirred something deep inside him. Something primal, some urge woke and demanded that he claim her in the most fundamental way a man could claim a woman.

His gaze dropped to her mouth, watching with fascination as her lips moved while she continued to lecture him. A faint scent caught his attention, and he breathed deeper, hoping to catch it again, and when he did, the analytical side of his mind noted that it was just the scent of a sun-warmed woman, as if she had been out lying on the beach. It was nothing extraordinary, nothing unusual, and yet it seemed to go straight to his groin, firing his desire as the most costly perfume had never done.

"—and you're not even listening to me!" the goddess yelled, drawing his attention from his contemplation of laying her down on his bed and burying himself in her glorious body. She gave him a particularly hard jab in the chest, and he captured her hand without thinking, idly rubbing his thumb over her fingers.

"Of course I'm not," he said, dismissively. "There's nothing further to discuss. The woman pursued Theo, not the other way around. She is not injured, despite her claims to the contrary."

She stared at him with stunned surprise for a moment or two, thick black lashes blinking over eyes he had first thought were gray, but now he could see were more hazel, the irises seeming to darken slightly as she looked at his hand. "What are you doing?"

"Trying to point out the obvious," he responded, his eyes on her lips, wondering if she tasted of the sea. She certainly looked like some goddess who had risen from the sea in vengeance, a tempest in human form.

"No, your hand. Your thumb. It's . . ."

Her gaze lifted to his, and he watched with primal satisfaction as her pupils dilated in sudden awareness of him as a man. How easy it would be to arouse her, this tempest. "What is your name?"

"Harry," she said, suddenly giving a little shiver as she pulled her fingers from his.

He frowned. That was not at all fitting for a goddess from the sea. "You have a man's name?"

"It's a nickname, actually," she said with a rueful smile.

His gaze moved instantly to her lips, a drawing in his groin warning that if he continued contemplation of her mouth, what he'd like to do to it, and what he'd like it to do to him, he would end up carrying her off to his bed. While that idea seemed just fine to him, there were other things to attend to . . . at least while Elena's party was under way.

"My name is actually Eglantine, but no one but my mother calls me that. It's just such a mouthful that everyone calls me Harry. What's your name?"

"Iakovos Panagiotis Okeanos Papaioannou," he said with a slight frown, as if he was surprised she didn't know it.

That floored her. She grabbed onto the first part. "Yackydos?"

"Iakovos. It's Greek for 'Jacob.'" When she gawked

at him, he continued. "My name is quite a bit more than a mouthful, yes. I would suggest that since you are this young woman's manager, you escort her back to her proper lodgings. I will attend to my brother."

"I'm hurt! I want to go to the hospital!" Cyndi cried.

"Don't be ridiculous. You don't need a doctor's care," Iakovos told her.

"I'm their *acting* manager, and if she wants to go to the hospital, then I'll take her to the hospital." Harry poked him in the chest again, not, she told herself, because she wanted to feel his fingers on hers again. Oh, sure, he was the walking epitome of sex on two legs, your standard gorgeous hunk, but he was also an extremely obtuse hunk—one who had a very large surprise coming if he thought he could just brush away Cyndi's (albeit minor) injuries.

"May I remind you that you are in *my* house," Iakovos said, his voice low and incredibly arousing. "On *my* private island."

Harry never really thought of voices as being sinfully sexy before, but the way this man's rumbled around in his chest made the hairs on the back of her neck stand on end. It was like he was a god, a Greek god come to life, standing right there in front of her, doing all sorts of things to personal, intimate parts of her that she didn't want to think about. He was a drunkard's brother, for heaven's sake! How could she find his voice arousing? "Look, Yacky—"

"Iakovos!"

"We may be in your house on your precious island, but we're also in a country that I'm willing to bet doesn't tolerate abuse to women, especially to American citizens, and double especially when the American citizen in question is just barely eighteen." Harry took a deep breath and leveled the Greek god a look that should have felled him. "I'm assuming that since we had to take a boat to get out to Smut Island, we're going to need one to get Cyndi to the hospital on the mainland. And since I also assume you own all the boats here, I'd appreciate if you could have one of your lackies fire one up for us."

"And if I don't?" Iakovos asked, his black eyes damn near spitting fire at her.

"You're going to be one sad little panda," she snarled.

"Are you *threatening* me?" He looked completely outraged at such a thing.

"You bet your incredibly attractive and probably hard-enough-to-bounce-a-quarter-off-of ass!" she snapped back.

An indescribable look flitted across his face. "You are the most irreverent woman I've ever met."

"And you're the handsomest man I've ever seen in my life, but that doesn't mean I'm going to lick you!" she yelled.

He stared at her in outright surprise.

"Sorry. That came out wrong." Color warmed her face as she mentally damned that odd twist in her mind that led her to speak without thinking. "Sometimes, the dialogue I write in my head comes out of my mouth instead of staying where it belongs."

"You wish to . . . *lick*?" he asked, the same odd expression on his face.

"Not *all* of you!" she said with dignity, straightening her shoulders. "Just that spot there, where your neck meets your collarbone. Where that little indentation is . . ." Her voice trailed off as he continued to look at her as if dancing boobs had just appeared on the top of her head. "Never mind. It's not important."

He opened his mouth to say something, shook his head, and, with a dismissive glance at Cyndi and the others still clustered together in silent shock, pulled out a cell phone, speaking rapidly in Greek into it. "A boat will be waiting for you at the east dock." His lips tightened as he looked at his brother before jerking him upright. "I trust that a visit to the hospital will reassure you that your charge has no injury beyond that done to her pride."

"Pride?" Harry grabbed his arm as he was about to leave. He spun around and pinned her back with an outraged glare, which she more than met with one of her own. "She's battered to hell and back again."

His black gaze flickered over Cyndi, who thrust out her chest and gave him an outraged look. "I see no signs of battery."

"She has red marks all over her chest and neck!" Harry said, pointing at Cyndi.

He looked at her steadily for a moment, and she could have sworn that one side of his mouth twitched. "Have you never had a lover who had heavy whisker growth?"

"Huh?"

"It is common among Greek men to have to shave more than once a day, and my brother and I are no exception to that fact."

She eyed his jaw, squinting slightly. He did have a slight darkness on his lower face, as if he was about to sport some manly stubble. He also had extremely attractive lips, the lower one in particular, with its sweet, oh so very sweet curve, and the upper with a deep indentation up to a long, straight nose. Like with the spot on his neck, she had the worst urge to taste that upper lip dip. She actually licked her own lips thinking about it before she remembered that ogling a drunk's brother, especially one who should have been on the cover of *GQ*, really wasn't the thing. "Er . . . what was the question?"

He sighed. "Whisker burn. That is all the red marks are."

"They are?" She turned to Cyndi. "Cyn?"

"He hurt me," she said, her eyes filling with tears. "Even if it was just his rough cheeks, I need to see a doctor."

Amy, Derek's girlfriend and the other singer in the group, immediately hugged her, her blue eyes worried. Even Terry—bright, cheerful Terry, who always had a joke on his lips—looked somber as he moved closer to the two women. All four sets of eyes watched Harry with an obvious plea in them.

"Whisker burn." She turned back to face the annoying god with the sexy lips. He raised an eyebrow, and she was thankful that he was clearly beyond such mortal things as saying "I told you so."

"I told you she wasn't hurt," he said with slight smirk.

She pointed a finger at him. "You just knocked yourself off your pedestal, buster. All right, I'm willing to accept that your brother didn't intentionally hurt her. But she's very upset, and she does have some nasty rashes, so I think it probably would be better for everyone's peace of mind if she saw a doctor. If you and Mr. Grabby Hands over there would just get out of here, I'll get Cyn dressed, and we'll take her to the mainland."

His lickable lips tightened as if he wasn't used to receiving orders—a thought that gave her immense pleasure. Oh, how fun it would be to take him down a peg or two, to remind him that he might think himself a god amongst lesser folk, but in reality, he was just nothing more than a man. An extremely rich, urbane, sexy, and probably quite fascinating man, but still a man.

She looked at the dip on his collarbone. Her tongue cleaved to the top of her mouth. "Temptation is a bitch."

"You can say that again," he muttered, giving her a dark look before turning on his heel and leaving the room, dragging his brother with him.

New York Times bestselling author

KATIE MACALISTER

Steamed
A Steampunk Romance

When one of Jack Fletcher's nanoelectro-
mechanical system experiments is jostled in
his lab, the resulting explosion sends him
into the world of his favorite novel—
a seemingly Victorian-era world of
steampower, aether guns, corsets, and
goggles. A world where the lovely and
intrepid Octavia Pye captains her airship
straight into his heart...

For videos, podcasts, excerpts, and more, visit
katiemacalister.com

S0045

KATIE MACALISTER

The Dark Ones Novels

Even Vampires Get the Blues

Paen Scott is a Dark One: a vampire without a soul. And his mother is about to lose hers too if Paen can't repay a debt to a demon by finding a relic known as the Jilin God in five days.

The Last of the Red-Hot Vampires

Portia Harding is stalked by the heart-stoppingly handsome Theondre North—who's also the son of a fallen angel. Portia's down-to-earth attitude frustrates beings from both heavenly and hellish realms—and gets Theo turned into a vampire.

Zen and the Art of Vampires

Pushing forty and alone, Pia Thomason heads to Europe on a singles tour, hoping to find romance. What she finds are two very handsome, very mysterious, and very undead men.

Crouching Vampire, Hidden Fang

Pia Thomason is torn between two Dark Ones: her husband Kristoff—who doesn't trust her—and his best friend, Alec, who is MIA. So Pia goes back to her humdrum Seattle life—but fate has other plans.

Available wherever books are sold or at
penguin.com

S0133